BY BRET ANTHONY JOHNSTON

Remember Me Like This

*Naming the World: And Other Exercises
for the Creative Writer* (editor)

Corpus Christi: Stories

Remember Me
Like This

Bret Anthony Johnston

Remember Me
Like This

A Novel

RANDOM HOUSE

NEW YORK

Published in the United States by Random House, an imprint and division of Random House LLC, a Penguin Random House Company, New York.

RANDOM HOUSE and the HOUSE colophon are registered trademarks of Random House LLC.

Library of Congress Cataloging-in-Publication Data
Johnston, Bret Anthony.
Remember me like this : a novel / Bret Anthony Johnston.
pages   cm
ISBN 978-1-4000-6212-6
eBook ISBN 978-0-8129-9616-6
1. Missing persons—Fiction. 2. Kidnapping victims—Fiction. 3. Families—Psychological aspects—Fiction. 4. Texas—Fiction. I. Title.
PS3610.O384R46 2014
813'.6—dc23
2013022805

Printed in the United States of America on acid-free paper

www.atrandom.com

2 4 6 8 9 7 5 3 1

First Edition

Book design by Victoria Wong

For
Jay Anthony and Donna Leah Johnston.
I remember.

Well, when one has no one, nowhere else one can go.

—Fyodor Dostoyevsky, *Crime and Punishment*

I've lain with the devil
Cursed God above
Forsaken heaven
To bring you my love

—PJ Harvey, "To Bring You My Love"

Remember Me
Like This

Prologue

THE HARBOR BRIDGE CROSSED OVER THE PORT OF CORPUS Christi. It was a high steel arc, tall enough to grant barges and freighters access to the ship channel, and stood where the old drawbridge once did. The city had hosted a contest to name the bridge, and the winner, a housewife who lived out by the oil refineries, was given the honor of riding in the first car to drive across. That was in 1959. She wore a pillbox hat and white satin gloves. She posed for pictures with the mayor. Years later, when she died, her family walked to the top of the bridge and scattered her ashes over the lilting water.

The structure was long and mellow, like a downturned crescent blade. A lattice of girders rose above the bridge's suspended deck, and the crisscrossing beams threw complex shadows on the lanes. After decades of sustained wind and salt from the bay, the joints were starting to erode and loosen. Rust flaked the girders. Each year, if the city could scrape together the money during the holidays, the bridge was strung with Christmas lights. An image of its illuminated reflection on the water had long commanded the cover of the Corpus phone book. A handful of couples had been married at the top, delinquent teenagers stole bowling balls to roll down the lanes or lob off the side, and a small group of citizens met on the first weekend of every month to walk the mile that the structure spanned.

The walkers started on the south side and crossed over to North Beach on the railed walkway that edged the bridge. At the foot of the walkway hung an engraved sign from the Coastal Bend Church of Christ: FEELING DESPERATE? "EVERYONE WHO CALLS ON THE NAME OF THE LORD WILL BE SAVED." ROMANS 10:13.

So, on the first weekend of September, it was the group of walkers who saw the body in the bay before anyone else. They didn't immediately comprehend the sight. The water was ragged and dirty from the previous week's storm, and the body floated facedown; it looked like a person snorkeling, except an arm and leg were bent at odd, harsh angles. One of the walkers retched and kneeled on the walkway. Another started praying. Another dug in her pocket for her phone. The rest of the group stared and speculated and tried to trick themselves into thinking the person might have survived the fall. No one could tell if it was a male or female, or how old, and none of them thought of Justin Campbell, the boy who'd gone missing years before. They knew only that the broken-up body was part of them now, that the memory would insinuate itself for the rest of their lives. Two Coast Guard cutters were soon speeding toward the ship channel, and police cruisers were parking on both sides of the port. A few of the walkers stood at the top of the bridge to watch, but most descended without a word. They walked single file, knowing they wouldn't return to the bridge, and held on to the rail as tightly as possible.

PART ONE

1

MONTHS EARLIER, THE JUNE HEAT ON MUSTANG ISLAND WAS
gauzy and glomming. The sky hung close, pale as caliche, and
the small played-out waves were dragging in the briny, pungent
scent of seaweed. On the beach, people tried holding out for a
breeze from the Gulf, but when the gusts blew ashore, they were
humid and harsh, kicking up sand that stung like wasps. By midday,
everyone surrendered. Fishermen cut bait, surfers packed in their
boards. Even the notoriously dogged sunbathers shook out their
long towels and draped them over the seats in their cars, the leather
and vinyl scalding. Lines for the ferry stretched for half an hour,
though it could seem days before the dashboard vents were pushing
in cool air. Porpoises wheeled in the boats' wakes, their bellies pink
and glistening.

After the short pass across the Laguna Madre, the ferry docked
on the north jetty and drivers moved onto the mainland through the
small, flat town of Southport, Texas. They passed an anchor-shaped
monument embossed with the words WELCOME ABOARD, then the
tackle shops and bait stands and the old rust-pocked pickups where
men sold shrimp from ice chests. To the west, behind the leaning
palm trees with their husks as dry and brown as parchment, the
soapy bay fanned into the horizon. There was the public boat ramp
and marina and the half-razed Teepee Motel, now nothing more

than a cluster of concrete teepees hemming a drained kidney-shaped pool. A faded vinyl banner for the upcoming Shrimporee sagged over the diagonal parking places on Main Street, then popped and opened up in the wind; the Shrimporee was in September. On the asphalt, puddles of heat appeared, shimmered, evaporated. The seafood restaurants and a spate of garishly painted souvenir shops lined Station Street, then just before the town yielded to the blacktop highway came the Whataburger and H-E-B grocery and Loan Star Pawnshop, whose rusted arrow marquee sign announced, WE BUY WINDOW UNITS! The pawnshop's crushed-shell parking lot was crowded this time of year—shrimpers hocking tools between good hauls, surfers hunting for wet suits, men from the Coast Guard quibbling over fishing rods. Today, the last Wednesday of the month, a man was trying to sell one of the pawnbrokers an old Cadillac, a cream-colored Fleetwood Brougham. The hood was raised and the ragtop was lowered, and the men stood in the pale sun—squinting, haggling, appearing stranded to everyone who passed.

ACROSS TOWN, IN THE VILLA DEL SOL CONDOMINIUM COMPLEX, Eric Campbell stood under a cool shower, listening. He thought he'd heard his phone buzzing, but either it had stopped or he'd been mistaken. He'd left the phone next to his watch and wedding band on the nightstand. He opened the shower curtain, leaned out, waited. The only sounds were the water pulsing through the showerhead and the air-conditioning unit whirring outside, so he drew the curtain and rinsed off. The afternoon sun slanted in through the bathroom's skylight. He wondered if they'd break a hundred degrees today, if they hadn't already. He was glad to have parked his truck in the garage.

The condo belonged to Kent Robichaud. He was a surgeon, and although he and his wife, Tracy, lived on Ocean Drive in Corpus, they'd bought the condo in Southport to be closer to the marina on weekends. They were in their late thirties, originally from the Midwest; they owned a twenty-footer named *Thistle Dew*. Eric liked Kent. He tried not to think about him when he spent afternoons with Tracy. With summer school in session, they'd gotten into the routine of him coming over after his Wednesday class. Tracy would drive in from Corpus and read the weekly *Southport Sun* in her breakfast nook until Eric's truck appeared on the street. Then she'd click open the garage door and make her way to the bedroom, undressing.

Eric always checked messages before stepping out of his truck. Usually there weren't any. At home, Griffin would still be sleeping, or he'd be playing videogames and waiting for the afternoon to cool off enough to go skateboarding. If Griff wanted to leave the house, he had to call his mother or father for permission; when Eric had thought he heard his phone in the shower, he assumed it was his son. His younger son. Griff had just turned fourteen. Of course, Eric worried it was his wife calling, but he also knew better. Laura rarely dialed his number anymore. Wednesdays were her early shift at the dry cleaner's, but she had, for the last few months, been driving to Marine Lab in Corpus after work. She volunteered a few times a week, stayed out there until dinner. Later, sometimes. When she came home, she was dog-tired and smelled of frozen herring. She wore an expression, so transparent to Eric (and, he feared, to Griff), of practiced contentment. She would update them on Marine Lab—currently, they were rehabbing a bottlenose dolphin that had beached on the National Seashore—then listen to Griff and Eric talk about their days; Griff usually told them about his skateboarding, and Eric spoke of his seventh graders or other faculty members. If there was nothing to report, he'd invent a sweet or comic story to buoy their spirits. On Wednesdays, he always steeled himself for the question of what he'd done after class, but Laura never asked. It was just another thing they didn't discuss. Eventually she would excuse herself from the table, kiss Griff on his head, then retire to the bedroom. More often than not, the sun was still in the sky, syrupy and molten, coppering the early-evening surfaces.

When Eric shut off the shower, there was only the steady hum of the air conditioner. Tracy might still be lying across the bed, her eyes closed and her dark hair wild on the pillows, or she might have already stripped the sheets and taken them to the washer. He dried himself with a thick towel, stepped too carefully from the tub. For years, he'd had an unfounded fear of falling in the bathroom, of cracking his skull on porcelain. He'd known no one who'd suffered such a fall, and yet the risk felt familiar and menacing, as if he'd suddenly grown ancient and infirm in the shower. In Tracy's bathroom, the vanity was marble-topped, sharp-edged and expensive. The whole condo brimmed with upgrades—Saltillo tile, a Viking range, one air-conditioning system for the first floor and another for the second. Every week, the lavishness sullied him; he wouldn't let his gaze settle on anything. Now, pulling on his boots, he wished he'd already left.

VILLA DEL SOL HAD BEEN BUILT AFTER SOUTHPORT LOST ITS BID for the naval station. Most of the sandstone condos were owned by people from Corpus or by snowbirds, silver-haired retirees who wintered on the coast and caned their way through the souvenir shops on Station Street. "It's snowing," Laura used to say when they'd get stuck behind an elderly driver. They lived in a three-bedroom ranch, a few blocks from the house where Eric had grown up and where his father still lived. Their house was drafty, in need of a new roof, double-mortgaged to put up the reward money. Every couple of years he had to raise the foundation with bottle jacks.

But when Villa Del Sol first opened, Eric had driven Laura and the boys to an open house. Justin was nine, Griff was seven. Everyone wore church clothes.

"Who can afford one of these?" Laura said in the living room of the model unit. "No one we know."

"We're not that far off," Eric said, trying to sound assured. "Besides, no charge for looking."

The boys were in the courtyard, hunting rocks. Griff had recently started collecting them, because Justin did. Laura watched them through the bay window. She said, "Guess what Justin asked me last night."

"If Rainbow could sleep inside?" he said. Rainbow was their black Lab, a dog Eric had bought from a man selling puppies out of his truck bed on Station Street. Rainbow was a good, affable dog, but she'd recently been relegated to the backyard after Eric woke to find her chewing one of his boots.

"Yes, but something else," Laura said.

"About cusswords? The other day he asked me if there were any he could say without getting in trouble."

"He asked me to marry him."

"Oh," Eric said. "Smart boy."

"You don't think it's weird?"

"He's got good taste in women, is what I think."

Laura paced across the room with her hands clasped in front of her. She looked like a woman in a museum, taking care not to bump into exhibits. Were she a stranger, Eric would've been struck with longing as he watched her languid movements. His wife—it still shocked him—was beautiful. She returned to the window to watch the boys.

"What are we doing here, honey? We're not—"

"I thought it'd be fun," he said. He crouched in front of the fireplace, trying to figure if it worked. Just for show, he thought.

"I don't want to live anywhere else. Neither do the boys. We love our house."

"It was just something to do."

"Sometimes I worry you feel like you need to give us more."

He couldn't remember *not* feeling that way. Though he hadn't yet told Laura, he'd just agreed to teach summer school. His plan was to surprise everyone with a vacation over Christmas break. The boys had never left Texas.

"We have everything we need," she said. Outside, Griff was trying to show Justin a piece of limestone he'd found.

"What did you tell him?" Eric asked, pushing himself up from the fireplace.

"Who?"

"Your suitor."

She smiled as if he'd paid her a compliment. Her eyes stayed on their sons. "I said I loved him very much, but I was already married."

"He must've been heartbroken."

"Crushed," she said. "Utterly crushed. But then I helped him sneak Rainbow into his room and he seemed to recover."

WHEN ERIC STEPPED FROM THE BATHROOM, TRACY WAS STANDING with her back to him. She peered through her bedroom blinds, watching the two sisters who owned the condo across the courtyard. The women were in their eighties, stooped and wire-haired. Tracy loved spying on them. She'd wrapped herself in a sheet that puddled around her ankles and exposed her back. The knuckles of her spine looked like shells in sand. Laura's body, he thought, might resemble Tracy's now; she'd lost weight over the last four years. Twenty pounds, maybe more. And ever since Justin had gone missing, she'd let her hair grow out, a protest of sorts, or a show of solidarity. She'd stopped shaving her legs and under her arms, too. Eric couldn't remember the last time he'd seen his wife naked.

"I think the sisters' air conditioner's busted," Tracy said. "They're just sitting at the kitchen table, fanning themselves."

He was tempted to say he'd walk over and take a look, but

checked himself. He didn't want to run into the sisters later. For old girls, they got around just fine. They drove a Lincoln Continental. Eric said, "After I leave, tell them to have someone check the Freon."

"Sexy handyman," she said. "I was just going to visit the pawnshop and see if your father had a window unit I could buy for them."

"He had two yesterday. They're marked at eighty, but he's only got thirty into them. He'll take sixty."

"You're just full of helpful information. Give me ten minutes to repay you?"

Eric slipped his phone into his pocket, clasped his watch around his wrist. He put his wedding band back on and said, "I need to head out."

Tracy raked her fingers through her hair, then parted the blinds again. She said, "How's the whale this week?"

"Dolphin," he said, correcting her. "Running a fever, I think."

"Poor thing."

"I need to pick up some new flyers and make the rounds."

"They don't last long, I guess."

The flyers hung in most storefronts in Southport, taped among the rummage sale notices and advertisements for windsurfing lessons. They were also posted from Corpus to Ingleside and all the way up the I-37 corridor into San Antonio; there were a few donated billboards, too, one standing just outside Southport. If the flyers went unchanged, the sun bleached the image and the words. Eric checked them vigilantly. In the last four years, he'd put forty thousand miles on his truck, most of them within a twenty-mile radius. Today he wanted to leave a stack of flyers at the Alamo Fireworks stand out on the highway. Early on, the flyers had generated a lot of leads; now, they were down to four or five a month, usually from crazies or pranks. They'd used Justin's fifth-grade yearbook photo. In it, he wore a western shirt and his hair was too short. Eric had cut it in the garage the night before; then to make amends for the botched job, he'd handed Justin the clippers and let him go to town on his father's head. When they'd come inside, Laura had said, *Did y'all use the lawn mower instead of scissors?* and Griff had fussed until Eric and Justin took him into the garage and buzzed his head, too. For months, clippings from his sons' hair would wisp onto the workbench like daddy longlegs. When the detective wanted a DNA sample, Eric spent hours on his hands and knees in the garage, but turned up nothing. It was Laura who'd simply pulled strands of hair from the brush on Justin's dresser.

He'd been eleven, almost twelve, excited to start middle school. He'd been a skateboarder, a boy who loved the Blue Angels and hated the beach.

Now Eric said, "I also need to swing by the marina and pick up some shrimp for supper."

"Your famous recipe," Tracy said.

"Griff hasn't been eating. I think he's in a dustup with his girl."

"The one who's a little older."

"If she heads for the hills, he'll be one lonely cowboy. Most of his other friends have gone AWOL."

"I remember," she said.

"He does okay during the school year. He gets invited to birthday parties and little camping trips. Summers are tougher."

"At least he's not getting in fights anymore," Tracy said.

"At least," Eric said.

She let the blinds snap shut. As she turned from the window and crawled back into bed, Eric saw that she'd been crying. His throat closed. He looked at his boots.

"Sorry," she said.

And then this familiar thought: How did I get here? The pieces that made up his life seemed pulled from another man's existence— the berth he and Laura afforded each other, these bleak and sweaty afternoons with Tracy. Even that he was in his forty-fourth year confounded him; most mornings, he woke feeling like the boy whose thin arm could inexplicably send a tight, perfect spiral seventy yards. And, of course, Justin. Sometimes he'd pass the closed door of Justin's room and forget for a beautiful moment that he was gone. How often in the last four years had he almost knocked? Then, when his thoughts fitted themselves to reality, he felt cored out and drugged, groping awkwardly through his days as if he'd lost a limb in an accident, an arm or leg whose weight he still anticipated. He recognized its absence, and yet he could still feel the arteries as they dilated, the nerves as they burned.

Tracy rustled under the sheets, bunched a pillow under her head. She was fingering her hair, twisting it, looking for split ends. He smiled so she could see. Maybe she smiled back a little, furtively. His phone started buzzing in his pocket. It was loud against his keys.

Tracy said, "It rang while you were in the shower, too. If you want privacy, I can take the sheets to the washer."

"It's Griff saying he's going to skate," he said without checking. "I'll call him when I leave."

"I wasn't crying about you."

"I'm glad," he said.

"I *do* cry about you, but I usually hold those pity parties after you've left. They're very exclusive."

"I'm not worth—"

"I'm in Alaska this month," Tracy said. She wrote articles for a travel magazine, though she never visited the destinations. Each month, her editor sent a manila envelope pregnant with statistics and featured attractions that Tracy shaped into a story. "I'm in São Paulo," she'd say. Or "I'm in Sag Harbor." Now she said, "And watching the sisters fan themselves, I started thinking about polar bears, how the whole world's melting around them."

"I don't know," he said. "Alaska sounds like a mighty fine place to spend the summer."

"North to the Future," she said.

"North to the Future?"

"State motto."

He averted his eyes to the window, the blinds laddering light across the bed. The air conditioner droned. Tracy was still studying her hair.

He said, "I should get going."

"Leave the garage door open. I'll close it when I put the sheets in the wash."

"Sure thing."

"You're a good father, Eric," she said. "You think you're not because of what we're doing, but you are. You're a good husband, too."

Tracy said such things occasionally, and Eric always suspected she was trying to convince herself as much as him. They'd been sleeping together for a year. More and more Eric had the sorry sense that he and Laura were both just treading water, trying to stay afloat until Griff graduated high school. A good husband. A good father. He only knew he'd filled those roles at one time, though he could hardly recall it now. He watched shafts of lurid sunlight slant through the blinds, the dust motes eddying like galaxies.

"It's the pads of their feet," Tracy said.

"Do what now?"

"Polar bears," she said. "Something about those black pads on their white feet makes me really sad."

He leaned across the bed, pressed his lips to her cheek. As always when he was leaving her, he felt at once restored and ashamed. *This can't be my life. This* isn't *my life.* The feeling he had was one of erasure, as if their time together diminished him, stripped him down to some essence he could concentrate on rebuilding. He would do better from here on out. He'd check the flyers, run by the fireworks stand and the marina, fry shrimp. After dinner, he'd run a hot bath for Laura. They were both off tomorrow, so maybe they'd take Griff to the skate park in Corpus, get his mind off his doomed heart.

Eric passed through the condo and into the garage like a man who was late, a man who'd kept his family waiting too long. As he was backing his truck out of the garage, his phone started up again.

Years later, he would remember very little about that afternoon. Not how he'd parked on the street to dig the phone from his pocket, or how he'd assumed Tracy was calling to elaborate on the polar bears, or how the disparate parts of an idea about taking Laura and Griff to Alaska were crystallizing in his mind. *North to the future.* The light that afternoon washed everything out; the asphalt looked chalky under tremors of heat. Eric could feel eyes on him—maybe Tracy was peeking through the blinds and calling to say he'd forgotten something on the nightstand—but when he reached his phone, the caller ID showed a Corpus prefix, so he assumed Laura was calling from Marine Lab. He thought she'd tell him she was staying late so he and Griff should go ahead and eat. He thought her voice would drip with grief, and despite his earlier resolve, he didn't want to hear her just then. What Eric would remember for the rest of his life was how he almost didn't answer.

ACROSS THE STREET, RUTH AND BEVERLY WILCOX WERE STILL fanning themselves, waiting for their air conditioner to kick in. Bev had woken up worried about money again, so they'd left the air off until Ruth finally said phooey and lowered the thermostat. Now they were watching Justin Campbell's father in his truck. They thought his engine had stalled again, but eventually realized he was taking a phone call. Ruth called his afternoons with the married gal "The Soap." "Time for The Soap," she'd say, and Bev would break out the Lorna Doones. They knew what he'd endured, what he and his poor wife had lost. Everyone knew. Sipping their midday coffee, Ruth and Beverly wondered silently how you'd go on, how you wouldn't just up and die. They were both widows, Ruth to cancer and Beverly to Korea, but to lose a child was an altogether worse kind of hurt, a scar that would absolve all manner of sins. And they did think of him as scarred. Grief had disfigured him. He looked slackened. Each week there seemed a little less of him. Ruth had been the one to notice how, all these years later, some folks at church still stole pitiful and sadistic glances at him, like he'd been burned, like his face was mottled and waxy with misfortune. She had also noticed how his wife had stopped coming to services. So let him diddle, she thought. So let him find some respite.

"Who's he talking to?" she asked now.

"How in the world should I know?" Bev said.

Ruth hadn't meant to speak the words, or if she had, she'd meant them rhetorically. The truth was she'd been curious about the young man's life even before he started parking his little Toyota truck in the garage across the street. Maybe he reminded Ruth of her own son, maybe she was a little sweet on him, maybe his sadness mystified her the way it did Tracy Robichaud. Once, before his son went missing, he'd held a door open for her and Bev at the Castaway Café by the marina. (His father drank coffee there every morning, Ruth knew. Cecil was a tall man with hard, sad eyes. There were stories that he'd known violence. Oh, she'd like to sop him up with a biscuit.) After she and her sister stepped inside the café, his wife and two sons followed; the boys were rambunctious, slicing around her legs like trout. One of them knocked into her—Ruth believed it had been Justin, but Bev maintained it was the younger brother—and she'd almost toppled. Justin Campbell's father made the boy come back and apologize. It was embarrassing. She could feel her cheeks turning to apples. But Ruth remembered how he kept his palm on the boy's back, how he'd been trying not to smile as his son made amends. After supper, the boy came over to the table and shyly placed a piece of flint in her hand. "I found this for you," he said. She'd made an excited face and told him how pretty it was—he grinned, looked at his feet, then back at his family's booth—then she made a big production of letting Bev see the rock before slipping it in her purse. Today, as the missing boy's father's truck suddenly rocketed up the street and around the corner ("Wife must be coming home early," Bev said and cackled), Ruth wished she knew what had become of that small stone. She'd like to give it to him some Sunday at church, tell him she remembered how he'd been trying to raise a good boy. Or maybe that would only wound him more. It didn't matter. She hadn't seen the stone since they moved into Villa Del Sol. No, you don't think to keep an eye on a little thing like that.

2

SHE WAS A YOUNG BOTTLENOSE, MAYBE FIVE YEARS OLD. ON an unseasonably cool morning in April, Eddie Cavazos, a park employee on sea turtle patrol, had found her stranded near Mile Marker 18 on the Padre Island National Seashore. He believed the dolphin was dead until he stepped closer and she slapped her tail on the sand. He jumped. He looked around for help, but the beach was deserted. He knew not to push her back into the water, knew she'd either drown or strand herself farther up the coast, but his knowledge of beached dolphins ended there. He radioed the ranger station, and the dispatcher paged Marine Lab. Eddie waited. He kept hearing phantom trucks that never approached. He called the station again, then again. Two hours passed, endless and harrowing hours in which he continually doused the dolphin with water, stroked her sides and pectoral fins, even sang songs his grandmother used to sing because the melodies seemed to calm the animal's breathing. Then the crew arrived, trucked her to the converted warehouse, lowered her into a four-foot-deep, forty-thousand-gallon aboveground pool. She was diagnosed with pneumonia, severe dehydration, an intestinal infection. And, most distressingly, she wouldn't swim. Unassisted, she would sink to the bottom of the rehab tank, water folding over her like thick cloth. She weighed almost three hundred pounds, so keeping her afloat took four, sometimes five, volunteers. They wore wet suits and surgical masks while cradling her in the water. When she refused to eat, they gave her fish gruel through gastric tubes. No one expected her to live.

Then, a week later, in the middle of an overnight shift—murder shifts, they were called—the dolphin bucked and broke free from the volunteers' arms and went slicing around the pool. She swam along the bottom, breached for air, dove low again. The volunteers— including Laura Campbell—vacated the tank, then stood watching from the observation deck. Swimming on her own, the dolphin looked sleek and ethereal, like the shadow of a cloud gliding on the water. Within days she was eating solid food, fatty herring and capelin injected with antibiotics. She gained weight. She played with balls, a hula hoop, even an inflatable alligator that Laura had found wadded up in her garage. The dolphin clapped her jaw and chuffed when angry, and skyhopped when she wanted attention, extending her head from the water like a periscope. Laura had a picture of her magneted on the fridge among coupons and Eric's summer teaching schedule and the postcard from California. In the photo, the dolphin peered out of the water with her mouth open. Her teeth looked like a string of small, perfect pearls.

Pinning down why she'd stranded was impossible. Blood work ruled out morbillivirus and meningitis. Maybe an algae bloom or red tide was floating somewhere in the Gulf, or maybe she'd been fleeing a shark. Or she may have just gotten lost, exhausted. Her body mass was too small for a far offshore pod, but some of the barnacles she'd brought in were found only in deep water. The barnacles would, in fact, make returning her to open water a logistical and bureaucratic nightmare—Fish and Wildlife would require a battery of tests to determine where she'd come from and where she might safely be released—but those were distant, possibly moot concerns. She'd stay at Marine Lab for six months, maybe a year, depending on her progress. More pressing was the need for extra volunteers, donations, a name. The tradition at Marine Lab was that naming rights fell to whoever found the animal, so once the rescue director felt confident the dolphin would live, he tracked down Eddie Cavazos. Eddie's first instinct was to name her after his daughter, but he quickly reconsidered: If the dolphin took a turn for the worse, the name might seem an omen. Instead, he chose Alice. It was his grandmother's name, the name of a sturdy and stubborn woman who'd died in her sleep twenty years before.

Volunteering at Marine Lab consisted mostly of taking notes. Some twelve volunteers a day systematically logged how many breaths Alice took, when and what she ate, what direction she swam in, when she vocalized or played with a toy or moved her bowels. It was tedious work—"Your job is to pay attention," Paul Perez, the rescue director, always told new volunteers—but the monotony comforted Laura. Before she started volunteering, she could feel too pent-up and find herself doing things she'd never imagined. Once, she'd been detained for pocketing some nail polish at the drugstore in Southport. Both the police officer and the store manager knew her—meaning, they knew about Justin—so they let her off with a warning. How to explain she'd never actually wanted the nail polish and that not being arrested had been a disappointment? That it had left her livid? Over the years, she'd purposely slammed her fingers in a desk drawer; she'd thrown sweet tea in a fat woman's face at the Castaway after the woman said, *I'm still just so broken up about your boy.* And then there were the times when she locked the bathroom door and sat in the empty bathtub, watching the day succumb to night. Twice she'd come so unglued in public that someone had to call Eric at school to come get her. "Maybe we should think about seeing someone," he'd said, and she'd nodded to appease him, thinking, Maybe the world is too much for me. Maybe I'm too small for this place now.

But the hours at Marine Lab calmed her, stoked her optimism in ways that nothing else did—certainly not the church-basement support groups: Beyond Grief. Comforting Other Parents Who Have

Experienced Sorrow (COPES). Anger Management. Bereaved Families. Work could occasionally prove distracting if a customer brought in a challenging stain, a blotch that would take time and ingenuity to remove, some soiling that seemed impossibly permanent, but she mostly saw shirts that needed laundering, slacks that required pressing. Only Marine Lab brought her any peace. Eric, she knew, believed she volunteered to clear her mind, but it was the opposite: She went to nourish herself, to absorb and metabolize that which would sustain her outside the warehouse. "Like blubber," she'd once said, trying to make him understand, or at least laugh. He did neither. Occasionally, she'd felt obligated to invite him to volunteer with her—maybe it would help to repair the countless fissures in their marriage—and yet she was always shamefully pleased when he declined. It was like getting away with something. In the warehouse, no one knew who she was. When she first filled out her volunteer paperwork, she used her maiden name.

On the last Wednesday in June, Laura stood beside the pool and watched Alice swim in silent, lazy circles. Her shift had ended twenty minutes earlier, but she'd lingered after the next volunteer arrived. The air in the warehouse was clammy, salted; much of the space lay in shadows with only a grainy, diffused light canting through random fiberglass panels on the roof. Marine Lab was just over the Harbor Bridge and the Corpus Christi Ship Channel, an hour's drive from Southport. If she left right away, she'd get home by six-thirty or seven, depending on traffic. She wasn't ready to head out, though. Alice had been running a fever the last few days, and the vet was due to stop by with an update. Five more minutes, she thought. Her back ached from sitting on the pool's wooden observation deck, and her veins thrummed with exhaustion. She hadn't slept well the night before—she rarely did, unless she allowed herself an Ambien—and then she'd worked the early shift at the dry cleaner's. Thinking of it made her yawn. She snapped a rubber band off her wrist and pulled her long hair into a loose ponytail. A sparrow bounced around the warehouse rafters, then landed on a beam and started chirping. Laura wondered if Alice could hear the bird underwater, if she was whistling back. Last night, when Laura couldn't sleep, she'd done the dishes and then stayed up reading about dolphins' acoustic signatures.

She was about to leave when she saw that the current volunteer had missed something crucial. He'd been texting. On principle, Laura always left her phone in the car, and it riled her when volunteers checked messages or took calls on the observation deck. It happened a lot. What, she sometimes wondered, had volunteers been too distracted to see when they'd been looking for Justin? No way to know. The police rarely allowed her or Eric to participate; the parents of the missing child were themselves a distraction. This volunteer looked to be in his mid-thirties. He was Mexican with a thick neck and arms. He reminded Laura of an army recruiter.

"Excuse me," Laura said. "We're supposed to make a note of that."

"Of what?"

She pointed toward the loose black swirl dispersing in the water. The volunteer looked, but didn't see.

Laura said, "She pooped."

"Crap," he said.

The man checked his watch, then jotted the note on his data sheet. Overhead, the sparrow started batting around again, knocking into walls. Alice swam counterclockwise. Laura hoped she'd roll onto her side and make eye contact as she passed, but she stayed beneath the surface.

"I'm covering for my wife. She's sick today," the man said, his gaze following Alice. "She just texted. She wants jalapeño corn bread and a milk shake. She's pregnant."

Oh, Laura thought. She peered into the drab, cloudy water; the pool needed more chlorine. She said, "Congratulations."

"Thank you." He sounded sheepish, like he hadn't yet cottoned to the idea of fatherhood.

Alice rubbed her back and dorsal fin on the stiff orange rope stretched across the water. She glided against it slowly, then turned around to work her other side. The volunteer made a note. By the end of his shift, the log sheet would be dark with thatches marking how many times she'd gone to the rope.

Laura glanced at the clock above the grease board that outlined Alice's med schedule. Maybe the vet had gotten delayed at his clinic, but more likely he was stuck on the Harbor Bridge. Traffic always backed up in June, so no telling when he'd finally pull into the parking lot. Now, suddenly, she just wanted to get the drive home behind her. She thought to stop at the grocery store and see if a new skateboard magazine was on the newsstand. Griff had been having a hard week. Girl trouble. Her gentle, radiant son. They called him Lobster, a nickname they loved more than he did. When he entered a room, her heart rose, like a sweet old dog, to greet him.

She was stepping away from the pool when the volunteer said, "My wife has a dolphin tattoo on her ankle."

"Cute," Laura said.

"She got it in Cancún on our honeymoon. We went swimming with a few dolphins in a little cove, then next thing I know we're at a tattoo parlor. I almost passed out. I'm a tough hombre, but needles get to me."

Laura could've told him about the dolphin pendant Eric and Griff had given her, but she didn't. She knew she should wear it more often, knew they worried they'd picked out the wrong gift. She actually loved it. She just preferred to look at it in her jewelry box. Jewelry had lost its appeal; anything that drew attention had.

Alice made another pass, hugging the side of the pool, then returned to the rope. Small waves rippled the surface, catching and throwing the overhead light, then petered out. Tonight Laura would tell Eric about meeting the volunteer, about the couple's honeymoon. It felt refreshing to have something to share. He'd get quietly excited about Cancún, start imagining a vacation. Maybe she'd wear the necklace. Her husband, so beautifully and intimidatingly stalwart in his dreams. When he entered a room, something inside her receded.

"Man," the volunteer said, "she really loves that rope."

"She's exfoliating," Laura said.

In the back office, Paul Perez was on the phone, negotiating for more bags of salt to be donated. His voice rose and fell, rose again.

The volunteer swiped his brow with his forearm. He said, "We hit a hundred today and still didn't break the rec—"

"Was your wife pregnant on your honeymoon?" Laura asked.

"Depends on who's asking," he said, then laughed.

Overhead, a wispy commotion: the sparrow darting around, bonking into corners, looking for a way out.

"Well," Laura said, "the dolphins in the cove knew. They would've been doing sonograms while you were swimming. They like pregnant women, and people with metal in their bodies. They see through us."

"Wait, I know this: the clicking stuff?"

"Bingo," she said. Probably his wife had told him about echolocation. Maybe her nightstand, like Laura's, was cluttered with overdue library books on cetaceans. Some of Laura's books had been checked out for over a year and never renewed. She had yet to receive a late-return notice, though. When the librarians saw the books had been borrowed by Justin Campbell's mother, a woman who used to be pretty and capable, they likely just marked them LOST.

The pool pump chugged, a quick deviation in its rhythm that reminded Laura she'd been hearing it all afternoon. Her mind was dull, gummed up, and she had a sense of being on a precipice, precariously balancing between reason and collapse. Time to go, she thought. Eric was frying shrimp tonight. Laura couldn't remember if she'd eaten anything since breakfast. Actually, she couldn't re-member if she'd eaten anything since yesterday.

The sparrow flew to another rafter, started chirping. Alice ex-haled a mist that hung in the air, a silvery cloud. The volunteer marked the breath, and Laura realized that he'd been talking.

"I'm sorry?" she said.

"I asked how long you'd been working here."

"I'm just a volunteer," she said, flattered. Then she added, "And a mother. That's all I am."

BEFORE LEAVING THE WAREHOUSE, LAURA SIGNED UP FOR TWO more shifts over the weekend. She also left a note on the grease board about the chlorine—*Are the tablets fully dissolving?*—and put a bag of frozen herring in the sink to thaw, ran warm water over it. She washed her hands and dried her palms on her shirt, one of Eric's old button-ups she kept in her car to wear at Marine Lab. The shirt had come from the dry cleaner's. She'd brought it home after the customer failed to pick up his order. She got a lot of Eric's clothes that way. Hers, too. Alice exhaled, and Laura watched the volun-teer mark the breath on his sheet. She waved goodbye to Paul in the office—he was still on the phone and made a show of rolling his eyes at the conversation—then stepped out of the warehouse and into the brilliant sun.

The sky was alabaster, the sun swamping and wet-wool-heavy on her skin. She shelved her hand over her eyes, and the depth of her fatigue hit her. She stood still, mindful of her body's emptiness. The feeling wasn't unpleasant. When she and Eric first started dating, he used to take her floundering at midnight. She never actually fished, but she loved pulling on the waders and walking into the brackish, moonlit water, then feeling herself sink a little as the sand slipped beneath her heels. They wouldn't come home until dawn, her skin tight with dried salt water, her hair matted with sand, her every cell vibrating with fatigue. He would fry flounder for breakfast while she showered. They ate it with lemon and Tabasco sauce. When they finally went to bed, the waves were still rolling in her stomach.

She heard a car pull into the driveway from the road. The driveway, a long stretch of caliche that ran alongside Marine Lab's redfish hatchery, was on the opposite side of the warehouse, and although she couldn't see the car, she knew it was Dr. Frye. A pair of seagulls banked around the building, scared from their perches when the vet steered into the lot. Pebbles pinged against the car's undercarriage. He was going faster than she liked. Bad news, she thought. Maybe there were signs of infection in Alice's blood, or another intestinal parasite. Now that he was here, she couldn't leave without hearing what he had found. Five more minutes, she thought again, and turned back toward the warehouse. One of the gulls landed in the blond grass edging the parking lot, the other on the dumpster where volunteers disposed of unused capelin. A raised 4x4 truck was parked near the dumpster, probably the volunteer's. A breeze kicked up, pulling in the soily smell of the ship channel, and gently lifting and spreading the branches of a nearby red mulberry.

Maybe Laura recognized the sound of her husband's truck as he pulled up beside her, but maybe not. She would never be sure. Even when he was upon her, when she was looking into his wild eyes and he seemed to be saying, *Get to Corpus. We need to get to Corpus*, she wasn't positive that she understood whom she was seeing. She knew only that nothing good could come of it. Light was narrowing, dimming; it was as if the sun were being hastily put away. He was lowering his window, or it was already down. His face was flushed and bloated, the way it sometimes was when he came in from the garage and refused to admit his sadness. Seeing him— seeing him *there*—dizzied her. She dropped her keys. She heard a garage door in the warehouse rolling up: A pallet of salt bags would be delivered soon. Inexplicably, she remembered Griffin dressing as a sheep one Halloween, a costume they'd made by gluing pillow stuffing to a wet suit his grandfather had brought over from the pawnshop. The garage door rose, the chains clattering. The tickle of dust in her nose, the slow and distinct feeling of her knees buckling, her ankles going to mud. Her stomach turned. The truck was idling. She wanted to speak, but her mouth might as well have been full of sand. She knew no words. Language itself had atrophied. She was suddenly—fiercely, wholly—grateful that her own parents were dead, grateful that they wouldn't have to live through this, wouldn't have to watch their daughter live through it.

Eric opened his door, came toward her, called her name as her vision was smearing and blurring and exploding into countless specks of light. Had she been thinking clearly, she might have recalled the sick beauty of those early night searches for Justin in the dunes, all of the flashlights playing over the sand like a single fluid body, bright as a bloom of luminescent algae. Or she might have thought of the night sky, how she sometimes sought in vain the dolphin-shaped constellation Delphinus. But there was no clarity to her thoughts. Nothing made sense. She was detaching from herself, rising and rising until she was peering down on everything. She saw a man gathering his wife in his arms, the glint of dropped keys in the sun, the water in the ship channel as gray and still as a lithograph. Then, just before the world went black, she saw a tiny sparrow swoop through the warehouse's garage door, a flutter of wings that caught a current of wind and was carried skyward.

3

CECIL CAMPBELL WAS NOT SOMEONE WHO RUSHED. HE WAS sixty-seven, a widower and grandfather, a pawnbroker with a felony gambling conviction, and what he'd learned of the world was that impatience might as well be called arrogance. Smugness. Vanity. So when Ivan Martinez handed him Eric's phone message—written in Martinez's clean print, on the back of a triplicate pawn ticket—Cecil read the few words deliberately, as if translating them into a new language: *Pick up Griff. No TV, radio, computer.*

Okay, he thought. Okay. I can do that.

This was behind the jewelry showcase at Loan Star Pawnshop, amidst the whir of various fans oscillating around the shop. The air felt so cool and clean Cecil wanted to close his eyes. Ivan was talking in a hurried and apologizing way, saying he'd asked Eric to hold the line so he could run and grab his father—Cecil had been in the parking lot buying the Cadillac from a sailor fixing to go AWOL—but Eric couldn't wait; he got another call and hung up. Cecil nodded. Someone had tied tinselly ribbons to the fans; he was noticing them now for the first time. He lingered a moment longer, then slid the keys to the Caddy across the counter to Ivan and rapped his knuckles against the glass and started for the door. His Ford pickup was parked beside the arrow marquee: WE BUY WINDOW UNITS!

When he pulled out of the parking lot, there was no spray of dust behind his tires. He eased onto the road slowly.

Cecil drove the speed limit. He considered backtracking to his house to pick up his cell phone, but decided it wasn't worth the time. Patience wasn't procrastination. It wasn't lollygagging. Still, he wished he'd brought the phone to work. When everything had first started, they'd all carried the phones everywhere, but now Cecil mostly left his at home. People knew where to find him. The grooves of his life were deep and rigid. He drank black coffee every morning at the Castaway Café, then went to Loan Star, then home for supper after work; he usually ate tamales, or beans and rice, or steak in a bag, but occasionally a shrimper would swap swordfish or shark meat for something in pawn, and Cecil would drag out his hibachi. Some evenings he'd piddle in the garage or play solitaire or go floundering, but most often he'd drive around checking the flyers at the filling stations and rest stops. On those nights, he took the phone with him in case something turned up. The phones had been donated, the unlimited minutes too, and early on, Cecil thought they'd make a difference. You clung to what you could. His hadn't rung in years, though. He wasn't sure he knew the phone's number anymore. He stopped carrying it because the weight of the thing in his pocket reminded him of what they'd all lost.

The Ford's steering wheel was baking, so he drove with a handkerchief cupped under his palm. Sweat tracked down from his armpits; the thin cotton of his shirt went damp and sticky between his back and the vinyl seat. He scanned radio stations, but found only music and commercials and a preacher from Corpus. The station he liked most was doing the surf and fishing report, which was sometimes followed by news, so he left the dial there. He was heading toward his son's house on Suntide Road. Griff, he knew, played videogames on summer afternoons, and with the heat still coming on, he could easily imagine the boy sprawled on the couch, working his thumbs on the controller. He should have stopped in the office before leaving Loan Star; over the weekend, a man had pawned a couple of videogames and he'd stashed them away for Griff. Probably Griff already had them—mostly people hocked the same ones—but Cecil would have liked to have been holding something when he knocked on the front door, something to distract the boy from the miserable randomness of his grandfather's visit.

Traffic lurched on Station Street. He thought of being in a funeral procession, not something that had come into his mind before, and he wished it hadn't now. According to the radio, the surf was flat and the drum weren't biting. The mercury had crossed the century mark. No other news. Cecil was idling behind a beach buggy, its chrome tailpipe rattling and angled toward the sky like a rooster tail. The ferries were running slow with folks leaving the island. In his mirror was an RV towing a boat trailer, and behind that a Jeep with surfboards stacked on its roof like warped pallets. He scrolled back through the radio stations. On any other day, he would've been listening to one of the classical CDs he took from Loan Star. He liked unaccompanied pieces, the calming austerity of the notes— his favorite was the Prelude from Bach's Cello Suite no. 1—but now he didn't want to associate the music with whatever was coming down the pike. He cracked his knuckles, one at a time, with his thumb. He wiped his forehead and slid his handkerchief back into his pocket. A gull was balancing on the Shrimporee banner strung over the road, raising and lowering its wings, but it soon wheeled off toward the marina.

He glanced at his watch, the gold nugget band refracting light. A group of tourists walked along the road with umbrellas to block the sun; a truck full of shirtless young men was trying to nose into the line up ahead. He should've anticipated the traffic and taken a different route.

"Goddamn," he said.

A horn bleated a few cars behind Cecil's truck, and then others started sounding. Like dogs, he thought. When the brake lights began blinking off ahead of him, he was leaning forward and reaching beneath his seat. He felt his spotlight, some paper trash, the cool and heavy links of a tow chain. Then, the waxy leather of the holster. The pistol was a Smith & Wesson .44, loaded with Short Colts, unregistered. It had come through the shop a few years back, and Cecil had paid for it with cash money from his own pocket without filling out a pawn ticket. No one knew it existed, certainly not Eric or Laura or Griff. This was another thing he'd learned over the years: Sometimes a man's obligation was to tell his family what he knew of life, but more often his duty was to keep it to himself.

Every surface seemed flattened by the strong sun, as if a thin white sheet had been laid over the landscape. Cecil lowered his visor, looking for his sunglasses. They weren't there. Nor were they in his shirt pocket or on the seat or in the glove box. He squinted at the road ahead, remembering the countless times Connie had lost her sunglasses and how he'd let it annoy him.

He tried to imagine where Eric was right now, what he was enduring. Cecil worried about him. Not merely because he was his son, but because, of everyone affected—save Justin, of course—Eric seemed the most vulnerable. Laura was tougher than she let on, and Griff took after her; you could see years in their eyes, the conviction to persevere. With Eric, Cecil didn't know. His son carried himself stoically enough, and he'd done the hard, right thing of buckling down in these last years, but Cecil wasn't convinced the façade would hold up. There was some softness in him, a naïveté, a capaciousness of the heart that Cecil wanted to admire but could only see as liability. Before his mother died—Eric was seventeen when the Corpus doctor found the tumors lighting Connie's X-rays—they'd been raising him toward a life opposite of theirs, an uncomplicated life of college and vacations and starting a family outside of Texas. After she was gone, Cecil understood how they'd cheated him: His son was a smart man, a kind man, not quite a strong one.

At Eric's house, Cecil expected Griff to answer the door right away, but he stood on the porch for a few minutes without a response. He knocked again on the screen, then opened it and rapped on the door itself. Nothing. He pushed the doorbell, knowing full well it hadn't worked in years, then knocked again, louder.

"Griffin," he called. "Son, it's Papaw."

He turned to look out into the yellowed front yard, then up and down Suntide. Across the street, the Daweses' driveway was empty and he wondered if there was anything to read into that. Some people believed that Ronnie Dawes, the retarded man who lived there with his mother, might be at fault. Cecil hoped not. He listened for noise inside the house, but heard nothing beyond the wind soughing through the leaves. Maybe Griff had gone back to sleep. Maybe with school out, he'd stayed up all night and hadn't woken yet, or maybe he and his mordant girlfriend were holed up in his room, giggling at the old man sweating on the porch. Cecil had never seen the girl wear a stitch that wasn't black. She came into Loan Star occasionally and shyly flipped through the CD bin. He knocked again, hard and fast and serious. *Come on, boy.* He squinted through the door's small, leaded window. His son's house lay in darkness; the couch and recliner and coffee table were just darker patches of dark. He turned around again, as something put him in the mind of being watched. He tried the knob, then stepped off the porch and crossed the dry lawn.

The gate to the backyard was tethered with a looped piece of rusted wire. He unhooked it and walked along the western side of the house. The air conditioner wasn't running, which likely meant the boy had raised the thermostat before leaving. Cecil hadn't entertained the possibility of his grandson being anywhere but at the house, though he should have. Stupid, he thought. Just flat-out stupid. When he came to Griff's window, blacked out with foil, he knocked on it and called out again, then moved into the backyard itself. There was good shade, a nice canopy of tallow and chinaberry and retama, but the grass was knee-high in places, overrun and tangled with weeds that snagged at his boots. Walking took concentration, as if he were fording a river. Twigs popped under-foot. The yard looked tired. It made *him* tired. The odor of dry dirt, dog shit. Under the faucet, Rainbow's water bowl looked recently filled, but not cleaned. It was rimmed with green-black algae.

Beside the three steps that rose to the kitchen door, the lattice had been jigsawed so Rainbow could steal under the house and stay cool when she wasn't inside; after Justin went missing, Eric and Laura had allowed the dog back in the house to sleep with Griff. Cecil pressed his forehead to the glass in the door, knocked, peered inside. The countertop had been wiped down, plates and bowls and glasses drying in the dish rack. Washing dishes, he believed, was Griff's chore. On the fridge hung the picture of Laura's dolphin and the arrowhead postcard that had raised everyone's hopes. It had ar-rived two years earlier, shortly after the second anniversary of Jus-tin's disappearance. The face showed nine arrowheads, and on the back, in handwriting everyone strained to see as Justin's, were the words *Don't Stop Looking*. A red light was blinking on the answer-ing machine under the cordless phone. Cecil believed—hoped—that meant the messages hadn't been played, but he could certainly envi-sion his grandson standing next to the machine, listening as the call was being recorded. Maybe he'd heard something, gone to pieces, run off.

"Griff," he called, knocking on the door. "Lobster, you in there?"

The glass was smudged with sweat from his face when he pulled away. He tracked back through the yard the way he'd come.

Before he relatched the gate, he stood with his hand on the sun-grayed cedar fence, trying to figure his next move. You're wasting time, he thought. The air felt dense with humidity and smelled of a trapped, particulate heat. Think, old man, think. A breeze swelled, tallow branches scraped against the side of the house. A yellow jacket bobbed over the dog's water bowl. Cecil tried to remember when he'd last seen the backyard, but he couldn't recall stepping through the gate in months, maybe a year. Then, at once, he understood that wasn't by chance: Eric hadn't wanted him to see the state of the backyard. After a moment, he slipped his thumb and forefinger under his tongue and let fly with a whistle as sharp as glass.

He was walking toward the truck when Rainbow bounded around the house and broadsided his legs. She was panting and clueless and excited. Her fur smelled of the cool, moist air between the house and earth.

"Let's go," he said, opening the driver's-side door.

She jumped onto the bench seat and sat down. Her tail went to thumping. The gate to the backyard was wide open when they left; Cecil checked it in his mirror.

HE DROVE BACK TOWARD TOWN, DIALING THE RADIO. THE SURF report was unchanged, the temperature had risen a degree. Rainbow sat upright, looking out the window, still panting. The cab smelled of her mucky breath, a scent some folks hated but one Cecil had always found reassuring. He pointed one of the vents toward her. She sniffed the air with her dark, wet nose.

Traffic had lightened. Heat waved over the asphalt. Cecil pulled into the Whataburger parking lot, cruising slowly around the A-frame restaurant to see inside the windows. Condensation, dripping and streaked, blurred the glass, but he could still make out who was eating. Some people he knew, some he didn't, but none was Griff. He moved on. He passed behind the H-E-B grocery, where the kids rode their skateboards off the loading docks, then drove over to the junior high, then past the Lazy Acres trailer park and into the neighborhood of bungalows south of the school. The lousy, familiar sense of how wide open the world was. And a constant, dreamlike readjustment: He was looking for *Griff,* not Justin. Cecil tried to pop his knuckles again, but they were still limber.

Rainbow circled herself, dropped to the seat. He watched for movement outside the truck, anticipating how he'd brake or accelerate or swing a U-turn when he caught sight of the boy. The feeling he had was one of false calm, a fleeting sense of lassitude. It was like the eye of a hurricane. The last four years had been the first wall and soon, after this current stillness collapsed, they'd get hit with the storm's second, harsher side. The dirty wall, it was called. The one that uprooted trees and twisted off roofs and turned cement foundations to mud.

Briefly, it occurred to Cecil that whatever was happening might have nothing to do with Justin. Maybe something had gone horridly wrong at summer school. People regularly told Cecil what a fine teacher his son was, and Eric had won a teaching prize from the school district, so maybe there was a crisis they needed his help to sort out. Maybe the dolphin in Corpus had died, and Laura had lost herself again. But these possibilities lacked ballast. Cecil had known this day would come; he assumed they all had, though they seemed to have a tacit agreement not to give voice to such inevitability. And he'd known the day would come when they'd lower their guards, when they'd begin to allow themselves to believe the draining heat was their worst trouble. That was the inconceivable and debilitating shock: You could grow accustomed to what had once seemed so miserable and alien. You could feel a foreign presence in your body, endure the pain and deep threat of it, and not notice as it turned to bone.

And he knew that most everyone believed Justin was dead. For some, the belief had taken hold four years ago when word of an unaccompanied minor going missing first spread—when they saw the initial flyers posted in shop windows, when the call for search party volunteers was first broadcast, when the vanished boy's mother fell apart on the evening news. For others, the resignation came gradually, insidiously, like a slow leak. Cecil watched it happen. As each year passed, the town's awareness of the vanished

Campbell boy grew more and more faint, thinning into nothingness, until people remembered only that they'd forgotten about him. Yes, the memory surfaced every year when the *Southport Sun* marked the anniversary of his disappearance. And yes, people would recall him when they happened upon one of his broken parents wearing a shirt with Justin's picture on it—HAVE YOU SEEN ME?—and when they glimpsed Griff skateboarding alone in the drained pool at the Teepee Motel, but Cecil knew the jolts of memory only preceded the inevitable assumption that Justin had died. Some felt sure he'd drowned, and some thought he'd been killed—by a stranger or a family member or Ronnie Dawes. All of it sickened Cecil. Worse still, he suspected people found a peculiar relief in thinking Justin was gone for good. He hated them for it.

He was out by the rut roads and stilt houses when the hourly news update came through the radio. Cecil braked in the middle of the two-lane road, then pulled onto the shell shoulder and turned up the volume. His heart was rubbery in his chest, thick and heavy as a hot water bottle. He closed his eyes and concentrated until he got an image of Connie, his habit when he was afraid. His version of prayer.

There was a report of backed-up northbound traffic on the Harbor Bridge in Corpus, and the National Weather Service had issued a drought warning. Tomorrow the heat index would reach 108.

When the music started up again, he whipped the truck around to head back toward the marina. Rainbow raised her eyes to him, but not her head.

"We're not thinking," he said, accelerating.

4

LAURA SAT SIDEWAYS ON THE BENCH SEAT IN THEIR TRUCK. She'd taken off her seat belt, or she'd never put it on, and she watched her husband drive. The truck was vibrating, shaking, the speedometer needle tilting toward eighty, eighty-five. Eric had both hands on the top of the wheel. He looked like a man begging for food. They were descending the Harbor Bridge, dropping down into Corpus. The windows were open. The cab was full of wind and noise and the cloying odor of the ship channel below. Some of her hair had come out of her ponytail. It was swirling around, blinding her, whipping into her mouth. She couldn't tell if she'd stopped crying.

"You need to wear your seat belt," he said. His voice was weighted with the drawling accent that emerged only when he was nervous. He'd always hated his accent. She'd always loved it.

Then the truck was swerving around a sedan—it seemed they were on ice, seemed they were in free fall—and Eric was laying on the horn. Laura grabbed the seat and dashboard; she felt the tendons stiffen in her wrists. The truck jostled. She thought she would vomit.

"Do you think this—"

"Please," he said. "Your seat belt. Please."

She twisted to face forward, reached awkwardly over her shoulder for the seat belt, buckled it. A scattered feeling in her arms, a rattling along her nerves. Her thoughts still couldn't gain purchase in her mind. She had the sense that she couldn't be trusted, that she was going to come unglued and let everyone down. She couldn't remember what she'd already asked, what he'd already answered. Her hair, like sand lashing her face.

"Should I call someone?" she asked.

"Who?"

"I don't know," she said. "Your father?"

"I left a message at Loan Star. He'll pick up Griff. I said no computer or TV or radio."

Griff. Lobster. She'd forgotten about her younger son, completely and ruthlessly, and hearing his name stopped her heart. Occasionally, to punish herself over the years, to exact a new pain that would distract and focus her, she'd tried to imagine that it was Griff, not Justin, who had gone missing. She tried to imagine how she would answer if she'd been forced to choose which child to lose. There was no answer, of course, no redeeming logic to any of it. Now, in the truck, she was freezing, shivering under her skin, a hard coil of ice between her eyes, dripping into her throat.

"I don't know what to do right now," she said. "I don't know what I'm supposed to be doing to prepare."

"Stay calm. We don't know the lay of the land."

He honked the horn again, hit the brakes and then accelerated. A car had come into their lane.

"Tell me again what he said," Laura said. "I want to know everything. It was the DA this time?"

"He said we needed to get to Corpus. He said things were happening. He said there'd be more to know when we got there. Remember, they won't—"

"I know," she said.

They'd been summoned to Corpus before. Early on, the trips had been frequent, and seemingly replete with promise, though they never knew what awaited them. The sheriff's office wouldn't betray any vital information on the phone, and neither would the district attorney's; they worried about litigation, worried there'd be an accident and the city would be held liable. It was infuriating, demoralizing. On one occasion, Eric and Laura had been asked to meet with a runaway who somewhat matched Justin's description. Two other times, they'd had to view the bodies of adolescent boys—one had overdosed and the other had been hit by a car—and make sure neither was Justin.

Now she said, "Did he sound upset? Sad? Did he sound happy? Remember, that one time you could tell it wasn't good news. The time with the boy who'd been hit—"

"He sounded rushed, just rushed. We lost the connection, got cut off. Then a few minutes later he called back and told me to park in the back."

"It might be another body. Or a runaway. Is that what you're thinking?"

"We just need to keep our heads. We need to stay composed."

"Where were you?"

Eric checked his mirror, then his blind spot. He swerved into the passing lane without signaling. He said, "Do what?"

"When he called, where were you?"

"School. I was just leaving school."

"Okay," she said. "That makes sense."

They were off the bridge now, slowing down and curving into Corpus. The world was quieting. The sense Laura had was that they'd crossed a threshold and they'd soon cross another. This is when it happens, she thought, on a Wednesday afternoon when you're wearing a button-down shirt that smells of dead fish. She smoothed her hair. It was wild, sticky, and blown out. She wanted to retie her ponytail before they reached the police station—they were just blocks away, she knew from all the previous trips—but Eric reached for her hand, took it into his. He was trembling a little, like he'd been straining too hard, like they were in an airplane that was about to take off or go down.

5

GRIFF DIDN'T KNOW IF FIONA MOORE WAS HIS GIRLFRIEND. Last Saturday night, while he was skating the curb at Whataburger on Station Street, she'd sauntered across the parking lot and said, "I need your help with matters of the heart." Then she led him by the hand around the building and, without a word, kissed him hard and long against the dumpster. He didn't understand what was happening; she almost seemed angry with him. His eyes closed. The dumpster smelled of old food, acrid and rotting and metallic. Her mouth was sugary, but also tasted of something sharper; maybe she'd spiked her Coke with rum again. Then the ugly food odor fell away and he inhaled the faint and familiar scent of her perfume, the sweat in her hair. He thought he could hear the sounds of the marina a mile away: the heave and slosh of the waves against the pylons, the hollow clanging of cables hitting the masts of docked sailboats. When she was finished, Fiona bit the tip of his nose and skipped back into the restaurant. Griff stayed where he was, trembling. His first kiss.

That night, he had gone home and stared at her class photo for an hour, thinking *You just kissed me.* Now the school annual lay like a dirty magazine between his mattress and box spring. Most everything she wore was black. She'd covered the windows in her room with tinfoil to block out the sun, and then the next day she'd done the same to Griff's. She was a member of the National Honor Society who'd gotten a week of detention after a teacher caught her writing I PUT THE SENSUAL IN NONCONSENSUAL on the bathroom wall. She loved Halloween, hated Christmas. Fiona was old enough to drive, two years older than Griff and a few months older than Justin would have been, but she rode her bicycle everywhere. The bike reminded him of the kind characters rode in black-and-white movies—wicker basket behind her seat, squeeze horn on the handlebars. When Griff had asked why she didn't take her driving test and get a car, she said, "Because I like to smell the world." Ever since, he'd been helpless with love.

Until Saturday night, they'd just been friends. She towed him on his skateboard with her bike. They went to the beach to make fun of the sunbathers and catch hermit crabs; they'd let the crabs crawl over their backs until the chills were too much to bear. They closed themselves off in one or the other's blacked-out room and talked about how much they hated Southport, about strange or sad things their parents had done, about Justin. Fiona had been in his grade. She'd once admitted to having had a crush on Justin, and Griff felt not jealousy but a pulse of embarrassing recognition. He realized that ever since his brother had been gone he'd nursed something of a crush on him, too. He pined for him. He both avoided and invoked his name, sometimes in the same conversation; Fiona, he'd noticed, did the same thing. They filled up shopping carts with odd combinations of items at H-E-B grocery, then abandoned them, and they sneaked into the pool at Villa Del Sol. They spent so much time together that everyone already assumed they were hooking up. One bright afternoon, riding her bike past the Teepee Motel, where he and some other skaters were carving around the drained pool, she shouted Griff's name and when everyone looked, she lifted her shirt and flashed her lacy black bra.

But the guys she went out with were older—college kids from Corpus, a pilot from the air base in Kingsville, a Coast Guard cadet who rode his motorcycle around Southport and whose tattooed arms were roped with muscle. She called them her "lovers," a word Griff had never heard anyone else use. Fiona grew tired of them quickly, then acted put-upon until someone else swept her up. She confided everything to Griff in her room. He listened, nodded, tried to offer advice that both was sound and made him appear desirable. She cried. She chewed her nails. A month ago, after she'd broken up with the cadet, she'd asked Griff why she couldn't just have *him* as her boyfriend and when he said she could, she rolled her eyes and said, "In my wet dreams." Then she went to swipe rum from her parents' liquor cabinet and left him alone in her room. Immediately, he peeled off his socks, doused them with her perfume, then stuffed them in his backpack. Smell you later, he thought. The socks had mostly stayed in the back of his closet, in a Ziploc bag behind the two fishbowls housing his old rock collection. Now they were with his yearbook under his mattress. His room was starting to smell like a girl's.

And yet they'd barely talked since she'd kissed him on Saturday night. His calls had gone unreturned. He'd floated through the first part of the week in a fog of ecstasy and paranoia. His foot seemed to constantly be tapping against the floor, and moments came when he felt like he'd concocted the whole fantasy. When he felt like he was dissolving. When he felt like he could run full tilt for miles. His parents thought he was coming down with something, so finally, on Tuesday evening, he said his stomach hurt. Not a complete lie. For days, he'd felt ravenous but lost his appetite when he started to eat. He'd tried to distract himself with skating and videogames, but nothing worked. He would remember how she'd moaned, how right before the kiss ended, she'd gently touched their mouths with her fingers, traced the inside of his lips. How she could do that and not want to talk with him every waking moment—for that matter, how she could sleep at all—baffled him. He worried she'd done it because she was drunk or had lost a bet with her girlfriends. He worried he'd botched the whole thing with poor technique. He'd always assumed he'd be a bad kisser.

Mostly, he worried that she'd kissed him because of his brother. The kids at school still sometimes regarded Griff with the same pitiful distance as they had the seagull a junior had pegged with a rock last year in P.E.—they'd watched the bird grow exhausted trying to take flight with a broken, bleeding wing and then fed it pizza crusts until the coach wrapped it in a gym towel and took it away. His brother's disappearance got him picked for teams, invited to parties, allowed to cut in the lunch line. It was awful, and it was the reason he'd started avoiding other kids, the reason they'd made it so easy for him, the reason he'd gone through a phase of picking fights he couldn't win. But Fiona had never pitied him. "To everyone else," she'd said, "you're that poor boy with the missing brother. To me, you're just a blockhead." She was right. He couldn't recall an interaction where he wasn't aware of the other person's awareness, where his brother's absence wasn't encroaching. In the presence of almost everyone except Fiona, he felt two disparate pressures—to convey his certainty that his brother would come home, and to intimate that, were that not to happen, his family would withstand the loss. They would survive. Really, he was sure of neither.

Since his brother had vanished, he'd watched his parents fall away from each other; he'd listened to their affection turn to arguing and then to strained silence, and he often pictured a future where they lived in separate houses, in different towns or time zones. He could imagine his parents giving in and buying a gravestone for Justin, and then all of them starting lives where no one knew everything that had happened. He could feel himself bracing for all of it, doing the dismal calculations of what the years ahead held. Sometimes he stared at himself in the bathroom mirror and said, "My parents are divorced." Other times, he'd peer at his reflection, his brown, unkempt hair and large eyes and slack shoulders, and say, "My name is Griffin Campbell. I'm an only child." He said it over and over until it sounded real.

Last night, his father had knocked on his door, then stepped awkwardly into the room. Rainbow's tail thumped on the comforter. She started panting. Griff had been looking at his yearbook and now he felt caught. It wasn't unusual for his father to come in to talk before bed. It was unusual for him to knock.

"Mom's gone on to sleep," his father said, as if Griff might be wondering, as if it were new. "Tomorrow's her early shift, and then she's volunteering with Alice."

"Sounds right," Griff said.

His father absently picked up a skate magazine from Griff's desk, then put it down. He surveyed the room—Griff's cluttered bureau and the skateboarding advertisements tacked to the walls and the two stacks of folded clothes that had been waiting to be put up since his mother brought them home from the dry cleaner's last week. He glanced at Griff, smiled, then turned to the foiled-over window and gazed at it, as if seeing the night sky. His hands were in his pockets. Then Griff understood: His parents thought he was upset about Justin. They thought it a lot.

His father said, "What say we sneak out for Whataburgers? You didn't eat much tonight."

"I'm still a little queasy, I guess," he said.

Rainbow rolled onto her side, groaned, smacked her lips. Griff liked when she did that.

"Or I can go through the drive-thru. Or if you have a taste for something else."

"No, I'm good."

Griff wanted to apologize for worrying him, but it wouldn't accomplish anything. His father was always working to rally everyone, like a mascot at a football game.

"Lobster," his father said, "if you want to talk—"

"My stomach's just thrashed, Dad. I probably drank too much milk."

His father turned to the wall, hands still in his pockets, and regarded the poster of a skater riding the wave of banked bricks under the Brooklyn Bridge. He asked where the photo had been taken.

"Brooklyn," Griff said, then added, "It's in New York."

"Thanks, son," his father said with a laugh. "It looks cool. Is that the best place to skate in the world?"

"I don't know. It's in a lot of magazines."

"Maybe we'll take a vacation," his father said. "Your mother and I will see a Broadway show and you can skate in this strange, mythical land called Brooklyn."

Griff smiled to be nice. Sometimes when his father started talking about vacations, Griff and his mother would sneak a glance at each other, a wink. They'd never gone farther than Houston or the Hill Country, and they hadn't gone anywhere in years. Fiona's family traveled a lot; she'd been to both coasts and to Hawaii.

His father said, "Does it smell like perfume in here?"

"I have a harem of ladies in my closet."

"In other words, 'Dad, time for bed.'"

Griff shrugged. He thought: Yes.

"You're sure there's nothing I can get you to eat? Nothing in the whole of South Texas sounds good?"

"I'm sure."

His father snapped his fingers, like he'd solved a riddle. He said, "I'll pick up shrimp tomorrow after class. If you don't clean your plate, we'll assume you're staging a hunger strike."

Later, Griff woke to the sound of his mother washing dishes. The chore was actually his, but some nights he shirked it so she'd have something mindless to do if she couldn't sleep. Most nights, she'd look through photo albums or read about dolphins or browse missing-children websites. Some nights she rode the ferry back and forth from the island, and others she sneaked into Justin's room to punish herself. He considered going to talk with her, maybe tell her about the New York vacation idea, but he worried she'd feel guilty about waking him. In the dark, he checked his phone and saw that Fiona had left a message. His heart surged. She told him to meet her at the Teepee tomorrow afternoon because she had something to show him. He replayed the message three times, saved it. He clutched the perfumed socks to his chest and listened to his mother working in the kitchen. Whether she was upset or just sleepless he couldn't tell. He only knew she was trying to move quietly, trying to let her family rest.

From this distance—four years, two weeks, four days— Griff had only blurry recollections of his brother. He saw Justin the way he saw constellations; his image was hazed, made up of somewhat recognizable points of light that occasionally emerged from darkness—long eyelashes, top row of teeth a little bunched, skinny legs. Just before he disappeared, there'd been talk of Justin getting braces at Dr. McKemie's. Griff remembered that his brother hated clipping his fingernails and the smell of canned dog food, and he always ordered his Cokes without ice and his favorite things to watch on television were *Wheel of Fortune* and Animal Planet. But he thought he should remember more. His parents' minds were so full of the past that he knew they assumed his was too, but in truth his memory was emptying.

Worse, Griff's most assured memories were of his brother behaving badly: Justin stealing candy and comic books from H-E-B, Justin copying other kids' homework on the school bus, Justin emptying a shaker of salt into Griff's Coke when he was out of the room, Justin kicking Griff between the legs after he threatened to tell about the salt. It had happened the day he went missing. Justin quickly turned remorseful, apologizing profusely, and invited Griff to go to skate on the seawall by the marina. Griff said no. Build a fort in the backyard? Go to the pawnshop to see if Papaw would let them strum the guitars or cast fishing rods in the parking lot? Catch a matinee, then sneak into a second movie after the credits rolled? No, no, no. When at last he suggested they head to the beach to look for shells for their rock collections, Griff told him to go to hell, the worst thing he knew how to say. He was nine, his brother was eleven. Justin laughed. Then he set off toward the beach with his skateboard and never came back. A year later someone brought his board into the pawnshop, and though none of them admitted it, Griff saw how the development had gutted the family. He saw how they had to work harder to appear hopeful.

No one knew about the salt or Justin kicking him or how he'd tried to make amends. Griff hadn't told his parents or Papaw or the detectives. Occasionally, he thought of telling Fiona, but he always stopped himself. At first, he'd thought Justin was staying away to punish him, to make him regret not accepting his apology, and his absence only addled Griff. Go to hell, he thought, just go straight to hell. Even after the search parties convened and Southport was papered with MISSING flyers and the orange-and-white Coast Guard boats were trawling the bay, Griff expected his brother to stroll through the door, smirking and refreshed, as though he'd only been gone for a short while. It seemed the kind of prank his brother would pull. When it became clear that Justin wasn't coming home— although Griff still sometimes endured excruciatingly hopeful surges—their having argued felt simultaneously urgent and insignificant. But he kept the information to himself because he thought Justin would want him to. He was scared the knowledge would contradict the image his parents had of their older son, and of Griff for not having forgiven him, for not having accompanied him, and he was scared that telling would awaken some dormant guilt inside his heart, that he'd no longer be able to believe he was blameless in the ruining of their lives.

JUSTIN HAD TOLD GRIFF THAT THE KARANKAWA INDIANS HAD fashioned the Teepee Motel's concrete teepees from real animal hides. This was two years before he disappeared, and Griff believed him. Their parents, no matter what they said, couldn't convince Griff that his brother was snowing him, that it was just an old motel, a cheap and kitschy place for tourists to stay near the marina. Griff knew better now, but he still associated the Teepee with his brother. The place reminded him of the time in his life when his allegiances had pivoted, like a sundial, away from his parents and toward Justin.

Now, half-demolished, the property resembled a quarry. After the first of the year, the demolition had halted because the developer who'd bought the property was backing out. Seven teepees remained. Mounds of pale rubble stood where others had been; they were jagged and tall clusters, with jutting slabs of concrete and rebar. Snakes of dust fell from the mounds when a wind blew from the bay, sidewinding across the parking lot or into the drained pool. The left-handed kidney was flawless: ten feet in the deep end, three feet in the shallow end, with two concrete steps and an embedded ladder. The coping that rimmed the top of the pool was so pristine— exactly the kind that skaters with private backyard ramps coveted— that Griff always expected it to be crowbarred loose and stolen. Even on days when he didn't skate, he tried to check the coping.

The coping was still there on Wednesday afternoon, but Fiona wasn't. Sunlight splayed over the long slab of concrete, the ground absorbing and expelling the insistent heat. Already Griff was glazed in sweat. Every few minutes, a heavy wind blew ashore and sprayed him with dust from the rubble. It was too hot to skate, but if Fiona showed up, Griff didn't want it to seem as if he'd been waiting pathetically, so he took the broom the skaters kept hidden under a pile of palm fronds and occupied himself by sweeping out the deep end. He inched around the pool, extending the broom up the transitioned wall, then dragging it down again like a painter. After each swipe, he stopped and listened for Fiona. He tried imagining what she had to show him: A car? A new bike? A tattoo? What if she'd tattooed his name on the small of her back? He remembered how she bit his tongue, his bottom lip, and then his nose, and how she'd skipped away. He pushed the dust and pebbles into the drain. His shoes and calves looked powdered. When lines of traffic passed on Station Street, the tires sounded like waves.

Then, a wash of memory: A year ago, his mother had come into his room while he was sleeping and sat on his bed. He didn't know how long she'd been there before he woke up, but he suspected it had been a while. Griff could smell the night on her, the dew and the still air. His stomach tightened. He thought she'd learned news of his brother. When he asked if she was okay, she said she'd read something before bed that had gotten her curious, so when she couldn't sleep, she'd decided to conduct an experiment. She walked to the marina and listened to the waves with her eyes closed, seeing if the noise would console her. According to one of her library books, the reason babies were comforted by the *ssshhhhh* sound was because early humans had lived close to the ocean and the sound reminded infants of waves; it returned the listener to some vestal state, soothed anxieties in a primitive, essential way. When Griff asked if it worked, she said, "No. No, Lobster, it most certainly did not."

Now, after sweeping the pool for almost an hour, he felt dejected and gullible. He thought he might stink a little, too, and wondered if he'd been in such a rush that he forgot to use deodorant. Sweat ran into his eyes, burned. He sailed the broom like a javelin onto the pool's deck.

"Missed me," she said.

"Fiona?" He jogged up into the shallow end. He said, "I didn't know you were up there."

"I'm a ninja. Hence my all-black wardrobe."

He climbed from the pool and started to ask how long she'd been there, but when he saw her, he stopped, stunned. He said, "Your hair."

"You'll have to be more specific," she said.

She'd dyed it. Bright green, almost fluorescent. She looked like a different person, older and more severe. He hated it. He said, "I love it!"

Her face opened up, brightened. She'd been kneeling by the edge of the pool, but now she picked up the broom and began sweeping her way toward one of the teepees. The sun was laying long cones of shadow on the concrete. Griff followed her. The back of her neck was white as porcelain. Blood jumped in his veins. He hoped he hadn't done anything weird while she was watching him.

They sat in the shade, Griff on his skateboard, Fiona leaning against the teepee with the broom across her lap like an oar.

"I lied," he said. "I knew you were here, especially if I did anything weird."

"You're a very thorough sweeper. When George and Louise fire our current maid, I'll slip them your name."

George and Louise were Fiona's parents. That she called them by their first names, even when they were in the same room, had always saddened Griff. A stream of cars came off the ferry and passed on Station Street. Griff didn't know what to say; he wished he'd planned things to talk about, phrases and jokes to deploy. He wanted to make her laugh and to kiss her again and to ask why she'd disappeared these last few days and if she'd kissed him because of Justin. He didn't want to betray how overjoyed he was to see her, how relieved and nervous. He thought to tell her about the *ssshhhh* sound, but instead he asked if she remembered the seagull with the broken wing.

"The one that idiot Blake Boggs hit with a rock? I brought it scraps from the kitchen."

"I wonder what happened to it."

"Coach Cantu wrung its neck behind the gym, that's what happened to it."

"I thought maybe he took it to one of those people in the phone book who rehabilitate hurt birds and then release them."

"Blake was trying to impress Rhonda Smirnoff, who is, by the way, a rampant slutbag."

Griff had seen them making out by the lockers. Rhonda always smelled like cigarettes. He said, "Isn't she his girlfriend?"

"She wasn't before he hit the bird," Fiona said. "Why are you thinking about such an uplifting story?"

"Where's your bike?" he asked.

Fiona regarded him, squinting and smirking, as if deciding how to answer.

"Well," she said, "after our dumpster date, I went home and was too heated up to sleep. So I did what any normal girl would do and turned myself into a radioactive brussels sprout. When I came down for breakfast on Sunday, Louise spit out her grapefruit juice."

"Then she took away your bike."

"You're a boy on whom nothing is lost."

There were clouds in the sky, thin and tattered. He stole glances at her hair; it was growing on him. He could hardly picture how she'd worn it before.

She said, "Are you having a seizure?"

"What?"

"Your foot."

It was tapping again, though Griff hadn't noticed. He looked toward the marina. A gull was twisting over the water.

"Griffin Campbell," she said, her voice full of dark surprise. She grabbed the edge of his skateboard and wheeled him toward her. "Griffin Michael Campbell, are you *afraid* of me?"

"No way," he said.

She pulled him closer, scooted around so that she was in front of him. She leaned in, pressed her forehead against his. His eyes had closed, but he thought she was smiling. She said, "No way?"

"A little, maybe."

"A little?" she whispered. "Only a little?"

"I'm sorry about your bike," he said.

"I don't care about my bike."

"I don't either," he said. Her hands rested on his thighs. He could hear her breathing, feel the heat of her skin. To anyone seeing them, he thought, they would look cold. He said, "I care about you."

"And you like my hair."

"I do," he said. "I love it."

"And you want to kiss me again."

"I do," he said.

"How much?"

"A lot."

"You want it so bad you can—"

A hard, sharp whistle cut her off, and they sat bolt upright. Griff's heart kicked. He couldn't tell where the whistle had come from. The cadet she'd dumped? A cop? Someone from the construction crew?

Fiona said, "It's your grandfather."

Papaw was sitting in his truck, idling just outside the Teepee's chained-up driveway. His window was down, his elbow hanging out like a fin. Even from across the parking lot, Griff could see Rainbow panting—her tongue pink as candy—in the passenger seat. It was all disorienting, defeating.

"He doesn't look like the happiest camper," Fiona said.

In his head, Griff was making sure he'd called his father before coming to meet Fiona. Not calling one of his parents before leaving the house was the offense for which they had no tolerance. But he knew he'd called. He was positive. He said, "Rainbow must have gotten out again."

Griff stood, trying to remember when he'd last been in the back-yard. He skated around the pool, hoping he looked cool and un-afraid from where Fiona sat. When he reached Papaw's truck, he said, "Did I leave the back gate open?"

"Nobody pawns anything when it's this hot, so I was going for a drive and saw her making a break for it."

"I changed her water before I left," he said. "Maybe—"

"You been here long?"

"A little while. It's too hot to skate. Fiona and I were just talk-ing. She dyed her hair."

Rainbow lay down on the seat, her muzzle on her paws. Papaw clicked off the truck's radio. He said, "You talked to your folks?"

"I just left a message like I'm supposed to. Leaving a message counts."

Another wind came off the bay, kicking up more dust. Griff had to close his eyes until it died down. He wondered what he could say to get Papaw to take Rainbow home and leave him alone with Fiona. He imagined himself sitting down beside her, saying *Now, where were we?*

Papaw fixed him in his gaze—it was as if he were seeing Griff from far away—then turned to look through the windshield. Rain-bow groaned. She liked car rides. Sometimes when his father went out to look for Justin, he took her along.

"I need to move some things around in my garage," Papaw said finally. He shifted the truck into gear. "If you'll help an old man out, I'll kindly keep Rainbow's escape to myself. I've got steak in a bag if we get hungry."

"Sure. Should I come over after you're done with work?"

"Ivan'll close up," he said. "Hop in."

"I need to walk Fiona home," Griff said. "Her bike had a flat."

"Lobster, my boy, that tide's already gone out for the day."

When Griff turned to look back at where they'd been sitting, he saw that Fiona was gone. She might have left before he'd even reached the truck. He felt exhausted by everything, confused and goaded by the turns the day had already taken. Papaw rapped twice on his door with his knuckles, and Griff walked around the back of the truck, dragging his fingers along the tailgate.

6

IN THE INITIAL SEARCHES, THE TOWN OF SOUTHPORT HAD cleaved to the hope that Justin had just gotten lost in the dunes. Or he was hiding. Children did it occasionally. Maybe he'd twisted his ankle in the hummocky sand. Maybe sunstroke. It seemed possible that if volunteers sprawled wide enough, if they stayed alert and confident enough, he would soon be found. He'd be sunburned and dehydrated and scared, but unharmed. The mood was serious, not maudlin; at the time, imagining a happy ending required no great effort. They thought of the ordeal as a storm that would, despite its present course, spare them.

But he never returned. The days turned to weeks—then months, then years—and they couldn't ignore how naïve they'd been. They had been, they realized, like Justin himself. Or almost like him, for they had to work to stay naïve. He'd had an easy smile. Neighbors asked him to water their plants and take in the mail while they were away. They remembered the photo of Justin and his younger brother in the *Southport Sun* after the boys had set up a table to sell rocks and shells the way other children sold lemonade. They remembered how, on Halloween, the parents would wait hand in hand on the sidewalk while their boys trick-or-treated; hadn't the younger brother dressed as a cloud one year? His father, the Texas history teacher whose class students jockeyed for, always remembered your children's names and asked after them. His mother, if she recognized you, would launder four shirts for the price of three at the dry cleaner's. After the ordeal began, she'd sometimes refuse your cash altogether. They were good people. After Justin Campbell set out for the beach on his skateboard and never returned, people donated money to the rescue efforts, papered their storefronts with his image, volunteered for search parties even when they knew the best thing would be to find nothing at all. They answered detectives' questions and feigned optimism when they rounded an aisle in H-E-B and saw one of the shattered parents picking out frozen dinners. Then they went home and thanked God the Campbells' lives weren't theirs.

The state police combed the dunes with cadaver dogs; the Navy deployed divers; the Coast Guard sent out boats and a helicopter with infrared cameras. An unsolicited psychic—a curandera named Ms. Esther who owned a curio shop in Corpus and who everyone believed was only interested in the reward money the Campbells had put up—said she'd had a vision of violence at the marina, an image of Justin's body being dumped in deep water from a shrimper's boat, but renewed searches yielded nothing. Laura visited Ms. Esther twice by herself, offering more money for more-definitive information, but the vision remained unchanged. Cecil had visited her, too, and ordered her to stay away from the family.

The Campbells' every conversation was strung with snares: Who would avoid Justin's name too conspicuously? Who would invoke it too often, drawing too much attention to his absence? Who would be the first to speak of him in the past tense? Some nights they went to bed feeling as though they'd been holding their breath for hours. Other nights, they fought; they threw accusations of surrender and apathy like knives. When they woke, they found no relief. Their world was discolored, muted, perforated by helplessness. The search parties dwindled to just a few volunteers every weekend, or if it was too hot, none at all. The detective they'd liked was reassigned, and

Justin's case was handed to a junior deputy. Media coverage dried up. When they'd first installed the 800 number in the kitchen, Eric and Laura could stay up half the night logging tip-line calls, but now it rang so infrequently they sometimes lifted the receiver and checked for a dial tone.

The mail had all but stopped, too. In the first year, that miserable wash of time when every noise in the house sounded like the front door opening, mail had come from Justin's classmates and from Griff's, from congregations of churches, from parents and relatives of other missing children, and from strangers from all over. After the second year, the arrowhead postcard had arrived: *Don't Stop Looking*. It had been postmarked in Bakersfield, California. Laura became obsessed with having the postcard dusted for fingerprints, but it'd been handled so many times that none of the prints were usable. Now, if any unusual envelope arrived, it was addressed to Justin. He would have turned sixteen this coming November, so credit card companies and car dealerships were appealing for his business. Laura dropped the advertisements into one of the plastic bins she'd bought to collect his mail so he could read it when he returned. She was filling her third now. The bins were in Justin's room, beneath the Christmas and birthday presents that had accumulated over the years. Continuing to shop for him, to buy gifts like wallets and CDs and books, was an exercise in faith. It was easier than not shopping.

His room was the only space not consumed by his absence, and with the exception of the bins and presents, it still looked much as it had when he'd left for the last time: the lumpy high-top shoes cluttering the closet floor, the fishbowls of rocks and shells atop his dresser, the plaid comforter that had, just months before he vanished, replaced the one with the cartoon airplane print. (Laura still had the airplane one packed away in a box.) A Blue Angels poster commanded the wall beside his bed, and above his desk hung his honor roll ribbons and the print of a car he'd made with a potato in art class; he'd given the potato prints as gifts that Christmas—Eric's was on his desk at school, Cecil's was in his office at the pawnshop, Laura's was framed on her nightstand, crowning the stack of over-due marine biology books from the library, and Griff's was tacked among the skateboarding photos. Sometimes, if his parents were out, Griff stole into his brother's room and tried on his clothes, charting how long Justin had been gone by how fully he'd grown into them. He'd even taken a couple of his T-shirts and kept them in his room; every week he transferred them from one secret place to another. If his mother came in to clean or put up folded clothes or just to snoop, he didn't want his brother's shirts to blindside her.

Laura had known about the shirts since the day Griff had taken them. She sneaked into Justin's room daily and had immediately noticed the drawer Griff hadn't completely closed. She struggled with the knowledge, wondering if he'd so poorly covered his tracks because he subconsciously *wanted* her to confront him. Her son, about whom she knew everything and nothing. Some days she sat on Justin's floor and wept, others she lay on his bed with her knees clutched to her chest. The room comforted and tormented and con-fused her with its permanence. One night, after almost two years of sneaking in, she told Eric how she sometimes buried her face in Justin's closet, how she pressed her nose into his hanging shirts searching for a shred of fabric that still held his scent. She expected Eric to balk, to try pacifying her with a wretchedly upbeat speech, but he did neither; instead, he admitted the same habit. She felt dis-armed. And at once she understood that she'd only confessed in hopes of starting a fight. But that he'd been sneaking in, too, that he'd sought shelter—or was it oblivion?—where she had, seemed a kind of communion, a renewal. They made love that night, the first time since their son had disappeared. Initially, the sex seemed an-other renewal, but soon it turned too raw and desperate, too obvi-ously freighted and inadequate. They'd wandered directionless ever since, stumbling into separate and skeptical lives.

And so, in a tight, boxy room at the police station in Corpus, when the deputy said a fifteen-year-old boy who matched Justin's description had been located at the Tradewinds Flea Market, Eric went under a wave. The simplicity of the logic, the absurd and easy ordinariness of the scenario, displaced him. A vendor had thought the boy resembled the picture on Justin's flyers, so she alerted a security guard. He'd been with an adult male, a man who was at present being interviewed by detectives. The deputy said the FBI was coming in from Houston, and the sheriff had a team searching the man's apartment. The boy, he said, was undergoing a medical exam.

All of it left Eric feeling blunted, saturated to the point of numbness. He told himself to focus. He and Laura were sitting in folding chairs, while the deputy leaned against a steel desk. Laura's hair was greasy in its ponytail, her eyes wet and worn out. She looked pale, woozy, as if she'd lost something vital on the drive from Marine Lab. He wondered when she'd last eaten. When they'd entered the police station, he'd spied a vending machine in a lounge area. He wondered if he had time to backtrack and buy her some candy. She liked M&M's and Milky Ways, but not Snickers. Knowing this, at that moment, in that room, was a comfort.

"How long before we see him?" Eric asked.

"Not long, I wouldn't think. An officer will escort him over after the exam."

"Okay, sure," he said. His voice was timid, disappointing. He said, "Thank you for bringing us in."

"This is great news," the deputy said. He'd already said it once, closing the door behind them. Eric nodded. His pulse throbbed. He was clasping and unclasping his hands, as if molding a ball of clay.

No one spoke. Eric could hear muffled voices on the other side of the closed door, shoes on the polished linoleum, approaching and passing.

"We broke a hundred today, but came up short on the record," the deputy said. "Next week we'll start giving out the free fans."

Again such banality was vexing. Eric understood the deputy was biding time, but it seemed obscene to mention anything that didn't relate to Justin. He could feel Laura growing morose. She was staring at her knees, and then the wall, trying to stay composed. He wondered if the dolphin still had a fever, wondered if talking about it would calm her. He wondered how it was that their lives had led them to a day where he spent the afternoon with another woman and his wife spent it with a sick dolphin and now they sat in a cloistered room, waiting for some reckoning.

"And if we're already this high in the mercury," the deputy continued, "I'd say we're looking at a pretty exciting hurricane season."

"It's been a while since we've had one. I guess we're about due," Eric said, trying to sound casual, engaged. Childishly, he wanted to mind his manners in hopes that they'd be rewarded with some fairness.

"The last named storm was—"

"What kind of vendor?" Laura interrupted. Her voice sounded weak, as if she'd gone days without speaking. In the last four years, she'd done exactly that; she'd done it more than once.

The deputy glanced at Eric, then back to Laura.

"At the flea market," she said. "You said a vendor recognized him."

"Yes, a woman who sells little critters—gerbils, hamsters. He was buying mice to feed to his snake."

"His snake?" Eric said.

"It's not him," she said, and immediately Eric realized he'd been thinking the same thing for hours. He'd been dreading meeting another runaway that wasn't Justin. He'd been dreading how it would undo Laura and how he'd have to resuscitate her spirits; he'd been dreading how he'd fail. He reached for her hand. Since the call had come, he'd wanted to be touching her.

"Ma'am?" The deputy cut his eyes to Eric again, a look that asked *What is your wife doing?*

"It's not Justin," she said. "Justin's afraid of snakes."

"You're right to be cautious, but let's—"

"Haven't we been through enough?" she said, rising abruptly. Her chair knocked into Eric's, slid, and clattered against the wall. In the small room, the noise was shrill. She said, "I'm leaving."

"Laura," Eric said and stood, "let's be—"

"No. They can't keep doing this to us," she said. She turned to the deputy. "Do you know how many times someone has matched his description?"

"Mrs. Campbell."

"Do you know that we've come in to ID bodies? Do you know that we've seen dead children, other people's dead children, in those bags? Those bags that are too big for their bodies. Do you know what it does to a person to hope your son is—"

"Laura, let's just wait—"

"Mrs. Campbell, ma'am, I do understand—"

"To hope your son is *dead*?" Laura continued. Her face was blotched red. She was crying, not wiping the tears. "To hope he's stopped breathing, to hope his body is somewhere decomposing? Do you know what that's like? How could you?"

"Laura."

"And if he were in Corpus," she said, ignoring Eric, "don't you think this would've ended by now?"

"Laura," Eric said again, louder. "Baby, we need to—"

Then the door was opening and Solomon Garcia, the district attorney, was stepping inside and Eric at once had the sense there was a long line of people behind him. Suddenly everything was quiet, not just in the room but, it seemed, in the hallways and corridors and the entire building. The idea of sound itself had fallen away, had never been.

And then, in the doorway, a young man.

THEY WERE NOTHING BUT TOUCH. As GARCIA AND THE DEPUTY stepped demurely out of the room, Laura held her son's face in her hands, then frantically pulled him close. To Eric, it seemed she was sliding down a hill, clawing at everything she could, trying to catch hold of something solid. Her fingers twisted in Justin's T-shirt. Eric had his arms around both of them. Laura said what sounded like "We never stopped." Justin nodded. He pressed his face against his father's shoulder. Eric felt a loosening inside, a rush of emotion that would fell him, and he choked it down: Showing his son and wife anything less than absolute resolve seemed unpardonable. He swallowed. He raised his eyes to stare into the fluorescent light box on the ceiling. Don't you cry, he thought. Do not fucking cry. His chin rested on Justin's hair, but just barely; he'd grown at least six inches. He smelled of a sweet, talcum-y sweat and soap. From the exam, Eric guessed. Laura was crying and squeezing so hard, Eric worried she was hurting Justin. She wasn't, though. He could feel his son smiling.

But then he *was* weeping, sobbing. For years, he'd coped with an awful, debilitating confusion: How could his son—a boy so precious that in first grade he'd paid a girl one dollar to be his girlfriend—how could that boy be eating a Pop-Tart when Eric left to run errands and then, just hours later, be gone? The coldness of it, the unassailable and disorienting finality of it, was crushing. That the world had nothing more to offer seemed inconceivable, and yet the days remained grimly unchanging. Now he felt the same confusion in reverse: How could his son—taller now and heavier, but still so much himself—be dropped back among them? He didn't know. Nor did he know how long they'd stayed in the boxy room—maybe a few minutes, maybe half an hour—but now they were moving through the glossy cinder-block halls of the police station. The white paint was as thick as cake icing. Eric walked in front with Garcia and the deputy, trying to pay attention to what they were saying, but constantly glancing back at Laura and Justin; they walked with their elbows hooked, knocking into each other awkwardly, smiling like they'd just left a movie. Eric thought Justin might be favoring his right leg a little. Was he limping, or had his foot fallen asleep? Eric didn't know where they were being led. Their path seemed haphazard, as if they were looking for someone who kept moving around. (They were avoiding a clerk who regularly leaked information to the press, but Eric wouldn't learn that until the following morning.) Each person they passed smiled. Eric had the sense that word was spreading through the station and people were seeking them out, maneuvering to catch a glimpse. When they stepped into a wide room mazed with cubicles and metal desks, the men and women stood and applauded. Eric started clapping, too, and then Laura did, then Garcia and the deputy. There was a sizzle in the air, of mirth and release. Justin smiled his shy smile—still the same!— and shrugged: *Pshaw. It was nothing.*

Eric tousled his son's shaggy hair.

"Dad," Justin said, smiling, "you're staring."

"It's really you?"

"It's me," he said.

Garcia poured himself a cup of coffee from a pot on a counter, and then he was stepping into an empty conference room and opening a folder onto a table and waving Eric in. Eric's impulse was to usher Laura and Justin in ahead of him, but then he sensed he shouldn't. Instead, he motioned for them to wait. Laura nodded, an almost conspiratorial gesture. She held Justin's hand, and a uniformed officer Eric hadn't previously noticed led them to an empty cubicle that faced the conference room.

The deputy shut the door behind Eric, then started to close the blinds in the window looking out into the cubicles, but Garcia said, "Not necessary, Mike. I'm sure Mr. Campbell will enjoy his view."

Eric could smell Garcia's cologne. Woodsy, musky. He knew that the scent would, for the rest of his life, recall this moment for him; already it was tattooed on his consciousness. The deputy offered Eric a desk chair. He sat and swiveled to look through the window. Laura had chosen to sit on the floor with her back against the desk, her legs extended and ankles crossed. Justin was lying with his head in his mother's lap. She stroked his shaggy hair.

"This is a good day in South Texas," Garcia said. "These things don't usually end this way, as I know you know."

"It's the best day of my life," Eric said.

"That boy of yours feels the same way. Your wife does, too."

"Thank you," Eric said.

"Mike," Garcia said, "is someone bringing up whatever Justin had with him?"

"Yvonne is, I believe."

"Beautiful." Garcia passed his eyes over a piece of paper in the folder, then another. He dragged his palm over his face. He raised his coffee cup, blew on it, sipped loudly. He lowered the cup to the table while reading something Eric couldn't see. Then he said, "We'll get you out of here shortly. Let you get home and start feeling like a family again."

"Thank you," Eric said. It seemed the only thing he knew how to say.

"We'll need to coordinate a press conference, but I want to hold off until tomorrow."

"Whatever you need."

Garcia closed the folder and watched Justin and Laura. Despite how much Justin had grown, to Eric he almost seemed younger than when he'd last seen him. Laura noticed the men looking at them and smiled. Eric waved, which felt juvenile and ridiculous, but he couldn't stop himself.

Garcia shook his head disbelievingly—*I'll be damned*—and turned back to Eric. He said, "What I need is for you and your wife to brace yourself. Justin's home, that's the bottom line, and I don't mind saying it's a goddamn miracle, but we're just starting to scratch the surface."

"We've been bracing for years," Eric said.

"I'd bet the farm on that. What I'm saying is we're not out of the muck yet."

"Okay," Eric said. "Sure, okay, absolutely."

"What I can say right now is we're interviewing a subject, okay? A person of interest, okay? We'll know soon if charges need to be filed."

"Is it Ronnie?"

"Who?"

"Ronnie Dawes. He's slow, mentally challenged. He lives across the street."

"No. Our man's name is Buford. Dwight Buford," Garcia said. "Single male. Caucasian, forty-one. He delivers newspapers in Corpus."

Through the glass, Eric watched Justin sit up, then stand and glance around as if someone had called him. Laura stood also, and looked at Eric. She pointed down the hallway and mouthed "Bathroom." Then they were out of his view.

Eric said, "He's been in Corpus the whole time."

"We're checking into that."

"Did he, did this Buford, did he hurt—" Eric said and stopped. He tried again. "Was Justin—" His stomach roiled and he felt like he'd vomit. He said, "I think I'm going to be sick."

The deputy brought over a wastebasket, set it by Eric's boots. He gagged, threw up. He swiveled away from the door in case Justin and Laura returned. His eyes watered. Through the exterior window, he could see the arc of the Harbor Bridge; it looked like a diving whale. He threw up again. For the first time in decades, he recalled how nauseated his mother had been in the last year of her life. She'd started carrying a green Tupperware bowl from room to room, in case she couldn't make it to the toilet. His father, Eric knew, still used the bowl.

Eric wiped his mouth, apologized. He said, "I don't know what to do."

"Take your son home," Garcia said. "Celebrate. Get some rest. Don't ask Justin about what's happened or about Mr. Buford, but if he offers up something, pay attention. Then call me."

"Okay. Thank you."

"Otherwise, we'll talk in the morning. We have a therapist— a real nice social worker with a master's degree—who will want to meet with him. Probably with you and your wife, too."

Eric almost thanked him again—he could've done it a thousand times—but he just concentrated on standing up. He felt frail and slow-witted, the way he had when stepping out of the shower at Tracy's.

"We've got a hard road ahead, we surely do, but your boy's home and we're going to work like hell to do right by him."

"I understand," Eric said, though he didn't. At that moment, he understood not one single thing.

"Do you need anything from me or my staff right now?"

"I need to call my father. He's with my other son."

"Sure thing," Garcia said. "Mike, can you find Mr. Campbell an office with some privacy?"

The deputy nodded and stepped out of the room. As the door was closing behind him, a young woman knocked and then peeked inside. She was carrying a small white paper bag, pinching it with her fingers and holding it away from her body, as if it stank. Eric could smell only Garcia's cologne, nothing else. She said, "I have Justin Campbell's possessions."

Hearing his son's name that way, divorced from anything relating to his disappearance, temporarily centered him. "Thank you," Eric said. "I'm his father."

The woman handed him the bag and said, "I'm glad he's back."

"You'd better get used to hearing that," Garcia said. He'd opened up his folder again and was squinting at a sheet of paper.

"I'll never get used to it."

"I don't suppose you will," he said, distractedly. "No, I don't reckon that'll be happening anytime too soon."

CECIL WAS IN HIS GARAGE WITH GRIFF. THEY'D BEEN CLEANING for two hours, organizing scrap lumber and spare parts and tools he'd accumulated over decades. They sorted old screws into one mason jar, nails into another. They filled a metal garbage can with trash, then started piling more in the bed of Cecil's truck; eventually, he'd have to drive to the landfill in Ingleside, but thinking of the future was currently beyond him.

He'd made bologna sandwiches and brought them out to the garage with glasses of iced tea that sat sweating on the workbench. While he'd been in the kitchen, he'd also checked for messages and slipped his cell phone into his shirt pocket. There was a landline in the garage, one he'd spliced from the house when Eric was still in grade school—*Cecil, you're going to go back to jail,* Connie had said, smiling—but having the cell still seemed prudent. They worked in near silence. Griff was sullen, stewing over how he'd been pulled away from his girl, so Cecil let him be, hoping his disappointment would preoccupy him, distract him from the conspicuous thoroughness of the cleanup. It was too hot for such work, but he could think of no other way to pass the hours. The air was musty, smelling of old sawdust, the half-empty cans of paint that had occupied the same rusted shelf for years. A few cockroaches scurried, then disappeared into the long, jagged crack in the floor. Cecil swept, made little mounds of dirt and pushed them into his dustpan. Rainbow snortled around the corners of the garage, her wet nose picking up cobwebs, and then she grew bored and went to lie on her side in the cool grass. As evening came on, the shadows collected on the lawn like rising water.

When the phone on the wall started ringing—the noise as harsh as breaking glass—Cecil leaned his push broom against the wall. He walked slowly, watching Griff feed Rainbow the sandwich he hadn't eaten, and he thought, Please. Please.

"Dad," Eric said.

"I'm here."

"Dad, I have someone here who'd like to say hello."

LAURA HAD WANTED TO FOLLOW JUSTIN INTO THE MEN'S ROOM. The idea of being separated again, of allowing a door to close between them, seemed negligent. Sickeningly so. Justin must have noticed the panic in her eyes. He said, "If I'm not back in three years, alert the authorities."

"If you're not back in thirty seconds," Laura said, "I'm coming in."

Then he smiled, squeezed her hand, and disappeared again. Laura stood with her back to the door, ready to stop anyone who might try to enter. "It's occupied," she planned on saying. But no one came, and soon there was the *whoosh* of a urinal flushing, then a faucet being turned on. Her son, who practiced good hygiene. When he reappeared, she took his hand again. His fingers were cool and damp and perfect.

She couldn't keep from touching him. She brushed hair from his eyes, pressed her palm to his neck and grazed her knuckles over his cheeks and touched her fingerprints to his, made steeples. Or her fingers were touching her own lips; her mouth wouldn't stay closed. *I'm in awe,* she wanted to say, but worried it would embarrass him. She felt deferential and pure, in the presence of something holy that was, moment by moment, delivering her. He had bushy hair and soft, clean cheeks; either he was shaving now or he was still a year away from picking up his first razor. His stride was relaxed and loping, giving the impression that his hands were in his pockets even when they weren't. Maybe he had a little limp—she couldn't quite tell. His voice had deepened, but his intonation and the cadence of his sentences were comfortingly, amazingly, familiar. He nodded as she spoke—babbled—and he held the doors open for her. A gentleman, she thought. They found Eric in the police chief's office, talking on his cell. He extended his arm like a wing, enfolded Justin and kissed his forehead, then gave him the phone. While Justin talked to his grandfather and brother, Laura stood with Eric in the doorway. She laced her fingers with his, brought his wrist to her lips and kissed it.

"We need to tell Griff not to ask anything about what's happened," he said in a hushed tone, watching Justin.

"I'm in awe," she said. "I'm in absolute awe."

"Garcia said we need to keep our guard up."

"I can barely breathe," she said.

And then they were driving home, shuttling over the Harbor Bridge with the moon lamping the dusk. They had a police escort, two unmarked cars. Laura knew Eric was disappointed that she was the one riding beside their son, but Justin was more comfortable with her in the middle; with the stick shift, his knees would have been wedged against the dash. He wore baggy shorts that hung to his calves; they were similar to some she'd bought Griff last summer. She'd also bought another pair for Justin. They were in his room. That the shorts might have come from the same store— a small surf shop at the mall in Corpus—knotted her throat. Justin shifted away from the passenger door, trying to get comfortable. The last time he'd ridden in the truck, he'd been small enough to sit with Griffin beside him and his parents on either side.

The small bag with the mice in it was on his lap. At home, she'd empty one of Justin's mail bins and let them run around in it. Because the mice were with Justin when he was found, she wanted to reward them. She wanted to give them bread and cheese. She wanted to name them. (She'd asked the D.A. for the contact information of the pet vendor and the flea market security guard—she wanted to call them after Justin went to bed—but Garcia said he'd have to get back to her.) Justin was watching through the window as they passed over the slatey water, his eyes half-lidded. Laura held his hand. She wanted to say so many things, to ask so many questions, but she didn't want to disturb any peace Justin was feeling. She didn't want to smother him. There will be time, she thought, and felt giddy as a schoolgirl.

As they came off the bridge, her hair started whipping around again. They passed Marine Lab. Paul Perez's truck was still in the parking lot. As was Laura's car. She kept quiet. For miles, she now realized, she'd been worried that Eric would remember they needed to pick up the car, worried that she'd have to follow him home and Justin would have to choose who to ride with—and yes, she was worried he'd choose Eric—but Eric passed the exit for Marine Lab. Whether he was being kind or had just forgotten she didn't know. She could feel her heart in her chest. At the police station, with his head in her lap, Justin had said, "Your clothes smell like chlorine." She told him about volunteering with Alice. Listening to herself—she was just nervously blathering, the sentences as slippery as eels—it occurred to her that he might take offense at how she'd spent her time, and she felt compelled to make excuses. But Justin was excited about Marine Lab. He said, "Do they let kids go in?" That he still thought of himself as a child filled her every cell with breath. Now his head was on her shoulder. She nudged Eric with her knee, and he leaned forward to look. He regarded Justin with a deep tenderness, his eyes aglow with reverence. Then she understood what she was feeling: It was like bringing a newborn home.

And like those first days after they'd brought Justin home from the hospital, she also felt closer to Eric. She knew there were rough patches ahead. She knew that whatever Eric had learned in the conference room had made him sick—he'd admitted nothing, but she'd smelled vomit on his breath when she and Justin returned from the restroom—and yet she couldn't ignore the sensation of being tethered to him again. For so long, she'd felt apart from the world. Each day was a wave that knocked her farther and farther adrift. There had seemed such awful and unbroachable distance between her and not just everything that mattered, but *everything*. Now the space was collapsing, imploding and dissolving with every mile they put between them and Corpus. When they passed the billboard with Justin's picture on it, she thought, Speed up. And like that, Eric accelerated. She squeezed his hand. She thought: We're parents again.

Justin said, "It's like when I got sick at camp and you had to come get me in the middle of the night."

"Camp Bandera," Eric said, as if he were on a game show. "We got lost coming and going."

"You were covered in chiggers," Laura said. "You found those arrowheads for Griff."

He laughed a quick little laugh in the dark.

"What?" she said. Then Eric said it too: "What?" They were both smiling, eager and hungry for whatever piece of himself he'd offer.

"I bought them at the cantina. Three for a dollar. I told him I found them, but really I just had dimes I didn't want to carry around."

"It's still sweet you thought of him," Laura said. "He still has them. They're in his rock collection."

Justin sat up. Laura's arm had fallen asleep under his weight, so when he moved, it felt needled. She wanted to ask about the postcard from California, when he'd stopped being afraid of snakes, whether or not he still collected his rocks. She wanted to ask if she'd been right in thinking he walked with a limp, and if so, what had happened. Justin yawned, then his father did, then finally she did. How to explain that this set a star of joy ablaze in her chest?

"I wondered if you'd still have the truck," Justin said.

"Of course we still have it," Eric said.

"Rainbow?"

"I can't imagine what she's going to do when you walk in."

"Sometimes I'd see a dog and it would have gray fur around its mouth and nose, and I'd worry."

"She's doing mighty fine," Eric said. "I'd watch your shoes, though. She still pees when she gets excited."

"Your room is just the way you left it," Laura said.

"Really?" he said.

"We wouldn't have changed it for the world."

"Sick," he said. "Awesome."

They passed Alamo Fireworks, then a long row of lantana bushes and dense stands of live oak that resembled giant sleeping animals on the roadside. A few cars were heading toward Corpus, probably people who'd spent the late afternoon at the beach. Shortly, those drivers would pass the billboard with Justin's face on it, and the knowledge dizzied Laura. She wondered when it would be taken down. Ahead, Southport was coming into view. The lights shimmered like buoys on the horizon. Justin's face was reflected on the inside of the windshield. What Laura hoped to see in his reflection, she couldn't say. A simple smile? His eyes lidded, his face peaceful and relaxed? Or maybe his gaze trained on the town ahead, his pupils lit with excitement now that he was finally coming home? In the coming weeks she would think of that moment in the truck and try to reconcile what she'd seen with everything that was yet to be learned, yet to happen. His face was just blank, expressionless in a way she thought he was allowing only because he believed no one would see. He was staring not at the road ahead but into his side mirror. He rode that way for miles, his attention focused on nothing except whatever lay behind them in the tight, whorling darkness.

PART
TWO

7

S OME SAW IT ON TELEVISION. THE PRESS CONFERENCE BROKE in on each of the three network affiliates that came in from Corpus, interrupting regularly scheduled programming. "It's a good day in South Texas," the D.A. said into a bouquet of microphones. The news ran briefly on the CNN ticker. People watched with their mouths agape, with their hands over their mouths, with an abrupt and complete stillness in their bodies. Others heard the news on car radios. They rolled down their windows and hollered into the sun. They laid on their horns, they flashed headlights. Disc jockeys played "Mama, I'm Coming Home." "Home Sweet Home." "Amazing Grace." Word spread through intercoms at H-E-B, Walmart, and McCoy's lumber. Customers looked to one another in the aisles, dumbfounded. They asked strangers if they'd heard right. Found? That Campbell boy? Alive? Just over in Corpus? Then they cheered. They embraced. They closed their eyes and cried and thanked Jesus. They bought cake mix and congratulatory cards, white shoe polish to write messages on their windshields. Camera crews fanned out through the town and reporters taped interviews with jubilant, wet-eyed residents. They gathered footage of merchants ripping down the flyers in their shop windows, and of teenagers spray-painting FOUND over Justin's face on the billboard outside town. Drinks were on the house at the Black Diamond Bar, and dessert came free at the Castaway Café. Emails were sent, copied, forwarded. Parents drove their children to the Alamo Fireworks stand outside the town limits and bought Roman candles to launch into the bay that night. Bonfires dotted Mustang Island. Plans had already begun for a celebration at the Shrimporee in September. The letters on the rusted arrow marquee outside Loan Star, instead of advertising window units, read HE'S BACK!

In those first days, Eric was stunned. There seemed a hallucinatory quality to such abiding relief. Moments came when he was so unburdened as to feel weightless: when he saw that Justin still cut pancakes with his fork rather than a knife; when he overheard his boys staging a burping contest in Griff's room; when Laura took his hand and quietly led him down the hall to show him something private. She nudged Justin's door open, but Eric didn't immediately grasp what he was supposed to see. "The bed," she whispered. Then he understood. The comforter was wadded at the footboard, the top sheet twisted tight and draping to the floor, the feather pillow wedged between the headboard and mattress. The bed hadn't been used in four years, so to see it now in such beautiful disarray was to gaze on the meaning of their lives, the scope of love itself. Laura said, "I'll get the camera."

There were changes, of course. Justin's voice was deepening, barnacled with the raspy climb from youth to adolescence. He was taller, more filled out; he took up more space. The house felt smaller, gorgeously contracted and compressed, with him home. If he was coming down the hall, Eric leaned back into a doorway to let him pass. (He also reached to touch some part of him—his shoulder or hair or forearm. Laura did, too. They were incapable of not reaching for him.) He'd become lactose-intolerant, developed a taste for black coffee. Although nothing had been moved since he'd been gone—to scoot the couch three inches would have been blasphemous—Justin had to ask where they kept the towels, the garbage bags, the cereal that he liked to eat straight from the box now. He was more courteous, deferential. Before, he could be lazy with his chores; more than once he'd had his television and videogame privileges suspended for not washing the dishes; he'd had his skateboard taken away for not changing Rainbow's water. Now he offered, without fail, to help clean the kitchen after meals. He carried himself like a grateful guest, someone hoping to make a good impression and be invited back. (Griff almost immediately started following his brother's lead, straightening his room and taking out the trash without being told.) Justin squinted a lot, which made Eric wonder if he needed glasses. It also recalled for him how, as a child, Justin couldn't wink. He'd close both eyes. Suddenly, in Eric's memory, his son was always trying to wink. He limped occasionally, or he walked in a pigeon-toed way, so his gait could be slightly slow, slightly awkward, as if he were walking with his shoelaces knotted together. Nothing about the limp had come up in his medical exam; he was in surprisingly good condition, though he'd complained about a toothache, which the doctor could clearly identify as a cavity. If Justin really liked something, he deemed it *sick*. "These are sick," he'd said the night Eric made everyone silver dollar pancakes for supper. "They're the sickest thing I've ever tasted."

His sleep schedule was upended. He had yet to fall asleep before the tops of the trees were dappled with morning sun, and then he slept until late afternoon or early evening. Twice he'd stepped bleary-eyed from his room just as the three of them were finishing supper. He apologized, and although Eric and Laura assured him there was no need, he promised to do better. But each night, lying in bed, Eric and Laura listened to him move through the house. They heard Rainbow padding behind him, heard the toilet flush and the faucet run, heard the television buzzing on and the volume being hastily lowered. For the first couple of nights they crept sheepishly into the living room and asked if he needed anything, but ever since, worried that he'd feel undue pressure, they stayed in bed, pretending to sleep. Eric remembered the strain he'd felt those first nights when, as a toddler, Justin first began sleeping alone in the nursery. He remembered how not going to his son when he was awake and crying seemed as inconceivable as not drawing breath.

"Is it still insomnia if he sleeps during the day?" Laura asked in bed on Saturday night. Eric lay behind her, his hand lightly on her hip. They were listening to Justin make a sandwich in the kitchen. The knife swirling in the mayo jar was like music.

"His schedule will even out soon enough," Eric said.

"Insomnia can come from fear. Our minds won't shut off. We're reduced to our animal selves, too alert to sleep. We're afraid we'll be eaten. I read about it in one of my books."

"He'll get back on track."

"He must've been so scared."

"He's safe now. We all are."

A cupboard door squeaked in the kitchen. For a year, Eric had meant to WD-40 the hinges; now he knew he'd been right to neglect them. The sound confirmed that his son was alive, a healthy boy looking for a glass for juice.

Laura said, "Dolphins never sleep, not fully. They're always at least half awake. Each side of their brain sleeps at different times."

"Because they're afraid?"

"No," she said sweetly, proudly, taking his hand and rolling into his arm like a blanket. "Because they're smart."

The next day, Eric drove the boys by the Teepee Motel—Griff wanted to show Justin the drained pool and to make sure the coping hadn't been stolen—and then they went to pick up Whataburgers. In the drive-thru, the cashier gave them their order for free. It was something that had been happening to Eric: When he'd gone to the wireless store to buy Justin a cell phone, the manager gave Eric two high-end phones for free (the second was for Griff, so he wouldn't be jealous) and waived the activation charges. When Eric went through the checkout at H-E-B, the old couple behind him insisted on buying his groceries. When he returned Laura's library books, the librarian cleared all of her late fees. He tried to decline the offers, but it was clear his refusal would have been an affront. "We appreciate you thinking of us," he'd finally say. At Whataburger, he was about to thank the cashier when she glanced over her shoulder and passed a paper napkin and pen through the window: Justin's autograph. Eric thought she was joking, but then when he saw she wasn't, he was appalled. He was about to pull forward, park, and complain to the manager, but Justin calmly took the napkin and signed his name, using the pickup's dashboard as a desk.

"Dad, it's fine," he said, sounding more annoyed with Eric than with the cashier. His signature was spiky, like the logo of a heavy metal band. It wasn't handwriting Eric recognized.

As they pulled forward and turned onto Station Street, Griff said, "You're famous. That's so sick."

Justin shrugged, then pushed his straw through the plastic lid on his Coke. Eric steered into the sun. He drove slowly, carefully, as if he'd just avoided an accident.

HIS NAME WAS DWIGHT BUFORD. HE HAD BEEN BORN AND raised outside Dallas, and he'd lived for some five years in Flour Bluff, a stripped-down stilt-house section of Corpus Christi. He was unmarried and had no criminal record, not even a parking ticket. So far, he'd been charged with one count of the Class A felony of kidnapping, though more charges were expected. He was being held on a one-million-dollar bond.

"He's not going anywhere," Garcia had told Eric and Laura. "Not on my watch."

They didn't know what he looked like, and for Eric, not being able to fix an image of him in his mind was menacing. Sometimes he pictured him as obese and towering. Sometimes he appeared gaunt and wiry, his face made up of gruesome angles, concave cheeks and eyes. The first time they'd see him would be Friday morning when Buford's arraignment was broadcast on television and streamed on the Internet. The proceeding weighed on Eric; it seemed a cliff toward which his family was being inevitably—powerlessly—borne. A search of Buford's apartment in Flour Bluff had yielded weapons—pistols and rifles and knives. There were duct tape and a saggy cardboard box of pornographic VHS movies and rope and a pair of handcuffs. Cases of generic soda and shelves of empty aquariums with algae-smudged glass. Videogame consoles, a karaoke machine, a miniature foosball table. When Eric imagined the apartment, the light was soupy and dust-heavy. The air smelled of turpentine.

Garcia had shared what he knew with Eric and Laura, but he betrayed considerably less at the press conference. It took place in Corpus on the steps of the Nueces County Courthouse; Eric, Laura, Griff, and Cecil watched on television at home while Justin was still asleep. Just then his lopsided sleep schedule seemed a blessing; they could watch without fear of burdening or hurting him. When reporters asked pointed questions, Garcia claimed Texas rules of ethics prohibited him from discussing specific details of an open investigation. Good, Eric thought. Very good. The discrepancy of information, the void between what Garcia offered the public and what he'd confided to Eric and Laura, seemed vital. Empowering. Hopeful. Eric could imagine teams of detectives and lawyers being deployed, gathering unassailable evidence, devising legal traps and strategies; the mechanisms of the law, the relentless logic of the process by which justice is meted out, were inspiring. Even innocuous information seemed damaging if Garcia withheld it from reporters. Buford's parents were retired and living just outside Southport; they docked a boat, a thirty-two-footer named *Oil-n-Water*, at the marina; Buford was a registered Republican; he was a few credits shy of an associate's degree in business—all of this weakened Buford in Eric's mind. Knowing what Buford didn't know they knew was fortifying. Even that Garcia was the only person to appear on camera at the press conference, that he'd denied everyone but the family the opportunity to gaze upon Justin, seemed a sign of strength and confidence. It seemed something they were lording over Buford. When a reporter asked when they might glimpse Justin, Garcia said, "Our office's primary objective is a successful prosecution. Yours is to grant that boy some privacy. They've all been through enough."

Eric was nodding emphatically, as if at church.

AT SCHOOL ON MONDAY, ERIC'S STUDENTS PRESENTED HIM with a WELCOME HOME poster for Justin: a lime green background and a pasted newspaper photo of Justin's billboard with the word FOUND spray-painted across his image. Above the clipping were the words TEXAS HISTORY IS MADE! and around them were the kids' signatures. Some of the students brought cards and presents from their parents—gift certificates to the Castaway Café, plates of cookies, bags of tamales. He tried to act professional, lecturing on Santa Anna and Sam Houston and assigning a chapter on the Battle of San Jacinto for the next class, but it was no use; his every thought veered back to Justin. He started to feel that beautiful weightlessness again. "You should just let us go early, Mr. Campbell," Clarence Ogden said. "Justin probably wants to see you more than we do." So he did. In the hallways, teachers went out of their way to shake his hand, clap his back.

When he wasn't teaching, and while Justin slept in, Eric ran errands. He swung by the pawnshop and brought home a bigger aquarium for the mice Laura had decided to keep as pets; she'd named them Willie and Waylon. Eric and Cecil drove to Marine Lab and retrieved Laura's car, then stopped in Portland for fruit cups dusted in chili powder—a treat the boys had always loved. The running around afforded him a feeling of usefulness, just as hanging the flyers had before, and whenever he returned home there always seemed a new development. (Again, those early days of fatherhood came back, days when his sons seemed to grow an inch in an hour, learn five new words in the time it took him to mow the yard.) The governor's office sent a small palm tree and a signed card, welcom-

ing Justin home. Another five bouquets of flowers and balloons arrived, another ten. Another slew of stuffed animals. A producer
from CNN called, and Laura had kindly asked the woman where
the fuck she'd been four years ago when they'd begged in vain for
airtime. She made a dentist appointment for Justin and set up his
counseling with a social worker in Corpus named Letty Villarreal.
He'd have two sessions next week, and then they'd meet once a
week indefinitely. On Wednesday afternoon, an animal control officer from Corpus dropped off Justin's gray rat snake. She was four
feet long with slate-colored patches running down her back. When
Justin woke that evening, he set up her aquarium and heat lamp on
his dresser, adjacent to the mice. He outfitted the tank with pieces
from his old rock collection. The snake's name was Sasha. Laura
took a picture of her slithering into Justin's shirt, his face gorgeously
scrunched, as if someone was tickling him.

To Eric's surprise, the press respected Garcia's request and
largely left the family alone. He and Laura had both seen a photographer circling the block, each on separate occasions, and a handful
of reporters left messages and sent emails requesting interviews, but
that was all. Laura said she remembered reading about photographers posing as deliverymen, how they would come inside the house
with packages and floral arrangements and then take pictures with
cameras shaped like pens, but they were spared any such intrusion.
If anyone was being hounded, it seemed to be Buford's parents, the
district manager of his newspaper route, and his neighbors at the
Bay Breeze Suites in Flour Bluff. They said he was quiet and distant.
They said they were horrified. They slammed doors in the reporters'
faces, covered the camera lenses with their palms.

Laura was staying home from work. She'd also canceled her
shifts at Marine Lab. Maternity leave, she called it. She worked
around the house, dusting and waxing, opening windows to air out
the rooms. She packed away the excess flyers, the MISSING buttons
and T-shirts, the postcard from California that had been magneted

to the refrigerator door. She returned calls and wrote thank-you notes, cards she left out for Eric and Justin to sign after supper. Griff filled Hefty bags with the stuffed animals people sent. When enough time had passed, Eric would deliver them to the children's hospital in Corpus. Laura fried chicken and baked casseroles so Justin would have food to nibble on during the night. She called Eric to say Justin was still sleeping—something she'd also done when the boys were infants, when sleep was a scarce commodity—so she and Griff were going to wash her car in the driveway. Another time, they did a jigsaw puzzle together. Another, they tried to tie-dye some shirts, but everything just came out purple. They did anything they could to pass the long hours until he stepped out of his room, rubbing his eyes, smiling.

Once Justin emerged, it was as if all the lights in the house had been thrown on. Eric wasn't yet accustomed to seeing him again, and everything that his son came into contact with seemed to radiate, to shine in new and pure ways. What he understood now was that a stillness had crept into the house over the years—the tamped-down carpet, the scrim of dust that blurred the television screen—and he noticed it now because the stillness was gone, supplanted by a fresh energy. His vision was keen, his mind precise. If Justin recognized how he restored his father, he didn't let on. He cupped his hands around his coffee mug, asked what everyone had been doing while he slept. He would also ask about things he'd remembered overnight: What ever happened with Mrs. Harrison, the fourth-grade teacher who ate chalk? What about Tommy Benavides, the bully from grade school? When did the Teepee go under? His reactions were measured and opaque, but not uninvested. Even when they told him that Johnny and Jason Holland, his old best friends, had moved from Southport three years ago, Justin was unfazed. It was simply that nothing seemed to surprise him now.

"Keeps his cards close to the vest," Cecil had said. He'd always valued reticence, the strong contours of silence, and because his father could, Eric tried to find respite in his son's polite shyness. Most evenings, Cecil stopped by after work. He brought videogames and DVDs the boys might like from the pawnshop. One night they had to help him in with a thirty-gallon aquarium, an upgrade for Sasha. Fiona, her hair now shockingly green, would usually arrive as they were clearing the dinner table. Each night she brought some kind of present with her. A lemon pie, a book on sharks for Laura, a jug of Miracle-Gro for the plants that were overtaking the rooms. There was hardly a flat surface in the house that didn't host a vase or pot. "It's like living in the Amazon," Justin had said.

On Wednesday, two days before the arraignment, Fiona brought a Trivial Pursuit board game and set it up on the kitchen table to play after eating. Eric couldn't remember a time when the house had felt so full, so refreshingly loud with familiar voices. Fiona usually stayed until nine or so, when Griff would walk her home. They always invited Justin, but he was yet to accompany them.

"It's weird to see him with a girlfriend," Justin said after they left. "I guess a lot's changed."

"Not the important things," Laura said. "No one touched the things that matter. No one."

EXACTLY WHEN THE FIRST TREMORS OF INSECURITY SEIZED HIM, Eric couldn't say. Most likely they'd been dormant in his blood since he'd first seen Justin in the police station, but now he'd started noticing the porosity of his relief. Maybe the first symptoms had come when Laura offhandedly said, "You know who we haven't heard from yet? That nice Tracy Robichaud. Do you ever run into her anymore?" Or when she said, "I just wonder what was happening in the world. I want to know what everyone was doing. Somewhere, someone was washing his car. Someone else was making some horrible mistake." Maybe it was knowing that Dwight Buford would enter his plea on Friday morning. Or maybe as Eric grew more accustomed to seeing Justin, he grew less capable of ignoring what his son had suffered through. The pain Justin had endured, the fear and neglect and ruining shame, shadowed Eric's every thought. It was a kind of quicksand, a constant threat that emptied every promise from the bottom up. How disgusting, how humiliating, to realize that he was afraid to be alone with his son. They had, he saw now, hardly spent more than a few moments by themselves, and shamefully, Eric understood he'd always been the one to ensure that someone else was around—Laura or Griff or Cecil. He didn't know what scared him, but he felt the fear between them like an electric current.

When Justin had first gone missing, Eric had fantasies of a swift return, an absence so insignificant that his son would come home unaffected. Nothing more than a sleepover, he thought. A week at camp. He never stopped expecting to see Justin around every corner, never stopped scanning the faces of children for his son's eyes and mouth and cheekbones, but the fantasies of him emerging from the ordeal unchanged fell away. If they ever found him alive, Eric knew Justin would be so altered by the trauma that he'd bear no resemblance to the boy who'd disappeared. Of course they would accept the changed boy; they'd adopt him, offer up Justin's room, lend him their son's name. But Eric also knew there'd be a chasm between them. He'd never mentioned his lowered expectations— voicing them would have cast them in iron and he longed to be proven wrong—but they persisted. Now that Justin was home, now that he seemed so disorientingly himself, Eric was realizing that he hardly felt rinsed of doubt. Walking his father out on Thursday night, Eric confided this and Cecil said, "It's early yet. You'll cotton to it soon enough." Eric tried to believe him. He tried to accept that such profound relief was something that took getting used to.

That night, before Laura drifted off, they'd been whispering about the arraignment. If Buford pleaded not guilty the following morning, Justin would start meeting with Garcia a few times a week to prepare the state's case. Justin had agreed to this as casually as agreeing to buckle his seat belt, but the thought of requiring any more of him was abhorrent.

In bed, Eric's mind was surging. He sniffled. Years before, it had been how he and Laura would check to see if the other was awake. Sometimes they'd talk. Others, they'd make love. He sniffled again, louder. Nothing. He slipped out of the bed and crept into the house.

He expected his son to be watching television, but the living room was dark, the kitchen empty. He had a sense of having marshaled his nerve too late; he was, at once, absolved and a coward. The air conditioner hummed in the walls. The house smelled of potpourri. The air was cloying, dank. Eric felt seasick. Moving toward Justin's room gave him a jumpy, underwater feeling, as if he were swimming through the wreckage of a sunken ship, paddling from one ruined space to another. When he eased the door open, he saw that Justin's bed was still made. Moonlight reflected off the aquariums. The mice were skittering in their cedar chips. His heart constricted in his chest, pumping heavily. He peeked into Griff's room—maybe they'd stayed up talking or playing videogames, or maybe Justin had gotten scared and wanted to sleep with his brother—but he only saw Griff, balled under his blanket. Eric ran his hand over his face, leaned back against the wall.

Jesus, he thought. Jesus, no.

Then he heard Rainbow's tags in the backyard. He went through the door in the kitchen, stepped down to the porch and onto the patio. Humidity swamped him.

"She had to pee," Justin said, his back to Eric. He stood on the edge of the cement as if it were a pier.

"Me, too," Eric said, going for a joke. Justin made no response. Rainbow was invisible in the distance, but Eric could hear her parting the tall weeds and padding over the knotty grass. Even at night, the yard was an embarrassment. He said, "I let the yard go."

Justin shrugged, a gesture at once innocent and, Eric worried, judgmental. An easy wind came through the trees. Rainbow trotted along the fence line. Coils of gray clouds hung in front of the yellow moon, a gauze of light that deepened the darkness. It was as if parts of the sky were wet, blacker than usual.

"Are you hungry?" Eric said. "I can fix silver dollars again."

"I'm good," Justin said.

In the dark sky, the gray clouds were unspooling, fraying, giving up. Eric wished he hadn't asked about the pancakes, for now he suspected that Justin hadn't loved them as much as he'd claimed. He wished, too, that he'd stayed in bed. Maybe he'd always had such trouble connecting with Justin and he'd idealized their old relationship. There was an odd prospect of comfort in such thinking, but Eric couldn't remember the old life just then. Sweat pilled on his neck, glazed his chest. The seasickness returned. A tightening in his throat, desperate and dry.

Eric said, "Did you ever learn how to wink?"

Justin stayed quiet, maybe trying to wink. Rainbow trotted in the far corner of the yard. She sniffed hard at something, then moved away, swishing through the grass. A twig popped, then another. Justin said, "No, I still close both eyes."

"That's okay," Eric said. "It took me years—"

"I delivered papers with him," Justin said. "If you were wondering."

Eric became exquisitely aware of his bare feet on the patio. He remembered reading how there are some seven thousand nerve endings in the soles of your feet, and presently he could feel every one of them. He felt as if he'd drunk a gallon of ice water; he fought not to tremble. Justin said, "Our schedules were flipped. We slept all day, then went to throw the route at night. Right now feels like midafternoon to me."

"That's no fault of yours."

Justin picked up a stick and whipped it into the dark yard.

"I got to where I could sleep for twelve hours a day. More sometimes. Time speeds up when you're asleep, or it doesn't matter."

"You felt safer that way. It makes sense," Eric said, sounding lame. He wished they weren't alone, wished Laura would step outside. He said, "Dolphins never really sleep. Their brains stay awake. They're smart."

"That's pretty sick," he said. "Snakes sleep a lot, but you can't ever really tell. They don't have eyelids."

"Papaw got bit by a cottonmouth when he was about your age," Eric said.

"I think I remember him telling me that. Maybe when we went to the rattlesnake races that year."

How long since Eric had thought of that day trip to San Patricio County? The egg-toss contest, the diamondback hatbands and belts and boots, the cotton candy and beer in plastic cups, and the picture he'd snapped of Laura between the boys, holding their hands, as they watched the races. Justin had been afraid, hadn't wanted to stand too close, and Cecil had said it was okay to be scared, said he wished he'd been afraid as a boy and saved himself a nasty water moccasin bite. That Eric could access the same memory as Justin did was exhilarating. He wanted to gather his son in his arms, but he didn't want to call attention to the moment, didn't want to jeopardize how their pasts were fitting back together.

Rainbow loped onto the patio, her tail wagging. She pressed her wet nose to Eric's feet, tickling him, and he scratched the scruff of her neck. Her fur was soaked with dew. He wanted Justin to turn around, but he stayed staring into the yard.

"I'll do better on sleeping," he said. "On waking up earlier, I mean."

"You're doing fine."

Another wind kicked up, the warm smell of the bay floating over them. Eric didn't know what time it was, which struck him as odd. Nothing felt familiar. Laura had sometimes taken late-night walks when she couldn't sleep—she'd go ride the ferry or sit on the beach—

but he couldn't remember the last time he'd stood outside under a silent moon.

"I remember the rattlesnake races," Eric said. "You and Griff had a good showing in the egg toss."

"I still think those other kids were using a hard-boiled egg."

"You're probably right."

Rainbow jumped onto the back porch, circled herself, and lay down with a sigh.

"Dad?"

"Yeah, bud?"

"He'll plead not guilty."

"Beg pardon?"

"Tomorrow, he's going to plead not guilty. He told me he would, if he ever got caught."

"Okay," Eric said. "That's okay."

"I guess I just wanted you to know," he said.

"Thank you," Eric said. He was feeling turned around and trapped, like the wreckage he'd been swimming through was collapsing around him. He said, "No, I appreciate it. No, this is good. This is really good to hear."

8

THE PLEA DIDN'T SHOCK LAURA. NOR DID THE NEWS THAT Dwight Buford had retained a well-heeled lawyer from Houston, a French cuff–wearing man named Edward Livingstone who was donating his services. "Publicity hound," Garcia had said. Unless Livingstone successfully petitioned to have it moved, the trial would begin in Corpus in late September. Eric acted furious—which meant he was terrified—and Laura had pantomimed anger, too, but it was relatively baseless. She wanted Buford to pay, to suffer and die and rot, but now that Justin was home, she cared precious little about what happened in court. Times had even come when a nauseating wave of gratitude had surged through her, as if Buford had intentionally—graciously, apologetically—returned her son.

Her ambivalence surprised her. She'd long believed that the meridian that would define and divide her life would be Justin's disappearance. Before, after. Light, darkness. But no, the true division was his homecoming. Every previous experience grew formless, irrelevant. It was as if everything she'd known before had been covered in heavy black cloth. Her childhood in the Panhandle? Gone. The lives and deaths of her parents? Vanished. The tender ways Eric had courted her, the inexplicable pleasure she'd found in pregnancy, the stash of holiday and birthday cards by which she could trace her sons' penmanship (Justin's backward G's, Griff's R's that looked more like *A*'s), the summer when Justin refused to wear anything except the orange astronaut costume she'd sewn for him from a pattern in a magazine—all of it as insubstantial as puffs of air. Even volunteering at Marine Lab, even an experience as recent as Alice swimming to the side of the pool, breaching and then gently resting her beak in Laura's palm seemed no more real than fragments of a story she'd heard secondhand. If anything, thinking of all the hours she'd logged in that damp warehouse was discomforting. How transparent she must have appeared: the sad woman trying to save lost animals because she couldn't save her son. She hadn't been to Marine Lab since last Wednesday, the day Justin came home. She didn't know if she'd ever go back.

To spend any time away from him seemed duplicitous. And now, on the opposite side of the meridian, there seemed so much time. Every hour—every minute—contained new pockets of capacity. She made lists of things to do and meals to cook: Monopoly and Frito pies, charades and omelets, rented movies and homemade pizza. She felt reborn. Filled with vigor and mirth. With bottomless optimism. Watching the press conference, she'd remembered how some of the reporters and police officers in the room had maintained that Justin had drowned. Fuck you, she'd thought. Just fuck you now. The irony was that she felt as if *she* had drowned, as if she'd stayed conscious only long enough to watch her old haggard life blur and dissolve away. How shallow her existence had been, how selfish and lax and ungrateful. Behold the frigid wife, repulsed and repellent. Behold the bereaved mother, continuing to buy her missing son's favorite cereal, practically daring his brother and father not to eat it. Then, regardless of what she deserved, she'd been brought to the surface and resuscitated, revived into a benevolent world. Her elder son, the scaffolding of her heart, the blood within its soft chambers.

Part of Laura knew she was being idealistic. Knew the past was anything but vanquished. Knew the sham of her confidence would crumble beneath her and she'd plunge into the pit of guilt, of shame and despair, that came with having failed her son. Knew she should be more disgusted by the images of Dwight Buford standing before a judge and pleading not guilty. They watched it online, then on the newscasts. His patchy stubble and sallow skin and the girth packed like dough into his orange prison jumpsuit. Eric had watched the video clip countless times on the computer; he'd *studied* it. Laura took care to avert her eyes or leave the room. No, the past couldn't be ignored, but she had to believe that it could be controlled, quarantined. She wanted to focus on the future. Now that Justin was home, now that she'd been offered a reprieve—despite how ungrateful she'd been, despite how she'd deserved to have her heart cut out of her chest with a spoon—her sole concern was making good on the implicit oath of motherhood: I will keep you safe. Had Justin said he wanted to leave Texas, she would have packed their bags and made sandwiches for the drive. They would have left within the hour. Had he said he wanted Buford to die, she would have found a way to claw out the man's wet throat.

She took Justin to have his cavity filled. He wasn't ready to run into anyone yet, so Dr. McKemie was meeting them at his office at ten of seven on Tuesday morning. Justin hadn't slept at all yet. His eyes were heavy.

Justin said, "The treasure chest."

"You remember."

"He'll probably say I'm too old now."

"I bet he'll give you a one-time pass," she said.

McKemie was a wiry, mustachioed man who'd outfitted his waiting room with the mounted heads of a twelve-point buck and a pink-tongued javelina. He kept an old footlocker filled with cheap toys for kids to riffle through after appointments; they got one toy just for showing up and two if they were cavity-free. Laura didn't know if other kids called it the treasure chest, but hers always had. She was excited to see McKemie's face when he laid eyes on Justin.

Every time she saw her son now, Laura brightened—she felt it—and she remembered how it was in the early days after Eric proposed, how her eyes were drawn to her engagement ring, how possessing such a beautiful thing could convince her that she deserved it.

"He still lets Griff," she said now, carefully avoiding his brother's nickname. The other night, she and Eric had called him Lobster in unison when he surprised them with an answer during Trivial Pursuit. "Lobster!" they'd said and looked at each other with delighted surprise, but Laura had also seen a brief look of confusion—of *exclusion*—passing over Justin's face. Immediately, she knew the nickname drew too much attention to the years Justin had missed. Later, in bed, she told Eric they needed to start calling Griff by his real name. He wouldn't care. Laura had long suspected he tolerated the nickname only as a courtesy to his grieving parents. Oh, the mystery of what your children know, the scope and terrifying beauty of their perception. Now she said, "I think last time he got a Slinky."

Justin nodded, his head against the window. His eyebrows had thickened. His jaw had become more pronounced. She had to stop herself from stroking his hair.

Seagulls wheeled overhead. The streets and yards and roofs were dew-darkened, glistening and quiet. Shrimpers were heading out of the bay. When they arrived at the dentist's office, the parking lot was empty.

"I fed the mice some bread while you were in the shower," she said. She just wanted to get him talking. Being alone with him felt like a gift. She said, "They really love the crusts."

"Griff feeds them popcorn. He put some quartz from his rock collection in their tank."

Laura had wondered about those rocks, though she should've known they were Griff's. Since Justin had come home, Griff had deferred to his brother in every way. He seemed to be constantly ceding something, striving to make him more comfortable; it was as if Justin were in a wheelchair and Griff was always running ahead to move furniture and open doors for him. Griff, who'd gotten in those fights, whose friends had dwindled, who was fearless on his skateboard but so intimidated by most everything else. Then a memory buffeted her: Both of her sons had, for a time, been afraid of the dentist's chair in Dr. McKemie's office. They didn't like the hydraulic hiss the chair made when they were raised and lowered.

"The barbecue will be sick," Justin said.

The barbecue. Eric's project. Saturday would be the Fourth of July, so he wanted to have Cecil over and grill in the backyard. He'd bought sparklers, patriotically colored paper plates and napkins and streamers. Their freezer was overrun with meat. He liked the symbolism of Independence Day.

"We'll be eating ribs for weeks," Laura said. "Your father's eyes are bigger than our stomachs."

"The yard's looking good."

"It is," she said. Over the years, she'd watched the backyard succumb to dirt and choking weeds. Not only had she not minded the decline, but she could almost remember admiring it, how pure and undeniable the loss of essence. Now she said, "He wants to find someone to come and lay down new sod. It's too hot, and it'll be expensive, but his mind is made up."

"He doesn't have to."

"He just wants everything to be perfect."

Justin nodded. He seemed about to say something more, but turned to face the window. The morning was opening up around them. Laura hoped McKemie was running late or stuck in traffic. She even considered throwing the car in reverse and taking Justin someplace where he could further unburden himself. She longed to ask him questions: Did he hurt you? Were you here the whole time? Do you know how much we missed you, how desperately we tried to find you? Did you miss us? Do you miss him?

Instead, she said, "Lots of nights your father would go out looking for you in the truck. He'd take Rainbow. He'd say, 'Let's go find that boy.' And he always sounded so optimistic. He was convinced that would be the night, like he'd thought of a simple and obvious place where we'd all forgotten to look."

Justin was listening, fingering the hem of his new shorts.

"Some nights I think he'd just go off and cry. He'd come home, putting on a hopeful face, but his eyes would be swollen. A lot of times he slept in his clothes. His boots, too. He was too wrung out to change, but I think he also wanted to be ready if a call came to pick you up."

Justin nodded. It meant she should keep talking. He wanted to hear what she had to say.

"I don't think he really believes you're home," Laura said. "Probably none of us do."

"The yard and barbecue don't matter to me. I don't want him to think he has to do that stuff," he said.

"Just give him some time. He'll come around. And if there's anything you want to talk about, he's there to listen. So am I."

"It's cool that you kept getting presents for me. And that you kept my mail. Thank you," he said.

"Honey, you never have to thank me."

"I've been going through my mail at night and opening the presents. I wanted to tell you that."

"I probably won't remember buying any of it," she said.

"And I like your hair."

She thought she misheard him. "What? You what?"

"Your hair's pretty when it's long," he said. "I've been wanting to tell you that, too."

"Thank you," she said, drunk on love.

THAT NIGHT, SHE COULDN'T SLEEP. SHE LAY IN BED, EYES CLOSED, and breathed the air, which seemed sweetened. There was a potted azalea on her vanity, a vase of lilies of the valley on the dresser. Eric dreamed beside her, his legs occasionally twitching. Eventually, she realized her eyes were open and she was staring at the dark acoustic ceiling he and Cecil had blown in years ago. It reminded her of moonscape, and for a while she whimsically tried to imagine an inverted world, a world without gravity, where she was floating above the ceiling and looking down on the pebbled surface. The illusion never took hold, though, and finally she was more awake than before.

Two weeks ago, Laura would've cast off the thin sheets and sneaked out of the house and ridden the ferry back and forth across the ship channel. She would have searched the sky for the nine stars that constituted Delphinus, staying out until the sun rose and brassed the fog as the shrimping fleets went out. How heavy the salted air had been on her skin; how satisfying to feel the ferry push through the choppy water. Even now, sleepless beside Eric, she had the feeling of being lifted and dropped. And, like that, she was awash in time. The past and present were parting around her like currents, drawing her in the same direction, and the heavy cloth that had draped everything before was brazenly cast off. She remembered the first time Griff went to a sleepover party after Justin disappeared, a year after, how after days of deliberation, she and Eric had both consented, and how furious their agreeing had made her, how she'd been banking on one of them saying, *No, I'm sorry*, and how she'd desperately wanted it to be him. How Justin had called fried chicken legs "handles," and how he'd called carbonation "sparkles," and how Griff had, too, and how he'd stopped. How she could hardly remember a day since this began when she hadn't considered getting in her car and driving until she reached some place where she could assume a different name, a landlocked place with no memory of her so that her own memory might be bleached clean. How, once your son vanishes, you can't ignore how easy it would be to follow him into nothingness. How when she was clutching Justin in that cinder-block room at the police station, she wished she'd worn something prettier for him, wished she'd done her makeup, how she should have, every morning for four years, been dressed as if she were expecting him to return home that afternoon. How people avoided her in grocery store aisles. How she both resented and understood them not wanting to look at her, not wanting to see the hurt on her. How she hardly glanced at herself in the mirror anymore. How every afternoon of the school year she saw the kids walking home after class and their reliable presence mocked her. How Griff had called them from the sleepover and said he was sick and needed to be picked up, and how only just this moment, as she fell into sleep, as Eric rolled onto his back and the air conditioner cycled on, only now did she understand that Griff had been lying. He'd come home to spare them the shock of waking up to another son missing.

9

Thursday morning, three days before the Fourth, the pawnshop's fluorescent bulbs sizzled as they brightened. The counters and floors were tacky with humidity. Eric had met his father at Loan Star to borrow the expensive grill someone had in pawn. While Cecil was in the back counting out money for the till, Eric went around the shop turning on the various fans. All of them had tinselly streamers that lifted and vibrated once the blades started whirling; it made the shop feel oddly crowded, though Eric was alone. The air conditioner kicked on, a heaving metallic lunge in the ceiling and then the first surges of air coming through the vents, not yet cool.

The shelves looked thin. A few nights before, eating leftover chili at the house, Eric's father had told Justin that his return had been a boon for business. It had been something of a joke, Cecil's way of communicating how glad he was, how relieved. Only now did Eric understand he'd been serious. Last week there had been a wall of televisions on display, but this morning he could count where four, maybe five, had sold. A compound bow was also gone, one or two of the expensive fishing reels from the shelf behind the register, and a window unit. (He wondered if Tracy had bought one for the sisters at Villa Del Sol. She'd left a couple of congratulatory messages on his cell, but he hadn't spoken with her yet. He didn't know when he would. She seemed part of a different life now, a long fugue marked by guilt and dread.) The jewelry case was barer than it had been, the same with the racks that housed chain saws and musical instruments. The barrenness felt like a compliment; it helped make everything real. Eric would describe the picked-over stock to Justin later that evening. *Papaw owes you a commission,* he'd say. *You're better than the day after Thanksgiving.* Or maybe he'd wait until Monday when they were driving to the courthouse in Corpus so Justin could begin meeting with Garcia. Eric and Laura weren't allowed to participate for the same reasons they'd been precluded from so many searches: They were a distraction, a hindrance. During Justin's time with the D.A., they planned to take Griff to the mall, where he would help them pick out clothes and shoes for his brother. It was a surprise.

The glass case housing the pistols was so scratched that in places it appeared frosted. Eric had to lean forward to see the revolvers and semiautomatics through the cross-hatched counter. He couldn't remember it having always been so scoured, though he also couldn't remember ever having paid attention to the glass before. Even now, he wasn't completely aware of having gravitated toward the guns. The search of Buford's house had yielded a .38 and a 9mm, and Eric had wondered if he might find similar pistols in the case. He wanted to see them, to hold them and feel their heft. The sun came bright through Loan Star's storefront, pooling and glinting in the grooves in the glass like amber.

"Not on your life," his father said from behind him.

Eric turned from the guns. Cecil was pushing the stainless-steel grill from the back like a shopping cart. The wheels squeaked as he maneuvered around the counter. He was also carrying a set of bamboo tiki torches. He had them awkwardly trapped between his arms and his torso.

"Let me help," Eric said.

"You've never been interested in pistols before."

"I was looking at the glass," he said, relieving his father of the torches. "It's scratched to hell."

"You think it'll help your cause when someone sees Justin Campbell's father contemplating firearms?"

"I was just looking. I would never—"

"Good," his father cut in. "Now, open that door."

Outside, Eric had to squint as he pushed ahead of Cecil to lower his truck's tailgate. He slid the torches into the truck bed, then he and his father got a grip on the grill and, on the count of three, hoisted it. Eric would have been comfortable driving with it pushed against the cab of the truck, but his father fished a coil of twine from his pocket and busied himself with tying the grill down. Before he tied each knot, he gave the twine a hearty pull that rocked the truck. It was how Cecil did everything—deliberate, thorough, with an air of inconvenience.

"I've got some men coming over from Corpus this afternoon to put down the sod," Eric said.

His father met his eyes, then yanked on a piece of twine and tied it off. He was in a stew. A sedan passed on Station Street and honked. Cecil waved without looking at the driver. Maybe it was someone they knew, maybe not. People liked to honk when they saw the arrow marquee beside the road: HE'S BACK!

As Cecil went around the truck cutting off excess twine with his pocketknife, Eric said, "Dad, listen, I wasn't—"

"Are you paying through the nose for the sod?"

"Not too bad. A nursery in Corpus needed to get rid of its St. Augustine."

This wasn't true. He'd paid twice what he'd told Laura. She thought it was foolish and extravagant, and probably his father did too, but the idea of charcoal smoke and his family in lawn chairs with cool, fresh grass under their feet had become an oasis for Eric. Thinking of it could push the image of Dwight Buford and his orange jumpsuit and rangy beard out of his mind.

"Somebody just pawned the torches yesterday," his father said. "I thought Laura might like them."

"She will. She's enjoying getting the house back in order."

His father gazed toward the bay while a long line of cars passed. One honked, but Cecil didn't wave. A gust of wind came up, and they turned their backs to it. When it abated, Eric's skin felt filmy. He wiped his forehead on his wrist.

Cecil said, "He's never going to see the light of day, son."

"We don't know that," Eric said too quickly. Once the words were out of his mouth, he realized how long he'd been holding them in.

His father leaned against the truck, blotted his neck and face with his handkerchief. He looked like a man who'd already worked a full day, exhausted and short-tempered.

"Justin got to bed a little earlier last night," Eric said. "He and Lobster filled two trash bags with weeds from the backyard, so they were worn out."

"I thought we weren't supposed to call him Lobster anymore."

"We aren't. I keep slipping."

"It's good to get them working. It helps to sweat," his father said. He'd been saying it Eric's whole life.

"I hope so."

"Don't trip yourself running downhill."

"Do what?" Eric said.

"Let Johnny Law do his job, and you start working on putting this behind you."

"It feels too big. It feels like all there is."

"Well," his father said, "it isn't."

Eric looked down Station, saw another line of cars coming off the ferry from the island. He tried to affect distraction, ambivalence. It always surprised him how, at forty-four and given everything that had happened, he still needed his father's guidance. He'd long believed you outgrew such things, but a piece of advice or a kind word from Cecil could still prop him up the way it had when he was a boy. Even that his father had been short with him earlier about the guns was bracing. It meant he thought Eric capable of retaliation; it meant Cecil saw something in his son that was hidden to Eric, a store of resilience and strength and violence.

A light wind blew around them. The sun had started to feel good on Eric's skin, though he knew it wouldn't last. Soon the heat would tighten and become unbearable.

Eric said, "Think we'll break a record today?"

"I wouldn't be surprised."

"If it keeps up," Eric said, remembering what the deputy had said moments before Justin stepped through his doorway, "we'll have a busy storm season."

"That wouldn't be so bad," Cecil said.

Then he rapped twice on the truck and started crossing the parking lot toward the pawnshop. He picked up a flattened beer can. Eric expected him to wing it into the weedy lot beside Loan Star, but his father just walked into the shop and locked the door behind him.

10

EVERYTHING ABOUT JUSTIN BEING HOME SURPRISED GRIFF. Their mother had stopped going to work and to Marine Lab, but started cleaning the house and cooking meals again. Gone were the days when they'd heat up canned ravioli for supper, or when she'd wear the same T-shirt she'd slept in to her job at the dry cleaner's. Likewise the days when she had more hair on her calves than Griff did. (He realized—remembered—that his mother had been pretty, and he saw that she would be again; her eyes caught light in such a way that she looked young, mischievous.) Vacuum cleaner tracks in the carpet. Bathroom faucets gleaming so brightly he could see his reflection. His family started venturing into the backyard again, and there was a feeling of shared enterprise as they prepped for the barbecue. They spent evenings pulling weeds, cutting dead limbs from the trees, replacing split boards in the fence. While the workers laid the new sod, his father planted the small palm tree the governor had sent. Within hours, walking into the backyard felt like walking into a different life. Whether the life was new or old, Griff couldn't tell. He only knew the one they'd been slogging through was gone.

Justin looked almost exactly how Griff had expected. In the four years he'd been gone, the police had generated age-progressed photographs, but the images always looked warped and bulbous. It wasn't until Justin had stepped out of their father's truck that first night that Griff realized he too had been picturing how his brother would age. Justin was taller and his hair had grown out; he'd put on enough weight to dull his features, which made Griff feel as if he were constantly seeing him from far away. He asked for second helpings at almost every meal. He could beat elaborate videogames in two hours, usually without sacrificing any of his extra lives. ("Most kidnap victims are videogame wizards," he'd joked. "We're also really good at channel surfing and eating ramen.") His sleeping pattern was completely reversed. He limped a little sometimes, though no one seemed to comment on it, so Griff thought he might be imagining it. He'd developed a habit of cracking his neck and reading the newspaper. There was a capaciousness in him, an alluring air of knowingness, like a new student who'd transferred to Southport from a school in a bigger city. A glow, Griff thought. Justin was infinitely watchable; he sometimes seemed to glimmer, or the air around him rippled, the way it did over baking asphalt. Griff had long felt a secret significance as Justin's brother and now, with him home, the feeling was evolving, deepening. He often caught himself wanting to hug Justin, but not knowing if he should, and he'd again endure the awkward sensation of having a crush on him.

"Do I look that different?" Justin asked one afternoon. He was eating cereal from the box, watching ESPN.

"What?"

"You're staring again. Like you don't recognize me."

"Oh," Griff said. "Sorry."

"So do I?"

"No. I recognize you."

"Liar," Justin said.

ON THE EVENING AFTER THE NEW SOD HAD BEEN LAID, GRIFF suggested they go skate at the Teepee, but Justin wanted to practice before seeing anyone. They took their boards onto the back patio. Their parents were in the kitchen, cleaning up after supper. At first, Justin rode his old board. It had been under his bed for three years, his name graffitied onto the grip tape with paint pen—that had been the trend before he went missing. "This brings some things back," Justin said, and Griff wondered if his parents could hear. But the board's shape was cumbersome compared to newer models, and with all of the time passed, the deck had gone soft and lost its pop, so they took turns on Griff's. The yard smelled ripe in the humidity. Damp, turned earth. Griff had been looking forward to skating with his brother since he'd been found, though he realized it only now. He understood that every trick he'd learned had been to impress Justin.

And he'd learned a lot of tricks. Before, Justin seemed to ride away from a new trick every day. When Griff was just learning to ollie, Justin was clearing the six stairs behind the junior high's gymnasium; he'd even done boardslides down the handrail at the marina. Before Griff had become the Little Brother of the Kid Who'd Been Kidnapped, he'd been the Little Brother of the Kid Who'd Done the Marina Rail. Now Justin was awkward on the board. His weight was off, his timing delayed. Griff had been expecting Justin to dazzle him with new tricks, an expectation that embarrassed him as he watched Justin grow frustrated. It was disappointing, and being disappointed felt cruel. When Griff's turns came, he intentionally botched his tricks.

Justin was stuck trying kickflips, a basic trick where the board spirals once under your feet. He used to goof around with them, do them with his eyes closed or while taking a swig of Coke. Now he struggled. After a while, he landed one, but he was leaning too far back and the board shot out from under him and he fell backward, hitting the patio hard.

"This fucking sucks," Justin said.

"You're just rusty," Griff said. He couldn't remember having ever used that expression before. "And you need a new board. We can get Mom and Dad to buy you one."

Justin twisted to look at his elbow; blood was pilling from where he'd hit the concrete. He said, "Maybe."

Griff retrieved his board and spun the wheels, pretending to test the bearings. They sounded like rain. Again he wondered if his parents were listening. If not, he wondered if what Justin was saying was something he should relay to them later. When they had come home that first night, his father took Griff aside and made him promise not to ask Justin about what had happened when he was gone, but he'd also told him to listen for anything his brother offered. "Be a detective," his father had said, not sounding like himself. "You're on the case."

Justin took the board and tried another kickflip. He flicked his front foot too hard, so the board wobbled across the patio like a poorly kicked football. He said, "Can you do tre flips?"

"Only sometimes," Griff lied. A tre flip was a trick where the board simultaneously spun vertical and horizontal rotations under your feet. When Justin went missing, a tre flip was a new top-shelf trick, something only pros were doing; now it was commonplace. Griff had them dialed. One night last year he'd told himself that if he landed twenty in a row Justin would come home safe and soon; he did twenty-three before missing one. He said, "I can do them once in a blue moon."

Rusty. Once in a blue moon. Where were these words coming from?

"Why do Mom and Dad call you Lobster?"

"I broke my wrists a while back, trying the marina rail. My casts looked like lobster claws."

"That sucks," Justin said.

"Eating really sucked. You can't hold silverware with your thumbs in plaster," he said.

"I'd like to be able to slide that rail again."

"You will."

Justin stood at the edge of the patio, staring at the yard. He said, "You've gotten really good."

"I just skated a lot after you were gone," Griff said. "Like, *a lot*. It's kind of all I did."

"You should enter those contests they have in Corpus on the T-Head. You'd probably get top five."

His heart trembled, and he endured the same free-fall feeling he had when Fiona breathed into his ear. He *had* entered the Corpus contests. His parents had passed out Justin's flyers to everyone in the crowd, and they'd worn shirts with his picture on them. He'd tried to act like he wasn't with them, which had disgusted him. It did still.

"Did you ever go to those?" Griff asked. He tried to sound un-invested.

Justin took the skateboard again, tried another kickflip. "I wasn't allowed," he said. "But I had friends who went."

"You had friends?"

His brother laughed, an exciting sound Griff was still getting used to. Justin said, "Of course I had friends."

"I guess I never thought about it."

"My life could be pretty normal. Basic cable, fishing, midnight bingo. I was bored a lot."

A long wind blew. Justin was setting up to try another kickflip, but his wheel hit a pebble and he had to step off the board.

"Did you ever win?"

"Win?" Justin said.

"At bingo."

"Not even once, but we still went all the time. Sometimes I'd play three cards."

"Were your friends skaters?"

"No, they just went to check out girls. I was the only one with a girlfriend."

"You had a girlfriend?"

"You're like a half-deaf parrot," Justin said. He tried another kickflip, the board spinning more evenly but still shooting too far ahead of him. He said, "Yes, I had a girlfriend. She lived in our apartment complex. She's the one who named Sasha."

He had friends, Griff would tell his parents. *And a girlfriend. He lost at bingo.*

Justin came close to a kickflip. He said, "Why can't I just land one?"

"Did you tell your friends?" Griff asked. "Did they, you know, *know*?"

"I'm sure they do now."

The light was still on in the kitchen, but Griff couldn't see his parents. He hoped they'd gone into another room, out of earshot.

"Do you miss your girlfriend? The one who named Sasha."

"Would you miss Fiona if you were banned from contacting her?"

"That's how I felt with you," Griff said. "But worse, way worse."

Justin raked his fingers through his sweaty hair. He cracked his neck again. After a moment, he started carving around the patio on Griff's board. He said, "Y'all seem pretty tight, you and Fiona."

"I don't really understand what we are."

"Welcome to the wonderful world of women, little brother. Have you felt her tits yet?"

"I don't know," Griff said. His ears turned red, he could feel it. He raised his eyes to the kitchen window again.

"I think you'd remember. She has great tits."

"Thanks."

Justin tried another kickflip, but the board didn't spin.

"We went to a couple of those Corpus contests," Griff said. "Mom and Dad wore shirts with your picture. They passed out flyers."

"I used to see those things everywhere, the flyers," he said. "I hated the picture. My hair was all jacked-up."

"Dad cut it in the garage. He cut mine, too. And his."

"Everyone at school made fun of me—that's what I remember," he said. He was carving around the patio again. "How'd you do in those contests?"

Griff was looking into the new yard. He wondered what Justin remembered and what had already been supplanted by the changes. Did he recall the time he'd grabbed an asp on a tallow limb and Papaw pressed chewing tobacco to the sting? The night when Rainbow ate all of the Easter eggs their parents had hidden? Everything seemed so long ago to Griff. Probably there were countless changes that he couldn't see but were as obvious as Justin's old skateboard. He tried to picture four years' worth of boards lined up side by side, where the metamorphosis of shapes would appear gradual and inevitable. He tried to track the changes with the decks he'd ridden, but just then he couldn't remember how many he'd gone through while Justin was away.

"Hello?" Justin said.

"Sorry," Griff said, his voice loud in case his parents were listening.

"I asked how you did in the T-Head contests."

"Contests suck. The judges never know what they're doing," Griff said. He didn't want Justin to know that he'd won both contests, that no one else had stood a chance.

GRIFF HAD FELT FIONA'S TITS. SINCE JUSTIN HAD BEEN BACK, she'd hardly been able to keep her hands off him. When Griff walked her home in the evenings, they left early to make out on the dark playground behind the elementary school. He felt guilty leaving his brother at home, but not guilty enough to let Fiona leave alone. One night, on the merry-go-round, she pulled her shirt over her head and unclasped her bra. Griff was so worried someone would see them he felt nauseated. When he admitted his fear, Fiona said, "That wouldn't be so bad. Someone watching." Another night, when his whole family was crowded around the kitchen table playing Trivial Pursuit, she slid her hand between his legs and massaged his thigh.

He loved her aggressiveness, loved the distance he could feel spreading between this new phase of their relationship and what it had been before. There was a new breadth to his life, as if he'd discovered a door in his house that opened into a wing of rooms he'd never known existed. Although he knew he shouldn't tell anyone about what they did on the playground or under the table, he couldn't stop himself from imagining how he'd describe the events to Justin. *Her skin is like soft amber. Her hair smells cool and sugary.* Fiona had said she liked seeing the veins in his forearms, so before walking her home, he'd always slip into the bathroom to sneak twenty push-ups. He floated through his days as distracted by thoughts of Fiona as by those of his brother. They seemed the only two things that had happened in his life: Fiona sliding her long body against his, and Justin coming home. Moments came when doubt would rise in his throat, a confounding fear that Fiona's passion had more to do with Justin than with him, but he found ways to bury his doubts. He thought of the swell of her chest, how loud her breath could be in his ear, as if he were listening to the ocean in a shell. He imagined marrying her, imagined her name changing again. He whispered it to himself. *Fiona Campbell. Mrs. Fiona Campbell.*

The night before the barbecue, they fooled around at the Teepee. Griff hadn't been able to check on the coping since the night the woman at Whataburger asked for Justin's autograph, so he was relieved to find it intact. And he liked being near the empty pool again, the smell of plaster dust mixing with the sea breeze. He wished he'd thought to bring his board. There would have been time to sneak a few runs in the pool before his parents got worried. After skating with Justin on the patio, he didn't know when his brother would feel ready to try the Teepee, and Griff worried that if he went skating without him, Justin would feel slighted. As Fiona pinned him against one of the teepees and licked his neck, Griff thought of how off-balance Justin had been, getting so frustrated with not landing kickflips that he'd hurled Griff's board into the backyard and stormed into the house. When Griff came in, his parents were dousing Justin's scraped elbow with peroxide over the bathroom sink. They seemed thrilled by the scrape, by the blood as bright as finger paint, almost as if they'd been hoping he'd get hurt so they could bandage his wound. Justin found Griff in the mirror and rolled his eyes.

Fiona kissed him—hard and deep. She braided her leg with his, hooked her arms behind his back and pulled his hair. He tasted sweet tea on her tongue and smelled her perfume, a scent that recalled the socks he'd hidden under his mattress. He hadn't smelled the socks since Justin's return, and now he wanted to move them before he forgot where they were, before his mother found them. Fiona moaned. She bit his lip hard, a pinch of pain behind his knees.

"Where are you?" Fiona said.

"Between you and a teepee."

She was staring into his eyes, squinting, as if to gauge whether he was lying. She leaned in to kiss him again, but then paused and pulled back. Her face scrunched up. She said, "I'm not used to saying this, but am I moving too fast for you?"

"Justin had a girlfriend."

"So do you, and she'd like to get to second base before walking home."

"It seems weird to me. I never imagined him having a girlfriend."

Fiona pushed herself off him, smoothed her black shirt. In the distance, small fireworks crackled. Tomorrow was the Fourth.

"I mean, I want him to have been happy, but I guess I also want him to be happier now."

"Maybe he's lying, trying to impress you."

Griff shrugged. Earlier that night, they'd watched a movie Papaw had brought over from the pawnshop. They'd eaten popcorn. Sasha had been coiled in Justin's lap like a small plate. As Griff and Fiona were leaving, Justin was reading the newspaper. He had it in front of his face and, without lowering it, said, "You kids be careful."

Another small burst of fireworks. They sounded like paper being ripped from a spiral notebook. Fiona said, "Louise and George know his parents a little bit. Dwight Buford's. I guess I've met them, too, but I don't remember. George thinks someone is going to torch the Bufords' boat in the marina. It's called *Oil-n-Water.*"

"They'll probably move," Griff said, repeating what he'd overheard his grandfather saying a few nights before. "They'll probably sell the house after the trial and head to Florida."

"His mother's on oxygen. Lung cancer, I think."

"Did I tell you people ask Justin to sign autographs?"

"Only about fifty times," she said, smiling. Then after a moment she said, "Y'all took the postcard down from the fridge."

"One of my parents did," he said. "They don't want things around that draw attention to what happened."

"So you don't think they'll ask him about it?"

"Now that he's home I don't think the postcard matters anymore."

Fiona extended her leg and drew shapes on the ground with her toe.

"I went through nineteen different skateboards while he was gone. We were skating the other night and I saw how old his deck was. I didn't realize how much the shapes had changed, and so I've been trying to figure out how many boards I've gone through. It was nineteen."

"He was gone a long time," she said, her voice sounding frayed, as if he were hearing her from far away.

"Did you mean what you said?" Griff asked.

"Tell me what I said, doll."

"That I have a girlfriend."

"You're too good," she said. She bit his earlobe, ran her fingers through his hair. "You're just too, too good."

GRIFF SPENT THE AFTERNOON OF THE FOURTH HELPING HIS PAR-
ents ready the backyard, hanging crepe paper streamers and carrying meat from the kitchen to his father at the grill and then back
inside to his mother once it was cooked. He made sure the digital
camera was charged and the Handycam's discs were formatted, and
he sliced boiled eggs for the mustard potato salad his mother was
making. He answered the door when Ronnie Dawes and his mother
brought over a plate of cupcakes; he told Ronnie that Justin was
sleeping, but that he'd tell him they'd come over to say hello. Ronnie threw his head back and clapped, reminding Griff of a seal.
When Papaw arrived with a cedar picnic table in the bed of his
truck, Griff helped carry it into the backyard. "Smells mighty fine
back here," Papaw said to Griff's father at the grill. Smoldering
mesquite and peppercorn-rubbed beef. An offshore breeze was
blowing, pulling the smoke from the pit across the backyard like a
ribbon.

His father had on a Stars and Stripes apron and whistled a tune-
less tune at the grill. His mother brought out paper plates and napkins, weighted them down with bottles of ketchup and mustard. She
also placed two of the vases of flowers on the picnic table, and Griff
saw she was wearing the dolphin pendant he and his father had
given her. Her hair was out of its ponytail, brushed and shining.
Papaw tossed a ball for Rainbow to chase. After two throws, she
took the ball under the house, and he said, "I guess that's the end of
that." Then he went to water the new palm tree. Everyone was
waiting on Justin, but the waiting lacked pressure. They would eat

whenever he climbed out of bed, and until then, they'd munch on chips and deviled eggs. Today, the worst of their troubles would be keeping the flies away from the food.

Griff sat at the picnic table with his mother and grandfather. They drank sweet tea. Their red plastic cups left rings of water on the cedar. Griff's mother sprinkled some salt on a piece of celery, then took a loud bite and looked around the yard as she chewed.

"I'm always hungry now," she said. "I can hardly remember eating for the last four years. I remember going to restaurants, but I don't remember taking a single bite. I can't recall the taste of anything."

"There's never anything wrong with getting your appetite back," Papaw said.

A breeze came along, lifting the edges of napkins. The smell of charcoal smoke and pork ribs, of new grass and layered heat.

"We should buy Justin a new skateboard when we go to Corpus," Griff said. "His old one is lame."

"The one with his name on it?" Papaw said. "The one that came through the pawnshop?"

"Of course we'll get him a new one," his mother said. "Whatever he wants."

Papaw had started folding a napkin into triangles, concentrating on getting the edges straight and the corners tight. Once he finished, he said, "Is he all set to meet with the brass in city hall? Not too nervous?"

"Justin's fine," his mother said. "Eric and I can't see straight, but Justin's cool as a cucumber."

Papaw said, "He's due a long run of good luck."

"He had a girlfriend," Griff said.

Everyone looked at him, even his father at the grill. The world seemed to lean in around him.

"He told you that?" his mother said.

"His life could be pretty normal. He played bingo and went fishing. And he had a girlfriend. He hated the picture on the flyers."

"A lot of bingo parlors will have cameras installed. Might be something to have one of Garcia's boys look into," Papaw said.

"A girlfriend? In Corpus?" his mother said. She didn't sound pleased or displeased, but dazed.

Griff couldn't tell if he'd been right to share the information, couldn't tell if he'd said too much or too little. The day seemed fractured now, as if everyone was drifting away from each other in different directions. He wanted to say something that would pull them back, tether them together, but he couldn't think of what.

And then Justin was stepping out of the kitchen, and everyone turned toward him. No one spoke. They were trying to reconcile what they'd just heard with the boy standing before them. Griff wanted to apologize to Justin, to all of them, but he stayed quiet. Justin rubbed the heels of his palms into his eyes, then cracked his neck. He surveyed the yard and his stunned family.

After a moment, he said, "God bless America."

THEY ATE AS THE SUN DROPPED BEHIND THE FENCE, AND A heathered dusk fell over everything. Papaw went around the backyard, lighting the tiki torches, and soon the whistling and popping of small firecrackers started up. To Griff, the noises sounded like an expanding conversation, a complicated and widespread call and response that was happening all around them. His mother kissed the top of his head. Papaw squeezed his shoulder, and his father whispered, "Nice work, detective." The celebration regained the momentum it had previously lost, and Griff allowed himself to believe he'd been right to share what he knew. Rainbow lay under the picnic table for a while, but when the real fireworks began, she crept under the house. The pink starbursts and hot blue pinwheels, booming and crackling and hissing, left brief imprints of themselves on the sky, like the outlines of leaves on wet cement. Griff's father made a toast to independence. His mother took pictures: Griff waving a sparkler. Justin hiding his face with his hamburger. Then Griff set up the timer on the camera and they stood by the fence for a family portrait. Right before the flash went off, they all said, "Chicken-shit." It was something they'd done for every family photo before Justin disappeared, but Griff was surprised when he heard their voices. Maybe they were all surprised, shocked by the muscle memory of love. In the picture, everyone was laughing and above their heads, the sky was ablaze with streaks of sharp, colored light.

11

A GIRLFRIEND. LAURA KNEW SHE SHOULD FIND SOLACE IN THE news, knew it should throw a shaft of warm light on her son's time away. She knew it should evidence that someone had been kind to him when he so desperately needed kindness, but the knowledge that Justin'd had a girlfriend nettled her. For days—days when they ate leftover barbecue for lunch and dinner, days when she grew to hate its taste—the word would rise up in her mind. Girlfriend. Girlfriend. A wave of lethargy would overtake her. Girlfriend. Girlfriend. Try as she might, she couldn't understand what the word meant. The letters started to seem unfamiliar and puzzling, like a part of speech from a language she would never learn.

It had been different with Griff. When he and Fiona had started closing themselves in his room, she'd been nothing but proud. Laura assumed better mothers would have been concerned or offended, but it was all she could do not to congratulate him. Either she or Eric would have The Talk with him soon, and the prospect left her giddy. Not so with Justin. She felt preoccupied, slighted, taken aback. Threatened? Maybe threatened. Probably she was just being petty, enduring some hurt because Justin had confided in his brother rather than her. Hadn't there been a time when he told her everything—how he and Shane Rutherford found a toad on the playground, how he wished he had blue eyes, how lemons didn't taste the way he wanted them to? The idea had ballast in her mind, but it was also lacking. Something else bothered her. Then, on Monday morning while everyone was getting ready for the day in Corpus, she realized what it was: When she'd last seen Justin, girls were strange, prissy creatures to be avoided—a flash of memory: hadn't he, one evening, asked her to marry him?—so the fact that he'd returned having had a girlfriend was the sorriest, most irrefutable proof of how long he'd been gone.

She had thought she understood this. Those four years—the six inches he'd grown, the forty extra pounds—were the reason his old clothes no longer fit, the reason they were going to the mall to replace them. Those four years had gutted her family. How could she not understand such hideous gravity? Everywhere she looked, the absolute and crushing weight of the past. At times, she'd been bloated with sadness, leaden and unmovable. Other times, she would have sworn she was a sieve. Some days she'd felt swaddled in burlap so that every sight and sound came to her blurred and muffled and diluted by loss, and then, without warning, the tiniest sound would tear at her eardrums and the softest light would singe her eyes. This had been her life, wrestling with hope and hell until she'd come to think they were one and the same. Whoever believed hope was a gift had never lost a son. For four years, she was sure she'd known the emptiness of pretending, of feigning faith, the masquerade of appearing whole, and yet now she felt blindsided. And, yes, fine, she felt jealous, too—jealous of the girl, whoever she was, and jealous of Dwight Buford, who'd seen her son fall in love for the first time, who'd seen him blush and snicker when the girl started coming around. Did the three of them watch television together? Did Justin hold the girl's hand on the couch? (Laura had been waiting to spy on Griff and Fiona holding hands or pecking each other goodbye on the cheek. It was thrilling, like watching for a rare bird.) On his birthdays, did she bake him cakes, write him poems, ask Buford to snap pictures of them? A girlfriend, she thought. Of all things.

What else didn't she yet know? What would she never know? There seemed too much, and the depth of her ignorance, the force and expanse of it, made her want to rip her hair out in bloody clumps. Now that she knew he'd had a girlfriend, Laura knew she'd failed him there, too, having never once conceived of the possibility on her own. Just as she'd failed to find him when he'd been so close all along. If I were him, she thought, I'd slap me across the face. I'd turn and walk away, leaving me alone again. That's what I deserve. She wanted to scream, to break every plate in the cupboard, to kneel at Justin's feet and beg for forgiveness.

On Monday, after they left him at Garcia's office, Laura spent too much money at the mall. She bought Justin a new wardrobe, and Griff picked out a better skateboard for him. Each time she checked out at a store, Eric leered at the cash register total; she told him they'd return what Justin didn't want, but he probably knew better. Eventually, he went to roam the mall with Griff. "Call me when we're broke," he'd joked, then kissed her on the lips, which she took as license to spend more. She bought a bed-in-a-bag set for Justin, backpacks for him and his brother, and eel-skin billfolds for Eric and Cecil. She bought a heated rock for Sasha. She bought and bought and bought. At one point, a cashier ran her credit card and before the charge could be approved, she had to call Visa so Laura could assure the bank that her card hadn't been stolen and she was responsible for the shopping spree. On the way home, everyone rode with bags on their laps.

"Did y'all win the lottery while I was gone?" Justin asked, sounding half-serious.

"You needed new clothes," Laura said.

He adjusted the bag on his lap.

"Different things for different occasions," she said. "I wanted you to have plenty of options."

"Mission accomplished," he said, and Laura saw Eric and Griff trying not to smile.

"I just thought it would feel nice to put on fresh clothes, things that fit," she said. "Whatever you don't like, we can return. I saved the receipts."

"No," he said. "Everything looks cool. Thanks, Mom."

Maybe he was placating her, or maybe how much she'd spent would become a joke among the three of them in her absence. She didn't know. She'd thought buying as much as she had was unassailably right, and she was trying to hold on to such thinking, but Justin's reaction was undermining her. She wondered if he'd ever gone clothes shopping with his girlfriend.

After another mile, Justin opened a bag of clothes and stuck his face inside. He looked like someone bobbing for apples. Laura and Eric exchanged glances, then looked at Griff, but none of them understood what was happening. Justin took his head out of the bag, as if he were coming up for breath, then went in again.

Griff said, "What are you doing?"

"Inhaling," Justin said. "I'd forgotten how things could smell so new."

JUSTIN MET WITH GARCIA AGAIN ON WEDNESDAY, AND WITH Letty Villarreal, the social worker, on Tuesday and Thursday. Both the attorney and the social worker said spending more time with him early in the process was imperative. The goal was to have him tell the entirety of his story multiple times, to multiple people, and then once they had a sense of its scope, they could direct him to delve into the minutiae, the wrenching details. It repulsed Laura, as did her own dreadful curiosity about what he was sharing. She and Eric would meet with Letty on Friday, and eventually they would also be deposed, though possibly that wouldn't happen until much closer to the trial. "Right now," Garcia said, "your job is just to sit tight and get him to these appointments on time." After each meeting, Garcia's sleeves were rolled to his elbows and his collar was unbuttoned. He looked winded.

What words, she wondered, did her son have to utter in these meetings? What language formed in his mind? What vile combination of letters was he forced to hold in his mouth and then spit out? She worried it was all too intense, too draining and agonizing, and she watched Justin for signs that she should step in and call off the whole business, but each afternoon he emerged from the offices undaunted, almost more refreshed than before. Like he'd been swimming. Like he'd jumped off the high dive. Maybe he found the unburdening cathartic. Maybe, bless his heart, he understood that his efforts, however difficult, however taxing, could make a difference not just for his case but for others in the future. Or maybe it was all a sweet and stoic disguise, a courtesy to them. (*Did you wear disguises when you went to play bingo? When you went fishing?*) She had no idea. Every day there seemed more she didn't know. There seemed pieces of her son that would be lost to her forever, irrecoverable, and their absence was galling. What a peculiar and dislocating feeling to realize your teenage son knew what you never would.

On Tuesday and Wednesday, she and Eric picked Justin up together, and then Eric had a faculty meeting on Thursday, so Laura chauffeured him alone. The opportunity felt like a reward that she'd earned, that shouldn't be squandered. She wore a butter-colored sundress and a lavender cardigan, hoping to appear sunny. Before she left, Griff had said she looked like an Easter egg; he'd meant it to flatter her. Despite the heat, she wore her hair down. She arrived early and paced the hallways, readying herself to appear upbeat when Letty's door opened. Smile, she thought. Exude optimism. She brainstormed things to do before returning to Southport—throw pennies in the arcing fountains at the Water Gardens, or tour the USS *Lexington* or the Columbus ships in the harbor. They could stop at the tamale truck under the Harbor Bridge. They could go to Cole Park or walk along the seawall. They could just drive and talk. No denying the anticipation that Justin might confide or explain some unknown piece of his life, that he might grant her some private access to his tortured heart, but Laura believed there was also a selflessness motivating her. She hoped so.

Justin wanted to go to a pet store. He needed a mouse for Sasha. It was going on a month since she'd eaten. "And now that we're keeping the other ones as pets," he said flatly in the car. Laura was trying to find her way to Shoreline Boulevard or Ocean Drive, navigating various one-way streets that all seemed to send her in the wrong direction. She was feeling turned around and rushed. And she thought he sounded upset with her, critical of her having grown attached to the mice. She was trying to remember a pet store in Corpus that might sell mice; it wasn't something she'd ever considered. Of course the first place that occurred to her was the flea market where he'd been found, but it wasn't open on Thursdays. Immediately she recognized this as a blessing. Nothing good could come of him returning there.

Once they were out of downtown—she'd been driving parallel to Shoreline all along, and eventually found a residential street that conveyed them onto Ocean Drive—she remembered Pampered Pets on the south side of Corpus. "Would they have them?" she asked Justin.

"They usually do," he said.

She followed the lazy S curve, watched the lean palms stream by. Later, the implications of Justin's answer would fester in her mind: He'd been there before. The snippy old women who ran the store would have interacted with them, would have taken his or Buford's money in exchange for feeder mice without understanding that he was in trouble. Later, she would try to remember why they hadn't posted a flyer in the store, and she would decide for no good reason that the fault had been hers and it would feel like countless fishhooks piercing her lungs. But driving along Ocean now, she was safe, enjoying a swell of pride because she'd suggested a viable store.

The palm trees gave way to condominiums and sprawling homes behind brick fences. She said, "Was today okay?"

He nodded. He was wearing the sunglasses she'd bought for him at the mall, a shirt and cargo shorts, too. He said, "They're saying they might go after the death penalty."

There had been speculation about this on the news and in the paper, but she hadn't given it much consideration. She knew Eric hoped they'd turn it into a capital case. Cecil, too. Laura was ambivalent. Whether Buford lived or died didn't matter to her. She'd already gotten the only end result she needed.

They passed Cole Park and the fishing pier. She said, "Do you have feelings about that?"

"Him getting the death penalty? I think it'd be sweet. It'd be sick."

Laura turned right onto Everhart Road. She knew there was something to say here, but didn't know what it was. The subject seemed treacherous, not one she wanted to burden either of them with this afternoon. She wanted levity and sweet confessions; she wanted him to compliment her hair again, and she wanted to say she loved him and to hear him say it back. She wanted to hear about his girlfriend.

Pampered Pets was out of feeder mice, and so were PetSmart and Petco. None of the workers could explain the shortage, but each of them told her to check back in a couple of weeks after their next shipment. Justin stayed in the car at each stop, and Laura never went any deeper into the stores than she had to; she always kept the car in view. Not finding a mouse felt like a personal failure, and her head started to pound as she tried to think of another pet store to try.

"We can go to Aransas Pass. I think there's a pet store out there. Maybe Rockport," she said. They were outside of Corpus, heading home. "I remember we hung flyers in a place called Barks and More."

"It's okay. She'll be fine for a while longer. Snakes can go months without eating."

"We'll go to Pampered next week. We can make an afternoon of it. I'll make us a picnic lunch. We can eat by the Water Gardens."

Justin said, "Garcia doesn't think it will be a hard sell. He thinks a judge will go for it."

"The death penalty?"

"Yeah," he said.

"He'll get what he deserves. There's no doubting that. Either way, he won't hurt anyone ever again."

Justin's eyes were fixed on something well beyond his window, the opaque bay or the sun-hazed outline of the Harbor Bridge. He stayed quiet as she drove. Then, without looking at her, he said, "Sometimes you have to thin the herd."

"What's that, honey?"

"It's something he used to say when he'd read about someone getting executed. He'd always laugh."

"Oh," she said, her skin tensing. "Well, he's probably not laughing now."

"He might be," Justin said, still looking away. "He might see all of this as one big joke."

THAT NIGHT, SHE LAY AWAKE IN BED AGAIN. ERIC WAS ON HIS stomach, breathing evenly. He'd been more himself since the barbecue, and though she could still sense his nerves around Justin, he was doing a better job of masking it. She both admired and resented his progress. He seemed to have transcended what she'd suddenly found herself mired in, a bog of doubt. (Had he gotten himself out as a result of her getting pulled in? Exhausted, hovering between sleep and waking, she wondered.) The house was quiet, save for the air conditioner and ceiling fans, the constant hum that she could so easily mistake for silence.

Then, as if continuing a conversation they'd already started, she said, "I wonder where she was when they found him."

"What's that?" Eric said, his voice startled and sleep-heavy.

"His girlfriend. I wonder where she was when she learned the truth, learned he'd been rescued."

"What time is it?" Eric said, rolling onto his back, deciding whether he needed to swing his feet onto the floor, if he'd overslept.

"Was she happy for him, do you think? Or was she just disappointed, so disappointed she couldn't—"

"It's two in the morning. Let's talk about it tomorrow with the social worker."

"She must have felt like we did. Like the world just opened up and swallowed him whole."

Eric had already drifted off again, still on his back.

"The poor thing," Laura said. "That poor brokenhearted thing."

LETICIA "LETTY" VILLARREAL SPECIALIZED IN ADOLESCENT PSYchology. She didn't have a Ph.D., but Laura had to stifle urges to call her Dr. Villarreal. Letty was a pear-shaped woman with a penchant for floral-print blouses and tightly curled bangs. Ivies and ferns crowded the windowsills in her office. Thick white binders bowed the bookshelves. She kept a jar of candy on her desk, suckers and jelly beans and gumballs, and a wicker basket in the corner of the room filled with toys and stuffed animals. Laura liked her. Letty laid her palms flat on her desk when she had something serious to say— *Family reunification is a process, not a product,* or *Has either of you heard the term "Stockholm syndrome"? Traumatic bonding?*—and she steepled her fingers while others spoke. She seemed smitten with Justin, devoted to caring for him in a genuine way. She seemed to hold in her mind both the pain he'd endured and the courage that such endurance required. Laura regularly wanted to hug her.

And that Letty was now in their lives made the extent of Justin's abuse impossible to ignore. Sometimes the knowledge lit a scalding flare of anger behind her eyes. Other times, she was struck mute, no more capable of forming sentences than a woman who'd bitten off her own tongue. She was weak in the face of his suffering and weakened further by the necessity, the blood duty, of summoning strength. But it was as if her bones had been pulled through her skin, slid from her flesh one by one, until she was reduced to a formless puddle of herself. She was constantly shocked that no one seemed to notice how she'd diminished, how what remained of her was of no use.

On Friday, they dropped Justin at Garcia's office for his appointment, then walked two blocks from the county courthouse to the social services building. Eric had polished his boots and tucked in his shirt before they left for Corpus, and Laura wore her dolphin pendant. She put her hair up in a bun. She carried a Moleskine notebook the way she used to carry her textbooks walking to school, clutched to her chest. The heat was sluggish, torpid. Humidity dragged on her skin. Her purse hung from her shoulder, bounced against her hip as she walked. She had to keep stopping so Eric could catch up.

Letty was misting a fern when they arrived. Laura said, "Mine always die. You'll have to give me your secret."

"Turner's nursery," Letty said, putting the water bottle in her desk drawer. She motioned for Laura and Eric to sit, then lowered herself into her chair. She said, "I buy a new one after I've drowned or starved the previous one. Same pots, different plants—that's my secret."

Laura liked the answer, liked how the candor put her at ease. She wondered if Justin felt a similar relaxing. She also wondered if any of the white binders on Letty's shelves contained information about her son. Immediately, she had a fantasy of being left alone in the office and scouring the pages for an analysis of her son's psyche, his symptoms and prognosis.

"So," she said, "how's the little man today? I imagine this week's been a bear."

Laura wrote the words *little man* in her Moleskine, drew a box around them.

"He's holding up," Eric said, then looked to Laura for her assent. She nodded.

"He's sleeping a little better," Laura said. "I think talking with you helps. He seems to feel better afterward."

Letty's hands steepled. She wore two gold rings and a green Bakelite bangle. She said, "He has many admirers around here. He's become a source of great inspiration."

In her notebook, Laura wrote: *Admired! Source of great inspiration!*

Eric said, "How do *you* think he's doing? Has anything become clear in your time with him?"

"What's most clear is he's happy to be home."

"There's a lot of that going around," Eric said.

Laura's eyes went to the ferns on the window, the fronds lightly stirring in the air streaming from the ceiling vents. She wondered how long Letty'd had those particular plants—then it occurred to her that the story about Turner's nursery was very likely fictional. Letty seemed like someone who could keep ferns alive. Maybe the plants had been sent from patients she'd helped. Laura thought to bring one of the plants from home for her.

Letty had been talking. She said, "You're in the midst of a huge adjustment, and even positive adjustments come with confusing pressures. Some parents in your situation suffer from post-traumatic stress, depression, panic attacks, you name it."

Laura considered writing this down, but didn't. It sounded trite to her, and selfish.

"Treat yourselves from time to time. Go to a nice dinner, maybe a movie, or stroll along the beach. The boys can tag along, but it's not a bad idea to leave them alone occasionally."

"Justin hasn't wanted to get out much," Laura said, maybe too pointedly. She wanted the discussion to move back toward him. "We love having him to ourselves, but it's something we've noticed. He hasn't wanted to see anyone."

"Another aspect of Stockholm," she said. Her palms went flat against the desk. "It happens. He's afraid to let go of friends he had in the Away Life, and afraid the friends he had before won't embrace him. He feels tainted. But he's only been home a couple weeks. I'm not concerned right now. I suspect he'll thaw sooner than later."

Laura wrote: *Away Life. Tainted? Aspect of Stockholm. Will thaw.*

"It's also possible that his social development will become arrested. It can just stop. There can be disturbances of every kind— eating disturbances, disturbances in his sexuality and attachments, disturbances in fear-based behavior. Victims of childhood trauma often won't have the vocabularies to describe their emotions."

"He told his brother about friends he'd made in Corpus, but he hasn't directly mentioned them to us," Laura said. "He's pretty tight-lipped about everything. He doesn't say much at all."

"He hasn't shared much here, either. We have to be patient. My guess is Justin doesn't want to hurt your feelings, while at the same time he's coming to terms with losing his old friends. He knows he'll never see them again."

"Is that set in stone?" Laura asked. "With his friends? We know nothing could happen for a while, but if his friends were a source of, I don't know, *shelter* for him, is there a chance he could reconnect with them at some point? Is there a chance that would be useful?"

"The friends he was closest to in Southport have moved away," Eric said.

"I would strongly discourage any interaction, now or later. His friends in Corpus are, I'm sure, great kids, but they're best left undisturbed. When he's ready, he'll make new friends or reconnect with old ones from home."

"We just want him to feel loved, supported," Laura said.

"He does. He absolutely does," Letty said. "The children who survive this kind of trauma often do so because of what they were forced to leave behind. He was able to find meaning in each day, a reason to believe he should keep going, and more often than not, that was something instilled in him long before he was taken."

"Thank you," Eric said.

"Yes," Laura said. "Thank you."

She made a note to check the library for books on Stockholm syndrome.

The room went quiet, which made Laura feel rushed, as if she needed to squeeze more out of their time together. She said, "We're just worried he's bottling everything up. He seems really, I don't know, kind of *fine,* and I worry he's not."

"He's not fine," Letty said. "He's home and safe and things are getting better and better, but he's hurting. He's absolutely hurting. Maybe we'll see signs of this soon, maybe later, maybe never. This is a long and slow process. We can't ask the questions we want to ask. He'll open up when he's ready, if he's ever ready."

"We trust you," Eric said. "We appreciate everything you're giving him."

"He's a good kid, a strong kid, and everyone's working to give him the life he deserves. He's also a teenager, a boy who should be learning to drive and falling in love with a new girl every other day. He understands this better than we do. He absolutely does. Our job is to assure him that these terrible things that happened to him are not who he is."

"Driving," Eric said. His voice was light, dreamy.

"Do what?" Laura said.

"It hadn't even occurred to me. He needs to learn how to drive. He'll turn sixteen in November."

"Absolutely," Letty said. "You probably still think of him as an eleven-year-old. It's very natural, very understandable. The family's development can become arrested, too."

"He had a girlfriend," Laura said. "That's something else he told Griff."

"Marcy," Letty said. "The redheaded athlete."

"Is she in the same category as the other friends?"

"I think so. I'm sure she's sweet as can be, but I don't see her benefiting Justin anymore."

"Thank you," Laura said.

In her notebook, she wrote: *No friends. No Marcy. Never.*

WHEN THEY PICKED JUSTIN UP FROM GARCIA'S, HIS SPIRITS WERE high. So were his father's. It was as if they'd woken from a perfect sleep while Laura had been pacing the halls all night. She sat in the backseat, watching their car's reflection stream past on the windows of the downtown buildings. If anything, she thought she would've been pleased to leave Justin's girlfriend—athletic, redheaded Marcy—in the past. But she still felt petulant, passed over. It felt as though Letty had dashed some hope that Laura wasn't aware she'd been nurturing. She leaned her head against the window, closed her eyes. The backseat smelled vaguely of chlorine and fish; the shirts she'd worn at Marine Lab were still on the floorboards. Maybe she missed Alice. The possibility that her dourness had nothing to do with Justin was bracing. She pinched her dolphin pendant between her thumb and forefinger.

As they were ascending the Harbor Bridge, the girders overhead intermittently blocked out the sun as if Laura were batting her eyes. Justin said, "How many times did she say 'absolutely'?"

"I noticed that, too," Eric said, his voice full of energy. The car sped up, pulling against the bridge's incline. "Maybe four. Five?"

"She got nine in yesterday, but I wasn't counting in the first hour."

"She seems nice," Laura said. "Do you like talking with her?"

"Absolutely," Justin said. Eric laughed.

"She says everyone admires you. You're inspiring a lot of people."

Justin twisted his neck until it popped. Laura always grimaced when he did this, and she knew a time would come when she'd ask him to break the habit. She didn't know if cracking your joints was detrimental, but she'd say it was. She might claim to have read a study.

Justin said, "We just talk. There's not much to admire."

"That's nothing to sneeze at," Eric said.

They crested the Harbor Bridge. Its arcing silhouette rippled on the ship channel. Hazy late-afternoon sunlight dappled the water. Eric said, "Traffic's not bad right now." It sounded unlike him. Or maybe it sounded like the Eric from before. Laura couldn't remember. What she recalled was how Eric had once told her that his parents, during their courtship, used to steal bowling balls and roll them down the Harbor Bridge at night. Laura had never been able to reconcile the image of Cecil doing that with the man she knew now. When she and Eric had first started dating, she thought of the stolen bowling balls every time they crossed the bridge—she could close her eyes and see them gathering so much speed they bounced and went airborne down the ramp—and she always expected him to suggest they try it, but he never did.

They passed Marine Lab. Paul's truck was in the caliche parking lot. There were two other cars beside the building, though she didn't recognize them. She wondered how many volunteers had come and gone in the last two weeks. She wondered if Paul viewed her with the same disdain that he did everyone else who'd abandoned the cause. Or maybe he'd forgotten about her. She remembered the man who'd volunteered with her the day they found Justin, the one with the pregnant wife, and as Laura watched the wetlands pass, she wondered if the woman had given birth yet. That day seemed a lifetime away. She had a feeling of vertigo. Then they were moving through Portland, the bland shopping center and sprawling boat dealerships. Until recently, all of those windows would have had Justin's flyers displayed.

The clouds had dispersed. Light flooded the sky. Justin pulled down his visor. Eric eased off the accelerator somewhat, which made Laura think he'd spotted a cop idling in a stand of live oak ahead. She looked, but saw nothing. The road was open in front of them, sizzling, puddled with heat. A pickup hauling a boat on a trailer rattled alongside them, then pulled ahead. They continued to slow. Laura could feel the brake depressing. Justin glanced at his father, then at Laura. She shrugged. She looked through the back window, thinking they were being pulled over. The only car on the road was a sedan, a half mile back. Eric clicked his blinker on and guided the car onto the shoulder. She thought he was going to be sick again.

"What's wrong?" she asked. "Are we okay?"

"We're fine," he said, shifting into park and undoing his seat belt. "We're doing just fine."

"Is it overheating again? Are we out of gas?"

"Neither," Eric said. He switched the hazard lights on and looked in the rearview mirror. A few miles ahead stood the Alamo Fireworks stand, and just past that, Justin's billboard.

"Are you going to be sick?" Laura asked. She felt vulnerable on the side of the road. The hazards dinged, dinged, dinged.

Eric said, "What I'm going to be, in about five months, is the father of a son who'll be taking his driving test."

Justin looked confused, but now Laura understood. There was an exhilarating tremor between her skin and muscles. The sedan passed them. And then Justin understood, too. A smile like she hadn't seen in years. He cut his eyes to her, and she smiled, allowing him to believe she'd had something to do with this treat. He was beaming as he unlatched his seat belt. Laura was jealous of her husband's revelation, grateful for it.

"I think it's high time we got some miles under your belt," Eric said. "Sound like a plan?"

But Justin was already out of the car, jogging around the front bumper. Then his father was stepping out, too, and tossing him the keys.

12

ND THEN LIFE SLOWED DOWN. IT WAS GRADUAL, AND PEACE-
ful, bringing to Eric's mind images of floating down a long and
indolent river. He could call up the scene so easily that he wondered
if he hadn't recently dreamed it: the four of them, Eric and Laura
and the boys, maybe in the swath of the Guadalupe south of Austin.
The water is clear green, glinting in light that occasionally plunges
through a canopy of black hickory. His family lounges in inner
tubes, paddling lazily with their hands when the current lags, drifting toward the banks and then propelling back into the center by
kicking off from the exposed roots, the water eddying and clouding
and, finally, calming again. The surface is sun-warmed, but underneath there's an enveloping cool, and the contrast is refreshing. The
smell of sweet grass. There is the sound of rushing water in the
distance, maybe rapids coming over jagged rocks or a set of falls,
but it's growing quieter. In the weeks after he and Laura met with
Letty Villarreal, Eric could hear noise silencing. And with the quiet,
a crystallizing hope: Maybe his family was not, as he'd feared, being
swept toward a cliff. Maybe the worst lay behind them.

Most days he took Justin driving. Depending on their
obligations—Justin's meetings with Garcia and Letty, Eric's summer
school classes—they would set out either in the late afternoon or in
the early evening. They usually drove Eric's truck so Justin could get

comfortable with a manual transmission, but sometimes they took Laura's car. Laura and Griff had accompanied them on a couple of drives, and yet Eric always endured a rush of selfish relief when they stayed home. Cecil had taught him to drive, just the two of them on the bench seat of an old Chevy with a three-on-the-tree, so Eric thought of it as a father's duty and his duty alone; it was a tradition, and with Justin, also a prize. Justin stayed quiet, concentrating on the road, though once when they passed the yellowed field behind the high school, he confided that he enjoyed watching football and might eventually want to try out for the Southport Mustangs. "The team could sure use your help," Eric said. They drove the residential streets in town, the open highway toward Corpus, the narrow farm roads that meandered through the wetlands heading up into Refugio. Justin was a solid driver. He was confident behind the wheel, but not hasty. He didn't hit the gas as soon as a light turned green, and he didn't change lanes without checking his blind spot. Parallel parking gave him problems, so lately they were working beside the curb in front of the Catholic church. Eric borrowed a couple of orange cones from the school gym to stake boundaries. "You borrowed them the way I used to borrow clothes from the cleaner's," Laura had said, smiling. He'd also swiped a driver's ed textbook from the school's book room, and while everyone else slept, Justin stayed up memorizing the rules of the road.

One night on Farm Road 386, Eric asked, "If you're going down a steep hill, should you shift into neutral to control your speed?"

"No. Keep it in gear."

"Bingo," Eric said. The quizzes had become a regular facet of the drives, and though he hoped they might foster other conversations, that hadn't panned out. He said, "If you have a rear tire blow out, what do you do?"

"Slow down by easing off the gas. Don't hit the brakes."

"You're on fire tonight."

Dusk was coming down. The headlights of a car heading toward them illuminated, and Justin reached to make sure his were on, too. Eric was trying to think of another quiz question when Justin said, "It's pretty sick you teaching me to drive."

"You're a natural," Eric said. "With a student like you, there's not much teaching. Take a left up here at the light."

Justin clicked his blinker on, shifted into neutral.

"Good," Eric said. "Perfect."

LAURA READ BOOKS ON FAMILY REUNIFICATION AND STOCK-holm syndrome—and at least one on the intelligence of mice—and she scribbled notes in her Moleskine. She dug up her mother's old recipe book and made dishes she'd liked as a teenager: salmon patties, pot roast with honey and thyme, gazpacho. In bed at night, they whispered about the day: *I think Justin liked the German potato salad, but Griff mostly pushed it around his plate. Fiona, too. Parallel parking went a little better today. He only knocked the cone down twice! One of the worst things about Stockholm is what's called "learned helplessness." I made a note to ask Letty about it, maybe see if there's anything else we should be on the lookout for. He said Buford used to laugh and say, "Sometimes you have to thin the herd." What does that mean? It's ranching talk. You kill off cattle when the herd gets too big. Oh. While y'all were out driving, Griff and I let the mice run in the hallway. When I picked up Waylon, he latched on to my hair and started climbing it like a vine! Griff was cracking up, but it hurt! It did!*

The mice had become a source of joy for her. She sprinkled cornbread crumbs into their aquarium, cooed at them through the glass, and taped together old paper towel tubes for them to run through. She was still on her so-called maternity leave, and although Eric wondered how long she intended to keep from working, he hadn't broached the subject. He wanted her to enjoy her time with Justin, wanted her to feel supported. Laura was also starting to weigh the decision of what to do about Justin's schooling. Whether they went

with homeschool or enrolled him at the high school, he would graduate a year late. Maybe two. He would be tutored throughout the
fall. As far behind as he was and with the trial starting in September,
there was no other choice.

Griff was preoccupied with Fiona, and Eric was grateful for the
distraction she provided, even if guilt sometimes overtook him. He
worried that Griff felt relegated to the sidelines with all the attention being paid to Justin. How could he not? The house was crowded
with the plants and flowers that were still being sent, and their voice
mail was clogged with messages from reporters and photographers
wanting to come over. With Fiona around, though, Griff seemed to
exist in a heady daze of contentment. She visited the house regularly
enough that Laura started cooking supper for five, and her manners
were so refined that Eric wondered if she'd taken classes; he had
also started seeing her green hair and black wardrobe as camouflage, a hostile costume masking a timid soul. Each night, Griff
walked her home, and each night, they set out earlier and earlier
until they were leaving a full hour before her curfew. When Griff
returned, he seemed addled and secretive. "Do y'all think I should
follow them?" Laura had asked one evening after they left. "Do you
think he's scared to walk home by himself?"

"No," Justin said. "I think he's pretty happy with the current
arrangement."

"Oh," she said, and then seconds later, understanding, "oh!"

If Fiona wasn't around and Eric and Justin were on a drive, Griff
slipped off to skate the Teepee pool. He left soon after they did,
skated for a half hour or so, then returned to shower and change
before supper. When Justin and Eric got home, Griff was usually
playing videogames or running with Rainbow in the backyard. (The
backyard still pleased Eric. He could gaze at the grass and recall the
smell of burning sparklers and hamburgers, the sound of everyone
saying "Chickenshit.") It was Laura who pointed out that Griff
seemed to want to keep the skate sessions a secret from his brother.

"Justin's not ready for the pool yet," she said. "Griff doesn't want to hurt his feelings." She was proud of Griff, a light timbre of satisfaction in her words, and hearing it, Eric experienced a lift, too. Griff's discretion seemed evidence of how capable they had been as parents. Such sensitivity restored their confidence not just in their parenting but in an abiding decency that would see everyone through. Eric made sure Justin avoided the Teepee when they were out practicing.

At school, the students and faculty had largely moved past Justin's return. They still asked after him, but the kids were more concerned with tests being passed back and the teachers were focused on lesson plans for the following week, committees for the fall. Eric taught his students about Texas joining the Union, the King Ranch and the oil depression, and Judge Roy Bean. He assigned group projects that entailed students' developing election campaigns for previous Texas governors based on what they knew of the politicians' beliefs, policies, and events that happened during their tenures. It was an assignment he'd cooked up last summer, and as he distributed the handouts at the end of his Friday class, he was hit with how much life had changed in a year's time. The notion was suddenly incomprehensible. Eric felt seized by something so inevitable, so mysterious and unexpected that it seemed almost divine. For a moment, he thought he would collapse. His vision started to tunnel. Don't pass out, he thought, then worried he'd said it aloud. When the bell rang, the room came abruptly alive: Kids slid their chairs back from their desks and swung backpacks over their shoulders and moved toward the door in a long and loose huddle, squeezing into the hall, merging into the stream of students exiting the building. The door to Eric's classroom closed behind the last student. The quiet was immediate and immense, interrupted only by the rapid squeak of sneakers on the tile floor—someone running to catch up with the others—and the distant echoed voices of a few teachers making for the parking lot.

Eric usually walked out with the rest of the faculty, but today he took a seat behind his desk. His heart was racing and he'd broken out in a sweat. It was as though he'd outrun something and, now safe, needed to catch his breath. The poster his students had made him—TEXAS HISTORY IS MADE!—hung on the opposite wall. Even without Laura saying it, Eric knew she wanted the poster, knew she intended to laminate it and add it to her collection of cards and newspaper articles. A year ago, around the time he was devising the gubernatorial campaign assignment, she'd been hiding Valium and Xanax in her closet. One day when Laura was volunteering at Marine Lab, he'd gone to hang up a pair of jeans that had been draped over a chair for a week. When his elbow knocked one of her old purses down, the pill bottles came out of the bag like roaches. He'd been surprised at how unsurprised he was. He left a few pills in each bottle—not enough to do any damage—but flushed most of them down the toilet. For months, he'd been braced against the threat of her confronting him, but she never did. The purse had eventually disappeared from the closet.

Footsteps in the hallway, the click of heels approaching and then passing his door, the murmur of voices rising and falling, people talking over each other. A woman laughed, maybe Mrs. Norrell, the typing teacher, or Ms. Vasquez, the girls' basketball coach. Eric would leave once they were settled in the teachers' lounge. He didn't want to make small talk. The sun was bright through the classroom window. If Justin was still asleep, his head would be buried under the pillow to block the light; if he was awake, he would be drinking coffee and paging through the newspaper like an old man. Griff would be talking on the phone with Fiona, and Laura would be puzzling over homeschool requirements. They were all expecting him. They might already be wondering what was keeping him. It was flattering, astoundingly so, and as he started gathering the papers he'd need to grade before the next class, he wanted to repay his family's kindness. He would suggest they all go for a drive in Laura's car. Justin would drive and they would grab some sandwiches and have a picnic at the rest area just outside Corpus. He would tell them he'd been thinking of how everything had changed, how lucky he was to call them his family.

The door to his classroom inched open. A woman said, "Knock, knock?"

He expected it to be Mrs. Norrell, trying to enlist his support for one of her various projects—the ice cream social, the basketball booster club, the fall rummage sale to raise funds for new computers in the library. He was preparing to brush her off—*I'll get back to you after the dust settles on the trial*—when Tracy Robichaud stepped into his classroom.

"Tracy," he said. His voice sounded meek.

"Stranger."

He stayed behind his desk, his mind immediately calculating who might have seen her come into his room and how he could explain away her visit if asked. She wore a khaki blazer and white slacks, not clothes he recognized. Adrenaline poured into his veins. He steeled himself against whatever she'd come to say or ask or accuse, but also against the unhelpful and complicated tenderness he felt toward her. He should have called her. He should have thanked her for every kindness she'd shown him. He was about to apologize— for anything, for everything—when she gave him a little smirk, a private and sleepy-eyed expression he recalled with wonder and regret. Then she turned to shut the door, to lock it behind her.

"Stranger," she said again. "Howdy."

13

WHEN JUSTIN SHOOK HIM AWAKE IN THE MIDDLE OF A TUES-
day night near the end of July, Griff didn't understand what
was happening. At first, he thought Justin might be freeing him
from a nightmare. He had no memory of dreaming, but it seemed
possible that his brother would have heard him calling out in his
sleep. Then he worried that some new calamity had befallen their
family. He'd harbored fears that Papaw would die for as long as he
could remember, and for a moment, he could imagine nothing else.
But the house was dark and he knew that if there was trouble,
there'd be light in the hallway and Justin wouldn't be whispering.
"Get dressed," he said. "Meet me out front." Griff rubbed his eyes.
His thoughts slowed and narrowed to an idea that surprised him
with its force: Justin was running away. Griff didn't know whether
his brother had woken him to say goodbye or to enlist him in the
journey. Either way, he had the feeling he was about to do something reckless. He was flattered Justin had thought to wake him.

Outside, Justin waited behind the wheel of their father's truck.
Griff climbed in without a word. As he eased his door closed, his
brother shifted into neutral and the truck rolled backward down the
driveway. On the street, he cranked the ignition and they drove
down Suntide in the dark. Justin didn't turn on the headlights until
the end of the block.

They tacked their way through the neighborhood and eventually got to Station Street. They passed houses that Griff had seen all his life, some of which he'd been inside, but at that early hour, the lurid moonlight transformed them into unfamiliar shapes. Neither he nor Justin said anything, and illogical as it seemed, Griff thought they were still worried their parents might somehow hear them. There was the sound of the engine, of the tires on the road and the squeaking rattle of the truck's old struts. The streetlamps shone their amber glow, june bugs bouncing against the bulbs. A brown pelican was perched on a pylon. The bird watched the truck, its great head moving like a turret.

After they passed the anchor monument that read WELCOME ABOARD and entered the marina, Griff realized he'd expected Justin to park in one of the diagonal spaces along the seawall. That they'd kept driving opened countless possibilities. And a sense of liberation. When they'd been heading toward the port, he was—he realized suddenly—afraid that Justin intended to set fire to the Bufords' boat. Griff was also afraid he wouldn't be able to stop him, and afraid he'd run away and Justin would write him off as a coward. Now he assumed Justin was heading to the ferry and they'd cross onto Mustang Island. It seemed important not to ask where they were going. It seemed a sign of maturity, of trust. In front of the souvenir shops, they turned onto a side street and continued toward the water. Maybe he was simply practicing for his driving test, planning to have Griff stand outside and direct him toward the curb while he parallel parked. The speedometer needle hovered at just over twenty miles per hour. The cab started smelling of exhaust, so Griff lowered his window and the balmy air curved around the windshield and slipped inside.

Justin slowed alongside the walkway near the ferry landing and eventually stopped in front of a waist-high hedge that hugged the concrete leading down to the docks. In the distance, the ferry horn bellowed. There was fog over the water, fat and low, and the night's humidity was glazing the windows. The truck idled, and occasionally the RPMs spiked loudly. Everything else was still.

"I'd been trying to ollie it," Justin said. "I could get the speed and the height, and I was clearing it, but I couldn't keep the board on my feet."

"You were trying to ollie what?"

"That hedge."

At first, Griff assumed Justin was talking about something he'd tried to do recently, maybe earlier that night after their parents had gone to sleep, and the prospect thrilled him. It meant Justin was taking skating seriously again; it meant they could go to the Teepee together soon and Griff wouldn't have to sneak sessions while Justin was out driving with their father. It meant things were getting back to normal. But, no. Justin was referring to another time altogether. Griff looked at the hedge, a dense boxwood that everyone passed when they came off the ferry. He'd never thought to try ollieing it; the thing was too high. His heart surged and fluttered, as if a thousand small birds had jumped into flight, all at once, inside his chest.

"I'd been trying for an hour or so," Justin continued. "The sun was blazing. My shirt was drenched. When I tried it the last time, some sweat ran into my eyes and for a second I couldn't see. I ollied too late and my wheels clipped the top of the hedge. I landed with my ankle folded between my board and the ground. It sounded like a balloon popping. I remember getting really cold. Like, I was shivering."

"I got really cold when I broke my wrists," Griff said.

"I was just in a ball on the ground, holding my ankle, rocking back and forth, trying not to cry. It was stupid. I didn't know if I'd be able to stand up, so I was imagining rolling myself home, sitting on my board or lying on my stomach. I figured it would take an hour or two. I kept expecting someone we knew to see me, offer me a ride. Dad had gone to school that day to set up his classroom, and even though it wasn't on his way home, I thought I might get lucky. But I don't remember anyone driving by at all. It seemed like I was on the ground for a long time. I kept shivering. I felt like I was going to throw up. My ankle was swelling. I thought of a football being aired up. My shoe was getting tighter."

"Maybe the ferry was stuck on the island," Griff said. "You know how it sometimes—"

"He had a white SUV," Justin said flatly. "He never said so, but I assumed he was a paramedic, maybe in the Coast Guard. Just because his truck was white. He was parked right here, exactly where we are."

"Oh," Griff said. "Oh, wow."

"The engine was running. His hazards were on. He had these small scissors, and he cut the laces in my shoe, then slid it off. Then he cut my sock, and he started pressing on my ankle with his thumbs, asking if it hurt. He seemed to know what he was doing, but I couldn't feel anything, just numbness."

"That's why you limp."

"It gets really stiff sometimes. It didn't heal right. I never went to the doctor."

Griff wanted to say something more, for his sake and for Justin's, but he didn't know what. He also wanted to ask why he was telling him this. He looked out over the water. The moon had come through some clouds, giving the bay a metallic sheen.

"I don't remember how I got into his truck, whether he lifted me or whether I hopped over on my good foot. There were bundles of old newspapers. Everything smelled of paper and ink. He had me lay down in the back and he looked at my ankle. He said I'd probably broken it, maybe in more than one place, and he'd take me to the infirmary. 'Infirmary.' That was the word he used. We never went, of course. At his place, he cranked my ankle again. He made it where I couldn't walk at all. It wasn't until the next day that I realized we'd left my board by the hedge, but by that time I had bigger problems. I guess that kid found it shortly after we drove off."

"The shrimper's son," Griff said.

"The shrimper's son," Justin said. He cracked his neck. "I read the article in the paper, the shrimper trying to pawn it at Loan Star."

It had happened almost a year after Justin disappeared. The shrimper brought the board and a few other things into Loan Star, hoping to trade them for an air compressor. When Cecil saw Justin's name graffitied on the grip tape, he told the shrimper that he expected they'd be able to work out a swap, but he'd have to check in the back to see how many compressors he had left. In the meantime, he took the shrimper's driver's license and had him fill out a pawn ticket. He excused himself into the back room and photocopied the license; he found Ivan and told him to call the police in fifteen minutes, but not one second sooner. When he returned to the front counter, he invited the shrimper to follow him out to his truck. Cecil said he wanted to show him a compressor he'd planned on keeping for himself. It was there in the parking lot behind Loan Star, just as the shrimper was saying *Where's the compressor,* that Cecil took the pistol out from under the bench seat and pressed the barrel into the man's left eye, right into the socket and against the weak bridge of his nose, pinning him between the gun and the truck. The shrimper pleaded innocence, quivering and saying his son had found the board months earlier, maybe as long as a year, but the boy kept getting hurt, so his wife was making him get rid of the thing. When the police arrived, Cecil walked the man back into the shop and made him tell the story again. The shrimper had an alibi—he'd been out on a monthlong haul the Sunday Justin disappeared—and like the postcard that would arrive a year later, the board had been handled so many times that they couldn't pull any workable prints. When the police returned the board to Justin's family, Laura slid it under his bed. She said, "He'll want it when he comes home."

In the truck, Griff sat quietly, trying to figure how to respond. There were countless things he wanted to tell Justin, but he didn't know what to say. A sense of awe had overtaken him, the expansive feeling of a long wait coming to an end, and he couldn't yet apprehend the implications of what he'd heard, how or if it changed the past, present, or future. The night sky was brightening from the bottom, the first slashes of cobalt and lavender. It was incredible to Griff that people were sleeping as Justin was laying all of this out in their father's truck. His foot was tapping on the truck's floorboard. I might be dreaming right now, he thought. This could all be in my head. He had the urge to step outside and walk down to the black water and splash handfuls of it on his face. He felt starstruck. He understood why people would want his brother's autograph.

And then, just like that, his foot stopped moving. The thousand small birds that had leapt into flight in his chest dropped, all at once, from the air.

"It's my fault," Griff said.

"Do what?"

"It's my fault," he said again, louder. He'd been feeling this way for years, had stopped himself from uttering the words countless times. "If I'd gone with you that morning, I could have—"

"If you'd gone with me, he would've taken us both."

"I could've called Dad when you fell. I could've run for help. I could've gotten his license plate number."

"And if I'd ollied higher, I would've come home ten minutes later to rub your face in it. There are a million ways things could've gone differently. None of them matter."

"We'd gotten in a fight that morning."

"I'd dumped salt in your Coke and you were going to tell Mom and Dad. I kicked you in the nuts."

"I never told anyone. Not even the cops when they questioned me."

"The cops questioned you?"

"All of us," Griff said. "All the time, especially at first. They took Mom and Dad in separate rooms. They questioned me and Papaw, Ronnie and his parents, everyone. They came up with a list of registered sex offenders. They had me go into your room to look for anything unusual."

"Really?" Justin said, a light wistfulness in his voice. "That's pretty sick."

"That's nothing," Griff said and launched into a breathless catalog of what Justin had missed. He told him how some three hundred volunteers had done shoulder-to-shoulder searches in the dunes, and how the Texas Rangers had patrolled on horseback. He told him how the state police had, for a month, taken over the Southport VFW, and how the Coast Guard went out in boats and helicopters. He told him how aside from the volunteers and police, the town seemed deserted, like on Christmas, and how days would pass before you saw another kid in a yard or on the sidewalk because everyone's parents were keeping them inside. How entire blocks in Southport left their porch lights on so he could find his way home. How various people had tried to say that Justin had drowned, but Griff always knew they were wrong. How their mother had gone to psychics, how she'd been hypnotized and how she had, a few times, come into Griff's room and lay down in his bed while he slept and woke him up with her weeping. He didn't tell him how sad that made him, how neither he nor their mother ever gathered the nerve to discuss it. He told him how they'd all been given lie detector tests, how even when you told the truth it felt like lying, and how people seemed to suspect their father had something to do with his disappearance. How the police said Justin might have run away, how Griff wondered if he had, maybe because of their fight, and how they went around checking his friends' houses. He didn't tell him about their parents' fights or the fights he'd had with Juan Herrera and Toby Provost, nor did he admit he'd only tried to slide the marina rail because, with Justin gone, it seemed he didn't have anything to lose and when he broke his wrists, he'd felt something like gratitude. He told Justin how his friends had been kind and present at first, but then they started keeping their distance, as though Griff were contagious. How Griff, like an idiot, used to worry that it *was* somehow contagious, how he used to worry that he'd be taken, too. How, legally, parents had to wait twenty-four hours to file a missing-person report, but their mother had come so unglued that an exception to the law was made. How there'd been an Amber Alert. How the city council passed a curfew in Justin's name. How there'd been vigils on the anniversaries of his disappearance. How they celebrated his birthday every year, how it was Griff's job to blow out the candles on the cake. How their parents had taken out a second mortgage on the house to put up a reward. How, one evening last year, an insurance agent had called the house and tried to convince their father to list Justin as "deceased" so that they could access the money for the policy and use it as part of the reward, and how their father smashed the phone against the wall, shattering it, and they had to pick up the pieces before Rainbow tried to eat them. How Papaw had brought over a new phone from Loan Star, the one that was still in their kitchen now.

The words came out in a rush. He could feel his heart beating in his neck, in his ears. He desperately wanted something to drink.

Justin was resting his head against the driver's-side window. His eyes were closed. He looked like he was listening to quiet music.

Without moving, Justin said, "He said he'd kill you if I ran."

"Me?" Griff said.

"You," Justin said, his eyes still shut. "And Mom. And Dad. And Rainbow and Papaw."

"He knew about Rainbow?"

"One of the first things he had me do was make a list of everyone in our family. He had me write down everything I knew—birthdays, hobbies, places y'all liked to visit. He told me to write down what kind of food Rainbow ate."

The colors at the bottom of the sky were rising, spreading like ink into paper. Griff felt light-headed knowing that Dwight Buford knew so much about their lives. His stomach roiled. It wasn't like he was going to vomit, but like he already had. Buford, Griff realized, could be awake right now, lying in a cell just across the bay, thinking about their family. Griff imagined their parents, sleeping at home. He hoped they were asleep. If they were up, they'd be sick with worry and they probably would have already called the cops. The notion was sullying, but right then there was also no place he'd rather be in the world. Whatever punishment they'd mete out would be worth it.

"What else did he have you do?" Griff said.

"Is that a clever way of asking if he raped me?"

"No," Griff blurted. Then he said it again. "No. Not at all. I was just asking about other stuff like writing down our information."

"You don't want to know? You haven't been thinking about it every time you've seen me since I got back?"

"No," Griff said, hoping he sounded honest and comforting. His face was hot and panic was swirling in his chest, and he hated himself for wanting to know. "I want you to tell me whatever you feel like telling me."

"You sound like my therapist."

The RPMs spiked again, then came back down.

Justin sat up straight and twisted his neck. It didn't crack. His eyes were still closed. He swallowed. His movements were languid, like someone sleeping. After a moment, he opened his eyes wide and looked in the rearview mirror. He said, "You're sure there's nothing you want to know?"

"Do you do this a lot? Take the truck out while we're sleeping?"

"Pretty much every night."

It made sense to Griff, though until just then he would never have suspected what Justin was doing. He said, "Do Mom and Dad know how you hurt your ankle, how everything started?"

"Just you, Lobster."

"I won't tell," Griff said.

"I know," he said. "Anything else?"

"I want to know what you wrote down about me."

Justin turned to him and held his gaze. Then he looked away. He put his hands on the steering wheel and squinted, as if they were driving through rain.

"I said you were really into 4-H and junior rodeos, anything having to do with horses."

"Horses?"

"And baseball. I said you loved baseball and had your heart set on playing for the Longhorns. I said your room was decked out in orange and white—your sheets and trash can and slippers. I said you loved fishing, especially floundering, and you hated Mexican food. I said you liked country-western music and were learning to play banjo, and your birthday was August twenty-eighth."

"But none of that's true," Griff said.

"Mom was an accountant. Dad taught math and ran marathons. Rainbow was your pinto pony."

"None of that's right either," Griff said. When Justin didn't respond, he said, "Weren't you worried he'd find out? With the stories on the news and in the paper?"

"I didn't expect it to last four years."

"I don't understand," Griff said.

"Good," Justin said and cracked his neck.

Griff was waiting for him to explain what he meant, but Justin just watched the bay through the windshield. Then he shifted the truck into gear and they moved into the abating dark.

14

COME THE LAST WEDNESDAY IN JULY, HIS DAY OFF, CECIL WAS tired. Dead tired. *Bone*-tired, his father would have said. That seemed accurate. Exhaustion had seeped into his marrow. And yet, tired as he was, he hadn't slept past dawn. He never had been able to. With Connie, he'd always woken early and lay in bed trying not to disturb her. But as soon as his eyes opened, his muscles were bounding and he was fidgety and soon she'd say, "Well, go on, then, Mr. Early Bird." Now walking to the kitchen in the morning's smeared light was as slow as trudging through drying mud, and even after half a kettle of coffee, he didn't have any more energy than when he'd woken. He stood under a cool shower, then swiped menthol-smelling shaving cream onto his face with a horsehair brush and scraped a straight razor over his skin. He drank another two cups of coffee, and ate scrambled eggs and baked beans with brown sugar and crisp buttered toast. Nothing roused him. The paper hadn't even hit his porch yet, and yet he would've been happy to call it a day.

No, not tired. Old.

For the first time in his life, Cecil Campbell felt suddenly and profoundly old. It was in his flesh, in his eyes, in his joints and his concentration—the punishing accrual of age. There seemed an acute absence of some pull; whatever lateral gravity had been drawing him through the years was gone. Urgency was out with the tide. Another unbidden memory of his father: They were hunting dove near the King Ranch when, for reasons Cecil had never been able to discern, his father said, "Do you know the worst thing about being an old man?"

"No, sir."

"People stop seeing you as dangerous."

Cecil didn't know what people thought when they saw him. For the last few years, he'd been The Missing Boy's Grandfather, or The Father of the Missing Boy's Father, and so long as Justin was gone, there was no other way he wanted to be known. Maybe now anyone who looked at him saw just a tired old man, the widowed pawnbroker. It wasn't lost on him that this abrupt lassitude, this compounding of time and the sapping it had visited upon him, was hitting so soon after Justin came back; Cecil had experienced a similar weariness after Connie died. Before, though, he'd been able to throw everything he had into raising Eric, and it seemed he'd still been raising him right up until the bright morning Justin went missing. Since then, he couldn't remember a moment when his sole focus was anything other than finding the boy. Or bracing for not finding him. Or finding what they'd all prayed they wouldn't find. He had also been ready to step between his family and whatever trouble was coming, to absorb the impact with his body; he couldn't have been more poised had he watched any of them run blindly into oncoming traffic. No longer, though. With Justin home, with Dwight Buford incarcerated and staring down the death penalty, Cecil felt an abiding uselessness.

The morning paper slapped against the porch and Cecil read it at his kitchen table, finishing off the coffee. The only piece related to Justin was a short column promoting an upcoming event where parents could have their children fingerprinted. Most of the articles concerned the weather. They'd hit a hundred degrees for six straight days, broken two records. The drought was worsening and officials were seeking harsher water restrictions as lake levels dropped. If a hurricane hit—and with the heat and low pressure, the chances were high—inmates in the Nueces County Jail would remain in their cells because the city lacked the money and manpower to evacuate them. Cecil tried to imagine Dwight Buford in his cell with a hurricane blowing outside, but his mind wouldn't fix on any specific image or narrative. He simply hoped Buford would be afraid and hurt if a storm came ashore. He scanned the obituaries, then the classifieds, then stories about tar balls washing up on the National Seashore and the wars in the world. He rinsed out his coffee mug and watered the ferns Laura had given him. "Trust me," she'd said when she loaded his truck's passenger seat with potted plants, "ferns are not my forte. You're performing a lifesaving service." He stepped outside into the hard sunlight and the smell of salt water and crape myrtle. Or was it bougainvillea? He couldn't tell. A sticky breeze was coming through the palms and mesquite branches, rattling the tiny leaves. Elsewhere, the high-pitched squawking of gulls, the jostling of a boat trailer, the hydraulic hiss of a bus stopping on Station Street, the long low note of the ferry horn.

So, Cecil thought. So.

HE KNEW DWIGHT BUFORD'S FATHER. MAYNE BUFORD WAS A retired oilman. He had ruddy, gin-blossomed skin and wore a straw Stetson. Some mornings Cecil saw him standing outside the Church of Christ, drinking coffee from a Styrofoam cup with a handful of other men: AA meetings. (Eric and Laura had sampled a grief support group at the same location, but the meetings didn't take. "Closure?" Laura had said to Cecil and Eric one night. "They talk about closure like it's the Second Coming. Why would I possibly want closure? Selfish fucking hippies, the whole lot of them.") Mayne drove a white Mercedes with tags that read OIL-N-WATER, the name of the thirty-two-footer he docked in the marina. He collected nautical equipment and antique fishing lures, and every month or so, he

shuffled into Loan Star and poked around in the display cases, asking after scrimshaw and fishing net toggles. He always paid with
crisp twenty-dollar bills. Once, when none of the lures in the glass
case appealed to him, he chose a pair of opal earrings for his wife.
Cecil had never met her. She had cancer or leukemia, something that
was killing her slowly. They'd moved to the coast seven years ago
and soon after, she went on oxygen and refused to step outside.
Their house was a sprawling Spanish structure on Mustang Island,
deep-set windows and a nautical rope fence around the property.
It was an imposing place, resembled an old fort. A hospice nurse
lived in a bungalow behind the main house. Doctors drove in from
Corpus.

They'd had two children, both of whom, Cecil had gathered,
were sources of anguish. One of their sons had died in his early
teens in a car accident, and his older brother had estranged himself
from his parents after high school. There had been periods of recon-
ciliation, but according to Mayne, neither he nor his wife had heard
from Dwight since they'd moved down from Dallas. He'd told Cecil
this at Loan Star shortly after Justin went missing. Likely he'd meant
it as a vow of solidarity. A pledge to their unique brand of isolation.
A testament that such cruel distance could be endured. Over the
years, the Bufords had donated money to the rescue efforts, and
Mayne always asked after Eric and his family when he visited the
pawnshop. He'd also gotten in the habit of telling Cecil he hoped
Dwight would reconnect with them soon.

"I'm just not sure how much time the old girl has left," Mayne
said. "He knew she was sick, but he might assume the treatments
worked. He might think she's fixing to run a marathon."

"He'll turn up," Cecil said.

"I send letters to his old addresses, but they come back as un-
deliverable. My gut says he's still up Dallas way, but there's no
listing."

Cecil's mind was wandering, trying to make sense of the parallels in their lives: the wives with their grueling, insurmountable ill-nesses and the boys gone missing, seemingly just swept from the surface of the earth. He had never trusted anyone with the kind of money Mayne had—in fact, he'd always resented it, viewed the wealth as evidence of being soft and entitled—but he'd come to sympathize with him. He seemed like a man who was paying for the good fortune he'd enjoyed throughout his rosy life. Cecil remem-bered well the sorrow of outliving your wife, the cheap rudderless-ness of survival.

"His mother always thought he got tangled up with drugs," Mayne was saying. He said it every time the subject of Dwight arose. "I think it was losing Gilly, his little brother. My belief is he started running soon as that happened, and now he's run too far to get home."

It made sense. Wasn't that, in a way, what they were all afraid would happen to Griff? Wasn't that what Cecil was afraid would happen to Eric if the worst came to pass? Cecil shook his head, try-ing to keep the thoughts from finding purchase.

"I hope you find him," Cecil said to Mayne.

Yes, he could remember saying those exact words.

ON THAT WEDNESDAY MORNING, A FEW SALLOW MEN WERE LOI-tering on the steps of the Church of Christ, drinking coffee and blowing cigarette smoke into the breeze, but Mayne Buford wasn't there when Cecil drove by. He hadn't seen or heard from Mayne since everything transpired, but he expected to. For better or worse, it was inevitable. He still believed Mayne had been ignorant to the facts of Dwight's life, that he'd had no knowledge of his son's where-abouts or what he was doing with Justin, but there was also, when Cecil thought of him now, no compassion. Instead there was a feel-ing of jeopardy, of needing to take caution, like he was carrying an armload of old dynamite. Cecil no longer felt any sympathy about Mayne's wife—that he ever had was galling—and he understood that things between him and Mayne could go very bad very fast. Probably Mayne recognized the risk, too. Probably he was holed up in his extravagant house with his dying wife, drinking expensive liquor and waiting for Cecil to knock on his door with the barrel of a shotgun. Good, Cecil thought. Good.

It had come as a relief that Eric and Laura had been largely uninterested in anything having to do with Buford's parents. Their plates were full. Eric had first occupied himself with the barbecue, and now he'd moved on to teaching Justin to drive. Laura was scouring the house and looking into prospects for school next year. Cecil knew they were worried about the trial and what it would take for Justin to feel at home again, and while those were real concerns, he believed things would shake out for the boys. Griff was swooning over the girl who wore all black, and Justin, when he wasn't talking with the lawyers or the counselor, was tending to his snake and putting up with all of the affection his folks were lavishing on him. They were all settling in, calming down. They were immersed in the dull and pleasurable routines of family, the coded systems of loving and being loved. Had Cecil driven to their house on Suntide this morning, they would've been happy to see him, would have offered him coffee and juice and silver-dollar pancakes, but soon it would have dawned on them that he was only there because of the suffering Justin had endured. His presence would highlight everything they needed to ignore as their day got started. And yet he'd unconsciously been driving toward Eric's house ever since he passed the Church of Christ. He cut over to Beechwood by way of Drum Road and Monette Drive, then curved onto Station and headed toward the ferry.

Fishermen stood on the piers. An oil tanker made its way through the ship channel. It rode high in the water, which meant the cargo hold was empty and the captain would load up on crude in Corpus. Already, the line at the ferry landing was deep, curling out into the marina. The ferry docked and the long steel gate swung open like an arm. A few cars and trucks clattered onto the landing, and then the line of cars ahead of Cecil started proceeding onto the boat. He doubted he'd make the ferry before it was full and was preparing himself to wait for the next trip when the orange-vested attendant on the deck waved him aboard. Cecil eased off the clutch and pressed the accelerator. The attendant motioned for him to kill the engine, then threw a heavy wooden block behind the truck's rear tire as they were pushing off.

My lucky day, he thought.

The boat rose and fell on the water. There was no rhythm to the movement; the waves came randomly and with different lifts and drops. Occasionally the ferry driver gunned the engine and the vessel surged unexpectedly forward. A few gulls were hovering like kites tied to the railing. The engine rumbled. The horn blew.

That Cecil was driving to Corpus that Wednesday morning truly registered with him only when he accelerated off the ferry, the truck bumping over the lowered gate and onto Mustang Island. Now that he knew where he was going, he also knew he'd been headed in that direction since he'd climbed out of bed. The sky hung low, a washed-out blue strewn with downy clouds. Bach was playing, first the Prelude and then Suite no. 1. He passed the Bufords' property and saw Mayne's Mercedes in the horseshoe driveway. There were also a couple of NO TRESPASSING signs nailed to the fence that Cecil didn't remember from before. Then the stretch of grass-feathered dunes, the tidal flats, the smell of baking sand. A man lumbered along the beach with a metal detector. Behind him, a pair of surfers were trying to make the best of the chop. The Bach swelled. An SUV with words shoe-polished on its window approached, and Cecil hoped the writing would have to do with Justin—it happened from time to time, and he always got a charge—but when the truck passed, he saw that the owner had just listed the vehicle's specs and the words FOR SALE. Strip malls streamed by. Souvenir and sandwich shops, bait stands and convenience stores that sold beer, ice, and sunglasses. (Connie had sometimes said, "If I lost weight the way I lose sunglasses, you'd be married to a pin-up girl.") Vendors sold beach towels suspended from clotheslines. To Cecil, it appeared that each offered the same prices on identical inventory—towels that depicted the Confederate flag, the Texas flag, the Mexican flag, and towels with wolves howling at the moon and pink-bikini girls riding motorcycles, towels that looked like Budweiser cans. The vendors sat under tents, waiting like spiders for tourists. He briefly considered stopping and buying something for Griff and Justin, but he couldn't make up his mind and then he was on the causeway, looking down on the water and oyster reefs and spoil islands as he ascended.

CECIL USED TO TELL ERIC STORIES. THAT'S WHAT CONNIE WOULD say: "Oh, your daddy's just telling stories." If they took a drive somewhere—to the zoo in Brownsville or the rattlesnake races in Refugio—when Eric was too young to know better, Cecil would slyly honk the horn with his palm and then look around in confusion. "What is it, Daddy?" Eric would ask from the backseat, and Cecil would say an airplane had landed on their car's roof. The boy could laugh! Cecil told him there were swamps in Louisiana where spheres of fire bloomed nightly and rolled across the water like soccer balls, and he said there were caverns running beneath much of South Texas, tunnels with secret entrances and exits, and yes, of course, he knew where they were. One afternoon when they were driving home from an airshow at the Army Depot in Corpus, Eric asked how Flour Bluff got its name and Cecil invented a story about a pirate who covered the dunes in white flour so that his sons could pretend it was snow. "But," Cecil said, pleased by the way the tale suddenly fitted itself to the language, "it was all a bluff. It was a big flour bluff."

Years later, after Eric started teaching Texas history, he said, "You had the flour part right." He explained that the area was named after an event in 1838 when Texas forces captured a band of men smuggling flour and other contraband in from Mexico. "I like the pirate and snow version better," Cecil lied. He was already imagining how he'd dispense the information at the pawnshop, how he'd brag on his son having taught it to him. He also knew he would, for the rest of his life, think of Eric's story every time he came off the Kennedy Causeway and drove into the Bluff.

So it was on his mind as he passed the men fishing in waders in the cloud-gray water, but before long he was paying strict attention to the area. He turned off the Bach, concentrating. There were places to rent kayaks and Jet Skis, and places to get tattooed and pierced. A Baptist church was hemmed by a newly laid asphalt parking lot, so for half a mile the air smelled of piney tar. Tall, spindly weeds grew through buckled sidewalks. Highway barrels from a long-stalled road repair project had faded from bright orange to a translucent pink; one was doubled over like it had been hit with a baseball bat. Cars with sun-blistered paint, and bumper stickers that read GUN CONTROL IS BEING ABLE TO HIT YOUR TARGET and I CROSS + 3 NAILS = 4 GIVEN. The Army-Navy Credit Union anchored the corner of Waldron Road, and behind it loomed a Walmart, the lot already bustling. On the marquee of another church were the words FREE TRIP TO HEAVEN. DETAILS INSIDE. A nail salon, a palm reader, men selling watermelons and pecans and nets of oranges at the stoplight. Cecil turned onto Yorktown Boulevard, passing an abandoned shopping center. The storefronts were scrolled with elaborate gang tags that looked like calligraphy.

How many times had he trawled through here in the last four years? Eric, too. Or, worse, how many of these sorry places had become familiar to Justin in that time? Surely Dwight Buford had pushed a cart through the Walmart and bought cheap fried-fish baskets at the Boat 'n Net off to the west. Cecil remembered that Justin had loved hush puppies, and it was destabilizing to think the boy might have eaten countless quantities of them an hour away from Southport. Flour Bluff had been papered with the MISSING flyers.

Early on, volunteers had hung them, and once their involvement dwindled, Cecil and Eric had driven out with tape and staple guns. Maybe Buford had tooled around in his truck tearing them down before he threw his paper route—or more sadistically, he might have made Justin do it—or maybe if Cecil dedicated himself, he could scour the area and find one of the flyers still hanging in a window. He turned up the air conditioner and readjusted the vents to blow on him. He'd started sweating.

Bay Breeze Suites was a one-story complex about two miles beyond the Bluff's center. A slack chain-link fence bordered three sides of the property. The grass was patchy and blond. No trees. No shrubs or hedges. There was a gravel parking lot and a blue dumpster with trash bags spilling onto the ground. A young girl was lazily throwing a basketball at a rusted, bent-down hoop. The apartments themselves were painted brick, a neglected aqua. Each had a window unit and a screen door, and a few had folding lawn chairs out front. Residents used old coffee cans full of sand for ashtrays. The complex was horseshoe-shaped—Cecil thought it had been an old no-tell motel at some point—so the layout formed something of a courtyard. In the center of the dry grass stood a brick barbecue pit and a metal picnic table. There were empty beer bottles arranged on the table, maybe from a gathering the night before or maybe from as far back as the Fourth. Cecil parked his truck near the road, put on his sunglasses, and stepped out into the heat.

The door of Apartment 23 had been boarded up with three-quarter-inch plywood. The front window, too. Had it not been for the crime scene notices stapled in the center of the boards, someone might have surmised the apartment had been battened down for a storm and forgotten. Cecil had expected such a barricade, but he was still disappointed. Seeing firsthand the conditions in which Justin had lived seemed necessary. He had no intentions of telling anyone he'd visited Bay Breeze, and yet he believed he'd return to Southport with a perspective that would somehow prove beneficial.

What that might be, he didn't know. He only knew he'd expected to find something here, and he knew this now because he knew he wouldn't find anything at all.

When he turned to walk back to the truck, the girl with the basketball was blocking his path. Cecil bumped into her, was suddenly on top of her. He had to grab her arm to keep from knocking her down.

"Excuse you," she said.

Cecil dipped his chin in apology. His eyes scanned behind the girl, looking for people watching from between parted curtains.

"I'm going to start charging admission," the girl said. "Ten bucks a head. I'll be filthy rich by the time I'm sixteen."

Her hair was a dark, listless red. It hung to her shoulders and she had to keep tucking a hank behind her ear. She wore an oversized tank top and frayed cutoffs over a purple one-piece bathing suit. She started dribbling her basketball and the noise reverberated down the walkway. Cecil brushed past her and moved swiftly toward his truck. He walked with his head down as if it had started pouring rain.

The girl caught her ball and trotted close behind him, oddly reminding him of the seagulls that had hovered alongside the ferry. She said, "You don't want my tour? How about for half price? Five bucks gets you all the child abuse and pedophilia you can stan—"

Cecil stopped and swung around to face the girl. He said, "If you so much as *think* those words again, I'll put you across my knee and whip your little ass right here in the parking lot."

She smiled, her eyes alight and taunting. She said, "Big talk from a pervert."

He started toward his truck again, giving the girl a wide berth.

"Big talk from a dirty old man that drove into the sticks to see where a fat fuck used to give it to some sweet boy."

He halted again. He stood still not because he was angry, but because her voice betrayed a protectiveness he recognized. The girl was in front of him now, dribbling her ball. Her hair had fallen into her face, and although Cecil expected her to tuck it behind her ear, she left the lock hanging. He said, "You knew him?"

"So now you do want the tour? Classic indecisive pervert," she said.

"I'm asking if you knew him."

"Of course I knew him."

"Tell me," Cecil said.

The girl caught her ball and stared at him from behind her hair. A fan belt squealed a few blocks away. The girl never averted her gaze. Cecil thought she might be looking at her reflection in his sunglasses, but then he realized she was deciding what he was worth telling. She resumed her dribbling and said, "Everyone felt sorry for him."

"Y'all knew what was happening?"

"Nope." She watched the ball bounce between her palm and the ground like a yo-yo. "We thought Justin was his nephew. The story was that Dwight was his godfather and he was taking him in because Justin's parents had been killed in a car accident up in Dallas. That's the headline version. When Dwight told the story, it was all detailed and heartbreaking."

"No one suspected anything."

"It's not a popular view now that we know he's into ass-rape and all, but Dwight was cool. Like, he had karaoke parties and he'd give out free newspapers. He was rad at foosball. He'd always get the new videogames the day they came out. He bought Justin his snake. People, like, *admired* him for taking in his dead sister's kid."

"And what about Justin?"

The girl twisted the lock of hair and hooked it primly behind her ear. She said, "He was always real quiet, which totally made sense, given that we thought his parents had croaked. He never sang on karaoke nights, but he liked videogames and Sasha, his snake. I named her, by the way."

"He never tried to tell anyone? Never tried running?"

"Nope," she said. "And he had lots of chances. The three of us—me, him, and Sasha—used to go looking for shells and rocks. Once he found this really beautiful conch and gave it to me. It was pretty sick."

Cecil didn't know what to say. He was tired again, battered-feeling. An orange-and-white two-seater plane flew over and banked toward Cabaniss Field. The pilot was practicing touch-and-gos.

"Did you ever see a white Mercedes around here? The driver would have been wearing a straw cowboy—"

"Dwight's father," she said. "He came around last week for the first time. We'd never seen him before."

"What was he after?"

"I didn't talk to him, but I'm sure he's after what you're after, what I'm after, what everyone's after."

"And what's that?"

"Whatever will make all of this go away."

Cecil wouldn't have said that's what he was looking for, but the girl was right. He said, "Who talked to him?"

"Mr. Salinas," she said. "I wouldn't really call it talking, though. Mr. Salinas kind of gave him the old what-for. I'm given to understand a crowbar was involved."

A sudden jolt of pleasure, a sense of admiration, the need to suppress a smile. Cecil said, "That's a tough day."

The girl studied him again, then nodded. She said, "He never opened up, not completely. Justin, I mean. I knew he had all of these walls up, but I assumed it was because he'd lost his parents."

"You can't take it personally," he said.

"I swear I'm, like, really happy for him, I totally am, but I'm not stoked that he's over there and I'm stuck here."

The temptation was to placate her, to suggest that Justin would get in touch or their paths would cross again, but Cecil knew the therapist had told Eric and Laura that all the old ties needed to stay severed. The Coast Guard plane made another pass, but the girl seemed uninterested now that she was thinking of Justin. She was holding the basketball in front of her stomach, cradling it with both hands.

He said, "Well, I had better be—"

"Here's the thing," the girl interrupted. "My mom's pretty religious, right? She speaks in tongues at the drop of a hat—she did it for, like, an hour when we found out about Justin—and she's given most of our money to various TV preachers."

"You're losing me."

"So she's also all about the Rapture. She's convinced that the righteous are going to be taken up and the heathens are going to be left behind."

"Okay."

"I used to hide from her. I'd leave my shoes in the hallway so she'd think I'd been chosen."

"I need to head out. I do appreciate your talking with—"

"She hated it. I'd scoot under my bed and listen to her running around the house, screaming my name," she said. "It's exactly how I feel about Justin. Like, I know he's in a better place, but I really miss him. I keep thinking he'll call or stop by, but the only people who come around are perverts and cops and reporters."

"Not one shred of this is easy," Cecil said.

The girl pressed the heel of her hand to her eyes. She hadn't started crying, but the threat existed. She said, "We'd been playing videogames before they went to the flea market. We had the game saved on my memory card and were going to pick it up again once he got back and fed Sasha."

"But he never came back," Cecil said.

"I worried they'd been in an accident. I was trying to figure out if I could somehow throw their paper route, so they wouldn't get in trouble, you know? I wanted to help, you know? Then there were about a hundred cop cars in the parking lot," she said.

"It's okay," Cecil said. He was again tempted to offer some consolation—*You helped him, I know you did*—but he curtailed the impulse. Behind them, an apartment door opened and a woman in a terry-cloth robe stepped outside. She lit a cigarette, exhaled smoke. She walked in a small circle, watching her feet.

"Not my mother," the girl said. "That's Ruby. She's a substitute teacher and amateur alcoholic. Her son and Justin used to pass the football. I could watch them for hours."

Ruby drew on her cigarette and swatted away the smoke. Cecil said, "I appreciate you making time to talk."

"Tell him I said hey."

"Beg pardon?" Cecil said.

"Just do it, okay?" she said. "Tell him Marcy says hey and she, you know, misses him. Tell him I still have the conch and the game is still saved."

"Honey," he said, feeling a spasm of alarm. He didn't know how she'd picked up on his relationship with Justin, but he was suddenly certain that coming to the Bluff was a mistake. His heart was kicking in his chest. Sweat was running down his back. "Honey, I'm just here to take in the sights."

"Just do it," she said. "Please just do this one thing. Please."

15

SHE'D BEEN THINKING ABOUT THE MERIDIAN AGAIN, THE BE-
fore and after of her life. For years, she would have sworn she
hadn't imagined past the moment when Justin would be back in her
arms. Had anyone accused her otherwise, she would have balked.
Allowing herself to dream up how it would be to have him back
home, how it would be to watch him grow and love and marry and
prosper, or even to watch him rinse out a cereal bowl, would have
been too risky, decadent in its presumption. If anything, she had
bargained the other way. She had conceived of scenarios where he
was located but remained largely disconnected from his family. In
one, he talked with her on the phone, assured her that he was safe
and happy, but for some reason would always live apart from them.
In another, he met her in a secluded place—a park shaded by weeping willows and live oak, an isolated stretch of beach where the
heavy slosh of the tide washed out their voices—and he told her that
he was setting out on his own, but he would write letters. She had
even pictured a situation similar to one she'd read on a missing-
children website: A mother's daughter had been kidnapped by the
father, and when the police tracked the two of them down in another state, the mother flew out and sat in an unmarked van across
the street, watching her daughter play in the yard through blacked-
out windows. She watched her like that for almost a month while

the case was being built. Moments had come when Laura believed that was all she needed. Show me he's okay, she'd think, and I'll live.

But now she realized that she *had* granted herself more substantive fantasies. The realization was dousing to her spirits, for by denying herself such indulgence, by forcing herself to keep her expectations painfully low, she'd believed she was doing something right. She'd believed such restraint, such demeaning sacrifice, would pay off. A feeling of penance. Of fasting in her heart. But, no. She'd always envisioned Justin's homecoming in such easy terms that they were almost vulgar in their simplicity. Her notions of his rejoining the family were hardly more nuanced than all of them bounding over a fence, hurdling from despair on one side to salvation on the other. It was ridiculous.

And it was unfair to everyone, especially Justin. This hit her one evening while Justin and Eric were practicing parallel parking and Griff was at the Teepee. Whether talking with Letty Villarreal had brought it on, or seeing Eric turn the corner from awkward reticence to sure-footed confidence around Justin, or whether Laura had been heading toward such a realization all along, she didn't know. Nor did she care. She only knew she felt reanimated and clean, as if some sludge, some corrosive grime, had been inside her veins and now it had been purged. She vowed to think differently. She would see him as an animal in the ocean, a porpoise or whale or some sweet manatee, long submerged and scared, cautiously making his way to the surface. She would swim beside him, at his pace, rising as he did. The imagery had come from her time at Marine Lab, of course, the hours of watching Alice disappear and then come up for air, but Laura wondered if the image wasn't also rooted in something else she hadn't dared to think about for years: Justin's first word. Not *Mama* or *Mommy*. Not *Daddy*. No, Justin had been strapped into his high chair, pushing Cheerios around his tray, when she and Eric heard him clearly and emphatically say "Fish."

Which, in a sleight of association, reminded her of the photos she used to send to the detectives, to the police officers and sheriff's deputies, to the reporters and television stations when their investment in her son's disappearance ebbed. She chose photos of Justin as a toddler and young boy—Justin wearing a pair of underwear on his head (as a superhero mask), Justin asleep and using Rainbow as a pillow, Justin practicing the recorder, his eyes closed like a jazzman. Her aim had been for the new images to snap everyone back to attention, to refocus their anger, shake them out of their apathy. He was a baby once, the pictures asserted. He was a boy who could almost play "When the Saints Go Marching In." Don't give up. Find him. Please. The postcard from California had done the same thing for her, concentrating and repurposing her emotions, and that, she realized, was what she needed to do for herself now. She resolved to give herself a little jolt of perspective each day. She would remind herself of how far they'd come, how happy she should be, how grateful.

It worked. A shift inside her, one she could trust. Things that had previously isolated and wounded her—Eric's nightly drives with Justin, the fact that he'd had a girlfriend—were circumvented with relatively little effort. To consider Justin's options for his schooling was to consider the future. To fix a meal he liked enough to ask for seconds was to fill a void as only a mother could. It awoke in her a love of cooking, a desire to invent new recipes and buy new cookware. If either of the boys especially liked a meal, she immediately started planning when she could prepare it again. (No need to track Eric's tastes. He loved everything—sweetly, genuinely. If she warmed up fish sticks, he lavished praise on her like she'd toiled all day at the stove.) If the boys seemed lukewarm about a recipe, she fed the leftovers to Rainbow. When she wasn't cooking, she sorted through the articles and other ephemera she'd collected since Justin's return and started a scrapbook.

Life started to feel—what? Not normal. Not familiar. Inhabitable. Navigable. With time and effort, with patience and selflessness, she could find her way back to the vicinity of the familiar. She watered the plants. She plucked yellow leaves. She fed the mice, Willie and Waylon, let them sniff her closed eyes with their pink noses, and delicately scratched their necks until their heartbeats calmed in her hand. She was, she guessed, a week or so away from teaching Waylon to stand on his hind legs and twirl like a ballerina. She checked Marine Lab's website for news on Alice and took comfort in what little information there was; Paul was notoriously lazy about updating the online "Progress" page, but he was vigilant about listing any rescue deaths. That it was so easy for Laura to imagine Alice thriving seemed a promise unto itself. She read her library books, washed Griff's kneepads when they started to reek of their vinegar stink. She jotted ideas for Christmas gifts: a new lawn mower for Eric, kneepads for Griff, another snake for Justin.

On a Friday night in early August, for the first time in years, she woke Eric by twisting her fingers through his hair. In the soft moonlight, she recognized how gray he'd gone around his temples and above his ears. As he stirred, she felt an almost unbearable gratitude for him, for all the weight he'd carried, for his adamant refusal to let her slip away.

"Laura?"

"It's me," she said. "I'm here. I'm back now."

EVER SINCE TRACY ROBICHAUD HAD VISITED HIS CLASSROOM A week ago, Eric had expected her again. He felt on edge thinking of it, a fraught confusion. They'd done nothing more than embrace that Friday and she'd left his room within minutes. It had been a bolstering relief, like losing control of a car and then swerving safely back onto the road. He wasn't convinced they could manage such control again, though. He'd been leaving school right after each class to minimize the chance of another encounter. Time, he thought, would help.

She'd come for a meeting in the school's cafeteria about the

Shrimporee; Tracy was on the board of directors. Her husband was, too, but he skipped the meetings. In Eric's classroom, she said the board members were encouraging her to head up the committee organizing Justin's celebration at the Shrimporee, and because he couldn't bring himself to object, couldn't focus clearly on the variables her participation would involve because he was still focusing on who'd seen her enter his classroom and who would see her leave, he gave his blessing.

"Thank you," she said. "I think we'll be able to put together something terrific for him."

"I can't think of anyone better to be in charge."

"Careful," she said, smiling. "Now that I know where to find you, I might be tempted to stop by more often."

"I'm sorry I haven't returned your calls. With everything happening, I've just been—"

"I just want you to know I'm still here."

"I know that," he said.

"Nothing has changed. Not a thing."

But he hadn't seen her again, and with each passing day, it was easier to believe they could leave their old habits behind. To believe she knew his life had changed the moment he laid eyes on Justin again. To believe she knew he was afraid of pushing his luck—their luck—because he'd gotten so lucky with Justin. He briefly thought of this when Laura unexpectedly woke him up in the middle of the night, but soon he'd been unable to think of anything. Laura was ravenous, so consumed and consuming, that she seemed to be dreaming, loosed from who she'd always been. Eric was sore the next day—he felt like he'd been in a fight, one he'd likely lost—and when they tangled into each other again, his muscles and flesh ached a lovely ache. Laura was more herself the second time, more familiar, and he saw how shallow, how desperate and futile his afternoons with Tracy had been. Afterward, she lay on her stomach and he propped himself on his elbow, lightly grazing his fingers over her back. It was something he used to do every time, something he'd intentionally never done with Tracy, but he couldn't remember how many years had passed since he'd last touched his wife this way.

"Write something," she said. "Write something back there."

With his finger he wrote: *I love you.*

"I love you, too," she said.

He swept his palm over her skin as if erasing a blackboard, then wrote: *I'm hungry.*

"Me, too."

He wrote: *Justin's home.*

"Perfect," she said.

He wrote: *I'm sorry.*

"I didn't get it," she said. "Write it again."

He did.

She smiled into the pillow, then shifted to look at him, light in her eyes. She said, "I've missed you, too."

LAURA READ A BOOK EVERY TWO DAYS. SHORTER ONES SHE SOME-times finished in a single sitting. It seemed another good sign, like her renewed appetite and sex drive. She had a sense of reclamation. Of becoming or re-becoming. She'd always loved to read, loved it the way her childhood friends had loved riding their bikes. Her mother had assembled a set of Funk & Wagnalls encyclopedias with weekly coupons from the supermarket (she'd done the same with a set of dishes), and when a new volume arrived (usually on Thursday), Laura could spend hours reading random entries. Had she gone to college, she would have majored in literature; in fact, she knew people often assumed she *had* gone to college because she usually carried a book with her, something to read in waiting rooms or be-tween customers at the dry cleaner's. Before Justin went missing, she'd mostly devoured true crime—what Eric and the boys had called "Mom's death books"—but of course she later avoided the genre completely. Once she started volunteering at Marine Lab, she'd read almost exclusively about cetaceans. Really, though, what she read hardly mattered. Books on war and royalty, books on science and anthropology and politics, novels and story collections and Texana, even the occasional volume of poetry (though the poems always made her feel dense)—she just reveled in the act of running her eyes over lines of text, the feeling of dabbing her finger to her tongue and turning a page, the near-transformative sensation of reaching an end.

Lately, she'd gone on a tear with books about Stockholm syndrome. Some of the books she ordered online and others Eric checked out (and returned) for her at the library. She took notes on the books, made lists of things she wanted to monitor with Justin: his eating habits, any aversion to specific TV shows, any tendencies to grow angry or clam up around certain topics of conversation. Eric, she knew, worried she might read something that would pull the rug out from under her again. She could feel him studying her, silent and skeptical and beseeching, waiting for her to deliver terrible news, as if her reading about something would coax it into reality. As if she were tempting fate by what she chose to read, as if she'd be doing everyone a favor if she'd just stop. But the more she read, the better she felt. More at ease. Empowered, even. *Lucky.* The sheer mind-boggling luck of her life made her want to try harder.

So, when she finished her last library book late on Monday morning, instead of stacking her returns on the counter for Eric to take back, she decided to deliver them herself. The decision was immediately gratifying, the rush of accepting responsibility, and then the feeling redoubled when she decided against inviting Justin to drive her. That he was still sleeping and would have to be woken up wasn't the issue. If Laura invited him, she knew she'd be infringing on Eric's turf, elbowing her way into a province that wasn't hers. Eric's feelings would be hurt, and in sparing them, Laura was galvanized. When she poked her head into Griff's room, she found him on his stomach on his bed, talking on the phone to Fiona and flipping through a skate magazine. "I'm going to the library," she mouthed, and his face scrunched into an expression of sweet befuddlement. Then he gave her a thumbs-up. She saw in it more than simple acknowledgment. He was endorsing her, rooting for her. Her younger son, who knew how long it had been.

The interior of her car was sweltering, the trapped air still tinged with old chlorine. The seat burned, even through her jeans. If her car hadn't been parked under the chinaberry tree by their curb, the glue affixing her rearview mirror would have certainly melted, given way, and dropped it to the floorboard. That happened once or twice a summer. Not today, though, and as she turned onto Station Street, cool air started flowing through the vents. The perspiration dried on her skin, a film she'd enjoy washing off later that night in the shower. She'd think of how she'd ventured out on her own, running errands early on a stifling day. How she'd left her two teenage sons home alone, how nothing had happened, how happy they'd been to see her when she returned, the pride in their eyes like light reflected in a jewel.

Traffic wasn't bad for August. There were likely two, maybe three, ferries running, so the stream of people coming and going from the island was steady. Clusters of tourists waited at the crosswalks. They wore wide, floppy hats, sunglasses with coaster-sized lenses, and white zinc frosting their noses. Some surfers in a Jeep honked at a gaggle of bikinied girls, one of whom theatrically blew the boys a kiss and sent the others into a laughing fit. It made Laura want to slip out of her shoes and drive barefoot like a teenager. She felt that way now, young and liberated, living in a world that expanded outward with each mile she drove. Why not drive out to see Justin's billboard? Or back to Pampered Pets to see if the shipment of feeder mice had arrived? She could go anywhere and her family would be at home when she returned.

The line at the Whataburger drive-thru was ten cars deep. Laura thought to swing by after the library; she'd take lunch home. Maybe she'd go by the school first, surprise Eric with her being out and about, and then surprise him again by suggesting they eat lunch by themselves before taking burgers home for the boys. Hadn't Letty said they needed to do things together and without the boys? If she timed it right, he'd just be finishing up with class. She used to love watching him interact with his students at the annual assemblies or football games, and while she'd been derelict in her teacher's wife's duties for some time—she couldn't remember when she'd last rallied herself for a school function—stepping unannounced into his classroom would illustrate her commitment to improve. She'd see where he'd hung the poster the kids had made for Justin, and she'd see her husband seeing her try. At first he would be alarmed, but she would defuse his fear. *Everything's fine*, she'd say. *I was just out running errands and thought I'd say hey.*

Hey, she'd say. *Hey.*

SOUTHPORT'S LIBRARY WAS A LOW-SLUNG BUILDING COMPRISing three rooms. It boasted nice collections of Texana, naval history, and marine biology, and it was fiercely air-conditioned. Fresh- and saltwater aquariums lined the foyer and—Laura had forgotten this—there were a few terrariums mixed in as well, tanks housing turtles, lizards, and snakes. Seeing them was jarring in a way, given Justin's recent interest. Her first thought was that once he felt comfortable enough, she'd bring him here, but she quickly second-guessed herself and in doing so, she felt precariously balanced on the edge of anxiety: The D.A. had mentioned that a room in Dwight Buford's apartment had been crowded with empty aquariums. A wave of disgust rippled into Laura's throat. Would all aquariums recall what he longed to forget? Would an aquarium ever just be an aquarium again? The world seemed suddenly and acutely dangerous, booby-trapped and inhospitable. She had an urge to flee home, but she told herself to stay. She told herself Justin had aquariums in his room at home and he loved them. She told herself to breathe. To put one foot in front of the other.

And then the air deeper inside the library smelled of Saturday storytime, of puppet shows, of Halloween costume contests and cardboard Christmas tree workshops; it smelled of her sons' childhoods, of nothing less than happiness itself, and she relaxed. She slid her books through the return slot, recalling Justin's astronaut costume and Griff's attempts to re-create the puppet shows by putting socks on his hands and acting them out once they returned home. Changing his bed last week, she'd found a pair of socks sandwiched between the mattress and the box spring. They smelled of Fiona's soft lavender perfume and kept Laura smiling for half an hour. And she was smiling a little now, returning her books. She took her time, depositing them one by one, both to savor the experience and to survey the library. To her surprise, she recognized no one—not the librarian or the few patrons browsing the stacks, not the old men reading the paper or the women waiting in line at the circulation desk—and none of them seemed to recognize her. The anonymity was a relief, proof that life might return to what it had been. It was also, to her surprise, disappointing. She realized she wanted to run into someone she knew. She would've liked for someone to notice her brushed hair and clean clothes. She would've liked to brag about Justin, to leave the person struck by the transformation her family had undergone. She would've liked to think about people talking about her later, knowing how wrong they'd been.

So when she stepped into the parking lot—the heat as thick as wet plaster—and saw two old women waiting by her car, Laura felt something like satisfaction. They were snowbirds, dressed in ice cream–colored pants and long-sleeved polyester blouses. You must be so hot, Laura thought. As she approached, the women straightened their postures (as best they could) and arranged smiles on their faces. One of the women, the shorter of the two, was holding a package of Lorna Doone cookies.

"We wanted you to have these," the woman said, handing Laura the cookies. "We figured you'd be swallowed up by flowers about now, but we still wanted to give you a little something."

"Aren't you sweet?" Laura said. She thought she knew the women from the dry cleaner's. She might have laundered the bright outfits they were currently wearing. She said, "And yes, we're up to our necks in flowers. The house feels like a nursery."

"We were coming back from the store and saw you go in the library. We waited out here. We didn't want to pester you inside," the woman said.

"We'd rather fire from ambush," the other said, and Laura remembered. They were sisters, Beverly and Ruth Wilcox. Ruth, the one who'd pushed the cookies on her, was nicer, but Laura had always felt an affinity for Bev, as if she were the woman Laura might become. They'd aged considerably since she'd last seen them. Maybe the sisters were noticing the same thing about her.

"Y'all must be over the moon over there," Ruth said. "Y'all just must be walking on clouds."

"We are. We have to stop ourselves from smothering him with affection," Laura said, thinking she sounded like a little girl. Then, lifting the cookies: "Justin will love these."

"Some folks don't," Bev said. "But we have a couple each afternoon when we're watching the soaps. Sometimes I'll eat a handful for breakfast. They're sweet but not too sweet."

"Your boy gave me a rock one time, a little piece of flint," Ruth said. It sounded like she'd been gearing up to say it, waiting until she couldn't wait any longer. "We were eating at the Castaway, and your husband walked him over and he handed me the prettiest little rock. I remember showing it to Bev at the table. We both thought it was the prettiest little rock we'd ever seen."

Gauzy strands of memory, like she'd walked through a spiderweb: Justin had almost knocked Ruth down, rushing into the restaurant because he wanted to be the one to ask the hostess for a table by the window. Before giving Ruth the flint, he and Griff had various rocks arranged on the table. Eric had been adamant that Justin apologize, though Laura was less convinced, and she'd expected them to fight about it later, once the boys were in bed. It had been Justin's idea to offer the flint, his way of punishing himself.

"Thank you for remembering us," Laura said now. "I'll tell Justin when I get home. He'll be flattered you kept it all these years."

"It sounds like there's going to be a nice celebration at the Shrimporee," Bev said. "It sounds like they're taking it real serious over there."

"I haven't really heard anything yet, but I'm sure they'll do something special. We want to honor everyone who helped these past years, not just Justin," Laura said. "We're indebted to everyone."

"You don't owe anyone anything, not a lick of anything."

"We're just so happy he's home," Ruth said. "Oh, we're walking on clouds just like you are."

"Thank you."

"And we hope they put that dirty man in front of a firing squad for what he put y'all through," Bev said. "We hope he's real popular in the jail cells."

"He'll get what he deserves," Laura said. "Sometimes you have to thin the herd."

"Thatta girl," Bev said, nodding. "Amen to that."

"We're just walking on clouds," Ruth said. "We're just dancing in the air. We surely are."

GRIFF COULDN'T REMEMBER THE LAST TIME HE'D HAD THE house to himself. Justin was sleeping, so he wasn't completely alone, but with both of his parents gone, the rooms seemed cavernous. When his mother left, he'd been on the phone with Fiona. He'd invited her over, thinking they might be able to fool around in his room instead of at the elementary school, but her father was making her go to lunch at the yacht club. (Griff didn't entirely understand what the yacht club was, couldn't surmise if it was an organization or a physical building, but he didn't want to embarrass himself by asking.) Since then, he'd been walking from one room to another, trying to imagine how Justin viewed their house now. After they went for their drive that night, Griff had decided to be more vigilant, more aware. He wanted to perceive the world as his brother did. He wanted to look at something—their furniture, the hedge near the marina, Rainbow and their parents—and understand what Justin would see. He didn't want him to have to spell everything out if they took the truck again.

So far, though, Justin hadn't invited him on any more of his drives. It made Griff think he'd failed a test. He felt antsy and over-eager, the way Rainbow got just before feeding time, the way the mice got when someone unlatched the lid on their aquarium. They ran around like crazy, stopping to stand on their hind legs and sniff the air, trying to find the crumbs that were about to be dropped, then if nothing materialized, they started running again. "They're such little spazzes," Justin had said one night. He was holding Sasha, letting her slide from one hand to the other. She writhed like a hose with too much pressure, and Griff realized he was a little afraid of her. It was disillusioning, for being afraid of her was like being afraid of Justin. Griff wanted to change that, too.

He was standing by the sink eating a handful of cereal when Justin limped into the kitchen. Griff nodded at him coolly, as if they were passing on the street. He offered him the cereal box, but Justin declined and took a coffee mug down from the cabinet. He was wearing the bathrobe their mother had bought him at the mall. Griff had helped pick it out, and seeing him in it was always gratifying. Justin poured what was left in the pot and took a loud sip. He said, "What's Dad's deal?"

"He's at school. Mom went to the library. We're by ourselves."

"Dad's pacing in the driveway, talking on the phone. He looks pissed."

"He must have just got here," Griff said, sounding inane. "Do you think he knows we took the truck?"

"If he does, it's because you told him."

"I didn't," Griff said.

"I'm just fucking with you, Lobster. No, I don't think he knows."

"Me either," he said.

"I went to the island last night. I watched a coyote bark at the waves for an hour."

"You took the ferry? Someone could've recognized you."

Justin took another drink, shrugged his shoulders. He said, "Maybe that's who Dad's arguing with now."

"You can say I was with you last night. You can say it was my idea to sneak out."

"It'll be all right."

"And if you ever need me to go again, if you ever want company or something, just let me know."

"You want to go find the coyote tonight?"

"That'd be sick," Griff said.

Justin drained his coffee. He rinsed the mug in the sink, then stayed there for a moment, peering into the backyard.

Griff didn't want to say anything until Justin did, but finally he couldn't wait any longer and so he said, "Do you think he'll be in the same place? The coyote?"

"Maybe," he said, his back still to Griff. "They're creatures of habit. They're just like us."

ERIC'S TRUCK WASN'T IN THE FACULTY PARKING LOT WHEN SHE drove by the school. Laura wasn't disappointed; she was content to keep driving. She also decided against stopping at Whataburger. Part of it was the line in the drive-thru—now twelve cars deep—but another part was her wanting to live a little longer inside the memory of talking with Bev and Ruth. Of everything that had been sent to the house—the lush plants and gorgeous flowers, the stuffed animals and letters and balloons—she couldn't at that moment think of anything that meant as much to her as the Lorna Doones riding beside her on the passenger seat. Nor could she say exactly what, but something about the gesture floored her. Its innocence? Its practicality? The fact that no one else but two old ladies would think to offer those cookies, or that Laura understood they'd not been meant for her at all and were simply the only thing Bev and Ruth had in their grocery bags that they could feasibly cast as a gift? She didn't know if she'd ever open the package. If she did, she'd save the wrapping. She'd devote a page to it in the scrapbook.

When she pulled into the driveway, Eric was sitting on the front steps. It excited her to see him. She knew he would commend her getting out, knew he would be proud of her. She wanted to wrap herself around him, to tell him about the sisters, to hear his elaborate vacation plans.

"Guess who returned her library books all by herself," Laura said, sitting beside him. She could smell his sweat, a grassy scent she loved. "Before you know it, I'll be buying groceries and picking up take-out."

"Crazy talk," he said. The right words, the wrong tone. He was distracted, stewing.

"Who knows, there might even be a job in my future."

Eric smiled at her, snaked his arm behind her back and pulled her against him. Her head on his shoulder, her hair falling over her face, filtering the sun. She thought he would say something, but they sat in silence. Sweat beaded on her neck.

"Is Justin awake yet?" she asked.

"I haven't been inside."

"You were waiting on me?"

He kissed the top of her head.

"I ran into those two old sisters, the Wilcoxes. They gave us Lorna Doones."

"Big spenders," he said.

"They said Justin gave them a rock at the Castaway. I have a vague memory of it. You walked him over to the booth."

"He's getting out," Eric said.

She thought he was talking about Justin, but she didn't understand what he was saying. "Do what now?"

"Buford," he said. "His parents are putting their house up as collateral, as a bail. He'll be out within two days, maybe three."

She pulled back, sat up. She studied his face, watched as he looked away. She told herself not to cry, but her eyes were already wet.

"Garcia called," Eric said. "He's looking into ways to stall, but he doesn't know what recourse there is. I guess Buford's mother is dying. Maybe that has something to do with it."

"What happened to 'He's not getting out on my watch'?"

"I don't know," Eric said. "I don't know what's happening with anything."

"The boys haven't heard?"

"Not yet."

She knew it made no sense, knew she couldn't explain or defend it, but what Laura felt was punished. Punished for venturing out of the house. For leaving the boys alone. For courting attention and the façade of normalcy. For having once been so ambivalent about what became of Buford so long as Justin was home. Her pulse quickened. She wondered if Eric could feel it when he took her hand, wondered if he'd laced his fingers with hers because he'd sensed her urges to run screaming down the street, to slink back to her car, to drive into the bay. They sat without speaking, listening to cowbirds twittering in the trees. The air smelled of high tide and the sun was bearing down and Laura thought she remembered something menacing about cowbirds, but just then she couldn't recall what it was. She bit the inside of her cheek, bit down harder and harder, until the coppery taste of blood tinged her mouth. The pain neither distracted nor centered her. She spit a mouthful of blood into the yard. Her mind was scattered and numb. She could only focus on what she knew would happen next. Eric would squeeze her hand. He would stand and pull her up. He would lead her inside and they would deliver the news to their sons. They would sound strong, almost cavalier, as if they'd always anticipated such a development, as if they were brazenly pleased that Buford and his lawyers would make such a glaring tactical error. "It's actually a good thing," Eric would say. They would wear confident masks and go through the motions of hopefulness, and in turn, their sweet boys would rally, acting compliant and consoled and unafraid, and none of them would believe any of it.

16

THEY WERE AWAKE ALL NIGHT. THEY WERE DRAINED BY THE news and the effort of trying to sleep. The air was damp, bloated with gritty heat. The temperature barely dropped below eighty degrees, and the wind did little more than remind them of how stifling the rooms were. A sagging branch from the tallow tree in the backyard scratched against the house when a breeze swirled, a low and mournful creaking that would have woken each of them had they ever been able to drift off. But they hadn't. They twisted on the mattresses, cast off the sheets, tried to keep their eyes from adjusting to the darkness.

Laura wanted to think of the old women who'd given her the cookies, of Justin complimenting her hair, of Griff's socks under his mattress, but her mind found no traction on anything except Buford's release. It seemed another failure, like she'd incorrectly filled out a form and he was getting out because of a clerical error she, and she alone, had made. She imagined how people in town would again regard her with pity and gloom in their eyes, but now, for the first time, she also recognized something else in their gazes: blame. Yes, there had always been a poorly masked judgment, an indicting superiority and countless silent accusations of guilt, and she couldn't not see them anymore. *It would have never happened to my child,* their expressions said, and now they would say it again. And Laura imagined seeing Buford in Southport, glimpsing him driving toward his parents' house or browsing the shelves at H-E-B.

Beside her, Eric was trying to figure how to move his family three hours north to San Antonio. He was certified to teach anywhere in Texas, so it was just a matter of finding a position that hadn't yet been filled so late in the summer. If they sold the house and his truck, and if he found steady work substituting, they might be able to eke out a living through Christmas break. Maybe Houston or Austin, he thought. Maybe Dallas. His mind was trapped in a vise, and with each place he thought to run, it tightened. And he was thinking—helplessly, wretchedly, with a sense of having finally been cornered by something he'd long been eluding—of what Buford had done to his son. The man's weight on Justin's small frame, the vile odor of his body, the noise and force, the shame and terror, the degradation of being so close to home and never being found. Why shouldn't Justin be angry? Why shouldn't he hate them? Eric turned his face into the pillow and wept. He fought to stay still and quiet. Outside, the wind picked up and the branch scraped against the house, a sound like someone trying to push open a door.

Griff couldn't remember if his father had a handsaw in the garage, but he planned to look in the morning. He planned to climb the tallow and not come down until the limb was on the ground. Just then, the sensation of sawing held a powerful appeal. So did breaking glass. So did setting fire to something and watching it turn to smoke. Earlier, when he'd given up on sleep, he texted Fiona the news and she'd written back, "I found out where his parents dock their boat." The message had awakened in him the dangerous and disappointing feeling that he couldn't be trusted, and he'd lain in bed wondering if Justin felt the same way. Another gust of wind, another swipe of the branch. What he hated most about the noise was that every time he heard it, he thought it was his brother. He thought Justin was sneaking into his room, coming to collect him.

Rainbow lay in the hallway. Her tail thumped the carpet when

Griff stepped over her, but once he was in front of Justin's door, she just groaned and stretched her legs. A seam of light under the door, a flutter in Griff's chest. He hadn't known what he was going to say to his brother, but the light meant Justin was awake too and his being awake meant Griff was right to come to him. He knocked lightly. He waited, then knocked again a little harder. Rainbow moaned, opened and closed her mouth. Griff whispered his brother's name, then opened the door, slipped inside and closed it behind him. The motion felt fluid and efficient, and he was suddenly proud, eager to hear how Justin would praise such stealth.

Laura thought she'd seen a flash of light in the hall, but convinced herself she was being paranoid and it was nothing more than fatigue playing tricks with her vision. Eric was calculating their monthly expenses in his head, trying to make the numbers work for the move, and when it seemed a small, quick light came into the hall, he thought not of Independence Day, not of fireworks and tiki torches, but of his mother. Near the end of her life, after the cancer reached her brain and she forgot his name, after she forgot how to walk and chew and swallow, she claimed to see pinwheels of color in her peripheral vision. Eric remembered that his father had lied and claimed to see them too, so she wouldn't feel alone. At that moment, across town, Cecil was in his kitchen, spinning a wire brush into the barrel of his pistol. He cleaned the chamber. The hammer. The trigger. He rubbed fine oil into the steel and wiped it down with a dark swatch of cloth. He looked at the clock on his stove. He had less than two hours before dawn broke.

Griff hadn't expected Justin to be in his room, not really. The bed was made and the desk lamp was on. His window was open, so the room smelled of the muggy night. At first, Griff thought all of those things were what made the room feel unusual. The untouched bed, the glow of the lamp, the raised window. But it was something else—a vacancy, a stillness he didn't recognize. Every time Griff came into Justin's room, even late at night, the mice would start skittering around their aquarium, kicking up cedar chips. Now, there was no soft noise, no wild spray of cedar. He kneeled in front of the glass. They weren't in the paper towel tubes his mother had arranged in their tank, and they weren't behind any of Griff's quartz or under their plastic cave. Briefly it seemed clear that Justin was out looking for them. But when Griff looked in on Sasha—he was momentarily convinced she'd escaped, too—he found her coiled on her heat rock and he understood. Even in the dim light, he could make out two bulges in the snake's body. He had no choice but to see the sad and inevitable outlines of the past.

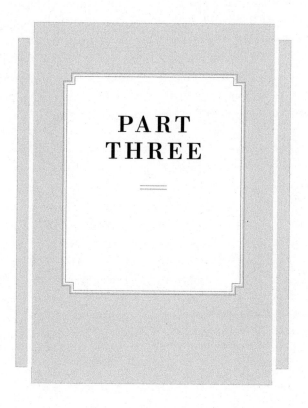

PART
THREE

17

IN 1836, NEAR THE HEADWATERS OF THE NAVASOTA RIVER IN Central Texas, a single Comanche Indian approached Fort Parker. He was unarmed, waving a white rag in surrender. No one inside the fort's walls trusted the gesture, nor did they believe the Indian was alone, but Benjamin Parker went out to negotiate. Or, knowing he would die, he went out to stall an attack long enough for the fort's few men to take up their weapons and for the women and children to flee through the back gate into the sagebrush. But there was no time. Instantly the fields were thronged with Comanche, their bodies slathered in mud and soot and bright berry juice, their war cries fevered and keening. They scaled the walls and dropped into the fort like spiders. Within minutes, all of the Parker men were scalped. Their genitals cut off with dull blades. Their throats slit. The women who hadn't escaped were stabbed and beaten, left for dead. Patches of the dirt were soggy with blood, a dark and mealy mire. Three Parker children were captured, two girls and a boy. They were spirited away on horses with shards of glass braided into their manes, sharp slivers that refracted the afternoon sun.

Two of the children were quickly ransomed back to an uncle who'd been away during the attack. The third child, Cynthia Ann Parker, spent twenty-five years in the tribe before Texas Rangers reclaimed her at the Battle of Pease River. She no longer knew her name, no longer spoke English. She'd married a Comanche chief and borne three children; one of her sons was himself a chieftain, and her infant daughter—Prairie Flower—was in her arms when the Rangers found her. Cynthia Ann denied having been abducted at all. The Rangers might have believed her if not for her blue eyes. They relocated her to Camp Cooper and then to Birdville, Texas, where everyone expected her to open up. She didn't. Living among the Texans, among people who seemed barbaric and gluttonous, made no sense to her. Again and again, she tried to return to the Comanche—once she disguised herself as a man, stole a horse, and rode through the night into Indian territory—but the Parkers thwarted her. They dragged her back. They watched her like a prisoner, set traps to snare her, and shackled her ankles. In 1864, Prairie Flower died of influenza. The loss proved too much for Cynthia Ann and she stopped eating. Eventually, she starved herself to death.

For a time, early into Justin's disappearance, Eric had worked the Fort Parker Massacre into his Texas history classes. He mentioned how Cynthia Ann's first son became the famed Comanche chief Quanah and how, after her rescue, the Texas legislature granted her a league of land; he offered extra credit to anyone who wrote a report on *The Searchers,* the John Wayne movie based on the Parker ordeal. Privately, at home, he plugged Cynthia Ann's name into Internet search engines. Whenever a new entry appeared, he got a rush of illicit, intoxicating resilience. The simple and galvanizing satisfaction of discovery, of efforts rewarded. He shared none of this with Laura.

Then, one evening he found her reading an article about Parker online; he hadn't cleared his Web history.

"What if he forgets about us?" Laura asked in bed that night. "The way that girl did? They were about the same age."

"She was missing for over twenty years. The world was different then."

"Different how?" she said.

"Technology," he said, trying to console her. "We have infrared lenses and forensics and billboards. We have missing-children databases and Amber Alerts—"

"He's been gone a year. Nothing helps."

"We'll find him," Eric said quickly, resolutely, trying to will belief. "I just posted another bunch of flyers around—"

"I liked one part of the article," Laura interrupted. She turned away from him and, despite the humid night, tugged the comforter under her chin.

"That they found her."

"Something else," she said.

"That her family kept looking. That they refused to give up."

"No," she said.

"What then?"

"That she starved herself after her daughter died. I understood that."

The next day at school, between fourth and fifth periods, Eric took a call from Kirk Bradshaw, who owned a souvenir shop on Station Street. Bradshaw, a kind man with a heavy Arkansas accent, said Eric needed to come to the store right away: Laura was on her knees beside the display of seashell wind chimes, sobbing. When Eric arrived, his wife was clutching a small broken conch, her eyes wild, brazen, unseeing. Blood was smeared on her hands, bright as paint. He thought she'd been holding the shell so tightly it had shattered and punctured her flesh, but he was wrong. She'd broken it and torn jagged gouges into her palms and forearms. For the rest of his life he'd wonder why she hadn't cut at her wrists, though he'd never muster the courage to ask.

ERIC RECALLED ALL OF THIS LATE ON A FRIDAY AFTERNOON THREE weeks after Dwight Buford's release. The sun was high and the sky pale, as if the color had been burnished away. He was parked in a fill-sand lot two hundred yards south of Buford's parents' house on the island.

He had binoculars, a solid pair of Pentax that a sailor had hocked at Loan Star and Cecil had passed along to Griff. Eric had been borrowing them without his son's knowledge. He wore sunglasses, a baseball cap. He'd been parking here for ten days. Despite the D.A.'s objections, the judge hadn't imposed house arrest. As long as Buford didn't travel more than twenty miles from his parents' home on Mustang Island or come near the Campbells, he was abiding by the law.

"He's free to go to an elementary school?" Eric had asked. "A children's museum?"

"I'm working on this," Garcia said.

Sometimes Eric watched the house for only a few minutes; sometimes he stayed for an hour. He staggered the times he watched, just as he switched up the vehicles he drove. Today he was in his truck. Yesterday, Laura's car. On Wednesday, after his class, he'd borrowed Tracy Robichaud's Volvo. He hadn't yet glimpsed Dwight. The longer he went without seeing him, the more he dreaded the moment he would. A sharp, agonizing worry squeezed his temples. His heart throbbed so fast that times came when he was short of breath. He felt pinned down by fear; it was a boulder on his chest. One careless move and he'd be crushed.

Mayne had emerged a few times—his arm in a sling, which made rolling the garbage cans to the curb difficult—and there was a Mexican woman, probably Mrs. Buford's hospice nurse, who regularly stepped outside to smoke under the chinaberry tree. A doctor had also visited the house. "I hope his mother dies in front of him," Laura had taken to saying lately. "I hope he sees her cough up blood and wet chunks of lung." Edward Livingstone, Dwight's attorney, had picked up an overstuffed accordion folder yesterday, and reporters had been taping spots for evening broadcasts. The news had said the family was receiving death threats, so Eric always expected to find police officers stationed on the property, but he never did. Maybe they were parked nearby, surveilling the house the way he was. Maybe they had their binoculars trained on him.

Why had he recalled the Parker story? Because the Buford house looked like a small fort? Because each time Mayne or the nurse ventured outside, his pulse spiked and he was shot through with the urge to attack? Because he wanted to wave his own white flag? He felt all of this, all at once. But if the memory was rooted anywhere, it was likely with Laura. After Buford's release, Eric had watched his wife withdraw. She seemed a shell of herself, brittle as old glass, moving through her days in a trance. She had started taking a few shifts at the dry cleaner's and volunteering again at Marine Lab, developments that should have been encouraging, but Eric suspected such initiative was all show. It worried him. Years before, when he'd approached her in Bradshaw's souvenir shop, the amount of blood was like nothing he'd seen. Patches of her jeans were soaked through, almost black. On the drive to the emergency clinic, she'd disinterestedly explained that to remove blood from fabric you had to soak it in cold water with salt and then try to draw it out with a steam pen. Usually, though, the stain was already set. Permanent. Ruinous.

The morning after they received news of Buford's release, Laura went through the rooms throwing out most of the plants that had been sent in the previous weeks. Two days later, Justin and Griff lugged the mice's empty aquarium into the garage. No one spoke of how disappointed they were, or how easily and often they were startled, how unexpected movements spooked them like horses, but the changes couldn't be ignored. There were sudden voids in the house, silences, cruel and conspicuous vacancies that had recently, beautifully, been full and alive. Eric stepped into them like cobwebs, like gorges. He continued taking Justin for his driving lessons in the evenings, but he was increasingly worried that they would pass Buford or his parents on the road.

"You don't feel like he's everywhere?" Laura had asked Eric after they returned one evening.

"Not at all," Eric lied. "I bet he's holed up with his parents. I bet he's terrified."

"I hope she dies in his arms," she said. "I hope he sees that bitch in grave pain."

ONLY TRACY KNEW ABOUT ERIC GOING TO THE BUFORD HOUSE. She was also the only one he'd told about the possibility of leaving Southport, but as soon as he'd given voice to the idea, he'd understood it would never happen. Perhaps he brought up watching the Buford house hoping that too would sound ill-conceived and futile. Instead, he felt emboldened. They were lying in her bed, and after he explained what he'd been doing, he asked to borrow her car. The room was bright, smelling of their bodies. Tracy said, "Keys are in my purse."

"I won't stay long," he said.

"You stay until you see what you need to see," she said.

It was the first time they'd slept together since Justin had been home. He knew he should feel guilty, and he did, but the emotion was distant, moldering in some locked-down place he couldn't access. Before, these afternoons had felt parallel to his real life, a base and shadowed rut he'd selfishly stepped into. Now, Eric was numb, barely present. In the moments before he took a shower and drove to the Buford house, his only thoughts of Laura were worries that she'd hurt herself while he was with Tracy. Maybe she'd torn at her palms again or swallowed a handful of pills or driven her car off the ferry. That he could even conceive of such grotesque possibilities was punishing. And yet not unfamiliar. Once when Justin was missing, Eric hadn't been able to stop himself from thinking how much cheaper it would be to put one son through college than two. An-other time, while idling at a railroad crossing with Laura and Griff in the car, he'd considered accelerating onto the tracks just before the train hurtled by. It had seemed a way to save everyone. For a brief and hideous moment, it seemed the only way.

Parked in the fill-sand lot, he called Laura and she said, "I'm flipping through recipes, deciding what's for supper."

"I vote for the famous Laura Campbell pork chops."

"Maybe next week," she said. "Coming home?"

"The kids are gearing up for the final projects," he said. "I have to stay a little late."

He didn't know what he hoped to see at the Buford house. Being near it, near Dwight, brought him both agony and a fleeting, con-founding comfort. Eric entertained fantasies of knocking on the front door, pulling Buford into the yard and cracking him open, but there were also fears that, given the opportunity, he would falter. He worried he'd reveal himself as a coward. Maybe he wanted to see Dwight Buford acting kindly toward Mayne or the nurse in hopes that it would allow him to believe the man had been, at times, kind to Justin. Or maybe if he saw him puttering around his parents' yard, saw him pushing his mother's wheelchair around the drive-way so the dying woman could feel the sun, Eric would experience such rage that he'd be transformed, emancipated from fear and logic and hesitation. Maybe, and this seemed most likely to Eric, he watched the house in hopes that watching the house would change him.

ACROSS THE LAGUNA MADRE, A MILE INLAND FROM THE FERRY dock, a new crew of skaters had claimed the Teepee. Griff assumed they were from Corpus, but they could've been from anywhere. They camped on the island at night, sleeping in tents and in the back of their rusted van, then skated all day. They were older, with patchy beards and six-packs of beer. Their clothes smelled of put-out cigarettes, a dank, melancholy odor that Griff tried not to inhale. They punched holes in the bottom of beer cans with ice picks, then duct-taped them one atop the other and drank from three and four at a time. The goal seemed to be to drain a whole six-pack that way, all at once, and if someone could do it, he would reach what the crew called "wizard status." Griff didn't understand. They skated the pool like surfers, slashing at the coping with too much torque and carving the walls with a lunging, herky-jerky motion. One of the skaters, a rangy kid they called Baby Snot, rode barefoot. It was hard to watch.

They were cool enough. They always nodded their glassy-eyed greetings to Griff, and once Baby Snot offered him a beer. But their presence wore on him, oppressed him. For the first few days after Griff started heading back to the Teepee, he expected skaters he recognized to arrive. None did. He wondered if someone had found a better skate spot. He rode the pool halfheartedly, uninspired to try new tricks and bored with old ones, so eventually he would just sit on his board in the shade of a remaining teepee. He pretended to text on his phone. The crew got louder the more they drank. They fell more. They laughed at each other, peed in the rubble of demolished teepees, poured jugs of water over their heads and shook out their hair the way Rainbow did after a bath. Baby Snot spoke in bad fake accents—German, British, French. Griff felt no affinity with them, or even with the Teepee itself anymore. Soon, despite what he told his parents and Justin, he stopped going there at all.

He went to the marina sometimes, to the hedge Justin had pointed out. He tried to ollie it without coming close, and yet he had the flattering feeling he *could* clear it if he really tried. The desire just wasn't there. He watched boats leave and return to their moorings, noticing for the first time that their wakes looked like fans of boiling water. The ferry slid across the channel, its horn bellowing, the engine coughing to a stop as the captain steered toward the landing. Minnows swam in skittish patterns near the docks. A few brown ducks paddled around, hesitant and hungry. Griff found the Bufords' boat easily, but after seeing the *Oil-n-Water* once, he avoided it. He worried that Dwight Buford or one of his parents would emerge from the cabin. He worried that something would happen to the boat and he'd be blamed.

After classes let out and his father's truck was gone from the faculty parking lot, he skated the curb in front of Southport High. He went to Whataburger to sit in the air-conditioning and drink free refills of Coke. Once, he skated out to Loan Star and visited with Papaw, but they had nothing to talk about except Justin and Buford, so being there felt too freighted. He read magazines and comic books at the grocery store, paid for one matinee and stayed for two, and played shuffleboard alone by the seawall. He combed the beach and found a striped horn shell, a tight cream-and-magenta spiral that he put in his pocket, but later threw away. He browsed souvenir shops. He tried to pretend he was a tourist, a kid from Chicago or Wyoming, but he felt sure everyone who saw him knew his whole crappy life story. He passed his old friends' houses: Jerry, whose father had a stash of *Hustler*s in their Airstream trailer; Felipe, who had a crossbow; Bill, who kids only liked because his older sister, Laura, a cheerleader, walked around the house in panties and half-shirts. Griff knocked on no doors. Had anyone come outside and called his name, he would've broken into a full run to get away.

On the days his mother worked at the dry cleaner's, he was tempted to visit her. Since Dwight Buford's release, she'd seemed both to have too much energy and to be in a constant daze. Every time Griff saw her, he wanted to hug her. When he did, she seemed to come apart in his arms and he had to take care that she was back in one piece before he let go. But if he went to the cleaner's, his mother would ask why he wasn't with Fiona, and he didn't have a good answer. He thought about her all the time. He missed her, but lately, as soon as they were together, he longed for solitude. "Is something up?" she'd asked earlier this week, and last week, and the week before. Each time, he'd said no and rallied himself and they both pretended he wasn't lying. He invented excuses for not being around: His stomach hurt, his parents wanted him to spend more time with his brother, he'd let the battery in his phone die, he was grounded for having forgotten to feed Rainbow. (He *had* forgotten to feed Rainbow one night, but no one noticed and he fed her double once he remembered. He also gave her some banana bread his mother had baked.) He tried to occupy his mind with memories of how Fiona had first kissed him by the dumpster, how her perfume smelled on his socks, on her neck and chest. Nothing took.

The last time they'd hung out, she said, "You're going to ruin this."

"I know," he said.

"Then don't," she said. "Just don't."

Roaming Southport on those grueling afternoons, his shirts sweat-heavy and his eyes squinting against the sun's raw glare, his mind eddying with Fiona and Justin, and with his parents and the trial, Griff felt bloated. But with what? Fear? Sadness? Ever since they'd found out Buford was being released, a kind of pall had fallen over his family. It made him want to scream, to never say another word. He kept expecting his mother to sneak into his room and explain things, kept hoping Justin would take him on another midnight drive and open up again, kept thinking his father would gather everyone in the living room and give one of his coach-y speeches or suggest an idea for a crazy vacation. But, no. His mother talked about being back at work, about Alice the dolphin. His father talked about the heat and how his students were struggling with their final projects. Justin asked about Griff's skating, if their father had taught this or that kid that he used to know, if his mother ever saw so-and-so's parents at the dry cleaner's. They never talked about anything real, certainly not about Dwight Buford. In that way, he was always there, watching and listening like a new member of the family.

Griff was walking on the wharf when his phone started vibrating. It was Fiona. He let it ring. *I love you,* he wanted to say. *I'm sorry. I'm scared.* But he couldn't make himself answer. The sky was the color of bone, depthless. The wind came in sour-smelling sheets. The sun was pounding, so hot it felt like there was a layer of thick, sweltering cotton under his skin. When his phone stopped vibrating, he waited to see if she'd left a message. She hadn't. There was only the sound of a far-off seagull, its cries plaintive and surreal and so familiar that Griff barely heard them.

18

A DREAM WITHIN A NIGHTMARE WITHIN A NIGHTMARE. A FUR-lough from grief. From a pain so deep and dense you wanted to cut your veins to let some blood out, thinking it would relieve the pressure. A pain so deep and dense you *had* cut your veins, but without relief. This was how Laura came to think of the weeks with Justin before Dwight Buford was released. They had been a gift, a reprieve, a short remission before the cancer metastasized.

She saw him everywhere. Everywhere. Even though he wasn't there, she saw him.

She saw him while she waited for deli meat in H-E-B, saw him taking free samples of toothpicked sausage. She saw him in the car next to hers on Station Street. He was riding the ferry, lobbing crumbs to seagulls. He was sunbathing on the beach. He mowed his parents' yard and washed their white Mercedes. She saw him at the library's circulation desk and leaning close to the reptile cages in the library foyer, watching the somnolent snakes and lizards, tapping the glass you weren't supposed to tap. She saw him strolling along the seawall with fishing rods over his shoulder and a bucket of bait. He was eating at the Castaway Café and shuffling his feet in the dust beside the Teepee Motel pool. He stood outside the D.A.'s office, wearing sunglasses, looking smug, smiling in the washed-out light.

Justin acted unfazed by the news and Griff followed his lead. Laura noticed changes, though. Griff was quieter, more deferential. Justin started picking at his fingernails and cracking his neck more. One night when Laura was washing dishes, a skillet slipped from her hand and clattered to the ground, and the noise was so startling to Justin that he jumped back and knocked a potted plant from the counter. The pot busted and scared him again. He almost slipped in the soil on the floor. He held on to the counter, pressed his back against the wall. His eyes were wide and madly roving. She could see his chest heaving with breath. She approached him slowly—her own heart going frantic—as she would a feral cat. "We're okay," she kept saying. "We're okay."

Eric claimed not to worry about Dwight Buford's new freedom, not to feel threatened or debased, but Laura knew he was lying. Or he was deluded, willing himself not to see. She looked for the man continuously. It struck her as perverse and revolting and about as fucked up an irony as she could conjure: She was now searching for Dwight Buford the way she used to search for Justin. She scanned every face for his eyes, every passerby for his gait. She expected him to round every corner and stand behind every door. Yes, it was precisely how she recalled the four years Justin was gone. The drain of constant awareness. The abiding sense that you'd always just missed him. How clearly she remembered walking into rooms, opening closets and drawers, only to realize she'd forgotten what she'd come to find. "Do you think you're looking for your son? Subconsciously, perhaps?" the therapist had once asked. Laura had gone as a favor to Eric—*See? I'm trying*—but she'd been so flummoxed by the triteness of it all that she left without a word mid-session. The difference now was that when she looked in a cupboard expecting to find Dwight Buford, he was there. He was always, always there.

Laura was also seeking out places to cry again. She wanted thick walls or open spaces. She wanted dark rooms and wide swaths of time. How many movies had she gone to in those four years? She always sat in the back. She bought buttered popcorn out of gratitude for the service the theater provided. She cried in the shower, in the pews of empty churches, in public bathrooms. She cried on the drive to and from Marine Lab; if the sobbing got too bad, she steered onto the shoulder. (But she never clicked her hazard lights on, lest someone stop to help.) And, of course, there were the times she'd broken down in public. How to explain that she felt no embarrassment? How to convey that she *liked* not being able to contain herself, *liked* that others had to see what she'd been reduced to? But she'd gotten better over the years, more disciplined. When she could feel the fits coming on, she'd start planning a trip to the movies, a late-night ferry ride. She almost looked forward to them. They became a way of marking the days that otherwise blurred into each other like fog.

She thought things should be easier. Now. Things should be easier *now*. With Justin home. With everyone having survived his time away. She thought the past should throw the present into a stark, palliative relief. She tried to focus on the beautiful mess of Justin's hair when he woke up, the way his shirts smelled before she washed them—woodsy, powdery, not unlike his father's. But the fear and anger and confusion came back with new force, with an intensified, rumbling vigor. She'd tossed out as many of the welcome home plants as she could. They taunted her, reminded her of how gullible she'd been. Had she really been jealous of redheaded Marcy? Had Justin's reticence really seemed so insulting? She appalled herself. Eric didn't like her throwing out the plants. She knew that. Maybe she was trying to goad him into a confrontation. If so, he resisted the bait. She admired and resented his composure. His resolute faith that things would work out, make sense, become clear. For her, Dwight Buford's being out in the world was incomprehensible. She couldn't figure where to fit such knowledge to keep it from consuming her, and so it was everywhere. Like him.

She'd been worried that she wouldn't be allowed to volunteer at

Marine Lab again. Worried that Paul, the rescue coordinator, would blacklist her for ditching the shifts she'd signed up for before Justin was found. Worried that Alice's condition would have deteriorated to such a degree that she would have been transferred to the facility in Galveston. Worried—selfishly, unforgivably—that the dolphin would have recovered and been released. Laura felt fairly certain she would've read about such developments in the paper or on the website, and yet she couldn't shake the feeling that she was being left behind. This was the reality in which she now lived. An essential faith had been stripped away. The assumption that what had existed would continue to exist was itself gone. Her life—everyone's life—seemed rigged with trapdoors and hidden, collapsible walls, panels that would open without warning and claim what had been yours, claim it only because you'd allow yourself to believe it couldn't be claimed.

But Paul told her to sign up for as many shifts as she could handle, asking nothing about where she'd been. Most of what was available were murder shifts, so Laura would often go straight from Marine Lab to open the dry cleaner's in the mornings. She didn't mind. She liked those quiet hours, how each angle of light took on significance. The track of the moon reflecting on the water like a jeweled path and the rising sun gilding the corners of the morning in nameless color. She liked being back at Marine Lab, the smell of chlorine and frozen herring and water spilled from the pool. The inflatable alligator she'd brought from home so long ago was still standing on its tail in the corner beside the life jackets. Paul was still constantly on the phone, jockeying for donations of one kind or another. Each time she interacted with him, usually when she sterilized her hands at the sink or turned in her shift notes before leaving, she was compelled to explain herself. *My son,* she would say. *My son came home.* She kept quiet, though. She was still signing up for shifts under her maiden name.

Alice's condition had worsened, though not to the point where she needed to be trucked to Galveston. Her appetite was diminished. She likely had another intestinal infection. Because she wasn't eating enough on her own, they tubed her twice a day, pumping a blended mixture of fish and liquid and antibiotics into her stomach. They wanted to keep her hydrated and make sure she had enough calories to maintain her strength. Laura took meticulous notes and watched for signs of distress, but Alice appeared strong. Maybe lethargic at times, and a little thinner, but healthy. She swam clockwise around the pool, occasionally rolling onto her side as she passed Laura on the observation deck. Sometimes she blew bubble rings that dispersed at the surface. Those were new. Alice gave no indication of recognizing Laura, but neither did she keep her distance the way she often did with unfamiliar volunteers. Laura clung to this, took it as evidence that she might be known again.

Every time Laura made a note on the log sheets she was reminded of how her handwriting had come to resemble her mother's. She'd started noticing the similarities when she dug up her mother's recipe box after Justin returned. It had been dislocating to see that the faded, ribbony script detailing how much celery to use in the potato salad so closely resembled the writing in Laura's Moleskine. Her mother'd had a bawdy, wide-open laugh and a love of Benson & Hedges cigarettes. She'd died young, of a heart attack, and Laura didn't think of her nearly as often as she believed she should. Nor did she believe she knew the details of her parents' lives that children—especially grown children—were supposed to. She knew the dates they'd died, but would be hard-pressed to name their birthdays or anniversary or how they met. Before Justin went missing, one of Laura's greatest fears was that the boys would ask about her own parents and she'd be forced to lie—to invent details of their grandparents' lives—or admit her ignorance, willful as it was. Unlike Eric, for whom history provided solace and pattern, she'd always sought to leave the past behind. She was insecure in the face of it, shamed by all she'd forgotten or never known.

But since she'd been dipping into the recipe box, and especially since Buford had been released, her mother had been on her mind more. She wondered how Patricia Wallace would have reacted to everything that was happening, how she would have felt about the way Laura had reacted. There was no telling. Her mother seemed to always be holding parts of herself back from those around her. She was most open, most herself, in the late afternoons when she and their neighbor Joyce would sit on the porch. Toddy Time, they called it. They smoked cigarettes, sipped beer, and ate apple slices dusted in salt. They gossiped about neighbors and people from church, and traded ideas about what to fix for supper. Laura played with her dolls in the flower bed.

On the afternoon Laura remembered most clearly, the women had been drinking and talking about some trouble at the jewelry store where Laura's mother worked. Laura was wearing a new dress, the first one she could remember picking out herself, one she had, in fact, chosen because it reminded her in some unidentifiable way of Joyce. (Joyce was prettier than Laura's mother, a fact that felt shameful to notice.) The dress was lavender with long lace sleeves. Laura was playing in the flower bed, hunting for woolly worms and ladybugs. She crawled between the house and the rose-bushes, taking care not to get dirty. She could hear the women whispering, giggling. She could hear the apple slices snapping between their teeth.

"Oh, he thinks he's a smart cookie," her mother said. "He thinks he's God's gift."

When Laura stood up, the lace of her sleeve caught on a thorn and the fabric was ripping, loosening around her shoulder and armpit, before she recognized what the sound was.

Had she gasped or cried out? The thorn had pricked her, too. Her skin was dotted with blood, but she was focused on having ruined her dress, on trying to keep quiet to think of ways to explain herself. Then the women were off the porch and in the yard. Cigarettes clenched in their lips, smoke rising into their eyes, and the branches of the rosebushes being gingerly pulled back so Laura could step out.

"Laura Leigh Wallace," her mother said. Her voice was low, but sharp. She blew smoke over her shoulder. "We just bought this dress. Your daddy'll have both our hides."

"It's not that bad," she said. "We can fix it."

The women stood her in the grass and studied her. Their hands were on her, dusting off her dress.

"Oh, baby girl," Joyce said. "All the pretty lace is ripped clean through."

Laura's mother flicked her cigarette into the street. She said, "You know what your daddy'll say? He'll say, 'If you can't take care of it, you don't deserve it.' We're going to hear that for a month."

"Can we sew it? Fix it up in a way he won't notice?"

Joyce laughed and said, "Noticing isn't a man's strong suit, you got that right. Just ask Mr. Handsy over at the jewelry store."

"Who's Mr. Handsy?"

"She means Mr. Clark," Laura's mother said. "She means he needs to pay more attention to his inventory and less to his lady customers."

" 'If you can't take care of it, you don't deserve it.' That's rich," Joyce said. "That's richer than rich."

What, Laura always wondered when that memory arose, had become of her pretty little dress? She had no recollection of what had happened to it, whether they tried to stitch the lace or just wadded the dress into a ball and tossed it in the wastebasket. Nor did she know what became of Joyce. She'd still been alive, still beautiful and smoking on her porch, when Laura left the Panhandle—this was the year after her mother died, when Laura went to live with her aunt in West Texas—but she was surely gone now. Everything about that time seemed cleaved from Laura's current life. Her handwriting resembled her mother's, yes, but even that seemed a kind of happenstance. The past was a bridge that looked solid and sturdy, but once you were on it, you saw that it extended only far enough to strand you, to suspend you between loss and longing with no-where to go at all.

ON FRIDAY MORNING, THE EARLY SUN BROKE YELLOW ON THE horizon. Murky light dappled the wetlands around Marine Lab. The smell of dew, a breeze already pitted with heat, every smooth surface streaked with condensation. As soon as she stepped out of the warehouse, she knew she'd have to let the air conditioner run to defog the windows before she could see well enough to drive. Crickets trilled, and frogs. They sounded far away. For a moment, to Laura, everything seemed distant, unknowable. It was as if she were at the bottom of a well.

As she made her way to her car, a man stepped out of a 4x4 truck parked on the opposite side of the lot. He cut a tall, broad silhouette against the rising sun; he left the driver's-side door open as he crossed the lot. Laura's heart sped up: Dwight Buford. His boots on the caliche sounded like tiny bones cracking. She didn't want to be afraid, didn't want to taste dread in her throat like bile. Sudden bursts of heat flared behind her knees. She kept her eyes on the ground, but knew the man was coming toward her rather than going to the Marine Lab door. The heat behind her knees had, like that, turned frigid, freezing, and yet sweat beaded all over her. She told herself it couldn't be Buford, that she was being paranoid and Eric was right, nothing to worry about, that no one knew she volunteered here, that she had used her maiden name, Wallace, that Buford would have no reason to come for her, that—

"Mrs. Campbell?"

Campbell. Not Wallace. She was ready to scream. She gripped her keys between her fingers, like spikes, thinking she'd try to gouge his eyes. She thought to turn back, unsure if she was closer to the warehouse door or her car, unsure which would be safer. The caliche cracked more quickly. He might have been jogging now. Her lungs felt shallow, seized up. She didn't look back, just tried to make it to her car before the man reached for her.

"Mrs. Campbell?" he said again. Then he touched her shoulder.

She spun around, gripping the keys, wondering if she would survive, wondering if she'd go to jail. Then, even in the half dark, she recognized him. Almost recognized him.

"Hey," the man said, looking remorseful. "It's Rudy."

She couldn't speak. Her throat was closed. Her fingers hurt from clenching the keys. The sense of being in a well returned, but she was farther down now, trying to see this man, this Rudy, from a great depth.

"Did I scare you? I didn't mean to," Rudy said. When she didn't answer, he continued, "We volunteered together a while back. I was filling in for my wife, remember? I told you about the tattoo on her ankle, a dolphin she had done in Cancún."

"Y'all were pregnant," Laura said.

"Still are," Rudy said and looked toward the wetlands. The sun was higher, glinting on the rippled water. With the light and with her heart quieting, Laura had a hazy recollection of having seen Rudy during that shift. Could it have been the shift when Eric had come to get her? The day Justin came home? She wasn't sure. It seemed years ago. Rudy said, "When you and I met, I think she was on a jalapeño corn bread kick. Now it's pan dulce. All pan dulce, all the time. But it has to come from a specific bakery in Portland."

"I liked anything lemon-flavored," she said. "I used to make my husband go to Luby's and buy three lemon meringue pies at a time."

"After my shift, I'm heading to Portland for the second time in two days. We live in Refugio, so I'll have an extra thousand miles on my truck before the end of the year."

"Just wait until the baby comes," Laura said, remembering other cravings she'd had when pregnant. With Justin, she'd had the urge to eat toothpaste straight from the tube. With Griff, she'd loved the smell of charcoal and she couldn't eat anything that wasn't drenched in Tabasco sauce.

"I wasn't on the schedule this morning," Rudy said, "but I'm at the top of the call list when someone cancels. I guess the person after you got sick."

I used to be that way, Laura almost said, but changed her mind. She said, "Paul's with her now. She's had a good morning. She blew a lot of bubble rings."

The sun was brightening, the crickets going quiet in the swamp grass. By the time she got to the dry cleaner's, the temperature would be in the high eighties, if not the nineties. On those afternoons in her youth, her mother would say, "Oh, it's hotter than a billy goat in a pepper patch."

"The bubble rings are new," Laura said. "Today she popped a few with her beak."

"She taught herself to blow them a couple weeks back. She's always surprised when she pops them, I think. It's like when a bubble-gum bubble bursts on a kid's face."

"Does she ever play with that inflatable alligator? The one that's standing on its tail in the corner?"

Rudy thought for a moment. "I'm not sure. Mostly I've seen her play with the beach ball and those floaty noodles. That was before she stopped eating."

"A girl has a right to go on a diet," Laura said, surprising herself. Because this man had turned out not to be Dwight Buford and because he cared for Alice, she wanted to make him feel better. "She's just trying to get her figure where she wants it. She'll bounce back."

"'On a diet,'" Rudy repeated. "I'll tell that to my wife. She'll enjoy it."

Something skittered in the grass—a lizard probably, though Laura couldn't see.

"Well," Laura said, "have a good shift."

"Sorry if I scared you," he said. "I just thought I recognized you and wanted to make sure."

"It's me," she said. "I'm still here."

LAURA DIDN'T CRY ON THE DRIVE TO WORK, NOR DID SHE DWELL on the implications of Rudy calling her by her married name. Days would pass before she even remembered it. Instead, she thought of the way a mother dolphin will swim with her newborn calf beside her. Echelon swimming, it's called. Until the calf develops enough strength and coordination, it will swim in its mother's slipstream. The positioning allows the mother to monitor her calf's breathing, and the slipstream pulls it along, preserving its energy and body heat. From there, Laura's mind slid to the accounts she'd read of dolphins seeing others in respiratory distress and lifting them to the surface so they wouldn't drown. There were reports of them saving other dolphins this way, but also dogs and seals and even humans. Pods would band together to take turns keeping the animal afloat, or they would swim so close to the shore that it could reach dry land on its own. How dolphins understood to do this, no one knew, and in her car, Laura found herself hoping it would always remain a mystery. The hour-long drive passed in an instant, the billboard with Justin's picture on it and the Alamo Fireworks stand hardly registering, and the only time Dwight Buford entered her thoughts was in those moments when she recognized that he wasn't encroaching. She knew he would, but briefly she felt as if she'd been buoyed, lifted to the surface where she could draw a breath before being pulled under again.

19

JUSTIN WANTED TO LEARN TO DRIVE ON HIGH BRIDGES, SO ONE Friday evening Eric took him into Corpus. Eric drove over the Harbor Bridge the first time, then they switched seats at a filling station. A long breeze, gulls crying and floating on vectors like choppy water. Eric tried to make out Marine Lab across the ship channel, but the screen of spruce around the warehouse obscured his view. A man in camouflage pumped gas into his dually truck; a woman leaned against the building with a cigarette in one hand and a Styrofoam cup in the other; cars idled in queue for the next available pump. Eric thought he and Justin would get back on the road right away, but Justin sat behind the wheel for a full minute without shifting into gear. At one point the truck's RPMs plummeted and Eric worried the engine would die.

"I guess I'm a little scared," Justin said. He picked at the bed of his thumbnail.

"It's no different than driving on the highway. Take it slow."

"I don't want to hold anyone up. I don't want people to be waiting on me."

"If they want to pass, they'll pass. You just go at whatever speed feels right. Keep your eyes on the road and it'll hardly feel like a bridge."

Justin cracked his neck. He drew a deep breath, then accelerated onto the street. The traffic had diminished, so he merged onto the bridge easily and settled into the middle lane. A flutter of pride in Eric's chest. He stopped himself from tousling his son's hair; Justin was concentrating so hard that the last thing the boy needed was his doting father distracting him. The car pulled against the bridge, gathering moderate speed as the girders overhead cast a lattice of shadows. Justin tapped the brakes often. More and more distance opened between their truck and the cars ahead. When a sedan passed too close on the left, Justin cut his eyes to Eric and then back to the road. Eric said, "You're fine." As they coasted down the bridge, a few more cars whooshed by, but Justin maintained his speed and steered toward the off-ramp.

"If that wasn't a successful maiden voyage, I wouldn't know what was," Eric said. It sounded like something Cecil would say, which pleased him, made him feel fatherly.

"It feels higher when you're the driver."

"You'll get used to it," Eric said. "You'll get to where you don't even notice."

They were stopped at an underpass. Justin was looking at the bridge in the rearview mirror. He was proud of himself, Eric could tell, and energized, the way he used to get when he found an unusual shell for his collection. Eric hadn't seen him like this since he'd been back. He wished Laura and Griff were in the car with them, and Cecil. He wished Tracy were there, too, and Letty the social worker and everyone who'd ever worried about Justin. Seeing him this way was a reminder and a reward, evidence of his son's capacity to recover.

"I'm proud of you, bud," Eric said.

"I bet the causeway is even easier than this was," Justin said. "It's not as high or steep, right?"

"It'll be a piece of cake," Eric said.

When Justin had asked about driving on bridges, the causeway entered Eric's mind first. The bridge there was about half as high—

the waters under it were open only to small watercraft—and the traffic out there was always lighter. To get to it, though, they'd have to pass the Buford house. If Justin had put that together, he didn't let on. Eric would have welcomed the opportunity to see what was happening at the house—he'd never been out there at this late hour—but he didn't want to risk Justin seeing anyone. Earlier that afternoon, Eric had watched the house through his binoculars for almost two hours, his longest session yet. (The truck's RPMs had plummeted then, too, and for a moment Eric was paralyzed with fear that he'd be stranded there and have to call for help.) Ultimately, he'd seen nothing more than the hospice nurse on her smoke breaks. He already wanted to go back.

In the sky, a perishing light. Drivers coming off the Harbor Bridge were clicking their headlamps on. Eric could see the corrugated roof of Marine Lab. He said, "If you hurry, I bet you can make it over the bridge and back again before it gets full dark."

"Really?"

"We'll just tell your mother we hit traffic."

"Sick," Justin said.

"She probably won't ask. She'll probably just be excited to see us."

"Don't worry, Dad," he said, dropping the truck into gear. "I'm good with a secret."

But when they returned home, Laura was already in bed. Griff was watching skate videos on the computer. He came into the kitchen and ate cereal from the box with his brother. Justin told Griff about having driven over the Harbor Bridge, portraying himself as more nervous than he'd actually been to amuse his brother. Rainbow trotted in and the boys fed her some cereal, then started trying to teach her to sit or raise her paw to shake.

Griff said Laura had gone to bed with a headache. Maybe that was true. She sometimes got migraines. Usually she could isolate

herself in a cool, dark room and sleep them off, but occasionally
Eric had to take her to the emergency clinic for shots of Demerol.
She hadn't suffered one in months, though, maybe over a year, so
Eric worried that something else had driven her to bed that early on
a Friday night. She could've seen Dwight Buford or his parents. The
district attorney could've called the house with news or questions
that unraveled her. Or something might have happened with the
dolphin. Or with Tracy Robichaud. Eric hadn't seen Tracy in a
week, but Laura could have easily run into her; Tracy was mired in
planning the event at the Shrimporee, and she might have contacted
Laura with questions. That Eric hadn't yet mentioned Tracy's involvement to Laura put him in a sweat. As he crept into their bedroom, he'd half expected the bed to be empty and their back window
open. But Laura lay under the covers, her breathing deep and even.
He went to sleep listening to her feather-soft snoring.

She rose in the middle of the night. Eric heard her and assumed
she was going to the bathroom. He drifted off again. Two hours
later, a little before dawn, he woke from a stiff, draining sleep to
find she hadn't returned, so he pushed himself up out of bed. It occurred to him that she might have gone for one of her midnight
walks down to the marina—he had a fuzzy memory of having been
afraid of something before bed—but he mostly expected to find her
sick in the bathroom. Migraines sometimes nauseated her.

She was in the kitchen, scribbling in her Moleskine at the table.
She'd made coffee and iced sweet rolls; the smells made Eric think
of winter, of Christmas, and for a moment it seemed he'd slept for
months. He was also struck, in a way he hadn't been in weeks, by
the absence of the plants and flowers in the kitchen, by how empty
the room was.

"I had a bad dream," she said. "I didn't completely remember it
until five minutes ago. I want to write it out. One of my books said
that can help."

Eric nodded, dragged his hand over his face. He had to yawn, but stifled it. He debated whether to pour a cup of coffee or to go back to sleep. He couldn't tell if Laura wanted him there. Outside, the night was eliding, splitting into the first soft rays of morning light.

"Is your head still hurting?" Eric asked. "Do you need a shot?"

"Did y'all have a good driving lesson?" Laura asked. She was still writing, not looking at him. Had there been an accusation in her tone? Eric wasn't sure. Just then he remembered Justin saying he was good with a secret, and the room spun a little. The window over the sink was open, which didn't make sense. Laura said, "I tried to stay up, but my head got too bad. I thought going to bed might stop it from turning into a migraine. I think it worked."

"Good. I'm glad," he said. She turned the page in her Moleskine—the sound was close and loud in the kitchen—and continued writing. Her pen moved so fast across the page that it put Eric in mind of his students when they took in-class exams. No—he thought of the student Laura had surely been, a smart girl who wouldn't have put her pen down until the bell rang. He could make out only one sentence at the top of the page: *If you can't take care of it, you don't deserve it.* Eric said, "We would've been home sooner, but he wanted to drive across a bridge, so we went out to Corpus."

"The Harbor Bridge?"

"He was scared at first, but he got over it."

"Clever," she said. " 'Got over it.' "

"I don't—oh," he said.

"We'll have to set boundaries when he gets his license. A certain distance he can't go without permission," Laura said.

She'd stopped writing, but sat looking at the Moleskine. Again, Eric could see her as a student, checking her work for errors. He hadn't thought of setting boundaries, hadn't even really grasped that teaching Justin to drive meant that he'd ever be driving without Eric in the passenger seat.

"We can write up one of those contracts," Eric said, remembering. "My parents did one with me. A piece of paper that says if he drinks or does drugs, he won't drive. The agreement is that he'll call us to pick him up wherever he is and we won't get angry. We all sign it."

"You think he's going to start doing drugs? Or drinking?"

"I was just saying we could do that along with the boundary rules."

Laura flipped a page in her Moleskine and wrote: *Parent/child contract. Drugs? Drinking?*

Morning was coming. The new light showed how tired Laura looked—her bagged eyes, her sallow skin. Crumpled tissues dotted the table. Eric hadn't noticed them before, but now he understood: She'd been crying before he got up. Crying while she baked the sweet rolls and brewed the coffee, crying while she tried to remember the dream that had woken her. He was overcome with deep affection for her, a sorrowful warmth.

"Can you get someone else to work today?" he asked. "If you can switch shifts, you might be able to get a little more rest."

"If Justin's still sleeping when I get home, I'll nap," she said.

"You ought to let him take you over the bridge."

"It was about him," she said. "About Dwight Buford. He'd come to deliver some salt to Marine Lab while I was volunteering. Nothing more than that, but it was terrifying."

"Sure. That makes—"

"I just feel like I see him everywhere. Absolutely everywhere."

"It'll ease up. And after the trial, he'll be in pris—"

"It wasn't the dream that woke me up, though. It was that I understood something, something I haven't understood since Justin came back."

"What?"

"Why he'd stay. I understand why he didn't try to run. Or call the cops or us or anyone. I get it now."

Eric didn't know what was happening, didn't entirely know

where he was. Everything was funneling and intensifying, as if the world was about to turn all of its attention on him. He said, "Why?"

"Because you feel like he's always with you. You feel like he's always watching you, hovering, always close enough to touch you. You feel like there's no getting away."

"You feel that way now? Right here, in the kitchen? You're worried he's that close this morning?"

She looked at him with equal parts pity and confusion. She said, "Isn't he?"

AFTER LAURA LEFT FOR WORK, ERIC DROVE OUT AND PARKED near the Buford house. He'd never been there that early, so he hoped to see something new—Dwight Buford taking his coffee on the porch or watering the lawn before it got too hot. There was nothing of the kind. The sun came up bright and molten—and fast, it seemed to Eric—and traffic clogged as the ferry made its way across the Laguna Madre. Soon the light was so bright that the glare obscured the quiet house. When the traffic thinned, he took the ferry back to Southport and picked up a bag of breakfast tacos. The boys would still be sleeping, but he wanted to have an excuse in case they'd woken and found both their parents gone. Later, after Laura returned home from the dry cleaner's, he said he wanted to visit his father at the shop, but drove out to the house again. He thought Mayne's Mercedes was parked a few feet farther back on the driveway, but nothing else had changed. The property might as well have been vacant.

Over the next week, the possibility that Dwight Buford wasn't in the house at all started taking hold. It was like catching the flu. The symptoms worsened each day, and the more aggressively they asserted themselves, the more he fought to downplay them. He spent two, sometimes three hours watching the house through the binoculars. His eyes grew tired. The bridge of his nose hurt. If he didn't have time to stop, he went out of his way to drive past the house, hoping to glimpse anything that would confirm Dwight Buford's presence. Nothing did. He saw only the hospice nurse and Mayne and the doctor. Edward Livingstone had visited just that once to pick up the accordion folder, and soon the lawyer's absence seemed to evidence Buford's absence. Eric wanted to alert Garcia or the police. He wanted them to assure him he was wrong or to start the manhunt for the fugitive. If he reported his suspicions, however, he'd have to admit he'd been watching the house.

He alerted no one. It would have worried Laura, irrefutably galvanizing her fears and breeding a new and desperate paranoia. Eric aimed to spare her that as long as he could. The same with the boys. He might have told Tracy, but almost two weeks had passed since he'd last seen her. They had slept together the once after Dwight Buford had been released, but when they tried again, it was empty and dismal and ultimately unsuccessful. It wasn't a problem he'd ever had before. He tried to lose himself in her eyes and body, in her scent and motion and breath, but nothing helped. He couldn't ward off images of Buford and Justin, couldn't help but imagine how impossibly difficult and fraught intimacy would be for his son in the future, how he would always feel soiled. From there, his thoughts went to Laura and the boys. He missed them with a raw and shaming force. He longed to be near them, to atone, to accept his punishment. As he showered, Tracy dressed and threw the sheets in the washer. She'd been kind about the trouble he'd had, but Eric knew she felt the same emptiness, maybe the same guilt, that he did. They parted as quickly as strangers.

And he didn't tell his father because he was afraid of what Cecil would do. Since Dwight Buford had been released, Cecil had been distant, beleaguered. He had hardly visited the house. Twice Eric and Justin had stopped by on their nightly drives, and although Justin didn't pick up on it, Eric had the sense that his father was eager for them to leave. He stood on his porch, blocking the door. On the next visit, he loaded them up with a couple of boxes of Eric's mother's things—ceramic figurines and photo albums and some of her clothes. "I've got roaches," he'd said. Cecil looked older each time they saw him, more haggard. He also seemed cornered, dangerously resigned, like a man whose choices had winnowed to a perilous degree and who had made his peace with the sad way matters would play out. There had even been a moment when Eric had thought the reason Cecil wasn't allowing them into his house was because he had Dwight Buford in there, strapped to a chair or bound to the stove. It was absurd, of course, but the notion had reinforced his feeling that he shouldn't share his concerns about Buford's possible absence. He was afraid Cecil would waltz up to the Bufords' door and demand to see Dwight. He was afraid to find out that although he couldn't do what needed to be done, his father could.

On Monday evening, a full month after Buford's release, Eric stood in the backyard watering the grass. Overwatering, perhaps, trying to make up for prior negligence. Laura was at work and Griff was skating at the Teepee. Eric had planned to take Justin driving, but when he woke up, Justin had only wanted to rearrange his room. Eric didn't mind. They moved the bed to the opposite wall, slid the dresser with Sasha's tank and the television to where the bed had been. So it wasn't so much rearranged as reversed, a mirror image of what it had been. The room looked odd, unfinished. Eric thought they would keep working, keep sliding one piece here and another there until they found the perfect layout, but Justin seemed content. It almost seemed like the setup for a practical joke, where Justin would invite his brother or mother into the room and pretend nothing had changed. But there was no hint of mischief in the air. Then, with the furniture situated, it became clear that Eric's services were no longer necessary. He told Justin that he'd be in the backyard and closed the door behind him.

The yard was saturated, the air thick with heat and mist from the hose and the coming night. A dust of pale stars hung in the sky. Gnats and mosquitoes were hovering. A few wasps. They were attracted by the spray of the hose. He looked at the yard obliquely, squinting his eyes to see it as it had been in its prime. After just a few weeks, the grass had yellowed in places, browned in others, and weeds had pushed up, started spreading. Eric didn't regret laying down the new lawn—the Fourth of July picture alone had been worth the money—but seeing it succumb to the sun dismayed him. He felt guilty, rash. In the last angled light of the day, everything looked slightly sloped. It was as if the yard had taken on more weight and was tilting forward and soon everything would slide down the pitched surface into darkness. He shut off the water and coiled the hose, then went inside to find something to fix for supper. Laura and Griff would be home soon.

Justin was in the kitchen, leaning against the counter and munching on cereal like popcorn. He extended his arm to let Eric grab a handful of corn flakes. The gesture seemed sweet and inclusive, affectionate in its way. How could he resist? For a moment there was only the sound of their crunching.

Then Justin said, "Do I need to tell Mom I'm sorry?"

"About your room?"

"About the mice."

"Oh," he said. He had to recalibrate his thinking, recall that night that seemed so long ago. Laura had been upset about the mice, no question. He remembered that she seemed to have taken it personally, but Eric was surprised it had made such an impression on Justin.

"I mean," Justin said, "Sasha needed to eat, but I could've waited. I could've ordered frozen mice online. I've done it before."

Before. The word was barbed. Behind and within it was every last thing Eric was trying to stave off. He turned toward the window over the sink, letting the word, the idea, sift away. He could still see the dense shapes of the yard, the odd angles of the little palm tree and the jagged fence line. An image of Laura came into his mind, his wife sitting at the kitchen table, scribbling in her Moleskine. *Because you feel like he's always with you.*

Eric said, "Just spend some time with her. That's all she needs."

"Letty thinks maybe I did it because I was angry."

"Like you said, Sasha needed to eat. That's proof enough for me."

"It was the last thing we talked about yesterday. She didn't say if she thought I was angry with y'all or with Dwight."

"The mice were bought to feed to the snake," Eric said. "Nothing seems mysterious here. Nothing seems malicious."

"The timing. I guess she was talking about the timing."

Outside, the sky hung low with clouds. Soon Laura would come through the door, or Griff would. Eric knew he wanted to move beyond this conversation, but something was nettling him: Justin hadn't said he disagreed with Letty. Aiming to keep his tone light, Eric said, "What about you, bud? Do you think you fed the mice to Sasha because you were angry?"

"I don't think so," Justin said. He was peeling flakes of dead skin away from his fingernails.

"I don't think so either."

Justin closed the cereal box and returned it to the cupboard, then dusted his hands over the sink. Eric had to again stop himself from touching him.

"I just couldn't believe he was getting out," Justin said.

"None of us could. It was a complete shock. And wrong. But there's nothing to be afrai—"

"And I just didn't want to look at the mice anymore. Mom liked them because I had them with me when I was found, and that's cool, I get that, but I was tired of seeing them."

"And Sasha needed to eat."

"But I don't think I was mad at y'all anymore."

Eric's breath caught, audibly. His gut turned over. It was like having his ribs kicked in. He said, "Anymore?"

"I guess not," Justin said.

"When were you mad at us?"

"When I was over there, I guess. When I was so close, and you couldn't find me."

"We tried, bud," Eric said. "We looked everywhere, every waking moment. You have to know that."

"I do," he said, his voice light with resignation. "You did everything you could. It just took a while."

Eric was unsure of what to say. What to do. What to feel. Everything seemed arrested, inert. Justin's expression reminded Eric of the look on Laura's face when she spoke of beached dolphins— the son's resemblance to his mother at that moment was uncanny, intimidating, and indicting—and Eric recognized the emotion that the expression always failed to mask: pity. What he wanted, what he needed, was for Justin to yell and curse him. Berate him. Punish him. Anything would have been more tolerable than pity. When Justin left the room, Eric was disgusted by the depth of his relief. Pathetic, he thought. Unforgivable. Then the beams from Laura's headlights sliced through the living room windows, flooding the house with a white glow. Eric crossed the kitchen and opened the fridge. He stood there for a long moment, the chilled air on his body, and pretended to be looking for something to cook. His eyes were closed the whole time.

20

CECIL WAS NOT A MAN WHO PLUCKED WEEDS FROM HIS WIFE'S grave. He was not a headstone cleaner, not a widower who laid sprays of lilies to mark the anniversary of her death or single roses for her birthday. He visited the cemetery so infrequently that he tended to forget exactly where she'd been buried. Her plot was under one of the slumped weeping willows—he always remembered that, but he could walk for twenty minutes before finding it. Knotty crabgrass had inevitably covered her marble plaque. Anthills dotted the ground, small cones of dry and granular dirt that were the shade of ash, puckered like bullet holes. He cleared the plot before leaving each time, but years would pass between visits, so it typically looked like he'd never been there at all.

But in the last month he'd driven out to the Coastal Bend Cemetery two and three times a week. He'd stop off at the Circle K for carnations—roses if they had them—and bottles of spring water. He doused her stone and polished the marble until the magenta veins and silver flecks took on a rich sheen. With his pocketknife, he cut away the weeds and dug caked sand out of the engraved letters: CONSTANCE LAUREL CAMPBELL. NOVEMBER 13, 1942–AUGUST 28, 1985. TENDER MOTHER, BELOVED WIFE. Mostly he'd visit in the early mornings before the day's heat locked in, but he'd also come in the evening to watch the sun drop into the bay. The cemetery was quiet, breezy. The weeping willow leaves lifted and fell. Cecil tried talking to Connie, tried narrating all she'd missed, but the words sounded childish, more like he was talking to himself than her, and he ran out of things to say far quicker than he would have guessed. If he wasn't yanking a weed or washing her plaque or arranging the flowers, he'd stand with his thumbs hitched in his belt loops and watch the doves and bitterns picking at the grass. Or he'd rest on one knee, squinting in the direction of the bay, listening to the tides convey what they could out to sea.

He'd started making the drive after Eric called to say Buford was getting out. Cecil's initial reaction was to dig the .44 out from under the seat in his Ford and clean it, then take it into the dunes for target practice on bottles or coyotes or whatever availed itself. But driving to the island that first morning, he'd gotten his mind right. He didn't want the game warden seeing his truck parked out where shots were fired. Without thinking, he drove to the cemetery. When he'd found Connie's grave—it had taken half an hour—he stood for a spell, trying to will tears that wouldn't come. The wide-open sky was a pale, expressionless blue, and the day was already heat-gripped. A few grackles perched here and there, openmouthed, like panting dogs. The ferry droned. Finally, apologetically, he said, "Honey, I'm fixin' to land my ass in prison."

He hadn't, though. He'd held off the first night, then the second, and by the third, he was thinking more deliberately. He made sure he was paid up on life insurance, double-checked his will, confirmed that Eric had access to his checking and savings accounts. He put together a couple of boxes of Connie's belongings, of photo albums and keepsakes, and gave them to Eric. "I've got roaches," he'd lied. "Once I get the house sprayed, I'll tote these back." Every couple of days he took a few of his things and sold them to the pawnshop. If Ivan wrote the ticket, Cecil said he was clearing out rooms, trying to make his house more appealing to his grandsons; if Ivan was out, he didn't bother writing anything up. He understood he might need

cash on short notice. He took one of the pistols Eric had been looking at, wiped the pawnshop's records of it, and stashed it under his
truck seat. He bought half a dozen jugs of water and loaded them in
the truck as well, along with a sleeping bag, cans of beans and soup,
a couple changes of clothes, and a map of northern Mexico.

Cecil couldn't say why he kept returning to the cemetery. He
only knew it brought him a kind of peace that was precluded in the
presence of his family. Around his son and grandsons, a wall went
up inside him. The objective of every conversation was to lead them
away from what he was truly thinking, away from what the future
might hold. Eventually, there could be questions, and for their sake
he wanted to make sure they didn't have the answers. When Griff
stopped by Loan Star or when Eric and Justin came by the house on
their drives, Cecil kept his distance. They regarded him like he'd
been diagnosed with an illness whose symptoms were becoming impossible to ignore. They thought he was down about Buford's release, somber and distracted by the injustice of it all, so he lived
behind that veil. Safer for everyone.

But at the cemetery he could drop his guard. He could breathe.
His thoughts banked off one another, moving from Eric to Justin to
Marcy—*Tell him Marcy says hey*—to Dwight Buford to Connie
until eventually his mind quieted. It was as if because Cecil hadn't
done what he'd thought he needed to do, it didn't need to be done.
As if because he'd been able to put it off this long, maybe he'd be
able to keep putting it off. He knew he might be rationalizing, suc-
cumbing to a fear too deep to feel, but still he allowed himself the
reprieves. In the cemetery, soft winds brushed over him, the scents
of lantana and salt water. He wished he'd spent more time here over
the years, tending her grave and sitting in the sun. He watched
women dab at their eyes with tissues and men remove their hats to
pray. Children chased each other through the maze of headstones,
workers in bandannas and sweaty long-sleeved shirts came through
with Weed Eaters. Twice, new mounds of freshly dug earth had

appeared—one plot for Harold Rattray, and a week later one for Whitey Mullen. If Cecil wasn't mistaken, Mullen still had a set of golf clubs in hock at the shop. The strange and scattered pieces of ourselves we leave behind, Cecil thought. Who could know what would still be in pawn when the world was done with you? Who could predict the legacy of small lives?

Cecil owned the two plots on either side of Connie. He'd bought all three shortly before Eric was born. She hated the idea of them, their implication and inevitability, but he never questioned the decision. He expected to die first and didn't want his wife and son burdened more than they had to be. He also wanted Eric to know that he'd always be welcome beside his parents, no matter who he was, no matter where life took him. The deeds to the plots were in the safe-deposit box at the Coastal Credit Union. Cecil had always assumed he'd be buried to the right of Connie, and Eric, if he so chose, would be laid to rest on her left, allowing space on the other side for his family. That Cecil's life had twisted in such a way that he himself might not be buried there at all was something he was still trying to swallow.

There had, of course, been a time when it seemed one of the two plots would go to Justin. Cecil had gone so far as to open the safe-deposit box and reread the deed in the bank's vault, checking for any fine-print stipulations about who could occupy the plots. He'd almost gotten sick on the bank floor, then again in the parking lot. He'd never broached the subject with Eric, but Laura had once asked if there was still space available around Connie. She'd pulled him aside at one of the annual beach searches, maybe the second or third year in, when most of the volunteers were deep in the dunes. Cecil had gone off by himself toward the National Seashore and she'd come up behind him.

"I like the weeping willow," she'd said. "I'd love for him to be in the shade."

Cecil hadn't known that she'd ever visited Connie's grave. Immediately he felt a new warmth toward her, and toward Eric for having shown her where his mother was buried. It was as if together they'd bestowed a great, unexpected kindness upon him. He also understood that Laura could've asked Eric but had come to him instead. They were each, in their own broken ways, trying to protect him, trying to gather what they needed to survive this long waiting.

"I think all those seats are taken," Cecil said.

"It's silly, I know it is, but I worry he'd be hot without some shade. I don't want the sun coming right down on where he'd be—"

"Like I said, they're all booked up," he said, firm. "When Justin gets home, we'll go sit for a spell under that shade tree, but that's as close as he'll get."

Laura reached over and squeezed his forearm. She started back toward the dunes and the other volunteers. As she was walking across the sand, she crouched to pick up a shell Cecil couldn't see. She blew on it and dusted it off, then turned and held it up to show Cecil. "A lightning whelk," she said. "I always try to pick something up on the searches, something we can add to his collection when he comes home." They never discussed it again, and although Laura had endured some rough patches, Cecil had always thought of the exchange as one that revealed a poise within her. She carried herself in a way he trusted.

He was thinking of this on Wednesday morning, driving back from the cemetery. He was thinking not of the lightning whelk or the cemetery plots, but of how Laura had squeezed his forearm. It had always seemed akin to how a child will squeeze your hand at the doctor's office, but now, in the truck, he thought she might have been trying to comfort *him*. Son of a bitch, he thought. The bay was dull and muddied, flat. He passed the Teepee Motel, where a group of stringy boys were climbing on the piles of rubble, chasing each other or some such. The Shrimporee banner over Station Street sagged, the morning dew still heavy on the frayed canvas.

When he rounded the corner to his street, he saw the white Mercedes parked in front of his house. Mayne Buford sat on his front steps, holding a Styrofoam cup of coffee with both hands. As Cecil pulled into the driveway, Mayne levered himself up from the porch and moved toward the truck. Cecil shut off the ignition, waited for the engine to rumble down before opening the door. He thought for a second and decided to leave his pistol under the seat.

"Coffee?" Mayne said, raising a second Styrofoam cup. "I stopped off at the Castaway. I figured you'd've already had your fill, but took a chance."

"You're taking a chance by stepping onto my property. If you think I don't have a Smith and Wesson loaded with Short Colts under the seat of this truck, I'd be happy to prove you wrong."

Mayne set the other cup on the truck's hood. He said, "I've just come to talk. I'm trying to keep things civil here."

"I kindly think it's a little late on that ticket," Cecil said. "I also think you've overstayed your welcome here. I won't ask again."

"Eric's watching our house," Mayne said. He averted his eyes when he spoke, looked at his shoes and the yard, as if ashamed. He sipped his coffee. He said, "He parks down the road and watches through binoculars. I'm wondering what the chances are of you asking him to give it a rest."

"I can't control my son any more than you've been able to control yours."

A truck with a camper and a struggling muffler rattled down the street. Not someone Cecil knew. In its wake came the hot and sorry smell of exhaust.

"Dwight's scared," Mayne said.

"Good," Cecil said. "I'd say scared is about one percent of what he deserves."

"My wife, too. And she hasn't done anything. She wakes up crying."

"Justin's mother probably knows something about that, too."

Cecil didn't like this talk, the back-and-forth of it. He wanted to get inside and fry some eggs and bacon in his skillet. He wanted to shut the door between him and Mayne before he lost his composure.

"I'd like to ask you for a favor," Mayne said.

"The answer's no."

"I'd like to take my family out on the water one last time, the three of us on the boat. We'd leave in the morning and be back later that night."

"You leave that dock and no one'll see you again. You can get to Mexico in a day. You can float to Galveston, tie the boat up, and drive to Canada."

"My wife would be with us. She'll run out of oxygen if we don't circle back."

"And you can't load a boat with oxygen canisters? You can't have a car waiting in Port Isabel with ten of the goddamn things?"

"I can get him to change his plea," Mayne said.

Cecil locked eyes with Mayne.

"Give me a day with my family and I can get him to plead guilty," Mayne said. "It would spare everyone the trial."

"If you can do that, you can do it at home. You don't need the boat for that."

"Probably I don't," he said. "But I want a day on the water with my wife and son. I want that memory. In a few months, I'll lose them both. I think it's a fair offer."

A skid of clouds moved past the sun and there was a gradual new light on the top side of the tallow leaves and puddles of shadows merging on the grass. The morning, the strange conversation with Mayne, felt like it was getting ahead of him, away from him.

Cecil said, "Like I said, Eric's a grown man. He makes his own choices."

"But you'll talk to him? Ask him about September sixth."

The date jogged something in his memory, though he couldn't

readily name the day's significance. Then he remembered. He said, "That's the Shrimporee."

"I figure we push off in the morning before the crowds get here and come back once everything winds down. It'll save us some hassle, and y'all can have that day to yourself. I know they're doing something special for Justin."

"You've put a lot of thought into this."

"I'd like to give this to my wife. We've been all over the world, but there's not a place she's seen that she'd trade for a day on the Gulf," he said. "I'm busted up about this. I'm drinking again. After the dust settles, I won't have much reason to—"

"If he comes near any of them, I'll kill him myself."

"He hasn't left the house. He barely leaves the couch."

"I'll take a hammer to every joint in his body. I'll pull his teeth out with pliers."

"Cecil, you don't need to—"

"I'll cut him and bleed him out, then I'll shove the barrel of a .44 down his throat and pull the trigger."

"Everyone will know it's you. They know the stories. The police will go to you before anyone else. I can probably call them right now and have you arrested."

"Hell, I'd call them myself," Cecil said. "But it'd be after I'd emptied the chamber."

Mayne nodded, sipped his coffee. Cecil locked the truck and started for the porch. To someone passing by, they might have looked like old friends.

21

L AURA HAD LIED TO ERIC THAT NIGHT IN THE KITCHEN. YES, she *had* dreamed of Buford showing up at Marine Lab, and writing out the dream *had* led to understanding why Justin wouldn't try to run away—*You feel haunted,* she'd written—but Buford wasn't the reason she couldn't sleep. It was Rudy, the volunteer. It was remembering how he'd used her married name in the parking lot. The memory had come unbidden as she was trying to drift off, when she was tunneling through the gauzy realm between knowing and unknowing. The sheets, damp with sweat, clung to her skin. There didn't seem enough air in the room, so she'd gone into the kitchen and opened the window over the sink.

She'd never told Eric that she volunteered under her maiden name. She hadn't wanted to risk his feelings, his questions or wounded silence; nor had she wanted to try explaining why she used *Wallace* in the first place. Would he believe that she'd never actually made the decision to use it? It was true. When she'd first signed up to volunteer, she'd written *Wallace* on the information sheet without thinking. A careless slip, the result of overeagerness. And yet she understood how tempting it would be to read more into the mistake. The seemingly sound logic was seductive in a shrink-y way: Since Justin had vanished, she hadn't felt like herself, like the wife or mother she'd been, so she'd found a way to erase her identity. What's more, in the last three years she had never corrected the error. She'd perpetuated it. She'd chosen to obscure herself, to free herself during each shift from the dreary connotations of her life. Laura knew how easily her position could be dismantled, and she'd always felt shallow and spineless when she wrote her old name. But she kept using it. If the choice afforded her anything beyond ano-nymity, it was simply this: the chance to believe that lost things could be found again.

And yet, the reason she hadn't told Eric about Rudy owed little to protecting herself or his feelings. She didn't understand what his using her name *meant*. She couldn't figure why it left her sweating and short of breath, and she worried that talking about it would wipe out her hopes of comprehending whatever there was to com-prehend. Did it mean others knew too? Were there implications be-yond Marine Lab? Surely not. Surely she was just being paranoid, her mind focusing on this tiny mystery to avoid thinking of Dwight Buford being, for all purposes, a free man. To avoid thinking of how Justin must despise them, how they deserved his anger, how he'd suffered indignities that made her long to be sick. So maybe Rudy had seen her on television or in the paper. So maybe she'd ac-cidentally signed up for a shift using her married name, having writ-ten *Campbell* as carelessly as she'd once written *Wallace*. So one part of her existence was infringing on another, the past colliding and collapsing and crushing into the present. So she'd never success-fully divided her existence after all. So what? So what, so what, so what?

Each time she volunteered she hoped to see Rudy, and when he didn't show, she searched the schedule to see if he'd signed up for future shifts. He was nowhere. It was frustrating, overshadowing. Thwarted. That was how she felt. Thwarted. Like when the post-card came from California and the detectives hardly gave it a sec-ond glance. Like when the 800 number would ring and the caller would hang up as soon as she answered. Away from Marine Lab, she did her best to put Dwight Buford and Rudy out of her mind. She plucked the dandelions and crabgrass that were taking over the backyard—sometimes one or both of the boys joined her—and she sorted through materials she would need to homeschool Justin in the coming fall. (She tried to mask how thrilling the prospect was. Both Griff and Eric would be back at school, so it would be just the two of them at the kitchen table, reviewing what he'd read the night before and solving equations. The image was so charged that it felt like a gift she had to wait months to open.) She gave Rainbow a bath with the hose, then another one when the dog, after the first wash, raced under the house and wallowed in the dirt. At work, she cleaned behind the machines, folded and bagged orders, flipped through the racks of clothes and called delinquent customers to remind them to pick up their clothes.

Justin was rearranging his room, trying one layout for a day, then changing it when he woke the next afternoon. On Wednesday, she and Griff helped him slide his desk to where his bed had been. They joked that they'd gotten so much practice in the last week that they could start their own moving and interior design company. Mom's Moving, they would call it. Their logo would incorporate Rainbow and Sasha.

"We could have an ad with a dog carrying boxes," Griff said.

"And a cartoon with Sasha stretched out like a ramp from the truck to the ground," Justin said.

The normalcy of the afternoon was intoxicating, buoying. The ratio between pressure and privilege was, in the moment, livable. They were all sweating. Justin took off his shirt and fashioned it on his head like a turban. Griff followed suit. Their hairless chests and arms and elbows and farmer tans were almost identical, and they looked so sweet that Laura flitted through the house to find her camera. The boys posed in mock strain, pretending to lift Justin's desk. Everyone agreed the picture would make a great image for the side of a Mom's Moving truck. They decided to move the desk to where the dresser had been.

As they were figuring out where to put the dresser, Eric called from school. The battery in his truck had gone dead while he was teaching, and he needed her to give him a jump. This too felt comfortingly normal, the beautiful everyday problems of an unscathed family. Such comfort was fleeting, Laura knew, and she knew she'd worry about leaving the boys alone as soon as she reversed out of the driveway, but she didn't cave. She told them she was leaving as nonchalantly as she would have told them to wear sunscreen. Justin said, "Mom's Moving. Where Mom's always on a union break."

The sky was lazy with sunlight. Driving, she kept watch for Buford, but there were only the tourists and fishermen and surfers making their way to the beach. Women walked around with visors and jute beach bags. Children licked ice cream cones.

In the parking lot of Southport Junior High, Eric was sitting on his truck's tailgate, swinging his feet in small circles. He looked young, like the last student waiting to be picked up. The easy problems of ordinary life, the effortless solutions: Your husband is stranded? Go pick him up. Battery's dead? Bring out the jumper cables and turn one key, then the other. She felt a brief rush of accomplishment for having temporarily shut the door on her grief, a rush of normalcy again, and of something like hope, the transient sense that people were capable of being rescued.

ALICE HAD AN INTESTINAL INFECTION. THE VET CONFIRMED IT. Normally, the problem wasn't serious, but given the weight she'd lost and her diminished appetite, Paul was concerned.

Laura had volunteered three times in as many days, two murder shifts and one early evening. Rudy never appeared. Most of the current volunteers were new, a cadre of marine biology grad students from Corpus. They were serious-looking, a little arrogant. She didn't like how they talked about Alice; their language was too clinical and their voices lacked affection. They seemed more fascinated by the infection than the dolphin, so much so that at times she wondered if they weren't hoping for worse symptoms. She didn't think they were as invested in Alice or her recovery as they should have been. If Paul called in the middle of the night because a volunteer had failed to show, she doubted any of the students would drive to Marine Lab to cover the shift.

Which was why, at one on Sunday morning, she dialed Paul's home phone number. If Rudy was, as he claimed, the first person Paul called to fill in for no-shows, she needed to cancel early enough for him to make the drive from Refugio.

When Paul answered, she almost hung up.

"Hello?" he said. "Hello?"

"It's Laura Wallace. I'm sick," she said. An hour later, she was on the road.

And, as she'd hoped, Rudy's 4x4 was parked beside the dumpster at Marine Lab. The lot was vacant otherwise, bathed in the lurid light from the single lamppost. Laura's heart was pulsing; she could feel her arteries widening. For a moment, she considered swinging a U-turn in the parking lot and driving home without ever confronting Rudy. But then she was cutting the ignition and walking toward Marine Lab. Insects knocked against the lamp. Frogs gurgled in the swamp grass.

The warehouse's exterior was humidity-slicked. With the night's heat, the door had swollen in its frame, so Laura had to use her shoulder and all of her weight to force it open. When it finally gave, the noise was a metal-against-metal screeching, as harsh as a car's brakes being slammed. Rudy spun around on the observation deck. He looked pissed.

"Sorry," she mouthed.

"I thought someone had crashed into the building."

"Just me," she said.

She closed the door softly. Water from the rehab tank was sloshing onto the floor, likely because Alice dove low with the noise and sent the water up and over. Laura's cheeks were warming. The light in the warehouse was intensely bright, garish against all the metal. She wondered if Paul had replaced some bulbs or if extra fixtures were switched on. A tall fan was oscillating, but the air was heavy and stagnant. Every surface was sweating. The wooden steps up to the observation deck were drenched. Laura held on to the guardrail, just to make sure she didn't flub up again.

"I thought you were sick," Rudy said.

"You called me Mrs. Campbell," she said.

"Do what?" He watched Alice circle the tank. She was moving fast, banking onto her right side, peering up. The water was still sloshing a little.

"The other night in the parking lot. You called me Mrs. Campbell."

He met Laura's eyes. She saw how tired he was. He looked thrown, too, squinting and cocking his head, trying to reconcile the data confronting him: Laura canceling, then showing up to chastise him for having called her by her rightful name a week prior. Rudy opened his mouth to speak, then stopped. He was cowed. He seemed to be considering not his response but the accusation. Laura waited. Alice swam a lazy lap. She exhaled a fine mist.

Finally Rudy said, "I'm sorry. I don't understand what you're asking, Mrs. Cam—"

"How do you know my name? I've never introduced myself to you that way, never signed up for a shift with it."

He swiped sweat from his brow with his forearm. Alice pushed herself against the orange rope in the pool, sawing herself forward, and Rudy made a mark on his log sheet. He looked at Laura, then leaned back in his chair, thinking.

"I guess I thought you'd told me your name at some point, or maybe I thought I'd seen it on the sheet, but I can't remember that ever happening. I apologize. I never meant to—"

"How did you know?"

"I'm a cop," he said. "Over in Refugio. I've been with them for going on five years now."

All sound peeled away, a steady quieting that left Laura feeling small and desolate. Woozy. She was suddenly aware that she could fall into Alice's pool. She put her hand on the deck's railing, stepped away from the edge.

Rudy stood and unfolded a metal chair. "Here," he said. "Sit."

She waved him off. She leaned against the railing, watching Alice. The dolphin kicked her tail once underwater, and the motion reminded Laura of a flag snapping in the wind. Alice was propelled forward, rising to the surface and issuing a loud breath. Rudy noted it. Laura's mouth tasted of copper, and though she desperately wanted some water, she didn't want to move. Her scalp burned.

"I saw you on the news or in the paper," Rudy said, nodding, remembering, his eyes still on Alice. "An older photo, I think. Your hair was shorter."

"We haven't done any press yet. We're trying to keep things low-key while Justin adjusts. The reporters have been good about it. They mostly focus on the Bufords."

"You caught a break there," he said. Then he started nodding again, energetically, and said, "It was the day I filled in for my wife. She was sick. I came home after having seen you and I saw some report. I told her I'd just volunteered with you."

"Probably," Laura said.

"It was. I'm positive," he said.

"Okay," she said.

"You know what's crazy? I knew about him being found before I showed up for that shift. If the news had been public yet, I would have mentioned it."

"You knew then? You knew before I did?"

Rudy kept nodding. He seemed to be getting worked up. Laura expected him to stand and pace, but he stayed where he was, nodding and nodding. He said, "I always listen to the radio when I'm driving, even when I'm off duty, and I remember the dispatcher saying he'd been found. She didn't give any more details, but I remember that coming through the speakers. I remember knowing it was true, but not believing it. If that makes sense."

"I think I will sit down," Laura said. Rudy stood and arranged the folding chair beside his, angled it toward the pool so she could see Alice. Presently, the dolphin was poking at a pink ball that Laura hadn't noticed before, nudging it along the tank's wall. Laura saw this, but she also understood that none of what she perceived at that moment was fully registering. Not the drone of the pool pump, the smell of chlorine or salt or heat trapped in the thick air, not the inflatable alligator in the corner by the life jackets. She was incapable of taking in anything else.

"Paul's not coming back for another couple of hours, if that helps," Rudy said. "He went home to nap."

"Okay. Okay, that's good to know," Laura said. "Five years?"

"I'm sorry?"

"You've been a cop for five years?"

"Almost five, yes."

"You started just a little before he went missing."

"I remember hearing about the case in briefings, and I remember seeing the age-progressed images."

"He hated the pictures we used."

Alice nudged the pink ball again, then submerged herself, which Rudy noted on his log sheet. He said, "How's he doing? If it's okay to ask."

She could have told him what she told everyone—*Justin's doing very well, better than anyone could have hoped, more progress each day*—but instead she said, "I don't know."

He offered a small, kind smile. It made Laura feel as though she'd gotten the answer right. He said, "Well, he's doing miles better than he was."

"It's like we were all on a sinking ship and now we're each in our own lifeboat, floating away from each other. Every few days I'll catch sight of one of them, or maybe they'll see me, but then we roll over the horizon and disappear again."

"Y'all have another son, right?"

"Griffin," she said. "He's currently avoiding his girlfriend, which makes zero sense to me. Eric, my husband, tries to act like everything is hunky-dory normal. Justin sleeps all day and watches television all night with a snake draped around his neck. The other night I dropped a skillet and scared him half to death."

"And what about you?"

"Me?" she said. "I'm here, watching a sick dolphin swim in circles in a humid warehouse."

"My wife and I have kept you in our prayers."

Laura averted her eyes to Alice. Whatever part of her was starting to open up to Rudy closed a little when he mentioned praying. When she'd gone to the support groups in the church basement, people were always advising her to pray. They made it sound as if the frequency and intensity of her prayers correlated to whether her son would be found alive. Once, after a woman said Justin's life was in God's hands and Laura only needed to trust His wisdom, she'd looked the woman in the eye and said, "Fuck God."

Maybe Rudy sensed her hesitation because he added, "And we've talked about you a lot, especially with the baby coming. We just can't imagine. And now, with the alleged abductor out, I don't want to think about what I'd do."

"*Alleged?*"

"Sorry," he said. "Force of habit."

Alice swung herself around and reversed her direction. The surface of the water had calmed and was only slightly disturbed when she breached to exhale and draw breath.

Rudy said, "I'd been wondering if you'd keep volunteering, if I'd see you again."

"I've been wondering how much any of us can take."

"The worst is behind y'all," he said.

"You'd think so, wouldn't you? Really, once the worst happens, it's always happening. It's never not happening."

Rudy sat quietly, watching Alice swim, then said, "Maybe talking to someone would help."

"Justin sees a social worker. She's a nice woman who will probably always know more about my son than I do."

"What about the rest of y'all? You and your husband and Griffin?"

She'd been wondering if Griff should see a therapist, maybe even Letty. Maybe, she'd thought, at least one of us can survive this. She hadn't broached the subject with anyone. She was afraid—afraid he would need therapy, afraid he wouldn't and bringing it up would make matters worse. As for Eric, she suspected he believed what she did: that they deserved all of the pain and sadness and guilt that was constantly marauding them. They deserved it for as long as it lasted and to seek any kind of relief would be craven and gutless.

Now she said, "You're right. It might not be a bad idea for us."

"There's no shame in—"

"Does anyone else here know?" she said. "Does anyone else know who I am? Paul or any of the other volunteers?"

"I think he's too wrapped up in Alice to notice much of anything," he said.

"I use my maiden name. I don't know why."

"It is what it is," Rudy said.

"What would you do?"

"Say again?" Rudy said.

"You said you don't want to think about what you'd do if it happened to your family. What would you do?"

The pool pump chugged. Alice glided against the rope. Laura thought Rudy was about to confide something private and true, but his only response was to shake his head, the motion slow and tight as if he were just then in great pain.

OUTSIDE THE WAREHOUSE, IN THE MILKY PREDAWN LIGHT, PAUL Perez tried to make sense of Laura Campbell's car being parked next to Officer Treviño's truck. He was still groggy from his too-short nap—despite having driven from his house since waking up—so he wondered if he was dreaming her car. He knew he wasn't, but that didn't clear anything up.

In the sky, clouds were stepped like cliffs.

Laura Campbell, that depleted woman. He'd recognized her the first time she'd volunteered, didn't doubt himself for a second even when she wrote *Wallace* in the info box. Like she was checking into a seedy motel, using a made-up name. He'd never expected her to stick around as long as she had, never expected her to devour so many books on cetaceans. No question she knew more than he did. She reminded him a little of a drug addict who quit using and got hooked on jogging. There was a level of desperation to her care, an urgency; there was something compelling her that every other volunteer—including Paul—was lucky enough to lack. She never mentioned anything about her struggles; she wasn't the proud kind of addict, not one to share war stories. She hardly mentioned anything about herself at all—most of what Paul knew had come from articles and news reports—and although he never pressed her, he could always sense a barely muted pain in her voice. How hard she worked to conceal it was as obvious as her long hair.

Who could blame her?

More than once he'd thought: If Alice dies, so does Laura.

If he had to guess, he'd say she used a different name to spare others the burden of offering sympathy. A kind of selflessness that saved her a little, too. Or would have if people didn't recognize her. But they did, almost always. How many times had new volunteers asked him—sheepishly, perversely, illicitly—if she was who they thought she was? Because he felt protective of her, because he saw how desperately she wanted to hide, he never outed her, but they still knew. Their stricken looks, their somber shaking heads, their conspicuous reaching for their phones to text their friends: "Guess who I just saw at Marine Lab." It made him hate them a little. Whenever possible, Paul arranged the schedule so that Laura only overlapped with the kindest volunteers—the shy honor students, the barefoot hippies, and the lonely women whose clothes were covered in cat hair. And, of course, the mothers or mothers-to-be, like Officer Treviño's wife. In fact, the only volunteer he'd talked about Laura with was Officer Treviño. He'd started volunteering right around the time when the Campbell boy had been found, and he was a cop in Refugio, so sometimes he and Paul would sit on the observation deck, watching Alice and talking about Laura. "What I'm hearing at the office," Treviño had once said, "is that the boy was raped practically every day. He was beaten with rolled-up newspapers until the ink smudged on his skin."

When Paul called him this morning and asked him to fill in for Laura, Treviño had said, "Copy that. I'm on my way."

Early light serrated the clouds. Gulls and sparrows and grackles were waking up, landing on the rails above the hatchery. Paul couldn't decide if he should go into the warehouse. He didn't know if he'd be welcome. It was what happened when you spent time near someone who'd suffered the way Laura had: You felt the stranger. You saw the void surrounding her, stranding and diminishing her, and you saw her seeing it, too. Undoubtedly, what everyone experienced around Laura was what she experienced around her poor, ruined son. You saw only the wounds. You couldn't ignore how their bodies betrayed the pain they'd suffered. They were, Paul thought as he eased his car into gear and pulled out of the parking lot, like dolphins. In the water, you could only tell them apart by their scars, the places they'd been hit by outboard motors or sliced by commercial fishing line or bitten by sharks. The gashes defined them.

Paul had thirty minutes before Treviño's shift ended. He pulled into the abandoned motel lot and closed his eyes, hoping to sleep in the truck for a few minutes. Around him, the morning was slowly rising. There were fragments of a dream—a girl from his youth, pigtailed Esmeralda, and woods strung with oak wilt, and someone welding, someone he knew but didn't know, the sparks from the torch as blue as ice. Sleep never came, not completely; he was already moored in the waking world. The sun was bearing down, heavy and molten even that early, and the bay was choppy and frothed, insinuating itself, offering up its countless wounded creatures.

22

"THEN BREAK UP WITH HER," JUSTIN SAID.

Griff had just helped him rearrange his room for what seemed the hundredth time. They were taking a break, assessing the layout, talking about Fiona. Sasha was on Justin's bed. She was inching under his comforter. Griff could see only her tail now, which bothered him. He thought it would be easy to lose track of her if she went all the way under. He thought she would disappear, for days or weeks, only to reemerge later where they least expected. He was scared of her scaring him.

"Sasha's going under the covers," Griff said.

"And?"

"And I don't want her to get too hot," Griff said.

"She's cold-blooded. If she doesn't get enough heat, she'll freeze to death."

Griff wasn't used to the room looking different. His parents had been so adamant that the room should stay how Justin left it that it had, Griff realized now, seemed fossilized, as permanent as a concrete memorial. He was afraid to ask why Justin kept changing it. Maybe the social worker had suggested it, or maybe the idea was all Justin's, something that would confound Letty as well. Maybe changing up the room was meant to signal a new beginning. Or maybe there was nothing to be read into it at all. Now, with Justin, there always seemed to be the promise—or threat—of a sign, a symbol that required decoding. Griff found it exhausting.

It was early evening on Monday. Their father was running errands and their mother was closing up at the cleaner's. Rainbow was under the house, lying in the cool earth; every once in a while they could hear her digging, kicking clumps of dirt against the floorboards beneath their feet. "Just think," Justin said. "That dirt hasn't been touched by the sun since the house was built." Griff didn't know how to respond when Justin said things like this, so he just nodded, trying to appear unaffected, like he'd thought the same thing before. He felt simultaneously older and younger around his brother, unsure whom their parents had left in charge. It was how he felt in general lately: clueless as to who meant what to whom.

Sasha was completely under the covers now, slithering in the furrows of the sheets. Justin wasn't paying attention and Griff stayed quiet. He looked around the room, pretending to ponder the best place for his brother's desk.

When Justin had asked him to help move his furniture again, Griff hadn't expected to talk about Fiona. If anything, he thought they'd talk about Dwight Buford or where Justin had been going on his midnight drives. Griff no longer thought he'd be invited along, but sometimes Justin shared things he'd seen. "Two people were definitely fucking on the beach. They were old, like in their fifties, probably having an affair," he'd said. Another time, he'd seen a group of kids they used to know shooting bottle rockets at each other's feet, the fireworks hissing and skittering across the pavement. But tonight, while Griff and Justin were pushing the dresser toward the wall near the closet, Justin had asked why Fiona hadn't been coming around. To his surprise, Griff admitted that he'd been avoiding her. He said he didn't know why, but being around her made him lonely and afraid. He didn't say that all of this had started after Dwight Buford had been released, but he sensed that Justin understood. That was something that hadn't changed, the feeling that his older brother was putting things together ahead of him.

Justin said, "Don't do it on the phone. And don't wait around for her to break up with you. That's what pussies do."

"That's not what I'm doing," Griff said, though he suspected it probably was.

"And, anyway, I don't think she's the leaving kind."

"She's left a lot of guys. Like, a whole lot."

"Says who?"

"She does," Griff said.

"Exactly," Justin said. He was surveying the room, trying to figure what to move next.

"I believe her. She used to tell me about all of her boyfriends."

"Boyfriends? Plural? I'd be surprised if she's had *one* boyfriend before you," Justin said.

"She likes pilots and Coast Guard guys. She calls them her lovers."

"I'm sure she does," Justin said.

"You think she's lying?"

Justin was glancing around the room like he'd forgotten something. Griff leaned against the dresser, hoping he looked bored and cool. He wanted to know why his brother thought Fiona wasn't telling the truth, wanted to know what his evidence was and how he'd found it. But Justin wasn't answering. He went over to the bed and lifted the sheets, then cracked his neck.

"Shit," Justin said. He looked around the room, biting at the nail of his index finger. Then he picked a piece of nail from his tongue and said, "Where's Sasha?"

GRIFF SNEAKED OUT OF THE HOUSE LATER THAT NIGHT. JUSTIN and his parents were watching television, passing around a bowl of popcorn. Sasha lay coiled in Justin's lap—earlier, they'd found her wedged between the box spring and mattress—and Rainbow was sprawled on the floor. Griff didn't need to leave so clandestinely, but he didn't want to alert anyone to where he was going. Or rather, when he eventually returned, he didn't want to answer questions about where he'd been. Before he crawled through the window in his room, he'd texted Fiona and asked her to meet him at the marina. She'd responded with "About time, jackass." He didn't know what he'd say once they were together. Part of him hoped she'd convince him that breaking up was a mistake. Another part hoped she'd be furious and erratic, hoped she'd dump him before he said a word. Who cares if I'm a pussy? he thought.

Lightning bugs flared in the air. Making his way toward the marina, carrying his skateboard instead of riding it, Griff tried to guess where the insects would next illuminate. He was always wrong. A few cars passed on Station Street, and far off, deep into the trailer park behind the raggedy soccer field, people were laughing. The smell of smoldering charcoal, of smoked brisket. Then, an odd and elusive thought: Griff wondered if the same lightning bugs he was seeing now had just flown through the trailer park, or if they were moving that way now and the people who'd been laughing would soon see their lights. It struck him as the kind of thing Justin would think about, but the notion gave him pause that had nothing to do with his brother. Just then, that he could share anything with anyone else, that he could be connected to them by a sight or sound was mystifying. Nothing seemed permanent. Nothing seemed to have a beginning or end; or, maybe, everything seemed only to have a beginning or an end, and lacked whatever qualities were required to last, to endure, to exist beyond the specific moment of Griff's regard.

Without meaning to, he'd stopped walking. He stood on the street and found himself surrounded by stillness, by a jarring silence. No cars, no movement or distant laughter, everything mausoleum-quiet. During the years that Justin was gone, there had been times

like this, times when the streets of Southport seemed utterly deserted. Lifeless. Motionless. No gulls overhead, no ferry horn in the
harbor, no tourists milling around or dogs panting behind fences.
The town seemed emptied, abandoned. People had retreated in-
doors from the withering heat, or they were already in bed or not
yet up, but Griff was out. He imagined the whole world this way,
imagined that he alone remained. It reminded him of the moments
when he used to try to think of himself as an only child, as a kid
who'd never had a brother at all. How disgustingly easy it had been.
How seamlessly loneliness took hold. The quiet and stillness un-
nerved him, taunted him. He envied everyone who'd disappeared.
He resented having ever been spared.

He lost track of time. Fiona was probably at the marina, fuming.
Again, he was torn. He wanted to jump on his board and skate to
her as fast as he could, but he also wanted to turn and bolt home.
How had his life reached this point? Just months before, he'd been
dousing his socks with Fiona's perfume, preparing to lose her to the
next pilot or sailor to come along. (That Justin doubted she'd had
other boyfriends was still a riddle he couldn't unpack.) And before
that, four years ago, he'd been where? Justin would have been gone
for a couple of months and the searches were already wilting with
disappointment; there was the pervading sense that anyone holding
out hope was pathetically deluded. Griff had certainly stopped expecting Justin to waltz back into their lives like it had all been a silly
misunderstanding; he'd stopped believing that their lives had been
paused as opposed to ruined. None of it had ever seemed real, and
it rendered everything that followed unreal, too. He remembered
someone, his father or grandfather maybe, saying he wished it had
happened earlier in the year, when school was still in session, so
they could have organized the upperclassmen into search parties.

"Two hundred extra eyes," he'd said. "That's what we could use
right now."

And yet here he was, walking through nets of humidity to break up with Fiona. Because Justin was home and had told him not to be a pussy. Because Dwight Buford was out of jail and crowding Griff's thoughts. Because letting Fiona go seemed somehow right. Because she deserved better. Because the world had stabilized to the degree that this was a worthwhile problem to have.

23

Sitting in the television's flickering light with his wife and son. A nearly empty bowl of popcorn on the coffee table, a movie full of rooftop chases and explosions on the screen. Eric thought he should feel more sanguine, more at ease. He was trying.

He felt good about having settled into the movie without the urge to vet it beforehand. For years, his habit had been to preview as many programs as he could before Laura or Griff watched them. Tonight he'd just started flipping the channels until they found something interesting. A small impulse remained, a low and constant concern that some plot twist would involve a kidnapping or sex, but it was endurable. Laura's feet were wrapped in an afghan. She had her Moleskine on the arm of the couch and a pen in her lap in case she needed to make a note. Justin sat beside her, his eyes fluttering as he tried to stay awake. Sasha lay in his lap. The air smelled of her scales, musky. Relax, Eric thought. Enjoy this.

Griff had been in his room all evening, so maybe his absence was the problem. Eric couldn't remember if Fiona had come over earlier, if they were holed up together. Or the problem could have been what he couldn't forget: Justin admitting he'd been angry with them while he was in Corpus. Eric had never entertained that possibility, though he should have. His breathing went shallow again. How was Justin to know they'd been tirelessly looking for him? How could he *not* assume they weren't doing enough? Then, the more trenchant and damning fear that Justin's anger was warranted, that they'd been sluggish and complacent when they should have been vigilant, monastic, relentless. Or maybe what was keeping Eric on edge was the worry that Dwight Buford had vacated his parents' house. That he was gone for good and they'd always expect him to come after Justin. Eric looked at the window. Lightning bugs fired in the dark. Had Griff ambled in at that moment, with or without Fiona, Eric would have paused the movie and told his family how much they meant to him, how he would spend the rest of his life striving to live up to their standards, how he'd never forgive himself for the ways he'd let them down.

And like that, he understood: He needed Griff in the room. He needed the four of them together. He said, "Griff would like this. I'll go draw him out of his lair and—"

"Shhh," Laura said, her forefinger to her mouth. Then she shifted her eyes and Eric's attention to Justin. He'd fallen asleep and in the half dark, he looked young and contented. He looked like the boy he'd been before.

Eric settled back into his recliner. He watched Laura watch Justin, watched her reach for her Moleskine and quietly flip to a page and write something out in her long, looping script. Or was she sketching him? He couldn't tell. Contentment still eluded him. The three of them seemed a surreal version of the family they'd been for the last four years. Justin had taken the place of Griff, and Griff was missing. There seemed an open circuit, an incomplete iteration. Everything felt ephemeral. Laura wrote in her notebook and Justin slept and Eric was trying not to acknowledge how vulnerable they all were. But if something can be lost, he thought, then its loss is always just a breath away. Then it's all but already gone.

24

THE WORLD RETURNED FROM SILENCE. CARS TRUNDLED OFF the ferry, their headlamps pushing through the dark. Griff was nearing the Teepee and could hear skaters in the pool. Urethane wheels groaned against the cement, rattled over the tile below the coping. There was also a dull banging.

Griff couldn't stop thinking about where he'd been four years ago. He remembered—in addition to the dashed hope of Justin returning, of him explaining everything away—how he couldn't decide if he should tell his parents or the detectives about the arguments with his brother. "Maybe it's a small thing that doesn't sound important at all," the cops were always saying. "Cases turn on the tiniest detail. One domino tumps another and then, bingo, everyone is safe at home." But he never mentioned their fighting, or how Justin had left the house because Griff had made him feel unwelcome. He remembered the filthy sense of empowerment, of feeling older and stronger, that came with exiling Justin. This was something else he'd never told: He'd been pleased with himself, proud even, for putting his brother out. What had Griff been doing four years ago? Hindering the investigation. Lying to everyone who could have helped find Justin. He might as well have been colluding with Dwight Buford.

Along Station Street, it wasn't dark enough for lightning bugs.

The streetlights were burning, casting a dusty glow onto the cement. A film of dirt and sand and pollen on everything; it had been months since rain. The dull banging fell and rose, and Griff assumed it was down in the marina, a mechanic working on a dry-docked boat. He was more focused on the noises from the Teepee pool, the harsh rumble of skaters grinding and the clatter of their boards when they fell. He could hear voices, too. Someone, maybe Baby Snot, said, "To the victor go the spoils, and tonight we're all named Victor!" Others laughed and clapped their boards against the concrete. Then, a new thread of a scent tinged the air: the sticky tang of marijuana. It grew more cloying with every step, and put Griff on alert. If he'd had more time, he would've doubled back and taken the long way to the marina. He didn't want to see the skaters, didn't want to nod and make small talk, didn't want to watch their expressions soften as they exhaled pale smoke. Call Fiona, he thought. Say you're sorry. Say your parents called you home. Say Justin did. Say it's an emergency.

But he was already in front of the Teepee, and Baby Snot was doffing an imaginary hat, saying, "Top of the evening to you, young Griffin. Unfortunately, the pool is closed for the night. No lifeguard on duty."

"It's cool," he said, thinking he was missing part of a joke. The pool wasn't closed at all. There were two skaters in the shallow end, and another was carving the round wall. Griff said, "I'm meeting my girlfriend."

"Ah," Baby Snot said. "The siren song of the snatch should never be ignored, should ye be lucky enough to receive it."

He was shirtless, sheened with sweat, aping a bad Irish accent. There was a crude black tattoo of a koi on his stomach. Behind him, the skaters in the shallow end waited to roll in. One of them looked familiar to Griff, but the others were new. They were older, maybe by ten or fifteen years, with stubble and bellies. Their van was parked close to the bowl. The dull banging started up again, louder.

Baby Snot said, "You enjoy yourself, laddie. And remember, when in the company of a lovely lass, always put a helmet on thy jimmy lest ye—"

"What's that noise?" Griff interrupted.

"It's Baby Snot sounding like an Irish pirate," one of the new skaters said from the pool. He had a graveled voice and rangy, board-straight posture, like he'd been in the army. He drained a beer and tossed the empty onto the deck of the pool, then said, "Do Irish pirates even exist? Is that a thing?"

"I thought he was a leprechaun," another skater said. Then more of the dull banging. It was coming from behind the van.

"No," Griff said. "*That* noise. What is it?"

"'Tis none of your business," Baby Snot said. "'Tis time you run and find the lass with the golden chali—"

"Shut the fuck up, Snot," the skater said. Then the sound of steel hitting steel hitting concrete.

Griff started toward the van. All of the skaters trained their eyes on him, like he'd dropped a tray of dishes. He said, "What's going on?"

"'Tis nothing to see here," Baby Snot said, stepping in front of Griff, blocking his path.

But Griff had already seen: Half of the pool's coping had been removed. The cement blocks were stacked like sandbags inside the van; they were so heavy that the back end sat lower than the front, the rear shocks depressed. Griff went cold. Everything seemed immediately fraught, changed, dangerous. Two skaters from Baby Snot's crew were working to pry the next block loose. They had crowbars and hammers. The banging was less dull now, more resonant and hollow. It was the same sound Griff's heart was making in his ears.

"Like I said, Mr. Griffin, it's best if you run along," Baby Snot said. His fake accent was gone, and his chest was inches from Griff's.

His sweat reeked of pot and beer, a thin and desolate odor that scared Griff. He said, "This is a carnival ride you're not tall enough for."

Griff couldn't take his eyes off the skaters sliding their crowbars under the block of coping, wedging them under and knocking them in with hammers, and then wrenching the piece off.

"Just get out of here," Baby Snot whispered. His tone was conspiratorial, like he was trying to help.

"Why are you doing this?"

"Dude," he said, "just split, okay?"

"Just leave the coping and skate here whenever you want. You're ruining the pool."

Baby Snot nodded, a glazed and dopey gesture, like he'd just taken a bong hit. In his accent again, and louder, he said, "The coping needed its freedom, and like the Pied Piper, we have come to liberate the—"

"Snot!" the old skater said. "Shut the fuck up and send the cocksucker's brother on his way."

"Oh shit," someone said from behind the van and stifled a laugh. Then everyone's gaze was back on Griff, boring into him. The guys working on the coping went still, crouched with their hands on their tools. Baby Snot seemed confused by what was happening. A car passed on Station Street. No one moved.

"What did you say?" Griff asked. "What did he say about my brother?"

"Mike's drunk," Baby Snot said. "Go find your girl. She's waiting on you."

"I said"—Mike, the older skater, was climbing out of the pool now, crossing the lot toward Griff—"I said you need to spend some quality time with your faggot brother. Let him teach you how to suck dick and then hurry back and show us what you've got."

"Ease up now, Mike. Be cool now," Baby Snot said.

"There's nothing wrong with going fag," Mike said. "And big brother must have liked it, right? Why else would he stay put for so long unless he liked a hard dick up his—"

Baby Snot tried to stay between them. He tried, Griff thought, to wrap his arms around Mike and keep him off Griff, but it was as if a cord had broken to turn everyone loose and they were all instantly tangled—Griff trying to get to Mike, and Mike trying to get to Griff. They were tripping forward, hitting the ground. Then the others were in the mix too, cinching in, constricting. The rubber sole of a shoe, sandy and somehow wet, on Griff's mouth, pinning him to the cement, maybe by accident. The sudden thick taste of blood, his mouth full of it. Someone's elbow in his eye socket and his nose running. He scratched at Mike's face with his nails, rammed his knee into his ribs, a heaving motion that released him from under the shoe. Blood and mucus and spit, now slick on his face, in his hair, and then he was down again, from behind, and someone was pulling at his arms, angling them up and behind him. The smell of beer and concrete dust. His face on the ground again, burning and twisting; he could feel every grain of sand against his cheek and forehead. More blood in his mouth. He could picture the wound perfectly, a dark gash between his teeth and bottom lip, deep enough that blood pooled in it. I'll need stitches. A sound like an animal in pain that Griff didn't know he was making. He thought, Is this what I deserve? He thought, My parents will know I snuck out. He thought, This is what they'll remember. He thought, I shouldn't give up Fiona. I'm sorry. I'm so sorry for all of it. Weight on him, so much weight that he couldn't breathe, and then his palm on someone's face. Then it was on a nose, and he hoped it was Mike's, and he pushed against his septum, feeling the head tilt back and hit the concrete, thinking of driving a stake into wet, hard earth, a pin into a stubborn cushion, and then he was on his stomach, his legs almost over his head like a scorpion, and everyone was rolling, and then a hand in front of him, and he bit at the wrist, tasted beer and salty sweat and gritty dirt and his own blood, and dug his teeth in, clamping down and down and down, trying to tear the skin until he heard the banging again, closer, behind his ear, and all at once the world was silent and black and gone.

25

AFTER FOUR YEARS, AFTER THE COUNTLESS TIMES THE NUM-ber had been called, Laura hadn't grown accustomed to the sound of the 800 line ringing. It still startled her. The ringtone was modern-sounding—futuristic and mellow compared to the clanging rattle of the other phone—and her heart always throbbed when she heard it. She'd never inoculated herself against the crazies who called, the pranksters or heavy breathers or wishful thinkers or the sadists who laid out horrifically plausible accounts of what they'd done to her boy; she listened to everyone with hope and terror, believing that life would be changed (not necessarily for the better) at the end of each call. One of the chores she'd assigned herself in the recent weeks was to cancel the phone line or surrender the number to the National Center for Missing & Exploited Children. She hadn't been able to bring herself to do it, though. She hadn't known why she'd been stalling until, near the end of the movie on Monday night, the phone rang.

She'd been watching Justin sleep, thinking he must still be so exhausted from all of it. She wondered if Buford had ever watched her son while he slept. Her poisoned thoughts. Her bleak heart, sagging with regret and vulgar, selfish need. The ringing phone was a kind of small salvation.

She jumped up from the couch out of habit, as quickly as she would have had Justin still been gone. Her movement, which reminded Eric of how she'd run to the boys when they started to cry as infants, had been so abrupt that she'd startled Sasha. Suddenly, Justin was fumbling to catch the snake, trying to keep her from slipping into the cushions, while Laura rushed to the kitchen. She answered before the second ring ended.

"Mrs. Campbell?"

Again, on blind memory, she'd flipped open her Moleskine and her pen was in her hand, hovering, ready to write down whatever information the caller offered.

Laura said, "This is she."

"I have your son," the caller said. It was a woman, maybe around Laura's age, maybe younger. The connection was clean and clear, an encouraging relief, and the woman's voice sounded urgent, but not crazy, not manipulative. For a fleeting moment, almost before the idea could gain purchase in Laura's mind, she thought these past weeks with Justin were nothing but a fantasy; she thought he *was* still missing and they were still searching. That she couldn't at that moment see or hear anything from the living room—probably Eric had muted the television to listen to Laura's reaction, probably Justin was pulling Sasha out of the couch like a magician's scarf— seemed to confirm that the woman was telling the truth.

Before Laura could think of what to say or ask, before she could ground herself in the proper moment, the woman said, "Your other son. Griffin. I have Griff."

"Who is this?"

A near-silence on the line, a hissing that seemed so long and encompassing that Laura thought the woman had hung up and the call was about to drop. She had also somehow known it wouldn't, had discerned from the meaningful quiet that the woman would speak again. Then, like that, the woman said, "It's Tracy."

"Tracy?"

"Tracy Robichaud. I volunteered on the searches for Justin. I'm in charge of the celebration at the Shrimporee."

"You have long brown hair," Laura said, feeling dizzy. "You're a surgeon."

"My husband is," she said. "But right now, Griff's hurt. He's been beaten up. We're at the emergency clinic on Station."

Griff's in his room, she almost said, but as soon as she opened her mouth, she knew she was wrong. At that moment, and as she was bringing Eric and Justin up to speed on the drive to the clinic, she was trying to remember when she'd last seen Griff. The most recent time she could recall was when they'd worked in Justin's room before she went to pick up Eric. That was days ago. The knowledge hollowed her. He could've been gone all along, could've been lying broken and afraid in the dark, waiting for his mother to come looking for him, waiting for her to at least notice that he too had gone missing.

26

S TITCHES. SIX OF THEM ALONG HIS SON'S HAIRLINE. GRIFF also had a blackened left eye, bloody swollen knuckles on both hands, and bruises on his back, legs, and ribs. He looked like a kid who'd jumped out of a moving car. He looked the way Eric and Laura felt.

Tracy Robichaud had been driving home when she saw the commotion at the Teepee. "My stomach has been upset," she'd said in the waiting room while Griff was in the back getting patched up. "So I'd gone out for a Sprite. We didn't have any at the condo." (*We.* The word seemed deliberate, but Eric wasn't sure if she said it for Laura's sake or his.) Tracy hadn't known that Griff was under the chaos of bodies, hadn't known he was bearing the brunt of the violence, but she knew there was trouble. She slammed her brakes and jumped the curb on Station Street. She threw her door open and ran toward the fight, screaming for them to stop. Everyone scattered, then converged at the van, jumped inside and sped away. Everyone except the boy lying on his back on the ground. Everyone except Griff.

"I remembered the 800 number from the searches and the billboard," Tracy said.

"Thank you," Eric said. There was a dispiriting drawl in his voice. His palms were sweating.

"I've been meaning to cancel that number for weeks," Laura said, as if she were talking to herself. She seemed in a mild state of shock.

Eric wanted to take her hand, wanted to say, *Everything happens for a reason,* but he didn't trust the notion any more than he trusted himself. He didn't want her to feel his sweaty palms, didn't want Tracy to see him holding his wife's hand.

"Thank you," Laura said. "Thank you for stopping. Thank you for calling us."

"Anyone would have done the same thing," Tracy said. Her voice was consoling but still rasped, dry-sounding, from having yelled at the Teepee; Eric wanted to get her some water. She never met his eyes, but stared at her hands clasped in her lap. Eric had learned that she did this when she was gearing up to say something that scared her. Moments later, leaning toward Justin, Tracy said, "I'm sorry we're meeting under these circumstances, but I wanted to say how happy I am that you're home. I've wanted to make your acquaintance for years."

"Thanks," Justin said shyly. Aside from his time with Letty and Garcia, this was the first occasion Eric had seen his son interact with someone outside the house. And, despite Tracy's kindness, despite what she'd just done for Griff and the safe harbor she'd so often granted Eric, a current of sad anger passed through him. How long would Justin have to abide strangers approaching him, congratulating and complimenting him? How long would he feel their stares? Hear their whispers? Justin appeared unaffected, but Eric thought otherwise: He thought his son was already resigned to the fate of people always thinking they knew him, seeing his pain as an invitation. Justin looked around the empty waiting room. There was a television with a cartoon playing, posters bleached pale by the sun, a few crinkled and coverless magazines. The fluorescent lights turned the glass on the automatic doors to mirrors. Eric took care not to gaze on who was being reflected.

Laura said, "You mentioned you're in charge of the Shrimporee event?"

"For better or worse," Tracy said.

"We're so grateful, just so grateful," Laura said. "We thought he was in his room."

"Boys will be boys," Tracy said, smiling. Then, after a beat, she said, "If there's anything you'd want or not want as part of the celebration, just say the word."

"It's great that you're in charge," Eric said. "You're perfect."

"I know people who'd fight you on that, but the event should be nice, something we can all look back on happily," Tracy said. It was her version of goodbye. She gave Justin an awkward hug and shook his hand, then Eric's. Then Laura rose and embraced her. Eric couldn't watch. He turned to Justin—just then he wanted desperately to tell him Griff would be fine, to assure him that despite every hurt they'd experienced, things would work out—but his son's eyes were locked on the cartoon. Two UFOs were bobbing through a starry universe, racing to a lumpy purple planet; Eric wished he recognized the show, wished he could share something about it with Justin. Then the automatic door was sliding open with a pneumatic whoosh, and Tracy was walking briskly to her Volvo. The soggy night rolled into the room.

"What would we have done if she hadn't called?" Laura said after a while, sounding mystified. Eric could tell the words had been scrolling through her mind for some time. "What would've happened if whoever found him hadn't known who he was, hadn't known about the 800 line?"

"We got lucky, no question," Eric said. "It's a small world, and things could have been far worse."

"For some people," Justin said. He was still watching the cartoon.

"Do what, honey?" Laura said.

"It's a small world for some people," he said. "Not for everyone."

GRIFF SAID HE HAD BEEN TRYING TO STOP THEM FROM STEALING the coping. Eric believed this, but he also thought his son's account sounded incomplete. Laura agreed. They didn't push, didn't ask why he'd sneaked out or why he'd take on five or six bigger guys. They were terrified by what had happened—to Griff, of course, but also by what Justin had said. *It's a small world for some people.* Fear blunted anger. There was the brief obligatory talk of grounding Griff, which they'd done in the past, but what would it accomplish? As it was, he did little more than move between his bed and the living room couch, watching television and sipping soup and eating ice cream. What his demeanor recalled for Eric was the period, shortly after Justin first disappeared, when Griff, only nine at the time, started wetting the sheets. How he walked around listlessly while his sheets tumbled in the dryer.

Justin doted on Griff. He woke up earlier and let Rainbow in and out of Griff's room when she scratched at the door. Justin never mentioned anything else about what he'd said in the waiting room, but his attention to Griff seemed a kind of apology, an effort to strike his words from the record. Why wouldn't he view the world as smaller for other people? Wouldn't his life have been better if someone had recognized him sooner, if it had been harder for him to move beyond his parents' reach? Again, Eric thought of how Justin had been angry at them, how he had no choice but to believe they'd failed him and how they couldn't dispute it. So, then, maybe another reason he was doting on Griff was because he didn't trust them to take care of his younger brother. Through it all, Griff remained sullen. Eric couldn't tell if he was feeling embarrassed about having been beaten up or if his glumness was the result of whatever he wasn't telling them. It could've been a side effect of his pain medication. When Eric asked him what was wrong, Griff just said, "The coping was perfect. It was what made the pool worth skating."

Neither Eric nor Laura had heard from Tracy. The silence made him nervous, though he knew he should see it as a good thing. Laura wrote her a thank-you card, had everyone sign it, and went back through the volunteer records to find her address.

"They have two houses, one in Corpus and one here, at Villa Del Sol," Laura said.

"Is that right?" Eric said.

"Where should I send the card?"

"I'm sure either place will work," he said.

"I'll do Corpus," she said. "I bet they're spending more time there now."

Laura worked her shifts at the dry cleaner's, but arranged for someone to cover at Marine Lab through the weekend. Cecil brought over tamales, and showed Griff how to play double solitaire. Griff played the game with Justin a few times, both boys sitting on his bed, looking young. Eric taught his class on Monday, then again on Wednesday, and when he could break away from school and the house, he parked in the fill-sand lot and watched the Buford place. Nothing changed. No one emerged. With each passing hour, there was a slow constricting in his throat, like he'd been crawling through a tight tunnel and gotten stuck, his arms trapped under his body. He couldn't decide if he should try to push forward or inch backward, if he should call for help or save his breath. At any moment, it seemed the walls would collapse.

"SEE WHAT HAPPENS WHEN YOU PLAN TO BREAK UP WITH ME?" Fiona said. She was sitting cross-legged at the foot of Griff's bed. He didn't know how long she'd been there.

He thought it was late afternoon, but it might've been later. Or earlier. The tinfoiled windows kept time out. So did his pain pills. Fiona wore perfume, and even in the half dark, he could see she'd put on makeup. His mouth tasted dry, medicinal. He patted his hair down, worried it looked bad from sleep. His stitches burned.

"What time is it?" Griff asked.

"Time for you to understand I'm not a chick to trifle with."

"Are my parents home?"

"Your mom's with the dolphin and your dad took the truck to the shop. Justin called me over."

"Justin called you?"

"What I want to say is that I'm sorry you got your ass kicked, I really am, and I hope whoever did it gets syphilis, but I'm still pissed at you."

"I'm sorry," Griff said. And he was. He was suddenly shocked at how sorry he was.

"You're forgiven," Fiona said. "But I'm still pissed. I will be for a while. Get psyched."

Griff's eyes were adjusting to the dark. He could see that Fiona had brought two milk shakes. They sat on his desk, beading with sweat, straws already in the lids. The thought of her inserting the straws before she'd come into his room, that she'd taken such pains to keep from waking him, was shattering. And now that he'd seen the milk shakes, he could smell them, too. Chocolaty, cold. It was a summer scent, not from this summer or any of the recent ones, but a scent from when he was much younger. He watched Fiona. She was worrying a loose thread from his comforter.

"I wasn't going to break up with you," he said.

"Yes, you were," she said, tugging on the thread. "But it's okay. You've had a lot going on. Abducted brother returns, asshole pervert kidnapper goes free, first official girlfriend. It's a big year."

"And they stole the coping from the Teepee."

"And you got the shit beaten out of you. Like I said, you're absolved."

"But you're going to be mad for a long time," Griff said.

"I am," she said. She was rooting under the comforter for his foot. She brought it into her lap and started to massage his sole with her thumbs. She clasped her fingers over the arch of his foot, then lifted his leg and scooted closer and closer, until his toes reached her shirt, the underside of her breast. Her hands were warm, soft. She'd never done this before, and her touch was much gentler than he would have guessed, like she was rubbing a baby's feet, taking care not to pinch or tickle him.

"Why?" Griff said.

"Why what?"

"Why forgive me?"

"The same reason I'm going to be pissed for, like, years," she said. "Because, against all odds, I'm probably falling into some low-grade version of love with you."

"You are?"

"Unfortunately," she said, smiling. "And here's some breaking news: you love me, too."

"I do?"

"Clearly. Irrefutably. Immeasurably," she said.

"This is maybe the best day of my life," he said.

After a moment, Rainbow pawed at Griff's door from the hall-way and almost immediately Justin was snapping his fingers and calling her name, luring her away.

"Did it hurt when you were in the fight? Or when you got your stitches? Were you scared?"

"Yes," he said.

"Yes to which?"

"To all of them," he said.

"Good," she said, reaching for his other foot and bringing it into her lap. "Good, that's nice to hear."

HE KNEW HIS PARENTS DIDN'T BELIEVE HIM, AND PROBABLY JUS-tin didn't either, but the truth was he didn't remember what had happened. Not exactly. He remembered Baby Snot's accent and the force of everyone's weight; he remembered the older skater—Mark? Mike? Mick?—insulting Justin and half of the coping being gone and the woman with the dark hair taking him to the clinic. He remembered not wanting to bleed on her car's upholstery, remembered thinking it was the nicest car he'd ever ridden in, remembered apologizing to her. He remembered feeling like he owed everyone an apology. But there were things that didn't fit, too: He thought the woman, on the drive to the clinic, had called him Lobster. He thought she'd said, "Y'all just can't catch a break, can you?" And on the way home, with his parents and Justin in the car, his mother had said, "You're right. The world is a lot smaller for some people. That's a smart way to put it."

Days later, every part of his body still ached. Fiona and Justin tended to him, as did his parents, but he sensed that they—his parents—were being pulled in different directions. Griff didn't know what was happening with Dwight Buford or the lawyers or his father's students or the dolphin at Marine Lab. No one talked to him about anything other than how he was feeling and what he wanted to do or eat. Griff knew he shouldn't, but he reveled in their attention. A better person would have rallied and told them not to pamper him. He did the opposite. When Justin was around, he acted more dismal. With Fiona, he exaggerated his pain. *Stop milking it,* he told himself, but he never did.

On Thursday night, Justin said, "It was really about the coping?"

"What?"

"You took on a gang of thugs just because they were stealing the coping. It wasn't because of anything else? It didn't have anything to do with me?"

"The coping was unbelievable," Griff said. "And it wasn't a gang. It was just a few guys."

"I would have helped them pry it loose. I would have helped them carry it away. Skating doesn't mean anything to me anymore."

"You just need to get back into it," Griff said, hearing how false the words were. He'd known for a while that Justin wasn't a skater anymore, but he didn't want him to admit it.

"I told Dad I liked football now, but I was lying. I made it sound like I lived for it. I wanted him to think I had a hobby. It seemed important at the time."

"Football's cool," Griff said. He hated football. Then he said, "Do you want to play cards? Or go work in your room? We can try a different arrangement."

"I hate football and I hate my room."

"That's why you keep changing it."

"And that's why it always feels the same."

"You can have mine," Griff said. "We can trade."

"We'll see."

Griff expected Justin to leave then, but he stayed. He looked around the room, studied the torn-out skate magazine pages tacked to the wall, the print of the potato car he'd done years before.

"Fiona said she loves me," Griff said. "She said you called her to come visit."

"Both of those are true."

"I thought you wanted me to break up with her."

"No, I told you *how* to break up with her and not be a pussy," Justin said. "I think she's a cool girl."

"You called her? You knew her number?"

"We went to school together, remember? I just looked her up in the junior high directory. I didn't want you to be alone."

"I'm not alone. You're here. We've hung out more in the last week than we have since you've been back."

"Trust me," Justin said, still looking at the skate photos, "you're alone. We all are."

ACROSS THE LAGUNA MADRE, CECIL WAS PASSING THE BUFORD house for the fifth or sixth time. He'd seen Eric's truck parked in the fill-sand lot after he'd departed the ferry, and he'd been driving in long loops for the better part of an hour. State Highway 361 was four lanes. Cecil drove a few miles to the south, then hooked a U-turn, passed the Buford house and Eric, then turned around to start again. On each pass, he hoped Eric would have driven away, but he stayed put. It was disappointing. Cecil hadn't ventured out on 361 since he'd gone into Flour Bluff, which just now struck him as strange. A betting man would have pegged Cecil as the one watching the property with an eye toward reprisal. Maybe he'd been staving himself off. Maybe he'd known better than to tempt himself, than to put Dwight Buford within reach. Even now, when he had other business to tend to, when the day was bright and people were out and his son was peering through his binoculars, Cecil could feel the draw.

He knew Buford had nothing to do with what happened to Griff, but nonetheless he held him responsible. It made Cecil feel old again, the full weight of his sixty-seven years bearing down. He was tired, just so tired, and he was tired of being tired. That was something else he blamed on Dwight Buford, the deep fatigue in his bones, the steady leaching at his marrow.

The sun fired off windshields. Loose curls of sand eddied on the pavement between the cars and then dispersed. The shoulders of the road sloped steeply, lowering into the scrub on the east and toward the narrow beach on the west. Cecil had his windows down. The air smelled of the dry, brittle seaweed strewn about the shore, of creosote and salt water. His shirt was damp between his back and the bench seat; the floorboards vibrated. He was thinking only about his son, how unfortunate the whole business was, how rotten and cruel, and how he'd soon be yoked to something else. For days Cecil had been trying to figure a different path out, some way not to involve Eric, but everything led back to where he was now.

When he came upon the fill-sand lot again, he steered the truck into the entrance. He slowed but never stopped. Eric saw him immediately; his expression went flat with humiliation, like a child caught stealing. Cecil raised his chin—*follow me*—and eased back onto the road. Sand kicked up behind his wheels and his son merged into traffic behind him, and like that, it had started.

HIS MOTHER HAD COME INTO HIS ROOM UNDER THE PRETENSE of putting away clothes, but Griff knew she wanted to talk. And as she placed his folded T-shirts in his drawer, saying that what he'd been wearing the night of the fight had been sent to the main dry-cleaning plant in hopes of getting the bloodstains out, he realized he'd been expecting her all along. He was happy to see her, almost relieved. She took the hem of her shirt, stood on her toes, and tried to wipe something off the top of his dresser.

"Fiona brings milk shakes over. We always forget to use coasters," he said.

"She's a sweet girl," Laura said. "She and Justin have really been looking after you."

"I feel guilty."

"Why in the world should you feel guilty?"

"I feel like they'd rather be doing something else."

"They wouldn't, trust me," his mother said. She smoothed his comforter and sat at the foot of the bed, Fiona's spot. "Justin's glad not to be the center of attention for once. You're doing him a favor."

"I'll try to get beat up more often."

"That won't be necessary," she said. Some of her hair came loose from her ponytail and hung around her face. "A mother's heart can only take so much."

"Maybe I should take karate."

"I'd rather you never leave the house. I'd rather cover you in bubble wrap."

Rainbow ambled into the room, glanced at Griff and his mother, then circled herself and lay down with a sigh.

His mother said, "How does he seem to you? Justin, I mean."

"Lonesome," Griff said. It wasn't a word he could remember ever having used.

"There's a lot of that going around. I think we've all caught the lonesome bug," she said. Then, after a moment: "You know, honey, if you ever want to talk with Letty or anyone else, if you ever feel the need to sort through your feelings with someone, we can arrange it right away."

"Sure," he said. "Okay."

"We know this is as hard for you as it is for anyone," she said.

What Griff remembered just then was how Baby Snot had dropped his accent and urged him to leave, how he'd seemed kind for a moment. He remembered how Mike had called him *the cocksucker's brother,* how Tracy Robichaud had said his family couldn't catch a break. All of this somehow proved his mother's point: He could see how lonesome everyone was.

Then Griff said, "Justin and I had a fight. That morning."

"That morning?"

"I was a jerk. Sometimes I think that if we hadn't argued, none of this would have happened."

"We all feel that way, honey. We each wish we'd done something differently. We're just being hard on oursel—"

"He'd put salt in my Coke," Griff said. "We were in the kitchen and I went to get something from my room. When I came back and took a drink, I gagged. He'd poured the whole salt shaker into the can. I got really mad, and we had a fight, and I wouldn't let him apologize. So he left and then it happened."

Laura's heart stopped. For a second, maybe two. She felt a tender but intense pain when it started again. If she had believed she could run out of the room without traumatizing her son, if she could make it into the backyard or out to her car without going to pieces in front of Justin—he was on the couch with Sasha, watching a football analysis show—she would have already bolted. But she was rooted to the bed, trying to stay composed, trying to keep herself from screaming or doubling over or slamming her head against the wall. She worried she'd vomit on his comforter, worried he'd assume her reaction meant she thought he *was* to blame. Say something, she thought. Tell him you love him or it's not his fault. Tell him he's being silly. But she couldn't open her mouth. She'd always suspected she was to blame for what had happened with Justin, and now she had proof.

The salt prank was hers. The week before Justin went missing, she'd taken him to the Castaway Café. Eric was off somewhere with Griff—she couldn't remember where. Justin had gone to the men's room and suddenly she had the idea to empty the salt shaker into his Coke. It wasn't something she'd done before, nor would anyone have expected it of her. Eric liked practical jokes, and he was cultivating that in the boys, but she'd never understood the appeal. She had always felt left out. When he came back and took a drink—how she had to fight not to smirk, not to cackle! How all at once she knew what she'd been missing all those humorless years!—he spit out a mouthful and then they were both laughing so hard they started to cry. She'd never felt closer to him, never felt more a part of a family, never felt more like a mother. A *good* mother. She'd told the detectives about the incident time and again, and Eric, too. He liked the joke, and seemed proud of her for making it. Over the years, she'd thought to do it again, to Eric, to Griff; she'd even once considered pulling it on Cecil, but no. It was hers and Justin's, theirs alone, and thinking of it now, in Griff's dark room, with her poor son waiting for her to speak, she realized she'd been waiting to ask Justin if he remembered the prank, if maybe he'd thought about it while he was in Corpus, if it had been a source of comfort for him. For her, it had been both a comfort and a torment. Now it was the noose with which she wanted to hang herself.

"Mom?" Griff said. "Mom, are you okay?"

"Of course."

"I think you're crying," he said, as if he was alerting her to a nosebleed.

"I just don't want you to blame yourself. That's something that's really important to me."

"Okay," he said. "I won't."

"Promise?"

"It's like you said, we're all just looking for—"

"I want you to hear me very clearly, okay? Listen to your mother, okay?"

"Okay."

"There's one person at fault here. There's one person who's responsible for hurting Justin, and it's not you."

"It's Dwight Buford," Griff said.

"It's just not you," she said. "That's what you have to understand. It was never you."

THE NEXT MORNING, ERIC SLIPPED OUT OF THE HOUSE TO WATER the backyard. It was just something to do. He'd hardly gotten any rest the night before, waking for hours at a stretch in the dark, unable to shut down his thoughts long enough to sink back into sleep. He was worn out now, more from his efforts to will sleep than a lack of it, but an exhausted calm had descended. A feeling like surrender. It was, he imagined, the kind of resignation that someone on death row would feel just before the needle broke the skin, before the poison washed into your veins.

A few cowbirds lined the fence. An iridescent rainbow in the spray of the hose, the wet grass glistening in the early sun, as if bejeweled. The palm tree the governor's office had sent looked sturdy and good; Eric could easily imagine it growing to ten or fifteen feet in the future, casting a long, top-heavy shadow against the house. What he couldn't predict was who'd be living here then. Maybe they would, or maybe just Laura and the boys, or maybe a family of strangers. He wasn't upset thinking this, not exactly, but curious in a detached way. It approached nostalgia, as if he were considering a visit to a place where he'd once lived. The sky was high, not yet its full color. A few contrails from jets looked recent and close, like they were falling toward the earth, slow as feathers.

He didn't hear Laura come out. Nor did she say anything when she stood beside him on the patio. She just offered him a cup of coffee. He wasn't surprised or disappointed to see her there—he thought she'd been awake most of the night, too, though neither tried to engage the other—but just accepted her presence as a given. Of course she would come out this morning. She was his wife, the mother of his two boys. The coffee steamed. It was too hot to drink, so he kinked the hose and dribbled some cool water into her mug, then his. Then he opened up the hose again and placed his thumb over the nozzle to arc water into the far part of the yard. The sungrayed boards on the fence turned a pleasing brown when the water hit. Until they dried, they would look new.

"Couldn't sleep?" Eric said.

"I talked with Griff yesterday."

"How's he doing?"

"He said Justin feels lonesome."

"Lonesome."

"His word," she said.

Eric pivoted away from Laura to wet down the other side of the yard. He took care not to let any of the water spray the boys' windows. He didn't want to risk waking them. Then, before he thought better of it, before he realized he'd been marshaling his nerve to speak the words all night, he said, "I've been watching the Buford house."

"The Buford house."

"Ever since he made bail," he said. "I park a little ways away. I've been telling you I was at school or running errands, but I've been watching their house. I'm sorry to have to admit that."

"You've seen him?"

"Not even once," he said. "I was convincing myself he wasn't there, but yesterday my father came and found me. I guess Mayne told him what I was doing. I guess he'd noticed me."

"You're lucky he didn't call the cops."

"I know," Eric said.

"You could've gotten arrested."

"Mayne wants to cut a deal. He wants me to stop parking out there and to let him take his wife and Dwight out on the water the day of the Shrimporee."

"The Shrimporee that's coming up? The one that's hardly three weeks away?"

"In exchange, he thinks he can get Dwight to change his plea."

"Cecil's been negotiating with him? This doesn't make sense to me," she said. She turned and took a few distracted steps toward the house, then walked along the fence and stood near the edge of the yard with the new distance between them. She started crying a little. She said, "What happens after they have their lovely day on the water and he doesn't plead guilty?"

Eric fanned the water over the grass. He said, "I don't think we can take a trial. Garcia said Buford's lawyer could tie this up for years with delays. I called him yesterday to ask his advice."

"Why am I not part of any of these conversations? Conversations about my son's life."

"Our son," he said.

"Why am I just hearing about this now?"

"I called from my father's, just to ask if what Mayne was proposing would even work. If he could still change his plea. He can."

"So it's decided? It's a done deal? They get to have their time on the water? A nice day celebrating what he's getting away with? What he did to Justin? How he hurt *our* son?"

"Cecil called him last night."

"Meaning?"

"Meaning yes. Meaning it's a done deal."

"None of this adds up," she said. She ran her fingers through her hair, crossed her arms, and she did, at that moment, seem more confused than angry. Quietly, she said, "I was coming outside to bring you coffee and to tell you what Griff had said and—"

"Cecil gave me a gun."

"He what?"

"It's a pistol he saw me looking at in Loan Star a while back. He gave it to me yesterday. It's in our truck now."

"You were looking at guns? I don't know who I'm talking to right now. I don't know what language you're speaking."

"Mayne wants to push off before sunrise that day. He wants to leave before people start gathering for the Shrimporee that morning," he said. "We'll be there before they are."

"Who's we?"

"Me and my father."

"And then what?" she asked.

"Then we drive to Mexico and drop him off. We tell him he's lost his American citizenship."

"Where does the gun come in?"

"To persuade him to get in the car."

"Eric," she said, but didn't go on. Then she tried again, saying, "I don't know . . . This doesn't seem . . ." But what could she say? The only sound was the water pushing through the hose and pattering on the grass. The morning came up quickly, the sky filling with color that overtook the jet contrails. *Lonesome,* Eric thought. It seemed another failure, something else he needed to make right. He was already off to a poor start. His father had insisted that Eric not tell Laura, and he'd vowed he wouldn't, but he wanted her to know what he was willing to do. *This is who I am,* he wanted to say. *Remember me like this.* He'd already said too much, though. He thought she might say something, or maybe just take his hand and lay her head on his shoulder until he finished watering the yard. She didn't. He couldn't hear or see what she was doing. His back was still to her. She might have retreated into the house, leaving as silently as she had come. To his mind, he was already alone.

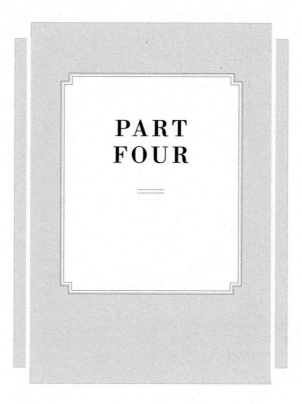

PART
FOUR

27

THE DAY BEFORE THE BODY WAS RECOVERED IN THE CORPUS Christi ship channel, the residents of Southport were scrambling to prepare for the Shrimporee. This was the first Friday in September. Blankets of heat, packed tight with humidity, lay over the town. Steam wafted from the still-damp asphalt. A ragged unnamed tropical depression had washed ashore earlier that week, and with it came days of rain. The storms were long and gray, messy at times, and loud, too, blurring and battering when wind got behind them. Station Street flooded for a few hours. Fences fell, and trees, snapping, exposed the blond wood inside the trunks, a color so raw it looked obscene. Tides rose. Ferry service was intermittent, then entirely suspended until the weather slacked off. A few boats in the marina got knocked around, bashed into the docks; one took on water and capsized. Lightning struck a tree out on the blacktop highway, and a driver swerved off the road, water sluicing and barreling over the car before it wound up in the ditch. The area needed the rain—lake levels were down and the fields were parched and the temperatures had been spiking day after day—but the weather had also halted the considerable work required before the mayor could ring the Shrimporee bell.

Now, on that boiling Friday, men were hustling to rig up the Ferris wheel and smaller carnival rides, to assemble the dunking booth and hoist the stage for the musicians, beauty pageant, and shrimp-eating contest, and to erect the remaining sixty-odd vendor booths. They'd started early, laboring under generator-powered lights long before birds began calling for morning. They didn't break for lunch, but ate sandwiches and tacos between hammer swings. They rubbed handfuls of crushed ice on the back of their necks, the inside of their elbows, and over their sun-ruddied faces. They soaked bandannas in thermos water, then tied them around their heads. They did everything they could to push through, to stand against the lost time.

When the storm had been at its worst, when it stalled just off-shore and whipped the coast with one gritty band of rain after an-other, there was talk of scrapping the Shrimporee for the first time in four decades. (The festival was founded by the Chamber of Commerce and the Fraternal Order of Eagles to commemorate South-port's centennial and to generate revenue for local merchants. That the Shrimporee had never been canceled was a point of pride in the community, a testament to its collective resolve.) But as the weather abated, talk turned to expediting the preparations. The Chamber called for volunteers—men with trucks and trailer hitches, bakers and electricians, anyone who was willing to sweep waterlogged debris from downtown sidewalks. Restaurants and families with kitchen space were asked to boil pots of shrimp for jambalaya and étouffée. Children were invited to blow up as many balloons as they could. Church groups pitched in, and members of the Coast Guard and VFW, the high school football team and booster club and 4-H club. By lunchtime on Friday, the prettiest stretch of Station was being cordoned off and lined with streamers and bunting and the children's balloons. The high school band rehearsed in the mucky baseball field. The Junior League put finishing touches on parade floats; the Castaway Coffee Club brought coffee and ko-laches to the volunteers. Everyone watched the sky and the bay—

now just smudged mirrors of each other—and tried to divine their future from the scroll of clouds.

Since his youth, Eric had associated the festival with the end of summer and the beginning of the school year, which always started the following week. It was a threshold. A line of demarcation. He always felt a little older on the other side of it, as if what had come before was suddenly unreachable. This year's festival was also imbued with a kind of providence. If it happened, if the weather stayed clear and the town could put the pieces together by late this evening, then he could believe that his father's plan would work. That it was just. That it was not simply right, but solely and absolutely right, that there were no other options. If the Shrimporee fell apart because some remnant of the storm came ashore or workers couldn't complete the job in such torpid heat, then he'd take it as a sign that the plan should be aborted and Dwight Buford should stand trial. Whether he hoped the festival would be canceled changed every half hour. Every fifteen minutes. Every five.

Laura had been distant and surly with him since they'd talked on the patio. With the boys, she was the opposite; she seemed relaxed, taking Griff shopping for school clothes and mapping out Justin's private studies. Having something to work toward had always grounded and invigorated her. For weeks she'd been wearing her dolphin pendant, earrings, and bangles that clacked together as she watered the remaining plants. She carried herself like a woman who'd gotten a raise, but when Eric tried to engage her, her affect flattened out. She went silent. Last week, she'd had coffee at the Castaway Café with Tracy Robichaud to discuss plans for the Shrimporee, but with Eric she would relay only that Justin's event would be short and sweet. Her reticence scared Eric, left him feeling vulnerable and paranoid. Their longest exchange had been her saying she didn't want him keeping the gun in the truck. She'd been adamant, confoundingly so. "Put it in the garage or under the house or in your sock drawer, I don't care, just get it out of the truck," she said. They were cleaning up after supper one night, and although he'd promised to remove the pistol after the boys went to bed, she wasn't satisfied. She said, "Now, please." So he'd wrapped it in an old bath towel and shoved it behind his dress boots high in the closet.

She didn't approve or understand, but he hoped she would eventually forgive him. Or he hoped she would eventually relent enough to see the decision from the perspective he was trying to convince himself was his. He had an opportunity to make their lives better, to restore some semblance of comfort and safety, an opportunity to prove—to his family and to himself—how much he longed for their happiness and what he was willing to sacrifice to ensure it. Had she given him the chance at any point in the past three weeks, he would have told her what had been going through his mind lately, the refrain of Texan soldiers leaving their families to fight at the Alamo: It's better for a son to grow up in a country without a father than to grow up with a father and no country. He wanted Laura to perceive his fear and watch him press on, to watch him carry it with him. So last night, when she returned from a late shift at Marine Lab, when the house was loud with the last of the rain on the roof and wind slammed against the siding, and she had, without a word, straddled Eric, he was stunned. And worried. Worried that his reaction should be less grateful, less shocked. Worried that he was being duped in some way. Worried, finally, that what had happened with Tracy would happen again, that his mind would fill with thoughts of Justin and Dwight Buford and guilt, and his body would fail, but soon Laura was guiding him inside her, and he could only hear their breathing and the storm. Her skin tasted of salt water and smelled of rain, of the violent clouds that had opened over her.

"You don't have to do it," she said, her head on his chest.

"I should've done it as soon as he was released," he said. "It should already be over."

Justin had been doing well with his driving. Parallel parking, driving over the Harbor Bridge, the rules-of-the-road quizzes—nothing fazed him anymore. He'd also settled on a layout for his room, a layout that seemed to Eric very similar, if not identical, to the original. His sleep schedule was starting to even out. Lonesomeness still surrounded him like a moat.

Griff's stitches had dissolved the week before, and he seemed more himself. Or he seemed himself, but a little older and more jaded, as if he'd emerged from a long sleep whose dreams had hardened him. His younger son, looming larger. Last Monday, Eric had peeked into Griff's room and glimpsed him holding Sasha, letting the snake convey from one hand to the next, and though he wasn't as confident as Justin, he no longer looked afraid. Curious, Eric thought. He looked curious. Then, on Wednesday night, when they were all playing a board game Fiona had brought over and lightning was scratching the sky and a clap of thunder rattled the windows and shook the house with such force that the girl jumped in her seat, Griff had impulsively reached for her hand to comfort her. There'd been no hesitation, no concern for who would see or what they'd think. Once the thunder had passed, he brought her wrist to his lips and kissed her pale skin. Eric and Laura and Justin exchanged quick, saucer-eyed glances—each of them thinking, *Well, look at that*—and they were bound furtively together by the sweet surprise of it all.

That Friday, the last day of summer school, Eric dismissed his students early. They wanted to link up with their parents and friends pitching in with the Shrimporee preparations. Eric usually made an end-of-the-term speech, encouraging them to pay attention to history as they moved into the future, but today he was distracted, thinking about the pistol on the top shelf of his bedroom closet. Thinking of all that it presaged, all that it might bring to bear by tomorrow. So he simply told the students to enjoy the Shrimporee and to get ready for the new school year. They left the room single file, hooting and hollering and high-fiving him. A few of the more sentimental students hugged him. As if they were sending him off to war.

When Eric got home, Griff was downing a glass of cranberry juice in the kitchen. He and his brother had spent the morning working in the yard, collecting fallen branches, while Laura went grocery shopping. "She wanted to go before the Shrimporee to avoid the lines," Griff said, rinsing out his glass. "Now she's taking a nap. Justin is, too."

"What say we take a drive?" Eric said. The idea hadn't occurred to him before that moment, and yet now he wanted it more than anything.

"Am I in trouble?"

"Of course not," Eric said. "We just haven't spent much time together lately."

"Oh," Griff said. "Okay, sure, yeah."

In the truck, Griff asked if they could go to the Teepee pool. He wanted to see if the rest of the coping was gone. To avoid the Shrimporee detours and stalled traffic, they tacked through back streets strewn with branches and toppled garbage cans. Eric watched for Mayne's Mercedes and Tracy's Volvo, and he tried to remember the last time he'd ridden with just Griff in the truck. He seemed to take up more space in the cab. He also seemed diffident, like he still thought the drive would end with his father accusing him of something, grounding him. The streets got worse closer to the water. On Beechwood, one of the snapped trees cut off the route completely, so Eric had to twist and look through the rear window as he reversed down the block. He turned onto Mary Street with its canopy of mesquite that he'd always loved, then onto Jackson and eventually Coral Road.

"Papaw used to like to drive around after storms, looking at what had gotten hit and what had been left untouched," Eric said. "My mother called those drives 'expeditions.' 'We're going on one of Daddy's expeditions,' she'd say. He liked to go through people's garbage, too. If he saw something he could use, he'd take it."

"That's probably why he works at Loan Star. Because it's full of things people don't want anymore."

"I bet you're right," Eric said. "I bet you're absolutely right."

They curved onto Sand Dollar Street, which ran parallel to Station. People were in the soggy yards, clearing debris.

Eric said, "The Shrimporee used to make me sad. I used to think of it as the official end of summer."

"I hope they have the rubber duck race again this year."

At the Teepee, Griff bounded from the truck before Eric had even shifted into park. Eric hadn't set foot on the Teepee grounds since it had been shut down. He remembered how the boys used to like to visit the place, how they'd chase each other around making Indian noises. The motel had been built shortly before he and Laura started dating; they'd stayed here one night, just as a goof. Now most of the teepees lay in chunks. Everything dusty, everything broken to pieces. Weeds grew through the seams in the cement, bearded the bottoms of the few teepees still standing.

The pool was half-full of brown water. A layer of chalky dust and yellow pollen filmed the surface, like powdered sugar. The walls were tagged with graffiti—some of it in bubble letters, some in cryptic single-line flourishes, some of it crude and crudely painted. He could read the words STEAM and EYE LEVEL and SKATE OR DIE, DIE, DIE, MY DARLING! There was an image of a rat with X's for eyes, and two large spheres that were either targets or breasts. A thin leafy mesquite branch floated on the surface, along with a couple of Styrofoam cups and a plastic bag, a palm frond that looked like a ruined fan. Eric found everything about the property depressing, not least the knowledge that it was where Griff had spent so much time in the last few years. It seemed exactly the kind of place where a boy would get pummeled. He wanted to leave, to forbid Griff from ever coming back.

Griff looked dejected, walking the perimeter of the pool. He reminded Eric of a lifeguard. "It's gone," he said. "They must have come back for the rest."

"The coping, you mean?"

"They took everything."

"Once the trial is over, we'll take a trip somewhere," Eric said. "You and your brother can pick the best place to skate in the country and we'll make it a vacation. We could all use a break."

Griff came around the shallow end of the pool. The sounds of the high school band practicing were in the air, a far-off cacophony of horns and drums.

"The bowl will still be skateable once it drains, but not like before. I probably won't come here again. It would just make me sad."

"I'm sorry, bud," Eric said.

Griff picked up a few rocks from the ground, inspected them, then lobbed one into the deep end. The plunk sent waves of concentric circles through the pool, small shivering ripples that folded back on themselves upon reaching the cement walls. Then he threw another rock, then another and another. The chalky skim dispersed into tiny concentrated islands that floated away from where the rocks hit, as if in retreat, and collected around the palm frond, the cups and mesquite branch. It made Eric want to toss rocks into the water as well, to start up some kind of game with Griff.

"Did you get in a lot of fights when you were a kid?" Griff asked.

"A few," Eric lied. "Not too many."

Actually, he'd been in only one fight, an awkward affair in junior high. There were more palms than fists, more taunts than blows, a lot of wrestling and very little pain. At one point, the other boy, Robbie Kuykendall, had taken off his shoes and thrown them at him. Eric had spent his life avoiding trouble, taking the high road, turning the other cheek. Not because it was the right thing to do, but because he was afraid. He'd long hoped no one recognized that about him. Even now, he'd lied to his son to throw him off his father's cowardly scent.

"They recognized me," Griff said. "They knew me. They were taking the coping, too, but one guy started saying these ugly things. About Justin, you know? They knew I was his brother, knew what happened."

"And that's why it started? You were trying to defend him?"

"It would've happened anyway," Griff said. "They were wasted."

"Well, I think—"

"I guess it's always going to be like that. With people recognizing him, saying things."

"It sounds like they were looking to stir something up. Not everyone's like that. Most people won't be," Eric said. It was a relief, a shock, to sound calm and sensible. To hear what Griff had endured was to feel small and inconsequential. His throat went stiff. He glimpsed a future where his sons, and Laura, and certainly Eric himself, were assailed by the past, and he was powerless in the face of it. The threat was brutal, but his powerlessness was worse; it was, he saw and then fought not to see, what he'd been staving off for four years, the sense that his best efforts would never be enough. He could protect none of them.

"Okay," Griff said.

"And once this all dies down," Eric said, hating the sound of his voice, the accent creeping in, the lie he was forming, "people will see him for who he is, not what happened to him. People have short memories. Trust me, I teach history."

Griff threw his last rock and dusted off his hands. He milled around the pool, kicked a long tube of beer cans bound together with duct tape. He said, "Don't tell, okay? Don't tell Mom or Justin. I don't want him to think people are talking about him, even though they are."

"I won't, bud," Eric said. "But next time, just let them say whatever they need to say and get out of there."

"You think there'll be a next time?"

Eric thought of Griff starting school the following week, thought of potential fights in the locker room or hallway, more trips to the emergency clinic. He said, "I just want you to know it's okay to walk away."

Griff was staring at the pool. He said, "Now that the coping's gone, I keep thinking of all these tricks I want to try, of everything I could've done here."

"You've got a good heart. Whatever happens, I want you to know that. You've got a good, good heart."

"Mom said something like that, too."

"We're your parents and we love you. And I'm just glad we get to spend some time together."

"We'll probably spend more time together now," Griff said. "There's nowhere to skate."

He was making a joke, trying to pardon his father. It made Eric want to say how sorry he was that he'd never come here to watch Griff ride. The heat cleaved to his skin and the air smelled of the stagnant water. Traffic was picking up, workers and volunteers arriving at the Shrimporee. There was the occasional whine of a circular saw in the distance. The marching band was still playing, struggling through a fight song that swelled and swelled and swelled but ultimately fell apart.

28

After Eric and Griff came home, Laura claimed to have forgotten a couple of items at the store and headed out again. It was another lie. She passed the pawnshop, but there were cars in the parking lot, so she went out to H-E-B and picked up a loaf of potato bread and a jug of laundry detergent. They were the first things that came to mind. When she swung back out onto Station Street, the only cars in front of Loan Star were the pawned Cadillac and a customer's beat-up hatchback, so she steered around to the rear of the shop and parked beside Cecil's truck.

She stayed behind the wheel, letting the air conditioner blow against her, hoping the hatchback would leave soon, hoping it wouldn't. The sun bore down, bright and lilting, and she closed her eyes in the heat. She hadn't slept the night before or this morning, and she knew she wouldn't sleep until after the Shrimporee at the earliest. Her hands had been trembling for hours, something she fully noticed only now that they had stopped. She longed for rest. The idea of closing herself in her darkened bedroom, of shutting her eyes under the ceiling fan, held an almost primal allure. And yet she knew the allure was a dead end. When she'd tried to take a nap after her first trip to the store, she'd just lain on top of the comforter thinking about the day ahead. After she'd said what she needed to say to Cecil, she was due to drive Justin into Corpus for his session with Letty. Then, tonight, they'd eat together as a family. Even if the meal was just a sack of burgers and fries, it seemed important that the four of them sit together at the table. After supper, Cecil would stop by, claiming to need Eric's help with something, and the two of them would go to the marina and ambush the Bufords. Then Laura would stay up all night, awaiting word. So this was her opportunity to rest, to breathe before whatever happened next happened. The knots in her muscles and mind loosened, lowering her into a soft pit that could become sleep. The ease with which she relaxed surprised her. Last night, after she and Eric made love, she could hardly close her eyes. She had, in fact, climbed on top of him hoping it would sate her, calm her, exhaust her. But, no. All night and all morning, she felt like she was being chased.

And yet, even in the last few hours, even with the Shrimporee looming, there had been short stretches of time when Dwight Buford wasn't foremost in her mind. Instead, she thought of Griff, of the scar that would surely form along his hairline and of what the coming school year might hold for him. She thought of Justin, how he worked so hard on his room, how he loved to drive, like every other teenager in the world. And certainly, she thought of Eric. Of how stoic he'd been these last few weeks, how he seemed to strut from time to time, his chest out and his shoulders back. If he found out she'd come to visit his father, he'd be mortified. Even with his newfound stoicism, Laura saw him as a child. He was a boy at the top of a high dive who couldn't bring himself to jump, a boy who'd stay up there until night fell and he could descend the ladder in the dark. No, he wasn't brave or strong, but now he was desperate enough, scared enough, so beside and beyond himself, that he was preparing to do what she knew he couldn't. She pitied him. She wanted to slap him across the face to wake him up, for he seemed to have dreamed himself into a life that didn't exist. And yet she couldn't recall a time when she'd loved him more. She hated how cold she'd been these last few weeks, how she wouldn't allow herself to relent. Another reason she'd pulled into him last night was to apologize. It seemed possible that it would be their last night together and she wanted him to remember that despite everything, he'd once had a wife who loved him.

Inevitably, thoughts of Dwight Buford would return. She'd start to sweat and shiver. Her gut churned with doubt, with guilty relief. She saw him getting into a car before dawn, riding silently toward the water that his father so badly wanted for him and his mother. Because of the storm, she saw skies dark and ugly and sagging with rain. She smelled the dampness in their car. He rode in the backseat without speaking, his reflection uncommonly large on the window, a distortion of slack cheeks and pale skin and tired, sallow eyes. They passed buildings and houses and signs that had stood there for decades, but everyone in the car, knowing their lives were on the cusp of change, saw them as if for the first time. The poor ruined woman in the passenger seat would have wanted to speak, but instead she just lay her head against the window, her mind riddled with the hollows left in the absence of hope.

Behind Loan Star, Laura's hands were shaking again. She clicked the radio on, hoping to hear something calming, but the deejays were just bantering about the Shrimporee. She got out of the car quickly and crossed the parking lot as if pursued by a wasp. Head down, no looking back. The hatchback and Cadillac were still there. Inside, Cecil was helping a customer, a woman wearing sunglasses and deliberating over a diamond-studded tennis bracelet. The air in the shop fluttered with all of the fans, and it smelled of Windex, as if Cecil had recently wiped down the display cases. A security camera hung from the ceiling. Laura knew it hadn't worked in years, a fact that Cecil had always bragged about, as if duping a potential thief trumped catching an actual one. Mismatched merchandise lined the long metal shelves. It saddened her, as usual. When she looked at what had been pawned, she was always bracing against an encroaching melancholy. It had been that way since the first time

Eric brought her here to meet his father. Seeing the necklaces and power tools—even seeing the guns and knives—that had once meant something to their former owners stymied her. What would it take, she wondered, for someone to give up that pretty silver tea set? The mounted javelina head? She couldn't stop herself from scanning the displays for items she recognized, rings she'd seen on her customers' fingers or paintings that had once hung in acquaintances' homes. Before, she'd always worried she'd recognize someone coming in to hock something, worried she'd see someone she knew reduced to the lowest possible point. Now she worried someone would recognize her.

"It looks dull. I'm not sure it'll clean up," the woman considering the tennis bracelet was saying to Cecil.

"Could be that you're still wearing your sunglasses," he said.

"Oh, right," she said, humorless. "What's the least you'll take?"

"I can't go any lower," Cecil said. "I've got that much in it. My partner paid more than he should have."

"Ivan," she said. "We see him at the Black Diamond. He likes tequila shots and married women."

"Those sound like hobbies of his," Cecil said.

"Can you hold it for me? I get paid next Friday."

"Layaway's ten percent down."

"Sometimes Ivan works deals with me," the woman said quietly, coquettishly. "I've seen the couch in the office a couple of times."

"He works Monday," Cecil said. "We're closed this weekend for Shrimporee."

She handed the bracelet back to Cecil. She lingered for a minute, hovered over the jewelry cases like an inspector. Laura thought the woman was watching her from behind the sunglasses, so she turned her back and studied a mother-of-pearl accordion on the shelf. She made her way to the front of the shop, passing fans that blew strands of her hair into her face. When the woman left, the bells on the door chimed. Laura watched her get into the hatchback. She situated herself behind the wheel, turning on the air and lighting a cigarette, then finally reversed out of the parking spot and pulled onto Station Street. Once the car was out of view, Laura flipped the sign in Loan Star's door so that it read CLOSED.

Cecil said, "Is this a stickup?"

Laura stood gazing into the parking lot, feeling the heat magnified through the glass. She wanted to close her eyes again. She could have fallen asleep right there. Cars passed on Station, and though she feared each one would turn in to the driveway, none did. The sun banked off the Cadillac's chrome. The arrow marquee still read HE'S BACK. Cecil must have taken the sign in before the storm, otherwise the letters wouldn't have survived. He was a practical, willful man, and just then she felt such affection for him that she wanted to spin on her heel and run to embrace him, as if he were her own father.

She didn't move. For a moment she thought she might faint. The world seemed to flicker. She said, "I love Eric."

"Beg pardon?"

"Your son. I love him."

"I'm pleased to hear it," Cecil said. "He's mighty partial to you, too."

"He's made mistakes, but who hasn't. He's done the best he could."

"Everyone has."

"He thinks he can hold everything inside, but he can't. He doesn't have a poker face."

"Laura," Cecil said, "if you'll say what's on your mind, I'll do my levelheaded best not to miss it."

"He's not built for what you're having him do. It's too much. I'm here to ask you to call it off."

"I see," Cecil said.

"The fact that I'm here proves he can't hold in what he ought to."

"Whatever he's told you, he told you because you're his wife, because you're Justin's mother."

"He shouldn't have," she said.

"We can agree on that," Cecil said.

"What happens when y'all show up and Mayne's got a body-guard with him?"

"A bodyguard? I think he'd more likely bring the Easter rabbit."

"Or a fleet of cops? What happens when something goes wrong and you can't go through with it? The two of you'll wind up in jail for attempted murder. Or kidnapping? Wouldn't that be something to read about in the paper."

"I needed him to ease up on watching the house. He wasn't doing anyone any favors out there."

"So tell him to stop," Laura said. "Tell him he's being careless. Tell him to go home."

"Mayne put something on the table at a fair price. It's no different than when someone pawns a television."

"And what does that offer have to do with tonight's ambush?"

A flatbed truck with a load of lumber jostled toward the marina, then another and another.

Laura said, "I don't deserve the blue ribbon for being a wife. Not even close. The same goes for being a mother. But I'm trying. I'm putting one foot in front of the other."

"So is Eric. He's looking for a road out of this. He's looking to do right by his boy."

"He is, or you are?" she said. Her hands were shaking again. She crossed her arms, curled her fingers into fists.

Cecil made no response other than to find a key on his key ring and lock the jewelry case.

"I'm sorry. I didn't mean that," Laura said. "I didn't sleep last night. The storm, I guess."

"It was a gully washer. What we used to call a toad-strangling rain. The farmers'll be happy."

"Can't you let it play out in court?" she said. "We're so close to an end we can all live with. I just keep thinking of everything that could go wrong."

"And I suspect Eric's thinking of everything that could go right."

That his father knew him as well as she did, knew of his cavalier optimism, was a comfort. There had certainly been times when she wished Eric had seemed angrier or more desolate, times when she questioned whether he truly understood the gravity—the finality—of their situation, but in the last weeks while she acted so frigid with him, she'd also come to see how much she relied on his hopefulness. Such reliance had brought her here this morning; she couldn't bear the thought of losing him.

Laura said, "Just because he thinks everything will work out doesn't mean it will."

"Doesn't mean it won't, either," Cecil said.

29

A FTER HIS SON'S WIFE TOOK HER LEAVE, CECIL LEFT THE CLOSED sign showing and locked the door behind him. Anyone stopping by would assume he was pitching in at the Shrimporee. The cab of the truck was baking. He'd always expected Eric to confide in Laura. He'd expected some resolve to come from it, some comfort. He hadn't counted on Laura to turn skittish. Truth to tell, he'd thought she would want to pull the trigger herself.

The blacktop outside of Southport was empty and wet. Overhead, a pair of frigate birds circled. They were the first ones Cecil had seen all year, likely flushed from the mangroves by the storm. Justin's old billboard threw a long, thin shadow across the road and over the snarl of mesquite trees in the median, their twisted and arthritic limbs. The roadside ditches brimmed with brown water; the grassy pastures and planted fields were darkly saturated. A broken-up tread from a tractor tire was scattered on the caliche shoulder.

Despite Laura's visit, despite the doubts she'd cast, he could still imagine driving out here tonight. He could still flash forward through everything he'd laid out for Eric: Cecil would pick him up after the boys were asleep, and they'd drive to Loan Star to get the Cadillac. Then they'd take it and the truck to the marina, snuff out the lights, wait. When the Bufords arrived, they'd show them the rollerboard suitcase full of clothes and the envelope full of cash. They'd hand them over with the Cadillac's keys and pink slip. Cecil would explain about the man he knew in Saltillo, Mexico, who'd agreed to pay Dwight cash money to clear brush from fields, a man who'd seen trouble himself and had a vested interest in not drawing any kind of attention. Then Eric would say they needed him out of the country. He'd keep his tone even, as if asking for a favor or calling in a friendly debt. He'd say that even the prison up in Huntsville would be too close for the Campbells' sanity. They would show them the gas cans in the bed of the truck. "If he skips bail, they'll take our house," Mayne would say, and Cecil would nod, not without satisfaction. They would allow his parents to say goodbye. Cecil would ride in the passenger seat while Dwight drove the Cadillac. He would admit to carrying his pistol, explaining he'd brought it only to discourage Dwight from wrecking the car or speeding in front of a cop or running off when they switched seats near the Sarita checkpoint; Cecil would deliver them across the border in case the guards asked to see a driver's license. Eric would follow in Cecil's truck. They would drive three hours into Mexico, then stop so Cecil could get out and drive back with Eric. Dwight would continue on to Saltillo while they crossed back into Texas and made it home in time for the Shrimporee.

Yes, despite everything, on the sodden roads that afternoon, Cecil could still see how that would make sense to someone. It required no great effort to see how you could allow yourself to believe that it would happen in just such a way.

30

G RIFF HAD JUST LET RAINBOW OUT INTO THE BACKYARD when his mother returned from her second trip to the store that day. She'd been gone longer than he'd expected. Since he and his father had come home from the Teepee, he'd been zoning out in front of the television, absentmindedly petting Rainbow. He would have been there still had the dog not jumped off the couch, given a long shake that began at her head and ended at the tip of her tail, and trotted to the back door. Both Justin and his father were in their rooms, and though he expected them to emerge, neither did. As his mother came into the kitchen and placed a bottle of laundry detergent on the counter, Griff tried to remember what he'd been watching for the last hour. He couldn't. His memory was so wiped that he wondered if he'd fallen asleep. An indistinct, viscous disappointment coated his thoughts.

"Need help?" Griff asked, thinking his mother had been gone so long that it might have turned into a bigger haul than she'd originally planned.

"Yes," she said, handing him a jug of laundry detergent.

"Is there more in the car?"

She pulled a loaf of potato bread out of a plastic bag and put it beside the other loaf in the cabinet. She wadded the bag into a ball, then chucked it in the garbage under the sink. She seemed rushed, like someone was coming over and she wanted to have everything put up before the doorbell rang.

"Mom?"

"Yes, Lobster?"

"Is there more in the car?"

"No," she said.

"Then what can I help with?"

"Do what?"

"You said you needed my help."

"Did I?" she said. "Is that something I said just now?"

A LITTLE LATER, GRIFF LET HIMSELF INTO JUSTIN'S ROOM— doing this felt bold and new, like a skill he'd only recently mastered— and said, "Mom bought laundry detergent and potato bread."

"Stop the presses," Justin said. He was leaning over Sasha's tank, rearranging her rocks.

"She said she'd forgotten those things, but there are two other loaves of bread in the cabinet and there's plenty of detergent in the garage. I just checked. And she called me Lobster for the first time in a while."

Justin was combing through Sasha's gravel. His fingers made long furrows along the bottom of the tank, then he smoothed them with his palm.

Griff said, "And earlier, when Dad took me to the Teepee, he said the Shrimporee used to make him sad."

"So our parents are weird. This is only occurring to you now?"

Griff was sitting on his brother's bed, looking at his shoes. He swiveled his ankles, feeling the joints click from all the times he'd sprained them, and then he was thinking of Justin trying to ollie the marina hedge and rolling his own ankle and Dwight Buford finding him that way.

"They're probably just nervous," Griff said. "They'll probably get back to normal after tomorrow."

Justin finished in Sasha's cage and then lifted her out. She wrapped herself around his hand, reminding Griff of a gray baseball mitt. Justin held her up, close to his face, and rotated his wrist to examine her from different angles. He squinted, moved around to find better light, squinted again and gently touched her skin with his fingers. Griff couldn't see what he was studying—Sasha looked the same as always—but then he noticed: The snake's eyes, normally black, had turned a cloudy, opaque blue.

"Is she sick?" Griff asked.

"Is who sick?"

"Sasha," Griff said. "Why are her eyes like that?"

"It's old skin. She's getting ready to shed. She can hardly see through it. Right now, she's really scared."

"That sucks."

"It really does," Justin said. "She can't see that I'm the one holding her. She doesn't know who I am. She doesn't think she's anywhere close to safe."

31

WHEN ERIC STEPPED OUT OF THE BEDROOM, THE HOUSE was still. *Vacant* was the word that scrolled through his thoughts. Laura had taken Justin to his session with Letty, and according to the note on the kitchen table, Griff was helping Fiona and her mother set up the Junior League's face-painting booth at the Shrimporee.

Midafternoon light poured in through the windows, heating the house. The air smelled stale. Eric considered brewing coffee, but the day was too hot for it. His skin was still tight with dried sweat from visiting the Teepee with Griff. He dragged his hand over his face, and walked from room to room, making sure he was alone. Rainbow followed him for a time, but then splayed herself on the cool bathroom tile and stayed there. Eric walked on. It was like touring a house he was considering for purchase. He tried to imagine how a stranger would assess their lives, given their furniture and the snake and Griff's foiled-over windows and the remaining welcome home plants. White trash, you might think. Or the house of someone who'd just gotten back from the hospital or jail. A family that needed a little more money and new carpet and a better air conditioner, a family with an old dog and dark wood paneling and sagging floors and a couple of cracked single-pane windows. That was the worst of it, though. Nothing else showed through. This came as a small revelation: You wouldn't know this was the home of the kidnapped boy or the woman who hurt herself in public. You wouldn't know this family had been torn asunder, that each of them was, in one way or another, scared of the other three. You'd think: These are just simple people, regular and steady and unafflicted. You'd think you could trust them. You'd suspect your own secrets were worse than theirs. Even if you reached to the top shelf of the closet and found the pistol, you'd hardly think anything of it. You might even be comforted to hold the gun, to feel its distinct and re-assuring heft. You might believe that the man who'd stashed it there was responsible and bold and true, someone you'd be proud to know, someone who could, when the time came, summon the will to do what no one else would.

OVER HIS LIFE, ERIC HAD NOTED HOW MEN AROUND TOWN watched his father, how they sometimes afforded him the same berth they would a growling dog. How they avoided eye contact. How they wouldn't interrupt him when he spoke. Whether the men had personally quarreled with Cecil or sensed some hardness in him or simply knew his history, Eric couldn't say. There were stories. The story of him breaking a shill's nose at a poker game in Refugio. The story of when, instead of calling the cops, he let a shoplifter keep the car stereo he'd swiped, but only after Cecil slammed his wrists in Loan Star's heavy back door. The story of him beating a man with a tow chain in the parking lot of the Castaway Café be-cause the man made some lewd gesture toward Eric's mother.

And the story of Rick Olivarez, the man who'd worked under Cecil at the pawnshop before Ivan. This was in Eric's youth. Rick had drawn cartoons for Eric, characters with long legs and short pants and oversized ears under jokey thought bubbles. He could make his voice sound like Donald Duck's. One Christmas Eve, Eric's parents had gotten Rick to wear a Santa Claus costume and visit the house with a bag of gifts. He'd presented Eric with a model train he'd been coveting in the hobby shop window. There were inevitably pictures of that night in one of the photo albums Cecil had given to Eric the other afternoon on his driveway. But on a muggy August morning Cecil, who was usually out of the house early, unexpectedly ate breakfast with Eric and his mother. He explained that he'd fired Rick the previous night. He told them to steer clear of him from here on out; Eric had to promise not to take rides from Rick or accept drawings or gifts, and to hang up if Rick called the house. None of it made sense, and though Eric kept expecting his father to fill in the blanks, he never spoke of him again. Nor did Eric or his mother ever see Rick around Southport. He just disappeared. His absence was so complete it was as if he'd never existed at all.

Years later, Ivan told Eric that Rick and Cecil had gone floundering after work that night, and Rick had gotten drunk and started confessing things to Cecil. "Upsetting things," Ivan said. "Sins, I guess you'd call them." Cecil kept opening beers for Rick, letting him talk. When their ice chest was empty, Cecil punched Rick in the solar plexus and grabbed a fistful of his hair and held his face underwater. He pulled him up, gasping and disoriented, and hauled him back to the truck and hit him again on the jaw, a blow hard enough to put him to sleep. Then he drove two hours up toward Karnes City and dumped Rick in a cotton field without his boots or shirt or wallet.

"Where is he now?" Eric had asked Ivan.

"Down in Mexico, somewhere near Saltillo."

THE ONLY CAR AT LOAN STAR WAS THE CADILLAC. IT WAS A FRI-day, typically a busy day at the shop—people who'd gotten paid came to clear their loans, and people who needed money for the weekend came in with things to hock—but with the Shrimporee coming, Cecil had probably assumed the store would be dead. Past the pawnshop, traffic was worse than earlier. A winding line of cars, stalled by construction and ferry delays, snaked down Station Street. Two cops in dark blue uniforms waved drivers through the detours and then stopped traffic when groups of tourists pushed into the crosswalks on their way to the beach. The high school band had stopped practicing, but the other sounds still hung in the air: swinging hammers, table saws, the steady beeping of a truck in reverse. In the distance, just before the water, the main stage was taking form. To Eric, the poles looked like masts of ships rolling over the horizon.

He didn't call Tracy to say he was stopping by. Nor did he worry about parking on the street instead of inside the garage. If anyone asked, he'd say he'd come to discuss last-minute issues with Justin's event at the Shrimporee. The risk was tolerable. He also hoped such blatancy would keep him honest while he was alone with Tracy. Later, in the years of uncertainty that followed, he'd wonder if he'd been courting trouble, trying to sabotage the night ahead. To think of it was to understand how close a different future had been. If Tracy's husband had come to the condo, or if Laura or Cecil had ventured out to Villa Del Sol, they would all have been so mired in pain and anger that everything would have been derailed.

"What's wrong?" Tracy asked and ushered him inside. She checked for anyone watching and closed the door behind him.

"I just wanted to visit," Eric said.

"Visit," she said, flirty. "Is that what we're calling it now?"

They sat opposite each other in the condo's living room, him on the love seat and her in a recliner that Eric thought probably belonged to Kent, her husband. The space was unfamiliar. They'd never lingered in there before, and more than anything, he was struck by the room's brightness. Sunlight reflected off all the polished surfaces—the cream-colored vase on the mantel, the small crystal chandelier, the granite-topped table. Eric felt dirty in the room, worried that he'd leave boot tracks on the carpet or smudge fingerprints on the upholstery.

They talked about Griff, about the wild and lucky coincidence of Tracy having found him that night. They talked about the storm and about the Shrimporee. She said she had a surprise in store for everyone.

"I didn't even tell Laura about it," she said. "I was going to, but then I started thinking she might enjoy a surprise, too."

"Laura hates surprises," Eric said.

"This one might get a different reaction," she said. "I liked her, for what it's worth. If things were different, I think we'd be friends. I think we'd get together and bitch about our husbands."

Eric leaned forward, rested his elbows on his knees, and clasped his hands. On the coffee table lay a fan of the magazines to which Tracy contributed her travel fictions. The covers showed pictures of Tokyo and Greenland and St. Petersburg, places neither he nor anyone in his family would ever see.

"Is there something you came to say, Eric?"

Because she asked him so directly, the idea appeared clearly in his mind: He'd come to say goodbye. He'd come to thank her and apologize and say that he loved her in a regretful way. He'd come to say he was scared of what would happen tonight, scared for his father and himself and Buford.

"I just wanted to thank you," he said. "For what you did for Griff, and for all the work you've put in with the Shrimporee event."

"That's what you came to say?"

"It is," he said.

"You're sure?"

"Of course."

"Because if this were a movie, I'd say this feels an awful lot like the part where the man cuts bait."

"I'm not cutting bait," he said.

"But you're not coming back to the bedroom. Not today and not ever."

"Things have gotten complicated."

"As opposed to before?" she said.

"With Justin back and with the trial coming up, I guess I'm feeling like—"

"An asshole?"

"Yes," he said. "I feel like an asshole."

"The feeling is accurate, I'd say. That's how you feel to me, too."

"I'm sorry."

"I'm not," Tracy said. Her legs were tucked under her in the recliner. She raised her eyes to the light, blinking, trying not to cry.

Eric studied the travel magazines. He remembered how she used to say *I'm in Tokyo* and *I'm in Russia,* how that was a joke she used to like.

"Where are you now?" he asked.

"I'm right here, wondering when you're leaving."

"I meant with your travel writing. Where didn't they send you this month?"

"You can only be in one place at one time."

"I'm sorry," he said again.

"I always knew you would be. I always knew."

32

"I SHOULD'VE LET YOU DRIVE," LAURA SAID.

"It's cool," Justin said.

"You can drive us back home."

They were on the long stretch of causeway between Portland and Corpus, driving to his appointment with Letty. On either side of the bridge, the water looked like mica. Had they been on solid ground, or if the causeway had sufficient shoulders, she would have pulled over and had Justin get behind the wheel. Letting him drive hadn't entered her mind until late, and she thought the oversight explained why he hadn't said much in the last twenty minutes. She felt dim, but also relieved to find such a handy explanation for how clammed up he was.

Gulls canted over the water. A few boats floated out near the ship pass. Laura could still feel the tremble under her skin, but with her hands on the steering wheel, she couldn't tell if they were actually shaking. The causeway bobbed with the traffic, a subtle lunge and sway that she felt in her stomach, as if each seam were a wave passing underneath. The road nauseated her a little, or it worsened a nausea she'd been feeling all along. Ahead, the steel arc of the Harbor Bridge came into view, along with the shipyards and the USS *Lexington*. Seeing them exhausted her, made her want to weep. She had no idea why.

"Are you still feeling okay about the Shrimporee?" Laura asked. "I had coffee with that Tracy Robichaud. I think she's putting together something really nice, but if you'd rather—"

"I'm not worried about it," he said. He was watching the water stream by outside his window.

They passed pelicans and herons, and the pilings from the old bridge that had come down in a storm whose name Laura couldn't remember. Her mind was sapped. She wanted to rally for Justin, for both of them, but she also wanted him to open up. She believed she deserved it. Believed she'd earned it. Soon she'd have to relinquish him to Letty for an hour, and just then, with the seams waving under them on the causeway, Laura didn't want to hand him over. Under normal circumstances, she thought she did a decent job of keeping such possessiveness in check. She knew she shouldn't feel this envy and resentment, knew she should be thankful that Justin had a professional he felt comfortable confiding in, but today, with all that was behind her and all that lay ahead, she couldn't fight it. Talk to me, she thought. Tell your mother something real. After his session, he'd be distracted by whatever they'd discussed, by whatever he'd told her that Laura couldn't know, and then he'd concentrate on driving, on crossing the Harbor Bridge the way his father had taught him.

"Is it Marcy?" Laura asked.

"Is what Marcy?"

"When you take Dad's truck at night, are you going to see Marcy?"

Justin cracked his neck. He kept his eyes on the water. Laura glanced between him and the road, but he never turned. Wind pushed small waves away from the causeway. The motion put Laura in the mind of a mason smoothing cement with a trowel.

She said, "If it's her, I can live with that. I won't say anything. If you're going to see someone else, I need to know."

"I'm not visiting Dwight, if that's what you're asking."

"Okay," she said. "Okay, good. Very good. That's very good to hear."

"Griff told you?"

"No," she said. "No, he hasn't said anything."

"Then how'd you know?"

The truth was she had no idea how she'd known, or for how long. She just did. She must have known when she'd forbidden Eric from stashing the pistol in the truck, and now she realized she'd been afraid Justin would take the truck out tonight while Cecil and Eric were at the marina, but her knowledge ended there. And yet if she didn't explain herself, he'd blame Griff. She said, "I touched the hood of the truck one night when I came home from Marine Lab. It was still hot."

"Clever," he said, as if proud.

"So, Marcy?"

"I want to, but haven't yet. I'm worried it'll be weird. Now that, you know, she knows."

"Is that why you wanted Dad to teach you how to drive on the bridge?"

"You should start a detective agency."

"Lots of practice," she said.

"You're not mad?"

"I'm supposed to tell you not to see her. I'm supposed to say she's part of a life that's gone now and you'll find someone better, but here's what I'm going to say: Don't take Dad's truck."

"Why not?"

"It stalls."

Justin kept watching the water. It was grayer the closer they got to the city.

"You can take my car," Laura said.

"I can?"

"Just promise to wear your seat belt and not to speed," Laura said.

"That's really cool of you, Mom. I promise."

She was nauseated again, feeling like things were moving too fast and she was making one crucial mistake after another, ruining everything. The exit for Marine Lab came up, and she had to stop herself from taking it. How nice it would have been to introduce Justin to Alice. But Laura didn't know who was volunteering, and the thought of seeing Rudy or Paul was too much. And it suddenly felt important to deliver Justin to his appointment with Letty, important for Laura to prove, if only to herself, that she could still pass as a responsible mother.

"And Justin?"

"Yeah?"

"Don't go tonight," she said. "Just stay in your room and try to get some sleep. Tomorrow's a big day."

"Okay," he said.

"Please, honey. I'm serious. Please?"

33

WITH THE WEEK OF RAIN AND THE NIGHT COMING ON, THE mosquitoes were too bad for them to eat outside. They hadn't specifically planned to have supper at the picnic table in the backyard, but each had come to suspect that's what they'd do, so moving into the kitchen was a letdown. Laura took in the glass dish of pork chops, and then the bowls of rice and peas, and the little tub of nondairy butter. Justin carried their plates and silverware, and Griff grabbed the salt and pepper shakers and the stack of paper napkins and the loaf of bread. Eric brought in their glasses, the pitcher of sweet tea. Everyone moved efficiently, in a swift and fluid unison, holding the door open for one another, making sure Rainbow stayed out of the way, then going out to retrieve what had been left behind: the saucer of sliced and salted tomatoes, the jars of mustard and pickle spears, the container of potato salad. The sky was clear, a variegated dark frosted with stars. A breeze laced through the tallow limbs like a ribbon. All of the weather had moved up into the Hill Country by now, but seated at the table, everyone felt as though they were still trying to outrun a fast-approaching storm.

Supper was a solemn affair. The kitchen was hot from the stove and oven. The round wood table was tacky to the touch. There was the scraping of utensils on plates, the clinking of glasses being lifted and lowered, and the quiet sounds of chewing and swallowing, but not much talk. Justin cut his meat with the edge of his fork instead of a knife, the way he always had, and dipped each bite in a dollop of mustard dusted with black pepper. Griff refused to eat any peas. As usual, he spent most of the meal waiting for his parents to force the vegetables on him. Neither of them did, though Eric had been considering it. He thought it was the right thing to do, the responsible thing, and he didn't want the obligation to fall to Laura, but more than that, he didn't want to introduce any additional tension to the table. The clock on the wall read a quarter to seven. It ticked loudly. In just a few hours, his father would be parked outside the house.

Laura pushed food around her plate, made it into a mound, covered it with buttered potato bread. She couldn't eat. The light hanging over the table burned too bright, too hot, too close. Her hands had stopped shaking, but her mind and memory were churning. If she'd had her Moleskine, she would have written: *My head feels like a dryer running with bricks in it.* She wanted to flee, wanted to pile everyone and anything they could fit into the car and truck and caravan out of Texas. Eric asked Justin to pass the pork chops. He stabbed one with his fork and dropped it onto his plate. He wanted Laura to see how much the meal meant to him. She looked piqued and scared and he wanted her to feel some peace before he left with his father.

Griff just wanted supper to end. He'd already finished his food, but was trying not to leave the table first. He hadn't thought the meal would feel this momentous, and yet the whole time his parents had been so withdrawn, so conspicuous when they glanced around the table, that he'd been bracing for them to say they were divorcing or Papaw was dying or the case against Dwight Buford was being tossed out. He was still trying to convince himself that they would return to themselves after the Shrimporee, but they weren't making it easy: His mother was hiding her food and his father wouldn't stop eating. Griff started sweating. He'd gotten sunburned helping Fiona and her mother, so at the table his skin felt hot and a size too small. He needed to shower—what did it matter if he left the table first? They'd all done it plenty of times—and so he was about to push back his chair when his brother wiped his mouth with his napkin and cleared his throat.

"Letty thinks I'm making progress," Justin said. "She thinks we're all doing a good job."

Immediately, Eric saw Laura's eyes welling. He saw that she would weep not only because Letty thought they were on the right path, but because Justin had said it in front of everyone. Because he'd acknowledged that there was something to acknowledge and they could no longer pretend otherwise. Because they couldn't snuff out this new life with silence, and they couldn't call back who they'd been by avoiding who they were now. Laura cocked her head like a small bird and she was smiling, trying not to cry, but tears were already on her lashes. He expected her to wipe them away. She didn't. Then she was reaching for Justin's hand, and then, on her other side, for Griff's. For a long and devastating moment, Eric was left out, utterly disconnected from his wife and sons. His stomach dropped and nothing in the world felt right and he saw that this was his future. Then Griff extended his hand, and then Justin did, and Eric took them, and they were all touching and moored together. It was almost too much, too good. Eric closed his eyes first, then Griff, then Justin, and finally Laura. They listened to their own breathing, and to each other's, and they felt the warmth of their clasped hands, the same blood coursing through their veins.

Then, one by one, they surrendered to circumstance and began to pray, to give thanks for the beautiful luck of their lives and to beg desperately for forgiveness.

34

LAURA DIDN'T NEED HELP CLEARING THE TABLE, BUT WHILE Griff and Eric watched television in the living room, Justin lingered in the kitchen. He could have situated himself on the couch, could have retired to his room and closed the door, could have lifted Sasha from her tank and worn her around his neck like an amulet to ward off everyone. But he'd chosen to stay with his mother. He returned the mustard and pickles to the refrigerator. He stacked dishes on the counter and toweled them off once she'd washed them. In the window above the sink, Laura watched his reflection. He looked content, concerned only with the task of drying the dishes. She washed the plates and glasses and flatware as thoroughly—as slowly—as she could.

She scrubbed the glass dish that had held the pork chops, rinsed it and handed it to Justin. He wiped it down until it squeaked. Laura was still reveling in what he'd said at the table. She wanted to know the social worker's exact words and what had triggered them, but she also thought it possible that Letty hadn't said anything of the sort. She might have even said the exact opposite.

Justin said, "Thanks for letting me drive home this afternoon."

"It was a test," she said.

"A test?"

"The good news is you passed. The bad news is you're now my personal chauffeur. It's a lifetime appointment that doesn't pay worth a damn."

Did she see a little smile in his reflection in the window? She thought so. She wished they'd dirtied more dishes. Behind her, the sounds of channels being flipped.

"And," he said, "thanks for what you said, you know, about the other thing."

"Just be careful," she said.

"I was thinking I could tell you when I might go over there, and that way you wouldn't worry."

"When did you get so sweet?"

Justin shrugged. And then he moved in a way that despite the soapy scent of the suds and the dishwater, Laura smelled him like she hadn't in years. It was staggering, profoundly and purely him, a scent without a trace of his father or her, the one she'd sought out so many times in the clothes hanging in his closet. With it, a kaleidoscope of memory: how they'd both laughed after she'd poured salt in his drink, how it had, for years, seemed she'd done something unassailably right; how, as a child, he used to sing along to the radio in the car, though he knew none of the lyrics; how the old weather girl from Channel 3 held weekly contests for weather drawings and he'd once won with a picture of an elephant sailing a boat toward a beach and how he had, for months after, wanted to marry the woman and how that tickled Laura and filled her with benevolent jealousy.

"Do you remember wanting to marry the weather girl?" Laura asked.

"Annette Maldonado," he said. "She broke my heart when she took the other job."

And then Laura was remembering that as well. Two years ago, two years into Justin being gone, Annette had announced she was moving to the bigger market in San Antonio. She cried during her final seven-day forecast and the morning anchors hugged her while confetti fell from above. Laura had cried, too.

Justin said, "I used to watch it after we came home from throwing the paper route."

"We were probably watching at the same time."

"That's why I put it on Channel 3. I knew it was the one y'all watched. Well, and because of Annette."

"I used to go into your room and smell your clothes," Laura said. "Daddy did, too. When we got your postcard, I held every speck of it up to my nose hoping to find your smell on it."

"What postcard?"

She looked at his reflection in the window again, thinking he might be smiling at the joke, thinking they'd crossed into a new phase of their relationship where they would playfully rib each other, but his face was expressionless, his eyes focused intently on the glass he was drying. In the living room, Griff and Eric were still surfing channels. Laura was suddenly afraid they were listening. Doubt quickened and pulsed through her veins. Her temples swelled. She said, "The one from California. With the arrowheads. The one that said *Don't Stop Looking.*"

"Someone else must have sent it."

"Are you sure?" she asked, hearing how ridiculous it sounded, how pitiable. Then, trying to sound upbeat, trying to stay cool, like self-control could make the difference, she said, "The handwriting looked exactly like yours. I had it on the fridge for years. I only took it down when you got home, so it wouldn't upset you. It was postmarked in Bakersfield, California."

"I wouldn't have been upset," he said. "But I didn't send it. I've never been to California."

She couldn't think, couldn't speak. In the sink, beneath the suds, her hands shook.

"I was in the Bluff the whole time," Justin said. "That's always right where I was."

CECIL REMOVED HIS WEDDING RING AND WRISTWATCH AND stashed them in the medicine cabinet above his bathroom sink. If things went sideways, he didn't want to give the law a crack at the gold. How many pieces of jewelry had he bought from booking agents over the years, rings and necklaces and watches that had gone straight into their pockets instead of into inmate possession bags? He took a blood pressure pill with water cupped in his palm and put the bottle in his pocket so he wouldn't forget it. Then he went into the front room, clicked the lamp on, and sat on the couch to wait.

He wore a dark shirt and jeans, though only his boots were true black. He didn't want a constable to pull him over at three in the morning and ask why he was dressed like a cat burglar. There were, Cecil knew, an infinite number of ways the night could go wrong and only one way for it to go right, but he didn't mind the odds. He would feel at peace with whatever befell him so long as it happened after he'd done what needed doing. The thought that kept surfacing in his mind was this: It's been a good run. It's been more than enough. Connie and Eric and the boys, they were beyond what he'd deserved. If it turned out that tonight was the end, if this was the vanishing point his whole existence had been building toward, then who could say he'd gotten a bad bargain? Not a soul. Not one goddamn soul.

GRIFF DECIDED AGAINST SHOWERING. HE JUST WANTED TO GET out of the house, to get away from his family. His father and Justin were in the living room watching a preseason Cowboys game, and his mother was flitting between her bedroom and the garage. He had overheard Justin deny having sent the postcard, so he assumed she was rummaging through her plastic bins in hopes of proving him wrong. Everything about the night felt unpredictable, like they'd spun off axis and were floating into uncertain lives. When they'd clasped hands and bowed their heads at the table—something they'd never done as a family, not even while Justin was gone—he'd been so shocked that the moment seemed to last an hour. It was like witnessing a car accident and not immediately knowing if he'd been involved.

In his room, he called Fiona. He said, "I think everyone's been replaced by aliens. Meet me at the Teepee?"

"You know who would say that? An alien pretending not to be an alien. An alien trying to lure me to the Teepee and feast on my brains. Thanks, but no."

"Seriously," he said. "We just prayed, all of us together, at the table. We held hands and closed our eyes and prayed."

"Interesting," she said. Then, after a silence in which she seemed to be assessing the veracity of his claims, she said, "Come to my house instead. The last time you went to the Teepee it didn't work out so well."

ERIC COULD SENSE THAT JUSTIN WAS ABOUT TO GO TO HIS ROOM, so he said, "Thanks for telling us about Letty, bud. That was good to hear."

"She wanted me to make sure everyone knew. I think because of the Shrimporee thing tomorrow."

On the television, the Cowboys were getting thumped by the Steelers. Eric couldn't pay attention to the game, but left it on because Justin liked football now. He hoped to keep him in the living room. Griff had gone to call Fiona; Laura had been rummaging in the garage for the last hour and was showering now. Eric couldn't hold a thought in his head. His mind was a dry field that had been touched by a lit match. He only knew it wouldn't be long before Cecil came to collect him and these might be his last moments with

Justin, and he needed them to count. For four years, he'd wished he'd said something meaningful to his son before he disappeared. Wished his last words had imparted some wisdom or the depth of his love, wished they'd been sturdy enough to endure and bring comfort when Justin needed it most. Now that he had the opportunity, now that he was faced with the possibility of being torn away from his son again, he could think of nothing worthwhile to say.

The football game was such a blowout that both teams had removed their starters. The Cowboys had the ball and the second-string quarterback threw an interception that one of the Steelers returned for a fifty-yard gain.

"It's too depressing," Justin said. "I'm going to bed."

"I'm sorry," Eric said.

"It's okay. The preseason doesn't mean anything."

"I'm just so sorry, bud," Eric said, a knot in his throat. "I wish it were different. I'm sorry it played out like this."

FOR MOST OF HER TIME IN THE BATHROOM, LAURA SAT ON THE closed toilet staring in disbelief at the California postcard. The door was locked and the shower was running, but she stayed in her clothes. The postcard had been in her dresser drawer since she'd swiped it from the fridge that first night. What she'd been looking for in the garage was samples of his handwriting, of Griff's and Eric's, too. If Justin hadn't sent the postcard—and she could see now that his *T*'s were more slanted and his *O*'s weren't as round— then she'd hoped his father or brother had. But their handwriting resembled what was on the card less than Justin's did. And there was the issue of the California postmark. She had to assume it had come from a stranger, the parents of another missing child or a nut-job taunting her family in a way she didn't understand. All Laura knew was that Justin hadn't sent it, and for no good reason, the revelation set her adrift. Her son was home now, safe in his room, but the night felt even more perilous than before. In the shower, she tried to give in and cry. No tears would come. She couldn't even figure how to do that.

When she came out of the bathroom, Eric was changing into a black sweatshirt by the window. The shade was drawn. She said, "You'll burn up in that."

"It's the only long-sleeved black shirt I have. Cecil said to wear all black."

Laura started brushing out her hair. She said, "Did the boys go to bed?"

"Griff's on the phone and Justin's got Rainbow in his room."

"I thought you might try to sleep a little. Just get whatever rest you could before he came to get you."

"I'm too wound up," he said. "I can barely sit still."

Laura tugged the brush through her wet hair, pulling the tangles apart one at a time until she could comb through in a series of straight, fluid swipes.

After a while, she said, "I don't want you to do this, and if the boys knew, they wouldn't want it either."

Eric didn't respond. Laura rubbed lotion onto her legs and feet. Her hair kept falling wet and heavy over her face, so she wrapped it into a loose bun. Eric was patting his pockets the way he always did before leaving, checking for his keys and wallet. Look at us, she thought. A married couple getting ready for a date.

"There's nothing you need to make up for," Laura said. "There's nothing you've done or haven't done that will fix this."

"What does that mean?"

"It means I don't care about the past. None of us do. Whatever's happened is behind us, and we need to get on with our lives, and I don't want you doing something like this because you think you need to redeem yourself."

Eric dug in his pockets, as if patting them hadn't been enough. When he didn't say anything, Laura said, "What if we left? What if we put everything we could fit in the car and truck, and the four of us just got out of Texas? That's something I keep thinking about. You've always wanted to go on exciting vacations, so let's just drive until we find a place we like."

"It doesn't feel like enough anymore. Like you said, he'll always be with us."

"We could start over. The boys could start fresh and we—"

"I used to go to the dump," Eric said. He leaned against the wall in his black shirt, not looking at her, and his voice was low, hardly more than a whisper. "Sometimes when I said I was going to hang flyers, I'd drive out there and dig through the garbage, looking for him. For his body."

"That's okay. We were all worried. We were all afraid of—"

"I'd follow the garbage trucks from one dumpster to the next, then out to the landfill. I wanted to get there before he was buried too deep to find. I'd shower at school so you wouldn't smell the trash on me. Do you hear what I'm saying?"

"Of course," she said. "Yes, I hear you."

"I'm saying I thought he was dead."

"Okay," she said.

"I'm saying I gave up on him."

"What happens if you don't come home? What happens when it's a cop knocking on the door tomorrow morning because you've been caught? Or worse? How do I explain that to Justin?"

"I'll come home," he said.

"We can't take any more, Eric. *I* can't take any more."

"It'll be done by morning."

"I feel like it's just starting over. I feel like I'm fixin' to get another call that will tear my world down."

"I'll come home," he said again.

"Do you know what I prayed for at the table?"

"No," he said.

"That I'd undercooked the pork chops or the meat was bad. I prayed that you'd get so sick that you would have to spend the night in the bathroom or the hospital."

"That's sweet of you in a way."

"I should have ground up a handful of my nerve pills and mixed them into your potatoes. I should have stirred them into your tea like salt."

"You mean sugar," he said.

"What's the difference?" she said. "What difference does any of it make?"

GRIFF CLIMBED THROUGH HIS WINDOW, WALKED DOWN SUN-tide, and once he was out of earshot, he dropped his board and started skating. He avoided the Teepee. He wasn't worried about Baby Snot and his crew, not really, but he didn't want to see the pool again, stripped of its coping. He hoped the property would get demolished soon, hoped the pool would be filled and paved over and he'd forget it had ever existed at all.

Fiona's house was frigid, and loud. She had the air conditioner turned to fifty-eight degrees, and music blared from the recessed speakers in the ceiling. She wore sweatpants and a zipped-up hoodie and thick socks. Her mother's two cats were snuggled together on the love seat, trying to keep warm. Candles burned on the wet bar and end tables. The room waved with soft, warping light. Shadows kept changing. The air smelled of candied flowers. "My parents are at the yacht club," Fiona said. "They're schmoozing it up at a pre-Shrimporee soiree." Griff thought they'd stay in the front room, but Fiona started blowing out candles and lowering the stereo's volume. Then she disappeared into the hallway and he followed.

Her bed was piled with stuffed animals, plush bears and hearts and dogs that guys had given her over the years. He'd forgotten about the collection since he'd last been in her room, and now, even more than before, he hoped the rubber duck race would still be at the Shrimporee. It was the only game where he'd ever won anything—a stuffed flamingo, two years ago, while his parents passed out flyers—and giving her something she could add to her menagerie suddenly seemed necessary.

Fiona lay on her back on her bed, using various teddy bears like pillows; they reminded him of all the stuffed animals people had sent after Justin was found, the ones that were in Hefty bags in the garage, waiting to be donated to a children's hospital.

She said, "So you're a Bible-thumper now, praying before meals and all? Does that mean we have to stay chaste on the one night when George and Louise decide to vacate the premises?"

"I don't think it means anything," Griff said.

"Heresy is very hard to resist in a man."

Griff walked around her room, looking at her knickknacks. Porcelain figures of babies and animals with teardrop eyes, photos in heavy frames, a trophy she'd won for selling raffle tickets, and a stein full of spare change. He'd never paid attention to these things before and, noticing them now, he tried to read what they said about a girl who dressed in all black and dyed her hair green. It seemed the kind of thing Justin would be able to do, but Griff had no idea. Fiona was still on her back on the bed. She was tossing a stuffed banana into the air. As soon as she caught it, she tossed it again. She might have been trying to hit the ceiling.

When Griff couldn't wait any longer, he said, "Justin told my mom he didn't send the postcard."

She tossed the banana again, unfazed. She did it twice more, flipping it end over end, then said, "That probably wasn't the feel-good hit of the summer."

"After he said it, she locked herself in the bathroom."

Fiona held the banana to her chest. Her eyes stayed on the ceiling. Every few seconds she blinked slowly. She said, "I did the best I could. With his handwriting, I mean."

"It was perfect," Griff said. "You did it perfectly."

The whole scheme had been Griff's idea. It wasn't so much an effort to help Justin, though of course he hoped it would, but rather an effort to give his parents a reason to stay together, to stay alive. Fiona's family was going to California for vacation, and while he worried the out-of-state postmark would send detectives in the wrong direction, the investigation seemed to have gone so dormant that the risk felt justified. Griff stole the arrowhead postcard from the rack at Sharky's Souvenirs and gave Fiona a folder of Justin's old school papers, full of his handwriting. They decided the message she'd write would be up to her. Her parents, in addition to visiting Hollywood and Disneyland, wanted to see Bakersfield Sound Museum and so when they drove out there, Fiona dropped the card in a curbside mailbox. When Griff saw the words she'd chosen—*Don't Stop Looking*—his eyes had filled with tears. He'd briefly allowed himself to forget who'd sent it.

In her room, she started tossing the banana toward the ceiling again. She said, "Are you going to fess up?"

"Should I?"

"Would it help her?"

"I don't know."

"I bet she already knows. Even if she doesn't know it yet. And I bet she'll never say anything because she'll realize we were trying to do something good. Ladies pick up on things that hairy-legged boys don't."

"The way you knew I was coming to break up with you."

"So you admit it," Fiona said.

"I thought it was the right thing to do. Justin said I should."

"He was wrong," Fiona said.

"He also doesn't think you've had a bunch of lovers. He thinks I'm your first boyfriend."

"So he gets kidnapped and comes back as, what, an all-knowing love guru?"

"It's okay if it's true. You're my first girlfriend, even though I used to tell people I'd made out with Melissa Uno and Kathryn Grosso."

She caught the banana and brought it to her chest again. She turned onto her side and met his eyes. Griff couldn't read her expression, which seemed both sorrowful and affectionate. He didn't know if it meant Justin was right or wrong. She stared at him for a long, quiet moment, then said, "You're a sweet boy, Griffin Campbell."

"What does that mean?"

"It means come here," she said, extending her hand languidly off the bed. "It means come here and I'll show you what I have or haven't learned from all my imaginary lovers."

CECIL STARTED PACKING UP HIS TRUCK A LITTLE AFTER MID-night. The suitcase full of clothes and an envelope of cash, two thermoses of coffee, a sleeping bag and Coleman stove and a tarp and a couple bags of canned food. The jugs of water and two gas cans were still in the truck bed, and the pistol was under the seat until he stashed it in the glove box. He passed through the house one last time, watering all of the plants Laura had given him and checking for things he'd want later. *Don't be sentimental,* he told himself. *Don't go down that road.* In the bathroom, he grabbed some old, thin sheets and frayed towels and balled them together, tucked them under his arm. Then he opened the medicine cabinet and retrieved his wedding ring and the gold nugget watch. He should have put them in the safe-deposit box at the bank; he understood that now, but he didn't feel right leaving them behind. If need be, he could toss them out of the truck window. He could drop them into the dark bay.

Outside, the cicadas were thrumming in the trees. Years ago, Ivan had told him that they sounded different in Mexico, that the cicadas down there sang in a different register. It was something he'd been curious about ever since. The night was thick and deep, draped with fog. Cecil stood on the porch for a while, breathing it in, accepting it. Then he locked the door to his house, checked the knob to make sure, and got into the truck. There was no more wasting time.

LAURA DRIFTED IN AND OUT OF SLEEP, FEELING HELPLESS. SHE remembered—or almost remembered, or dreamed or half-dreamed—those first weeks four years ago when she'd stay awake for days at a time until sleep insidiously claimed her. She never woke feeling refreshed or charged with renewed hope. No, she always opened her eyes to a world that had been further transfigured by guilt, knowing she'd failed her missing son, knowing everything would be different had she stayed awake just a little longer. Tonight, she trembled under the comforter and the trembling became a dream: She was a child, shivering and not necessarily herself. Her teeth chattered. She was naked and huddling in the dark. There was a cantilevered bridge. There was an ocean that looked like molten silver with birds skimming over it. No, the ocean looked like hammered metal. The moon beamed down in a cone of light like something she would draw with a yellow crayon. Her hair was soaked, dripping onto her bare shoulders, and long, cold winds passed over her, chafing her, whipping her. Then the ground was giving way, it had become the bridge and was now buckling, and she was tumbling and somersaulting through the dark until she landed back in her bed, gasping and sweating on the night before the Shrimporee.

Her heart quaked. Her eyes were wide and dry and stinging, stinging so much that she wondered if she'd slept with them open. The house seemed quiet. She didn't know if Eric had left yet. He'd taken the pistol down from the closet shelf. That, she remembered. Her mouth was sour and her head ached and she needed to push herself out of bed. She wanted to see if Cecil had come for Eric, but she also wanted to check on Justin, wanted to find him in his room or in front of the television, wanted to find that he'd kept his promise about not going on a drive tonight. Please, she thought. Please. But she only pulled the comforter up higher, bunched it under her chin. She could feel herself drifting off again. Her consciousness was thinning and dissipating, the way froth from waves soaks into the sand when the tide is pulled back into the ocean. She thought: After Eric leaves, load the boys in the car and go. She thought: Won't Mayne show up with a gun of his own? Isn't he a father, too? She thought: Call the police, or Garcia, and confess everything. She thought: The inflatable alligator I brought to Marine Lab, the one I took from the garage years ago, might have been blown up by Justin before he was taken; it might still have his breath inside it. She thought: I used to be a little girl who wore dresses with lace sleeves and now I'm something else, someone else, somewhere else, and once a stain sets, you'll never get it out, especially blood, and do I know anyone from California, didn't the handwriting on the post-card look familiar, and dolphins are descended from wolves, somehow that's true, and they rape each other, and kill each other, and when they beach, it's because they're sick or hurt or lost or just too tired to go on. Then she gave in, knowing it wouldn't be very long at all.

CECIL HAD WORRIED THAT WITH STATION STREET CORDONED off for the Shrimporee he'd have trouble getting his truck down to the marina, but the route was open. The barricades had been moved off to the side. He parked in a diagonal slot with a clear view of the *Oil-n-Water,* then clicked off his lights. He was hours early, but it was a relief to see the boat still tied to the moorings. The Bach Prelude undulated in the speakers, and as it played, the night stretched out. The moon was dull. The tide was in. Boats swayed in their slips, rising and falling on slowly lapping water. In his mirrors, the buildings that made up downtown Southport reminded him of what you'd see in an old Western, squat structures with high false fronts overlooking a wide street. He wouldn't have been surprised if a tumbleweed rolled by. There was no movement except for the boats gently knocking against the docks in front of him and the wind lifting the palm fronds and letting them down again. At some point, the Bach ended. He had no memory of the world going quiet.

Half an hour before he thought the Bufords would show, the moon slid behind a wide wall of clouds and he took out his cell phone to call Eric. His son answered after the first ring. Before Cecil could say anything, Eric said, "Where are you? We're late."

"I'm at the house," Cecil said, his eyes on the boats in front of him. "I'm going to get some rest."

"Rest? What does that mean?"

"I'm calling it off."

"Why?" Eric said, confused, angry. "I'm outside on the porch, like we planned. I've been waiting for you to pick me up."

"Laura came by the shop today. She talked sense into me. It's not worth the risk. I'm too old and you've got too much to lose."

"You have to be kidding," Eric said.

"Go inside and get in bed beside your wife. She's a good woman who's terrified of losing you. We need to let this thing run its course."

"You were so adamant. We had the whole thing worked out. I've been going over the variables in my head, feeling better about it. Setting him up with Rick in Mexico and—"

"Bring the pistol to the shop next week and I'll enter it back in inventory."

"I could go alone. I could do it myself."

"I'd ask that you not," Cecil said. "I'd ask you not to do that to your boys."

"*For* the boys. I'd do it *for* the boys."

"Someone could call the police. Someone could alert them where you're going, what you're planning. At best you'd be looking at possession of an unregistered firearm. That's half a year in County right there."

"You wouldn't call them."

"No, but I can't speak for Laura."

The moon came out from behind the clouds. The smell of the bay drifted in through the vents. Boats moved here and there along the docks, reminding Cecil of antsy horses in their stalls.

Cecil said, "Go to bed, Eric. It'll turn out all right."

"This feels wrong," he said. "This feels like we're rolling over. I was ready for whatever it took."

"Things will work out," Cecil said. "Trust me. Everything'll look different tomorrow."

HOW MANY TIMES HAD GRIFF IMAGINED LYING NAKED WITH Fiona? How many scenarios had he entertained over the years, how many strategies had he devised with this as his singular and ultimate goal? The number was unknowable, and yet now that her beautiful weight was pressing down on him, now that she was enfolding him in a warmth he'd never imagined, a warmth that somehow cooled his sunburn, he remembered every last thought he'd had about her. The distant smell of the candles, the seams of pale light framing her foiled windows, the fear that her parents would come home. She raised herself, straddling him, and brought both of his hands to her mouth. She massaged his fingers, gently kissed his knuckles and gently bit his thumbs and gently closed her soft lips around them. With her eyes closing, she said, "I like these thumbs."

But he also felt disconnected, off to the side, tethered only by the places where their bodies touched. The soft skin on the underside of her arm, the arch of her foot fitting itself over his ankle, sliding up and down over his shin, her fingers laced into his. He was thinking about his mother and the postcard, about the Shrimporee and the ruined Teepee pool and the woman who'd driven him to the clinic and Fiona, and Fiona, and Fiona, and about how he'd thought he'd probably always be a virgin, but now that he wouldn't be, the whole business seemed easy, fated. He thought about Justin and what he'd said at supper and what he'd said about Fiona. Who knew if he was

right? Who cared? As she crushed into Griff, dragging her tongue
up his neck and into his hair, as she traced her finger over his lips
and slid it into his mouth so that he could feel the ridges of her fin-
gerprint on his tongue, he wondered if Justin had ever had an experience like this. To his surprise, he was positive Justin hadn't. He
was almost as positive that Justin had embellished his relationship
with Marcy, that he was guilty of the same lies he'd accused Fiona
of telling. It made him acutely and intensely sad, and he wondered
what else he knew that his older brother didn't, what else Justin was
withholding. For a long and bleak moment, he imagined their lives
unfurling before him like a carpet and while Griff proceeded ahead,
he was leaving Justin behind.

"Are you cold?" Fiona said. She was beside him now, tugging
the covers up and over them.

"No, are you?"

"You're kind of shaking."

"Then I guess I am cold," he said.

"Here," she said. She pulled him closer, then closer still, and
wrapped them tighter in the sheets. His head was on her chest now,
her chin on his scalp. She started pulling her fingers through his hair.
She said, "Just come here, you poor thing."

"I don't want to stop."

"I'm not going anywhere," she said.

"That's hard to believe."

"Try," she said. Her fingers were still in his hair, tangling it into
a nest.

Then, before he realized he'd ever thought such a thing, he said,
"If you're not in front of me, I feel like I've lost you."

"I know," she said.

"I feel like you're going to leave me or find someone else when
school starts or your parents are going to get jobs in a different state
and you'll disappear."

"What can I say? What will make you feel better?"

"Tell me I'm wrong."

"You're wrong," she said. "You've never been more wrong, which is saying something because you're wrong a lot."

"Tell me you love me."

"I love you," she said.

"Tell me again."

"I love you," she said, pulling him closer. "I love you so stupid much."

LAURA WOKE DRENCHED IN SWEAT AND WENT FAST TO THE FRONT door, feeling faint and terrified and alive. She fumbled for her keys. Her hope wasn't to catch Eric before he left. Her hope was to bring him home.

When she opened the door and stepped into the thick early-morning dark, he was still sitting on the porch. He was holding his phone with both hands, staring across the street toward Ronnie Dawes's house. The pistol grip jutted out from the back of his pants. She thought to say something, but instead sat beside him without a word.

Eric said, "Do you think it's easier for someone like Ronnie? Do you think not knowing everything we know, not understanding or worrying about things the way we do, makes life easier?"

"I don't think it's easy for anyone," Laura said.

"I'd like to think he's happy," Eric said. "I'd like to think his mind is quiet, and he's dreaming of pleasant things."

"I bet he is. I bet that's exactly what's happening."

Overhead, tight gray clouds lined the sky like long bolts of cloth. Moonlight permeated them in places, but the glow was dusty and distant.

Eric said, "Cecil shut it down. He said we had too much to lose. I've been sitting here trying to decide if I should go alone."

"And?"

"And I figure I've got about fifteen minutes left before they're on the water."

"I meant what I said. Say the word and we'll load up the cars and be gone before there's light in the trees."

"I wouldn't take him to Mexico," Eric said. "I'd just kill him at the marina."

"That's what I'm afraid of," she said.

"I'm trying to figure how that would affect everyone, especially Justin. I'm trying to weigh what's worse."

Wind rustled in the trees. She wondered who else was awake at that hour. She wondered who was watching Alice and what she was doing. Laura's hands weren't trembling at the moment, but they'd likely start up again soon. Until then, she lay her head on her husband's shoulder.

HEADLIGHTS SWUNG INTO CECIL'S MIRRORS AN HOUR AFTER he'd hung up with Eric. Briefly, he worried it *was* Eric. The beams were long and bright, tipping and rocking as the Mercedes passed the car wash and pulled into the marina. They swept right through the cab of the truck, illuminating everything to the degree that Cecil had to squint, then the cab was dark again as the car moved on and parked a few spots away. Okay, Cecil thought. Okay now. He closed his eyes and conjured an image of Connie, and thought, Forgive me. Then he leaned across the seat to take the pistol from the glove box. He clicked off the safety, opened his door, and stepped out into the thick night.

Mayne was already walking toward him. Cecil looked to see that his hands were empty. Mayne said, "I figured you'd be here. Honestly, I'm not displeased."

"Where is he?"

"Gone," Mayne said. "All day I've been telling myself that if you were here tonight, then you didn't have anything to do with it."

Cecil stood where he was. The pistol felt heavy. He didn't know what he was hearing. "What do you mean 'gone'?"

"Since yesterday morning. Or the night before. When I woke up, he wasn't there."

Cecil studied him. Mayne looked wrung out, like he'd been up for days. He wore a wrinkled button-down shirt, shorts, and loafers with no socks. A wash of possibilities ran through Cecil's mind— that Mayne had driven Dwight somewhere and was just now getting back, that Dwight had absconded on his own, that he was still at home or already in the boat and Mayne had come to buy time, or that Dwight and his mother were in the Mercedes right now, watching from behind the blackened windows, eager to hit the road. For an instant, Cecil felt akin to Mayne. He recognized himself in him, the longing to protect your son, to do the hard thing on his behalf, regardless of right or wrong. He understood the pain this man was enduring before him, the fear and desperation, and with the understanding, Cecil's anger left him.

Then he raised the pistol and aimed at Mayne's forehead.

"I wish you would," Mayne said.

Cecil drew back the hammer.

"He was a good boy. He liked to collect baseball cards and to ride his bike down hills and—"

"Where is he, Mayne?"

"I don't know," he said, looking off and sniffling. "I just don't know. He was looking forward to today. He'd agreed to plead guilty. He was repentant. He knew this was the last—"

"I'll come to your house. I'll drop you in the water right now and drive there and if I find him—"

"He's gone. I don't know where or who with, but I don't think we're going to see him again. God help me, but he's my son and I still love him and he's just gone away."

Cecil thought to check the Mercedes, to throw the doors and trunk open, but knew he wouldn't find anything. He knew Mayne was saying what he knew to be true. Behind him, light threaded the horizon. Soon the morning would come up and the workers and volunteers would descend upon the Shrimporee. Cecil kept the gun on Mayne for a time, then he lowered his arm and moved past him. Walking toward the marina with the sky high and wide and already brighter, with the road leading out of town in two directions and the bay extending beyond itself, he felt tiny and weak and old. He felt too slow to do any good, outmatched by a long sight.

The gun kicked in his hand and the sound cracked in his ears and one of the windows in the *Oil-n-Water* exploded. Then another. Then he unloaded the remaining rounds into the boat's hull. The shots were close enough to open a hole the size of a child's hand. He didn't know if it was big enough to sink the vessel, but he knew the hole would require patching and every time Mayne saw it he'd think of this night, of what Cecil would do to his son if he ever had the chance.

Griff was skating along the seawall near the marina, trying to make it home before the sun came up, when he heard gunshots. They sounded like fireworks exploding in rapid succession. His insides went shaky, and though he hadn't actually seen the fired shots, there were flashes of brilliant yellow light in his eyes, the sound producing phantom visions that he would think were real for years. He kicked his board into his hand and ran into one of the stalls at the car wash. He flattened himself against the brick wall. His breath came in fits. His lungs felt as thin as paper sacks on the verge of tearing. Stay calm, he thought. Stay calm right now. The sky was brightening outside the stall, and Griff worried he'd be trapped by the coming light, worried that as soon as he took his leave whoever had the gun would spot him. It was hard to think that someone hadn't seen him duck into the stall, hard to think there wasn't someone waiting for him out there. He counted to ten. Then to fifty. Then to a hundred. He tried to catalog every skate trick he could do, but his mind kept drawing in on itself, as if it were curling into the fetal position. He summoned thoughts of Fiona, the long curve of her body and the sound of her voice, and he tried to guess how long it would be before his parents woke up, how scared they'd be to find his room empty. Run, he thought. Just run. He was rallying to bolt from the stall when he heard an engine start and a transmission drop into gear. He pressed himself flat against the wall again, trying to disappear, trying to keep composed and believe nothing like this could happen, not tonight, and then it wasn't long before his grandfather's truck came into view as it left the marina. Papaw was halfway down Station Street before he clicked on his lights.

35

DWIGHT BUFORD COULD HAVE BEEN DEAD FOR TWO DAYS. Maybe three. It was impossible to tell, given the salt water. When the Coast Guard crew pulled his body out of the ship channel, it was bloated and broken. Small fish and crabs had fed on him in places—his lips, eyes, and fingers.

Garcia called and relayed this to Eric and Laura just as they were about to leave for the Shrimporee. They were on different extensions, Laura in the kitchen and Eric in their bedroom. Laura wore makeup and a dress she'd gotten when she spent all that money at the mall, and Eric was in pressed jeans and shined boots, and to hear the news in their nice clothes felt fortuitous, like they'd gotten dressed up for the occasion. Garcia said only Buford's parents had been notified so far. His office planned to keep the news under wraps until tomorrow.

"But I thought you should get word right away," Garcia said. "I wanted you to go to the Shrimporee knowing there's nothing to worry about."

"How did he die?" Laura asked.

"We'll have to get official word from the medical examiner, but nothing about the body points to anything other than suicide. My gut says he jumped off the bridge."

"The coward," Eric said. Laura could hear him pacing in the bedroom. He said, "That fucking coward."

"Will there definitely be an autopsy?" she asked.

"The state requires that all unattended deaths be examined by a coroner. If the family disputes an autopsy for religious reasons, exceptions can be made."

"He knew he'd be found guilty," Eric said. "He gave up. The coward didn't have the sand for a trial."

"So what's next? What do you need from us?" Laura asked.

"Go to the Shrimporee and let everyone welcome Justin back," Garcia said. "If you want help sharing the news with him, don't hesitate to call Mrs. Villarreal."

"Okay," Laura and Eric said in unison.

"If the news leaks and anyone asks, just say today is about Justin and you have no interest in discussing Mr. Buford."

"Do you die on impact?" Laura asked. "If you jump from that high, is it the fall that kills you or do you drown?"

"Could go either direction," Garcia said.

"I hope it wasn't instant," she said. "I hope he got smashed up when he hit and then tried to swim. I hope it took him a long time to drown."

"Thank you for telling us," Eric said. "Thank you for everything."

"I would have liked to take him down in court, I'll be honest about that, but I'm glad y'all will get some peace out of this."

"I hope he almost made it to shore," Laura said. "I hope that's what the coroner finds out when he cuts him open—that he'd changed his mind and wanted to live. I hope he could feel the crabs eating his eyes."

THEY LEFT THE HOUSE WITHOUT TELLING THE BOYS ANYTHING and went to pick up Cecil. Laura gave him the passenger seat and moved to the back with Justin and Griff. They were both wearing bright T-shirts and shorts, and they smelled of soap and shampoo. Their hair was still wet from their showers. The backseat was tight with the three of them, but she loved feeling Griff pressed against her. He looked tired and preoccupied, but not unhappy, and Justin only seemed a little anxious, which was understandable. She wished she had sat between her sons, so she could feel both of them beside her. On the way back, she thought.

Laura felt as if she might float away. She wanted to laugh and scream and cry. She wanted to sprint for a mile. She wanted to dance. It wasn't just relief she felt, nor was the feeling as simple as happiness or hope or retribution, but rather something like acquittal. Like emancipation. It was, she realized in the backseat, what she hoped Justin had felt months ago when he'd first been found. A feeling of having thrown herself against a door again and again and again, and now, at last, the lock had given way and the hinges were cracked and she was breaking free. A feeling of finding the ones she loved, the ones she believed she'd lost, waiting for her when she emerged. She knew there would be other doors, some that would never open and others that would reveal truths all but impossible to bear. For now, though, her family was safe. And they were together in the car, breathing the same air. Laura closed her eyes and inhaled.

"Who's going to eat the most shrimp today?" Cecil asked. There was whimsy in his voice, a playfulness that none of them were used to hearing. He said, "I've got five dollars saying I can eat any two of the Campbells under the table."

Traffic was slow and dense, putting Eric in the mind of hurricane evacuations, when cars moved only half a mile an hour despite all of the lanes having been rerouted to flow inland. The closest parking space he could find was Nueces Street, still a good ten-minute walk from the festival.

On the sidewalk, Justin said, "You'd think they'd give the kidnap victim front-door service."

Cecil cuffed him on the head, then pulled him close.

Other people filed in, walking ahead and behind, families and couples and kids eager to ride the rides and play the games. Men wore guayaberas and cowboy hats. Women shaded themselves with umbrellas. Everyone in sunglasses, everyone smelling of sunscreen and insect repellent. A few of the people glanced at Justin. Some waved while others just proceeded toward the marina and looked over their shoulders. Griff expected kids to approach his brother and ask for autographs, but none did. His parents seemed a nervous kind of happy, and he could only figure that they were worried the Bufords would show at the event. Papaw was in a good mood, too, not at all sketchy or guarded or suspicious like Griff had been expecting. It helped. His demeanor made it easy for Griff to believe he'd been mistaken about the truck he'd seen last night. He didn't want to think—could hardly think—about anything except Fiona. The way she bit his thumbs. The smell of the candles. He wondered if she was already inside the festival gates. He wondered when her parents would leave the house again.

The line to buy tickets stretched down Station Street. Waiting, they could see the carnival rides and tops of the booths and the scaffolding for the stage. The smell of the bay and shrimp frying and cotton candy and roasted turkey legs was spreading on the wind, and the lively music of a Tejano band came through old and enormous speakers. Seagulls hovered, their heads swiveling to find dropped or tossed food. There was children's high-pitched laughter and the warbling tone of calliope music and a man talking through a bullhorn. Inching closer to the ticket booths, women started rummaging in their purses and men pulled out their wallets. Parents turned to count heads, as if they'd forgotten how many kids they'd brought. A man wore alligator boots with shorts and no shirt. Women in swimsuits and flip-flops. Boys and girls jumping in place, trying to peek inside, trying to get their parents to hoist them onto their shoulders. (Watching the children bounce around, Laura thought: That's how I feel inside.) A girl with ropes of curly hair blew bubbles from a pink wand. The bubbles floated up and around the crowd, and people tilted their heads to watch them rise and disappear. One of the bubbles landed on Cecil's hair and everyone around him clapped. Laura made him stand perfectly still—he felt like he had a wasp on his head and he'd do well not to disturb it—and she got her camera and snapped a picture. Then she had the boys and Eric pose beside him. Then a woman stepped forward and offered to take a picture with Laura in the frame too. Her name was Wanda Freeman, and though none of the Campbells recognized her, she'd volunteered at a good many searches. Seeing Justin up close was, for her, like seeing an angel. She wanted to cross herself and kiss her Holy Mother medallion, but didn't want to draw any more attention to the poor child. She took two pictures of the family, claiming the first one hadn't come out good, though it had. She wanted them to have two.

When they reached the ticket booth, Eric opened his eel-skin wallet and said, "Five adults, please."

"Y'all's money's no good here," the man said and ushered them through.

Inside the gates, Justin said, "Now, that's more like it."

They wove through clusters of people and the gauntlet of food vendors and game booths. The four of them glanced furtively at Justin. They couldn't help it. He hadn't been in a crowd like this yet, and they needed to make sure he wasn't overwhelmed, to make sure he didn't vanish when they weren't watching. Cecil bought a basket of fried shrimp to share, and Griff kept a lookout for Fiona and the rubber duck race. Kids ran willy-nilly and adults stopped walking without notice to sample food—frog legs and oysters and deep-fried Snickers bars. People knocked into each other. They sloshed frothy beer and dropped sticks of cotton candy. The ground was still soggy from the storm, and puddled in places; Eric's shined boots were already scuffed with mud. Game booths were bright with stuffed animals, loud with carneys barking at the crowds. There were shooting games and ring tosses, and a carousel where you sat on sea creatures instead of horses—dolphins and sharks and killer whales, shrimp and trout and catfish, mermaids and seahorses. Griff wondered if he'd overlooked the rubber duck race, if they'd passed it without his noticing. The Ferris wheel loomed by the water and he realized he'd been hoping to ride it with Fiona. He wanted to look down and see the bay and Southport and maybe his own house, and he wanted everyone to see him with Fiona. He looked around but couldn't find her. The petting zoo was nearby, the odor of goats and ponies and manure, and the sweet sticky scent of alfalfa hay. The Tejano band finished its set. The audience clapped and whistled.

Laura and Eric and the boys made their way to the back of the stage, where they were due to meet Tracy Robichaud for instructions. Cecil wasn't part of the event, so he went to find the best spot to record everything with Griff's video camera. In the ticket line, Griff had told him what button to push and how to zoom, but Cecil was still thinking about what Eric had whispered in his ear, so he wasn't sure he'd remember what to do with the camera. He positioned himself in front of center stage behind a plywood barricade. There were no chairs or benches. He stood in the tamped-down grass and rested his elbows on the barricade and felt the sun bearing down on the back of his neck. He wasn't surprised to hear about Dwight Buford. What he felt was more akin to contentedness, as if there was one less thing he needed to do now. He hoped it would lighten Justin's load, too, and his family's, and he hoped there wouldn't be much fanfare when the news broke. His mouth kept curling into a smile. After the Shrimporee, he'd head out to the cemetery and tend to Connie's grave. He'd tell her what he could.

"Are you psyched for the mosh pit?" someone asked from beside him. When he turned, he saw Fiona. "I bet it'll get wild when the Campbell Family Band hits the stage."

"I don't expect any shortage of applause, if that's what you're asking," he said.

"And I bet those old birds over there who keep checking you out will be the loudest," she said.

Cecil turned to his left and saw the small, hunched Wilcox sisters, Ruth and Bev. They met his eyes and though Bev looked away, Ruth raised her tiny hand to wave. They made Cecil wish he'd worn a hat he could tip at them.

The audience had started to fill in. A uniformed Refugio patrol officer and a pregnant woman ate pan dulce, and a large woman in a floral frock fanned herself with a rolled-up newspaper. Ivan was drinking a beer, talking with a gaggle of women in sunglasses. There were customers from the pawnshop all around, and a dozen or more teenagers. Joseph Anzaldúa, who owned the dry cleaner's, was talking on his cell phone while teachers from Eric's school and waitresses from the Castaway were mingling, trading stories. Ronnie Dawes and his mother stood off to the side; Ronnie held a homemade poster with a vivid red heart on it. A contingent of folks who'd volunteered in the searches was scattered around, donning their old search shirts with Justin's image on it. On each of them, the word MISSING had been replaced with HOME. Cecil wanted to remember to shoot video of them once they saw Justin. He craned his neck to look for redheaded Marcy, but he couldn't find her. The crowd was deep, though, and already large enough to fan out away from the stage, so maybe she was there somewhere. A part of him hoped so.

Fiona was still talking about the Wilcox sisters. She had a sweet and bawdy manner, like an actress in a play, and it was easy to see how Griff would fall for her. She said, "Piece of advice? Go for Bev, the one who didn't wave. That's the kind of minx that'll keep you guessing."

"Do you know how to work this?" Cecil held up the video camera.

"Push that red button to start recording and push it again to stop," she said. Then, in mock exasperation, she took the camera and said, "On second thought, you'll probably get all weepy, so I'll film. The last thing those boys need is to hear their grandpa blubbering like a girl. Don't blame me if there are a lot of shots of Griff's cute butt."

Cecil smiled. He could feel the crowd expanding behind him. He said, "Is Griff doing okay?"

"After last night, I'd hope he's doing a bit better than okay."

"I worry he gets lost in the middle of all this. I don't want him to feel out to sea."

"I'm watching him," she said, her voice tender, real. "I've been watching him for longer than he knows and I'm not stopping anytime soon."

"That sounds mighty good," Cecil said. Then, after a moment, he added, "Make sure you get a shot of the audience, all those people in their Justin shirts are a sight to see."

Backstage, as he and his family approached Tracy and Kent Robichaud, Eric's stomach coiled into knots. He worried about how he'd left things with Tracy yesterday, worried about her or her husband coming unglued, worried about what they'd say to Laura. He was also still trying to process Dwight Buford's death. That the man no longer occupied the physical world hadn't yet registered in Eric's mind. Maybe the reality would set in once they shared the news with Justin; or maybe the problem was not knowing how Justin would react, the fear that he'd feel anything except relief.

Kent Robichaud had a soft handshake but calloused fingers, which Eric thought might come with being a surgeon. He wore a shirt with a starched collar and smelled of cologne and had an easy smile. When Tracy introduced him, he turned to Justin and said, "Justin, she's been trying to get me to the Shrimporee for years, but you're the only reason I'd come."

Everyone smiled, laughed a little. People used the opportunity to look him over. If he caught someone staring, he smiled. He lifted his hand in a small wave. When Tracy asked if he was nervous, he shook his head *no* but said *yes,* and the laughter started up again.

Laura thought she remembered Justin making that same joke years ago, but wasn't sure. Or maybe Griff had and Justin copped it from him? Either way, she wanted to steal it and use it herself in the next few days. She thought Justin would appreciate such humor. His demeanor floored her. She liked watching him, liked watching people watch him. The admiration in their eyes, the respect in the way they approached him, as if he were royalty. And with everyone lavishing their attention on him, Laura could see how healthy Justin looked, the gained weight and the shine in his sweet, shaggy hair and the burgeoning confidence in his posture. It was as if he'd come to accept that people would want to study him and with that acceptance he had gained an undeniable poise.

Then, without anyone noticing, it was suddenly very crowded in the shade behind the stage. The mayor was there, and a news crew, and a reporter and photographer from the paper, and a man with a radio headset giving Tracy instructions. Eric watched her nod and push locks of hair behind her ears. The mayor was talking with Laura and Griff and Justin, stepping this way and that to let people pass on their way to the stage, and Eric was in awe of the moment, struck by the impossibility of what he was seeing. Flat blades of light cut through the stage rigging. It was loud outside—a cacophony of voices and music and machines. The Shrimporee was likely at full capacity. Earlier, after they got off the phone with Garcia, Laura had come to find him in the bedroom and she took his face in her hands, searched his eyes with hers, and said, "Starting right now, we're a family again. Going forward, it's just the four of us and we're going to be okay." Now, watching as she listened to the mayor saying something to their sons, Eric heard her words as a kind of beautiful threat.

Then Tracy was pulling Laura and the boys away from the mayor, and she was waving Eric over. He thought something was wrong. Thought the event was being canceled because news of Buford had been leaked or Mayne was there or the weather was about to turn. For an excruciating moment, he felt positive that the body found in the ship channel had been incorrectly identified and Buford was still in the world, making his way toward Justin at that moment. But Tracy was smiling. A woman stood beside her, a woman who'd been backstage the whole time, but Eric had assumed she worked for the Shrimporee. She was shorter than Griff and had thin silver hair longer than Laura's. The woman looked skittish, squirrelly. Eric wouldn't have been surprised if she'd bolted away. She kept smacking her lips, as if she were missing her teeth. She held a small white paper bag with both hands.

Seeing her, Justin said, "Oh, wow."

"You remember," the woman said, and smiled. It was as if she'd won a prize.

"Wow," he said again. "You came."

Laura looked from Justin to the woman to Eric, who was equally clueless, and then back to Justin. People were taking notice now. The energy backstage was being drawn inexorably to Justin.

"I was going to introduce everyone onstage," Tracy said, "but Mrs. Sheppard didn't want to wait."

Justin looked at his feet, then back at Mrs. Sheppard, then leaned forward and took her in his arms. He was taller than she was, so he had to stoop to bury his face in her shoulder and hair. Laura glanced at Eric again, thinking his face would betray something, but it didn't. They glanced at Griff, who could only shrug. Tracy wiped tears from her eyes. Her husband came over to her, pulling a maroon handkerchief from his pocket, and she folded herself into his arms. Then a photographer was crouching and snapping rapid pictures. The cameraman from the news ignited his light and started circling, moving in closer and closer.

After a moment, Justin stepped back. The camera light stayed bright. The photographer clicked away.

Then Griff understood. He met Mrs. Sheppard's eyes and said, "You're the one who sold him the mice. You're the one who found him."

Laura's hands flew to her mouth and she couldn't decide where to look and then she couldn't stop herself from grabbing the woman and wrapping her arms around her. Then she was reaching for Eric and Griff and Justin, and they were huddling together, laughing and starting to cry. Mrs. Sheppard smelled of cedar shavings. Laura was lost in everyone's embrace. She couldn't tell where her own body stopped and where others began, couldn't tell who was touching whom where, or how many people were involved. Someone was saying "Thank you." Someone was saying it over and over, or they were all saying it at different times.

The man with the headset returned to tell Tracy the stage was ready. It was time. The mayor ascended the stairs and disappeared into the sunlight—there was a smattering of applause—and the reporters followed. The photographer and cameraman positioned themselves at the top of the stairs, their backs to the crowd, their lenses trained on whoever would next climb toward them. Tracy's husband kissed her cheek and looked her over and said her makeup was fine; then he jogged through the rigging to make it to the front of the stage as she went up the stairs. The cameramen ignored her, which pricked Eric. At the top, she turned to look at him. She smiled and he knew she was telling him to hurry his family along, but she also wanted to see what he thought of her having found Mrs. Sheppard. Her face was open and full and beautiful, and to thank her, for everything, and to apologize, for everything, he held her gaze and then lidded his eyes. When he opened them, she nodded once with a small, subdued smile, and moved onto the stage out of his vision.

"Here," Mrs. Sheppard said, handing Justin the small white bag. "I thought your snake was probably getting hungry. I brought you a couple of feeder mice."

"Sick," he said. "She's about to shed."

"Then she'll be twice as hungry once she's done."

Laura said, "I will spend the rest of my life trying to make this up to you. I wish the reward was bigger, but I hope it will—"

"I told Mrs. Robichaud not to fuss with the reward. I don't need no money. We've got our apartment and a car that runs and I do okay selling critters at the flea market. You could come buy mice every so often if you had a mind to."

Then the headset man returned and guided them toward the stairs. Eric let Laura go first, then Griff, then Justin. As they stepped onto the stage, the cameramen crab-walked beside them, squinting and clicking, and the audience applauded. When Justin emerged, there was a roar. It was thundering, as if the town had been silent all these years, holding its breath, and only now was it crying out in joy. Eric started to choke up, just as he sometimes did when he attended school graduations. It was how he felt now, as if the world were momentarily balanced on an ending and a beginning, and soon it would tip forward and send everyone in a new direction and the life they were meant to have would commence. As he followed his family onstage and into the bright sunlight—he hadn't realized how his eyes had adjusted to the dark down below—he couldn't believe the luck of his life. He couldn't believe it at all.

Epilogue

IMAGINE KILLING A MAN. THE COMMITMENT. THE IRREVERS-
ible and unspeakable isolation in its wake. How you'd have to
relinquish yourself, the entirety of the life that had come before and
the dreamed-for future, knowing that nothing and no one would
remain the same afterward. How, by killing him, you'd also be killing yourself, and what would follow would be a hollow two-planed
existence. Both true. Both false. You would have come to see the
world as an animal does, without judgment or hope or mercy, and
believe that nothing—not grace or history, not consequence or
shame or God—mattered more than what you longed to protect.
Imagine how it would feel like surrender, like a narrative without
end, like a homecoming aborted.

This was what Eric was doing in the moments after they dropped
Cecil off and Laura lowered herself into the passenger seat. He
couldn't help it. The thoughts mounted like broken promises, and
he was defenseless, acutely vulnerable to their luminous and inces-
sant logic. What if, he couldn't stop himself from wondering, his
father had gotten to Dwight Buford after all? Maybe he went to his
house or found him at the marina without Eric. Maybe that had
been his plan all along. Maybe, atop the Harbor Bridge, Cecil had
held the pistol to the back of Buford's neck, in the soft pocket beneath the skull. Maybe they were both surprised by how perfectly

the barrel of the .44 fit there, how it seemed to have been made for exactly that purpose, exactly that place. Maybe that's why Buford jumped.

Then, unexpectedly, he thought of Laura. He knew he had to be wrong, knew how impossible the notion would seem to everyone else, but then again, how impossible was anything? Hadn't this very night seemed impossible just months before? Hadn't Justin's return itself seemed a kind of impossible resurrection? Eric drove slowly, waiting for the spell of doubt to subside. The last of the evening light remained in the trees, and stars were firing bright and low in the sky. Despite everything that had happened, the urge to make his way to the Buford house persisted. He'd never been over there after dark, something he realized only now, and with that thought came the late understanding of what Dwight Buford had been doing all those hours when Eric had been waiting for him to show himself: He had, like Justin, been sleeping. How long, Eric wondered, might Laura have understood that? How long might she have seen what he'd missed?

In the car, she was talking with the boys. Justin had promised not to feed the new mice to Sasha, which led Griff to suggest setting up the cage for them in his room. The boys wanted Laura to name them. Griff asked if anyone had seen the booth with the rubber duck race, and both Laura and Justin said yes but couldn't remember exactly where. Then the conversation turned to Alice the dolphin and Laura volunteering tonight. Eric hadn't heard everything, but the gist was that Rudy Treviño, the cop she'd introduced them to when they came off the Shrimporee stage, had been scheduled to volunteer later that night, but his pregnant wife wasn't feeling well after so much time in the heat, so Laura agreed to cover his shift. She expected it to be an easy, uneventful night. Eric thought she seemed proud, and serene, as if she'd relieved herself of a burden. His knowing wife, a woman who would never tell him she'd gone to the pawnshop to save him from himself. Listening to her now, something inside him braced.

How many of the nights when she claimed to be at Marine Lab could she have gone to the Buford house instead? Maybe she would have seen light pouring out of the living room windows, or maybe the whole house would have been dark except for a small room in the back where the unmistakable glow of a television flickered. At night, she could have parked far closer than Eric could in the daylight. Maybe she'd even pulled into his driveway. Maybe she'd seen Buford step out onto the porch. Maybe she'd watched him inhale the night's thick air or wipe crusty sleep from his eyes. Maybe when the morning paper arrived, he waved to the person throwing the route. Maybe he flipped the porch light on and read it outside. Maybe Laura was close enough to see him pausing over the pictures of Justin.

Or maybe Dwight Buford was as paranoid as they were, and getting him out of the house required more conviction. Maybe she would honk her horn from the driveway, or run up and ring the doorbell, or kick over the metal garbage cans, and because Buford didn't want anything to disturb his dying mother, he'd venture outside. Or maybe Laura would have to find someone else to ring the doorbell, someone who would leave Dwight Buford no choice but to open the door. Eric's first thought was Justin, but he knew better. Laura wouldn't put her son through such distress. Then his mind went back to Cecil—maybe that was why he'd called everything off this morning, because they'd already handled it—and then he thought of a sheriff or a policeman, and finally, incrementally, like clouds converging before a storm, he again started to see Rudy Treviño. A man who seemed so at ease with Laura, a man she'd never once mentioned to Eric. So after Buford opened the door, maybe Rudy said there'd been complaints or, better, a threat against Buford's own life, so his bail was being revoked for his safety. Maybe

Buford ducked into the cruiser willingly, gratefully. Or maybe he started to piece things together, just as Eric was doing now. Maybe when Buford caught sight of Laura in the passenger seat, he tried to run. Imagine Rudy taking him down, cuffing him, covering his mouth with a shirt Laura had taken from the cleaner's.

Or, if it happened on Thursday night, the last night of the storm, the night Laura came home trembling and wet and smelling of rain, then the weather's noise would have muffled Buford's holler-ing. When Rudy placed Dwight Buford in the back of his squad car, they would have been drenched. Ferry service was suspended that night, so they would have driven over the Kennedy Causeway and through Flour Bluff, where Dwight Buford had kept Justin those years, and then into Corpus. Maybe Buford started crying. Maybe he said, "You don't have to do this." Maybe Rudy turned on his flashing lights, maybe not. Maybe the only sounds were the wind-shield wipers and the tires on the rain-sheeted road and the wind buffeting the car.

Or maybe Laura said, "You've taken a piece of every last thing I love."

And was Eric mistaken or had she been overly interested in the autopsy? Maybe when the report came back, it would show Valium and Ambien in his system. Maybe Laura had started stockpiling pills again. Was it impossible to imagine after everything she'd en-dured? Was it impossible to imagine her and Rudy pulling over in the middle of the night in the middle of a storm to give the pills to the accused? Could anyone conceive of a scenario in which Dwight Buford would take them of his own volition? Maybe to keep from feeling the inevitable? To make it easier on himself? Or maybe he fought. Maybe Buford clenched his teeth and locked his jaw so that Rudy had to pinch his nose until his mouth opened. Maybe Buford started to get drowsy immediately, or maybe they had to drive somewhere and wait for his eyes to close. Maybe Laura told Rudy, who would soon be a father himself, how she and Eric sometimes used to drive Justin around the neighborhood to lull him to sleep when he was young. Maybe Rudy idled in the parking lot of a filling station, maybe the one at the foot of the Harbor Bridge where Justin and Eric had switched seats before he drove over that first time. Maybe he went to Marine Lab, where they'd rendezvoused hours earlier, where both Eric and Rudy's pregnant wife thought their spouses had been all night.

And then maybe, once Buford was out, they drove back to the summit of the Harbor Bridge and, with the storm keening, worked together to drag his unconscious weight from the backseat and pitch his body over the rail. Imagine the unyielding wind up that high. Imagine the sting of the rain and how your hands would tremble and how to anyone else there would still seem the option of turning back, but for you the option had never existed. Or maybe Buford had been only partially sedated and he walked with them, convinced he was being led to safety, somewhere dry and familiar. Or maybe they hadn't gone to the bridge at all, but rather to the docks along the ship channel. Maybe his body had started floating toward the bridge while Rudy dropped Laura off at Marine Lab and she drove home, passing Justin's billboard, and then crawled into bed with Eric, shivering and scared and longing to forget everything that had happened before that moment, longing to start anew. Hadn't he known then that something had changed inside her, that she was a different woman than just hours earlier?

Now, in the car, Laura was still talking about the dolphin. Her voice remained so light and airy that all of Eric's previous thinking atrophied. Buford had just jumped. Or someone had made good on the death threats the news had been reporting. Eric knew only that his own family had nothing to do with it, and Buford's hold on them was lessening.

"I have binoculars," Griff said. "They're somewhere in my room. Papaw gave them to me."

"Do what now?" Eric asked.

"Mom wants to be an astronomer, but she's not very good at it," Justin said. His tone was kind, approving.

"We can try tonight before you have to leave for Marine Lab," Griff said.

"Let me guess," Eric said. "Delphinus?"

"I just want to see it once," she said.

"Or maybe you've seen it but you didn't recognize it. Constellations never look right to me."

"Delphinus?" Justin said. "I thought it was named Arion."

"Arion was the musician," she said, then elaborated. Arion, the greatest lyrist Greece had ever known, had found passage on a merchant ship to Ionia for a music competition. Then, in the middle of the sea, the crew revealed themselves as pirates, robbed Arion of his silver, and started preparing to throw him overboard. He didn't beg for his life. Instead, he begged to play one last song. His foolishness amused the pirates, but because they knew of his talent, they agreed. Soon after he began playing, the pirates who'd been laughing at his frivolity were weeping at the beauty of the music. He improvised and elongated the song. He strung bridges of notes from one measure to the next. The longer the song stretched, the more the pirates wept. Eventually a pod of dolphins appeared in the water, drawn to the boat by his playing, and Arion jumped onto their backs to escape. The dolphins delivered him safely back to Corinth, where the king gave him a hero's welcome. The gods so loved Arion's music and were so grateful for his safe return that they staked a piece of sky with Delphinus, the dolphin-shaped constellation that guides lost sailors home.

"Sick," Justin said.

"I bet we can see it with the binoculars," Griff said. "I'll see if Fiona wants to come over, too."

"The binoculars are in my truck," Eric said. "I took them—"

"For one of the searches," Laura interrupted. "You thought they might help out in the dunes, remember?"

"It's a clear sky," Justin said, peering up through the window. "The storm pushed all the clouds away."

Above them, the sky was stitched with stars. Eric couldn't guess where to look for Delphinus, but he could imagine standing in the backyard with the boys and Laura, searching for what she needed everyone to see. A comforting order imposed on randomness. A pattern that arbitrarily shaped the darkness, made it bearable. He could imagine how they would pass the binoculars around and how they would try to coax the image out of hiding. Their minds would be teeming with secrets, with regrets and grave, unrelenting fears, and their bodies would be exhausted and corded with scars, and their gazes would be clouded by loss, permanently obscured. But they would be seeking the same thing, and in that, there seemed some small victory. The image was supposed to deliver them home, and yet Eric had a feeling of liberation, as if they were about to depart, as if they were soon to set out on a path lit by stars that would never fall. The prospect was buoying, sustaining. In the car, he reached for Laura's hand and braided his fingers with hers. He found his sons in the rearview mirror, their eyes still fixed on the sky, looking for signs and heroes. Eric gave the engine more gas, and they accelerated toward the half-known and desperate history that bound them together.

Acknowledgments

The working title of this novel was *The Unaccompanied*, but it's benefited from a lot of companionship along the way. So have I. I'm deeply grateful to the following people for everything they've given: Jennifer. Bill. Michelle, Camryn, Julian. Brie, Brad, Nathan, Austen. Joseph. Ivan. Jacob Rosenberg. Rodney Mullen. Julie Barer (and by proxy Beckett). Kendra Harpster. Susan Kamil. Gina Centrello. Avideh Bashirrad. Kaela Myers. Sally Marvin. Karen Fink. Leigh Marchant. Selby McRae. Joelle Dieu. Ron Koltnow. Toby Ernst. Rachel Kind. Steve Messina. Noah Eaker. Heidi Pitlor. Christopher Castellani. Ladette Randolph. Josh Emmons. Jorie Graham, Peter Sacks, Amy Hempel, Diana Sorensen, and my colleagues at Harvard University. John Irving. Jill McCorkle. Andre Dubus III. Tom Perrotta. Alice Sebold. Jenny Hopa. Mike Anzaldua. Cheryl Pfoff. Vanessa Jackson. Joe Wilson, Jan Williams, and everyone at the Corpus Christi Literary Reading Series. Steven Bauer, Eric Goodman, Kay Sloan, Constance Pierce, Tim Melley, and the creative writing program at Miami University. Ethan Canin, Connie Brothers, Chris Offutt, Marilynne Robinson, Deb West, Jan Z, and everyone at the Iowa Writers' Workshop. The National Endowment for the Arts, the Christopher Isherwood Foundation, the James A. Michener–Copernicus Society of America, and the Blackwood Residency. Michelle Kuo. Michelle Kim Hall. Eleanor Boudreau. Sorrel

Westbrook Nielsen. Lea Walker and the Texas Marine Mammal Stranding Network. Dan Menaker. Nina Collins. Sam Douglas. Judy Sternlight. Rob Torres. Paul Yoon. Ben Percy. Carol Campbell. William Boggess. Gemma Purdy. Anna Geller. Anna Wiener. Paul Buttenwieser. Sven Birkerts, Victoria Clausi, and my family from the Bennington Writing Seminars.

ABOUT THE AUTHOR

BRET ANTHONY JOHNSTON is the author of the award-winning *Corpus Christi: Stories,* which was named a best book of the year by *The Independent* (London) and *The Irish Times,* and the editor of *Naming the World: And Other Exercises for the Creative Writer.* His work has appeared in *The Atlantic Monthly, Esquire, The Paris Review, The Best American Short Stories,* and elsewhere. A graduate of the Iowa Writers' Workshop, he is the recipient of a National Endowment for the Arts literature fellowship and a 5 Under 35 honor from the National Book Foundation. He teaches in the Bennington Writing Seminars and at Harvard University, where he is the director of creative writing.

www.bretanthonyjohnston.com
www.facebook.com/bajbooks

About the Type

This book was set in Sabon, a typeface designed by the well-known German typographer Jan Tschichold (1902–74). Sabon's design is based upon the original letter forms of sixteenth-century French type designer Claude Garamond and was created specifically to be used for three sources: foundry type for hand composition, Linotype, and Monotype. Tschichold named his typeface for the famous Frankfurt typefounder Jacques Sabon (c. 1520–80).